Indulgence

SJM Westaway

SJM Westaway C/- Intertype
Unit 45, 125 Highbury Road
BURWOOD VIC 3125
www.intertype.com.au

Ordering Information:
Quantity sales. Special discounts are available on quantity purchases by corporations, associations, and others. For details, contact the "Special Sales Department" at the address above.

Indulgence/ SJM Westaway. —1st ed.
ISBN 978-0-6452042-7-8

Acknowledgements

I am deeply grateful to Kerry Laundon for her editing of this novel. She has made profound improvements to the original draft and I thank her for her professionalism, insight and friendship. I also acknowledge Shirly and Dani for their encouragement - and for leading me to Kerry. Thanks also to Hew and Kate for their technical assistance.

It is said that everyone has at least one novel in them. This is mine.

I have adopted the nom de plume of SJM Westaway for this work of fiction.

This book is dedicated to my brother, his novels an inspiration to complete my own.

.

CHAPTER 1

Thirty minutes left to live – what would I do with that time?

So mused Eva in indulgent contemplation of this oft-repeated challenge.

Today her answer was a simple one, continue doing what she was doing: looking outward, gazing down upon the small stream noiselessly caressing the smooth rocks along its path, its ripples glinting like small diamonds under the embrace of the early morning sun. It was worth getting out of bed early to sit quietly on the enclosed balcony of her apartment, admiring the early morning scene.

Some citizens were already walking or jogging along the dirt trail that separated the stream from the lush green of the overhanging vegetation. She could distinguish the colours of the clothing and the body outlines of the exercisers, their faces always too far away to analyse. With some familiarity, she wordlessly said good morning to Citizen Green, out again in her smart green leotard, and to Citizen Nice-Abs, his tight black t-shirt adequately displaying his attributes.

These precious moments, if not thirty minutes, gave her the courage to face the day. Who knew what the rest of the day would bring before she could once again slip between the sheets and find solace and forgetfulness in her bed?

Not that she didn't enjoy her work, Eva reminded herself as she moved to the small kitchenette, returning with a mug of hot strong coffee and a slice of toast. Still in her pyjamas, she pulled her wrap close to keep out the chill of the early morning.

She had chosen this particular north-facing apartment because of the view, the peace and beauty offered by the scenery immediately claiming her. The building, however, had been chosen for her due to its security.

She had minimal interaction with the other residents, usually passing them, her eyes cast down, without speaking. Similarly, others made no effort to engage her in conversation, each seeming to understand the sanctity that solitude provided.

Eva finished her light breakfast, showered and dressed. Today she wore an ochre-coloured top over black leggings. Stepping into her black stilettos with their trademark red soles, she gave her golden-brown hair a good brush, added lipstick to brighten her oval face, and lightly powdered her still-flawless skin. She felt her buzzer ping: her car awaited her. Resignedly, she knew the day was about to begin.

She took the lift to the basement, climbed into the back of the black sedan parked nearby, and settled into a plush seat on the left side of the car. No words were exchanged with the driver, not even a good morning: Eva knew the driver was not programmed to interact with a passenger. Aware it was for her own protection (so no-one under so-called 'duress' would be persuaded to inform on her movements), she still liked to pretend to herself that there was another human driving her.

The car skimmed along the well-maintained road. Through the tinted windows Eva recognised familiar sights: on her right, the turn to the Shopping and Entertainment District flashed by, quickly followed by the turn to the Sports District. A few kilometres later, the sign showing the Health District turning became visible. Today, her first call was not the hospital laboratory so the car continued onwards, maintaining its high speed. After a further ten minutes, the car took a left turn, slowing its pace until it paused at a monitored gate. Eva's car window lowered so her eye could be scanned, and a few seconds later the gate opened for the car. Eva was now in an area hemmed by tall trees, their branches leaning downwards, sighing as they moved to and fro in the wake of a slight breeze.

The car pulled up to enable Eva to alight next to a small sign stipulating that only authorised personnel had right of entry to The Departments. After further security checks, which were so much a part of her daily life that Eva hardly noticed them anymore, she entered her office. With a final look at the trees outside, she eased herself into the vegan leather chair at her desk, her back to the window. It was a narrow window in width, but as it ran from floor to ceiling, admitting light, the room could be thought of as quite pleasant.

First, she dealt with her communications, some of which required detail in her responses, so she was careful to check her statements and statistics. Eva's work was challenging, exciting and frustrating, with many steps forward and many steps back: characteristics familiar to those engaged in research. However, unlike some of her contemporaries, Eva had long ago (for the most part) learnt to block out any uneasiness and doubts about the morality of her research. She found the challenge of her job satisfying and could have been happy with her successes, had such an emotion seemingly not been cast aside along with her ethics.

A knock on the door interrupted Eva's focus. She ceased dictating, looking up questioningly as Cabut entered the room.

"Excuse me for the interruption, Major General Professor Baritz," he said. "We have a problem."

Eva focused instantly on Cabut's face, noting his seeming unwillingness to show emotion. Still so awkward, she thought. Out loud, however, she simply replied with a crisp "And?"

"There appear to be signs of shattering developing in the chromosome adjusted last week in the civilian receptor."

"Go on," she instructed.

Eva liked the succinct and impartial way that Cabut continued to put the facts before her. She paused to consider what she had been told. Then, looking directly at Cabut, she instructed him to authorise the immediate removal of the self-destructing chromosome and, if the civilian survived after six hours, to inform her straight away so that she could oversee a repeat of the original procedure. If the civilian did not survive then all working parts of the body were to be removed and frozen, the cadaver destroyed in the usual way.

"Very good, Professor Baritz, I shall attend to it," and, eyes downcast, Cabut left the room, closing the door softly as he went. The news was bad and she needed time to digest the implications – she hoped Cabut would have the good sense not to enter her office again for some time.

This was not the first time such an aberration had occurred. In the early trials, one of the receptors had been lost; but really, Eva admitted, this had been very helpful since much had been learnt from that event. Subsequent procedures both with lesser life forms and robotic simulations had gone perfectly smoothly, and the program had been refined to what she thought was as close to perfect as possible. This latest testing simply should not have failed; it should have sealed the end success of the research and allowed her to move on to its main purpose.

Could there still be a glitch in the program? Is there something in the DNA of this particular civilian that could have caused an adverse reaction? What went wrong? she asked herself.

Putting her other work to one side, she opened a file and studied its coding with intense concentration. There was only one very minuscule, almost negligible way the procedure could go wrong. She had always known this: no program could have a 100% guarantee of success. The probability of an error had been calculated to be extremely low, well within acceptable bounds. Sighing, she realised she needed to review the civilian receptor's genome profile, preferably while that person was still alive. She messaged Cabut that she was on her way to the laboratory. Closing her screen, she left her office.

*

A meeting was about to take place between the Country's President and the ministers who formed the Inner Cabinet, the highest seat of power in the Government – its ministers selected by, and answerable only to, the President.

Glancing around with satisfaction at the assembled ministers, the President mused that Revised Democracy had largely succeeded in preventing the appointment of unsuitable people or those of such minor intellect that they could do little to advance the Country. The citizens did not vote, while the President appointed the Government's ministers; an excellent system, she noted to herself.

Nor, under Revised Democracy, was there a formal system of political parties, where people of good intent too often had found themselves having to sacrifice their principles to toe a party line. The President looked around her, observing that the smartest people, those with track records of leadership, flexibility and agility, innovation, and the ability to think broadly, were seating themselves in readiness for the Cabinet meeting to begin.

Over the past few months, the locally based and far less powerful OCMs – the Outer Cabinet Members – had become increasingly restless, claiming that citizens were expressing unease about the Government's innovative replacement organs program.

Normally, any unwanted complaints could relatively easily be lost and the complainant ground down through the bureaucratic process deliberately designed to stifle dissent. This served the Inner Cabinet well, giving its ministers the time and scope for higher order business and ambitious planning for the good of the Country (without the unwanted distraction of trivial complaints from those who simply did not understand what was best for them). It didn't serve the OCMs so well, however, as it was their role to allay the citizens' fears.

As the Cabinet meeting proceeded, several ministers rose to report on the concerns that had been raised with them by members of the Outer Cabinet. This was very unusual, the President thought: the gossiping and griping of the OCMs rarely featured alongside the higher-level issues addressed in their Inner Cabinet meetings. She wondered for a moment whether the ministers actually shared the same concerns they were reporting.

Their words provoked others to speak in defence of the replacement program, particularly those most loyal to the President. The Minister for Health drew the attention of his fellow ministers to the fact that the organ replacement initiative had been considered to be a brilliant scheme when first mooted. "I remind ministers that the printing of new organs to replace those damaged by accident or disease has been hailed as one of the Country's great steps forward," he began, ending his contribution with the observation, "It would seem that some of my colleagues need to be more forthright and assertive in their discussions with members of the Outer Cabinet."

The Treasurer followed on, explaining that the costs of the program were not excessive once offset against a reduction in the long-term care needs of chronically ill or disabled citizens. She declared: "The effect on what had previously been an old and struggling health system, and its overburdened budget, is emphatic."

The Minister for Education observed that both the President and the Minister for Health had been widely acclaimed for the initiative, adding gently that perhaps the OCMs, and through them the citizens, needed to be so reminded. The minister's words received a muted round of applause from those of like minds.

President Gretel Nuewen briefly smiled at what may have been an attempt at flattery by Bethany, the Minister for Education. Inwardly noting that Bethany was a former OCM, appointed to the Inner Cabinet through her presidential selection process, she half wondered whether there was an element of self-interest in her words. As a Cabinet minister, Bethany's tenured position was secure; however, should Gretel so decide, Bethany could in theory be demoted back to her non-tenured OCM position. Not that Gretel had any such notion in mind, as Bethany was a highly valued minister.

The meeting continued to take its course until, having sat in silence, the most recent appointment to the Inner Cabinet rose to speak.

The President was really quite fond of her twenty-six ministers, with the exception of one: Timothy Augustine, the Minister for Roads and Transport. There had been good cause to question the wisdom of his appointment to the Inner Cabinet, so she knew it was important to listen carefully to what he had to say.

Acknowledging the points made by all the previous speakers, Timothy began by endorsing the conduct of both the former and the current governments. "I think it important we all pause to remind ourselves what these governments have achieved for our Country before we rush too hastily to criticise, as some OCMs seem to be doing," he said quietly, before proceeding.

"The Nuewen Government and, before it, the Homer Government, are able to draw attention to, and often had, and often do ..." He paused, allowing his colleagues a murmur of mirth over the constant use of Government propaganda.

Picking up his words, he continued. "These governments are rightly able to draw attention to such social achievements as the more even distribution of incomes, resulting in a rareness of poverty, homelessness and unemployment, and the lessening of drug-related social problems through both the decriminalisation laws and the treatment of addiction as a medical condition. Ministers will also be well aware that crime has decreased, and public vilification based on differences in racial background and gender orientation are almost unheard of – publicly, at least." Again, there was a trill of subdued laughter.

"Our older citizens can look forward to living long, healthy lives supported by a universal pension scheme, one that is not reliant on gambling on the stock market to service it. Gambling may have its pleasures, but not here, as legislated by these governments," he observed.

By now, the President was wondering where Timothy was heading. She didn't believe for one moment that his agenda was to praise the Government: he was too much of a strategist.

"I could go on, but I have made my first point," Timothy declared. "When there have been big issues to resolve, the Government has found solutions by facing the challenges, not by defensively dismissing the concerns."

The minister had chosen his words carefully, accentuating the positives while skating around the less flattering aspects. He steered the meeting back to the program and the rumours around it, repeating a claim that progress with the program suggested it could become possible to produce a comprehensive record of the replacements likely to be required throughout a citizen's life, to be pre-determined and recorded from birth through the study of a citizen's DNA.

"Who amongst us would disagree that such information would be extremely helpful for our planning and prosperity, both for the individual and for the Country?" he asked rhetorically.

"We are hearing that there is some unease about the impact on the right of the individual to privacy versus the right of the Country's need to know. And the rumours are growing. Would it soon be possible to make an adjustment to a person's DNA early on, thereby negating the need for the replacement?"

Timothy was no longer offering humorous asides. With his eyes sweeping around the Cabinet table, his voice quite hushed, he made his core point.

"To what extent would this actually be equivalent to requiring citizens to be programmed? This is the fear, ministers; this is the crux of the message from the OCMs. Is this signalling the beginning of the merging of two up-to-now disparate 'species'? We need to address the concerns openly and honestly, for all our sakes."

The President enjoyed debate; she listened to others respectfully, particularly as she herself disliked being interrupted when she was on-message. But Timothy was returning to type, his usual provocative self now on display. She chose to enter the discussion, cutting Timothy off from further speech, segueing into a rebuff by first allowing that he perhaps had raised a sensitive and contentious side issue.

"There is a wariness in our community, and perhaps even amongst ourselves, of android advancements, despite the appreciation of the many benefits that the use of robots in normal life has brought to us," she observed. "However, not only do these machine beings make our daily life safer and freer from menial tasks, but our Country's advancement depends on their use in research in so many fields, not least of which is in the domain of space exploration." She smiled.

It was dear to her heart that some magnificent discoveries about their universe had been made in recent research projects, and she hoped soon to be able to announce a major initiative in this domain. But that was for another day.

Her smile quickly vanished as she continued more sternly. "Let me state categorically that throughout our employment of the robot, there has never been any suggestion that these are equivalent to humans, however lifelike and cute their design. The thought that the two 'species' might one day merge, as the Minister for Roads and Transport appears to be suggesting, is beyond countenance," she firmly asserted, her rebuke of the minister not lost on his colleagues.

Thanking all her ministers for their participation, the President brought the meeting to a close. She confirmed they would reconvene when the Chief Scientist was able to appear before them to explain the ongoing replacement organs program and to address (and, hopefully, to allay any further concerns about) the matters aired by the ministers on behalf of the OCMs.

CHAPTER 2

It was late. Eva was still at her Department office. It had not been a good day.

The civilian had died before Eva reached the ward. Fortunately, the civilian was nobody and unlikely to be missed. If there were any enquiries about him, they could easily be deflected.

Nevertheless, this was a most frustrating mishap, all the more unexpected than the other, since this was a clean type 2 human being – *one of us,* or so she had believed.

Without a doubt, however, the real tragedy of the situation lay in the increasing likelihood of there still being an error in the program. *One might regret the loss of what had been a perfectly healthy case study, but one must learn from the loss and press on,* she rationalised. What could be achieved through this research would ultimately be of significant benefit to all the citizens of the Country.

Now, what are those benefits again, please remind me? Eva thought caustically.

She started to recite out loud. "Serious illness could be treated routinely and inexpensively through simple gene therapy. The reduction in healthcare costs would be significant, with the savings good for the Country's prosperity and productivity. Screening infants to identify future disease would allow gene vaccinations to bypass such disease before it could occur in the adult the child would later become …

"Yah-di-yah-di-yah," she ended, since none of the many benefits related to her true interest in the research. Shrugging, she did at least concede that, all things considered, her work could be considered altruistic and for the common good.

Or was it?

Eva suppressed the voice in her head asking whether the end benefits justified the means – and even if they did, how moral would the end benefits be? Wearily, she wondered, as she often did: *what defines a type 2 human being?* She shook her head, knowing she had to detach from such ethical and philosophical questions. Instead, she tried to focus on the challenge that such fascinating and intense work offered.

But ... what if people find out about the experimental stage of the research before the benefits of the program can be implemented by the Government? continued the tiresomely insistent voice in her head.

She told herself to stay calm. She, Eva Baritz, respected academic and officer of high rank in the Government's military and its Security Agency, was responsible for getting the program right. She knew she could do it, so long as no-one interfered in the current up-and-down stages her work was experiencing. Besides, what choice did she have anyway? She had no option but to continue; this was her life's work, and it was time to get on.

Eva engrossed herself in her work for another couple of hours until she felt the need for dinner. Closing her computer, she tidied her desk and wrote a list of things to be done first thing in the morning. Top of tomorrow's list was to prepare to meet with the Chief Scientist, who had phoned her earlier that day. The Chief Scientist had told her of receiving a summons to appear before the Inner Cabinet, so it was essential that Eva had the opportunity to provide an appropriate briefing beforehand.

Placing the list on her desk, Eva secured it carefully with a paperweight, noting how its pattern radiated; then, picking up her bag, she called out to Cabut that she was leaving. *Really,* she thought, *I must be kinder to Cabut and go home earlier one day. I know he cannot leave until I do.*

She quite liked Cabut in that he was reliable, discreet and uncomplaining. As her private secretary, he was efficient and helpful. She knew, as she walked towards the building's exit, that he would be alerting her driver that she was on her way. She also knew that Cabut had been appointed by the Agency: that he monitored and reported on her movements, that he would check her room after she left, that he would read her note and try to carefully replace the paperweight exactly as she had left it. It was a game they played, a challenge Eva felt they shared – whether Cabut could get the paperweight back into the exact position that she had left it.

Nestled in the back seat of the car, Eva watched with some pleasure the twinkling of the stars in the night sky. As a child she remembered hours spent cosily sat outside resting against her father's side, one of his arms wrapped around her, the other pointing out various constellations. Her father would tell her stories of the majesty and mystery of space, a simplified story of the beginning of time and of the incomprehensibly large distances that separated the planets. When she grew just a little older her father would take her to the observatory, where together they would view the sky through the telescope and those planets would seem a little less far away. On their return home, her mother would have warm cocoa and homemade biscuits ready for their shared supper, after which Eva would be tucked up in bed with a parent sat either side, each taking it in turn to read her a page from her storybook. It had been a beautiful, uncomplicated childhood.

Once ensconced back in her apartment, Eva slipped off her high heels and shed her clothing, letting the work clothes drop to the floor. For a sixty-six-year-old woman, she still possessed an attractive body. Clad only in her underwear, she peeked in the microwave to see what her maid had left her for dinner. After a quick shower she put on something casual and, returning to the living area, she poured herself a glass of red, zapped her food and settled on the couch to watch the news channel. The spicy flavour of the chickpea curry was warming and tasty.

She was not a bad person; she still felt fairly certain of that. Finding her attention drifting from the news, she lowered the volume and fell into a reflection about her better self, the one who had never needed to question whether she was a bad person or not.

She had been 'noticed' as a young undergraduate; she had high intelligence, considerable mathematical ability and confidence. After her undergraduate degree she had commenced postgraduate study, accepting a part-time tutorship in the Mathematics Faculty. There, she met the man she was going to fall deeply in love with. The six years she and Nolé had shared had been brilliant, both personally and professionally. She had felt so alive, so valued, so blooming with happiness. She'd completed her doctorate, receiving the university's annual medal (awarded to the candidate whose thesis was of the highest quality). A minor research position in astrophysics had followed. Her life had been full and joyous.

Taking another sip of her wine, Eva shrugged off the memories of those times with Nolé. Their relationship was over, a thing of the past … Nolé long since lost to her world.

The immediate post-Nolé period was hazy in her memory, although she remembered immersing herself in her work and quickly rising up the academic ladder and into a professorial position. She had been flattered by the attention she had received from some powerful members of the Government at the time, but she had managed to resist the enticements of a Government role.

On becoming head of an expanding research team in astrophysics and robotics, some of the happiness that had eluded her since Nolé left her life began to return. The stimulation of her work, the many successes she and her research team had achieved, and the collegiality and friendship she had fostered within her team had all left an indelible mark on her; those were times when her working life had seemed almost an honour, an indulgence.

By then, she had met Gretel. And Javier. Working with them had started to make her life more complicated, although the memory of her brief but intimate relationship with Javier still caused her to smile.

She and her fellow researchers had continued to make tremendous strides, finally proving the existence of gravitational waves, and from there … well, the rest was history.

The Government had bided its time, careful not to approach her again until she was ready for a new challenge. It was not only the flattering overtures and guarantees of generous funding that had finally won her over, but her desire to remove the friction that had entered her life. She had relinquished her Head of Research position and embarked on her present role within the Departments, becoming, at age forty-seven, the Departments' star recruit. Nineteen years later, her reputation remained formidable.

Responsible for the Government's space program, her work had come to encompass some of the more shadowy but developing areas of artificial intelligence and humanoid robotics, which had morphed into her current DNA research project, conducted under the military's secrecy pact. Her success in the new role had been accompanied by a rise in rank, with 'Major General Professor Baritz' becoming her formal appellation.

Even today, she could never quite understand why she'd done it, why she had crossed over: compromise, betrayal, cutting-edge research, unlimited funds, altruism, flattery and so on were all parts of it, but not the whole.

But, once in, there was no way out. She'd become important but invisible, invaluable but always considered a risk. Happiness was a stranger, now felt only in moments of fleeting appreciation for the early morning scenes she viewed from her balcony, or the starry night skies, or perhaps in the outwitting of Cabut over the placement of a paperweight or the time she spent contemplating the different ways you could spend the last thirty minutes of your life. Pathetic really, but she couldn't claim she was unhappy. Scared at times? Maybe, maybe not. Mostly she felt very little emotion; quite possibly, she had lost her own humanity. Did that make her a bad person? She still felt not.

Eva rose to rinse her bowl, placing it in the dishwasher. She selected a firm banana and a bunch of grapes from the fruit bowl for dessert and poured herself another half glass of wine. Settling back on the couch, she switched off the news channel that she'd let run in the background and started to think about how best to ensure that Berry, the Chief

Scientist, was well able to answer the questions the Inner Cabinet ministers might ask. She was going through the types of questions that might be put to Berry when her personal cell phone rang.

Immediately recognising the name of her caller, she said, "Gretel, how nice to hear from you. How are you?"

"I'm well; thank you for asking, Eva. I'm sorry to call you so late, but I have a couple of things I need to talk to you about in person. Is it convenient for me to pop over in about fifteen minutes?"

Oh blast! thought Eva, but she replied, "Of course that would be okay, see you soon."

Fifteen minutes later, having picked up her discarded clothing and quickly tidied the living area of her apartment, Eva found herself admitting Gretel.

"Hello darling, so sorry for the lateness of the hour, but I won't keep you long," said Gretel, as she breezed into the living area. "Yes, a glass of red would be lovely, thank you," she said in response to Eva's questioning gesture, followed by, "Love your furniture, you've always had such great taste," as she sat herself on the designer chair next to the couch.

Eva poured Gretel's drink, placing it and a cheese platter on the low table near Gretel's chair. Picking up her own unfinished glass, she sat down at the end of the couch closest to her visitor.

Her eyes had quickly run over Gretel the instant she'd appeared. *Why do women do this?* she wondered to herself. *Did men do this too?* Gretel had aged, but Eva quickly judged she looked good, nevertheless. Gretel's once-blonde hair now had streaks of grey, and she had changed the way it was styled to a short bob. She was wearing an elegant grey-blue jacket over tailored navy trousers, with low-heeled navy shoes. All this she'd noted from just one glance.

Eva was about to make some conversational opener, but she was forestalled by Gretel.

"Now, Eva, both of us are busy people, so let me come straight to the point. Tomorrow you are arranging to brief Berry, and I have complete confidence that you will do so appropriately and thoroughly."

Good old Cabut, thought Eva, *he didn't waste any time passing on tomorrow's planned agenda,* but she said nothing, waiting patiently for Gretel to continue.

"I'm also quite confident that you can hazard the more outlandish questions Berry may face." Eva nodded.

"So, it's not just Berry's preparation strategy that brings me here. I'm here, Eva, because I need to hear from you, in confidence, just between you and me, things that you may not be so directly informative about with Berry."

Gretel paused to sip her wine before continuing with a smile. "It will help me to know what I should avoid allowing Berry to discuss at the Cabinet meeting."

With a more serious face, she looked keenly at Eva, and asked, "Exactly what stage is the program at, and when do you expect it will be ready to implement?"

Calmly, Eva responded that the program had successfully passed the simulation stage without the need for any major adjustment, but it was still in the process of further ongoing testing. She assumed that Cabut would have informed Gretel about today's issue, but she thought better of raising this unless pressed. Instead, she clarified with Gretel, "I presume you're asking about the implementation of the part with relevance to Berry?"

"Of course, that's why I'm here," shot back Gretel.

Eva nodded. "It's difficult to be precise, but as a conservative estimate it could be ready to be passed on to medical companies within twelve months – dependent, as I say, on the completion of the current controlled tests."

"And who, Eva, is aware of the ongoing testing to which you so glibly refer?" questioned Gretel.

"Apart from the two of us, only Cabut has full knowledge," responded Eva.

"Are you sure about this, Eva? You know how important it is for me, that is to say the Government, to be able to announce the introduction of the next stage of our replacement organs program without any hint of controversy."

"Yes – to the best of my knowledge, I'm sure. The laboratory staff are programmed beings."

Gretel waited in silence for more.

Why does she always unsettle me? thought Eva defensively.

Eva admitted what Gretel would have already heard from Cabut about the incident that day.

"Cabut arranged for the matter to be cleaned up, and as the civilian was chosen with care it's most unlikely there will be any enquiry about his welfare," Eva said.

She went on to explain that she had isolated the likely problem with the procedure, and ended by reassuring Gretel that there was nothing in the program that should cause her concern.

"Thank you, Eva," said Gretel, "but, regrettably, that is far from true. I do have misgivings about what you are doing."

Eva was about to point out that Gretel had given the authority to proceed, before thinking better of it.

Gretel sighed. "How many other civilians are you likely to need as volunteers for your ongoing testing and refinement before we can put all this in the past? The more cases you use, the more likely it is that information will be leaked."

Gretel didn't wait for Eva to respond.

"Today I listened to concerns raised by some of my finest ministers. Should they get a whiff of the last stage of your testing, it could be most unfortunate for both of us. As the President, you know it is my overwhelming desire to do good and to support and promote initiatives that are for the betterment of our citizens. I also understand, as a former scientist, the need for thoroughness, and so it was with a heavy heart that I approved the final stage of testing."

Holding eye contact with Eva, Gretel calmly added, "I think there is scope for only one more test case, the details of which I continue not to wish to know. This brings me to reiterate to you, Eva, that should any knowledge of this testing get out, then I shall be able to honestly deny full knowledge of what you have been doing. As for you, Eva, you might face criminal charges, and do so alone."

Gretel paused for effect. "Do I make myself very clear Eva? You need to get the program right, and quickly, without any questions raised about the final stage of the testing."

Eva did not immediately respond, although this time she judged Gretel expected a response. When she did reply, it was simply to say that Gretel could rely on her to deal with the situation and that she was confident the program was nearly perfected. As an afterthought, she agreed that quite possibly only one more test would be necessary.

Gretel nodded, without further comment.

"Goodness me, just look at the time. I'm keeping you from that beauty sleep you so desperately need, Eva," said Gretel, rising from her seat while draining her glass.

"Why don't we catch up for dinner once Berry has given her performance and things are clearer at your end? Say in about four or five weeks? We can talk about old times – now that would be fun, wouldn't it?" And with that, Gretel swept out of Eva's apartment.

On her own again, Eva realised that Gretel was setting a time limit for her to identify and fix the error in the program. The offer of dinner was really a summons to ensure she had successfully complied.

Late though it was, she decided to message Cabut to ask if another potential test subject had been considered along with the civilian they had chosen for the unsuccessful test.

Cabut responded straight away: 'Yes, someone else was considered. Do you want the details now?'

She replied that it could wait till first thing in the morning and wished him good night, thinking to herself what a gem Cabut was – he was always alert to her needs, no matter the hour.

Was he in his pyjamas or did he sleep naked, and was he alone in bed? she wondered with a giggle. Dismissing these frivolously inappropriate thoughts, she readied herself for her own bed. While she did this, it occurred to her that, if necessary, she could always call in a favour to make things a little easier for herself. It was certainly worth bearing in mind.

Eva's last thoughts before sleep embraced her were: *What did she mean that I desperately needed beauty sleep? That woman really gets under my skin. And I would think old times would be the last thing Madam President would ever want to talk about.*

CHAPTER 3

Aneeka and Aleck were well-known at the Ensemble Café. When Aleck arrived a few minutes after Aneeka, Felix, the owner, greeted him warmly and pointed him in the direction of the corner table she'd chosen.

"Hello darling, I'm sorry I'm a little late," he said, leaning down to kiss her lightly on the lips.

"That's fine Aleck, I've only just arrived myself," she replied.

"And how's our little man coming on?" queried Aleck, patting his wife's distended tummy.

"Much to tell and some decisions to be made … but first, let's order: I'm ravenous, and I bet you are too," smiled Aneeka, knowing full well that Aleck's thin physique belied a very healthy appetite.

Aleck was a fit, not unattractive man of thirty-seven, with clear blue eyes and an unruly crop of sun-bleached brown hair that gave him a boyish charm. Aneeka loved that he was so fit and active, and she loved his body that she alone was privileged to share. During intimate moments, of which there were many, she liked running her fingers down the sides of his face, stroking his slightly raised cheekbones and feeling the friction from the fine stubble around his jawline, then moving on to his muscular hairless chest, playfully tweaking his nipples, dallying around his taut stomach while her tongue …

Goodness! she thought, collecting herself. *I hadn't realised that one of the side benefits of pregnancy was rampant libido. Here I am in the middle of the day with much to tell my husband about our-soon-to-be-born child, and all my mind is focusing on is how I shall bed him this evening … pity he's got to go back to work this arvo.*

Aleck continued to study the menu, seemingly unaware of Aneeka's sensual musings. She knew that, for him, the decision-making was a big part of the joy of eating out.

Felix wandered over with two glasses and a bottle of water. "No wine for m 'lady and her budding bub, and you sir must work hard this afternoon now that you will soon have a family to support, so no wine for you either," he quipped. "Please enjoy our best vintage water."

Over the years, Felix had become a friend. They exchanged pleasantries, asking after Felix's wife and daughter. Hearing her name mentioned, Felix's wife, Ivana, waved from the open kitchen area where she was busy supervising the food preparation.

"Now, what can I get for you today? Can I recommend the braised aubergine with lentil tagine?"

Aneeka accepted Felix's recommendation, while Aleck opted for gnocchi infused with a squid-ink sauce.

It wasn't long before Ivana delivered their food to them. She admired how well Aneeka looked, wishing her all the best for the remaining weeks. "Make the most of your time for sleep," she counselled. "There won't be much opportunity after the baby comes." They all laughed, then Ivana left them to enjoy their meals.

The gnocchi in its piquant sauce was delicious, and Aneeka gave full marks to the tagine. Each tried the other's food and agreed they had chosen wisely. For a few minutes they ate in silence, then Aneeka paused, resting her fork on the side of her plate.

"Now, darling, tell me your news," said Aleck.

"Well," she began, "Geraldine contacted me this morning."

Looking alarmed, Aleck also put his fork down, saying: "But we saw Gerry earlier this week for your check-up, and she said all was well."

"It's okay, worrywart, it's because all is going so particularly well that Geraldine, as my obstetrician, wondered if I would be willing to participate in some research that she and a colleague of hers are planning."

"What sort of research did Gerry say?" enquired her slightly sceptical husband, who had resumed eating his meal.

It was an ever-so-minor point of contention between them as to how they should address their obstetrician. To Aneeka, her heavily built, somewhat imposing doctor, Miss Geraldine Geary, looked more like a 'Geraldine' than a 'Gerry'; she found it hard to think of her as the sprightly and diminutive 'Gerry' that the more casual name conjured in her mind. As it was, she uttered the name Geraldine only rarely in the doctor's presence and would have been happy to have just called her 'Doctor'.

In truth, she was puzzled why she always felt somewhat intimidated in Geraldine's presence. Aleck seemed very relaxed during their appointments; he and Geraldine would happily discuss the progress of the pregnancy, joking and chatting together quite easily. This left Aneeka feeling invisible – or, worse, reduced to no more than a womb on legs, somewhat like she imagined a surrogate mother might feel during her antenatal visits. When she had tried to explain this to Aleck, he had laughed at her. "Gerry is an empathetic, open, warm and welcoming person and a highly respected and accomplished professional," he had said, pointing out that other patients greeted the obstetrician as 'Gerry' too.

So, Aneeka learnt to suppress her thoughts and allowed Aleck to take the lead during the consultations. And what did it really matter anyway, as she and the baby were doing great and she felt she was thriving at thirty-six weeks.

However, when Geraldine had contacted her personally, a very surprised Aneeka had seen it as a chance to earn the respect of the doctor. She would show Geraldine that she, Aneeka, was a person of intelligence, and there was more to her than her uterus. She was a worthy person who understood the importance of supporting research; she was a solid citizen too, willing to play a responsible role.

At least that's what she'd thought afterwards. During the call, Aneeka had been so flustered that she was neither able to think clearly nor articulate any meaningful comment. As a consequence, she was a bit vague on the details.

"It's something to do with collecting together the results of amniocentesis procedures to enable research into the early detection of problems in pregnancy," she said lightly, pausing to finish the last morsel of her food. She sighed happily. "That was so delicious."

Knowing that Aleck's forensic legal mind would need more information than that, she added, "Geraldine said that since our baby and I are doing so well, our results would be part of a control set of data against which results from more difficult pregnancies can be compared. All that we need to do is authorise the release of the data to the research group."

Aneeka felt cross with herself that she hadn't asked for more details. "And maybe attend a session with the research group, if required," she finished lamely, trying hard to dredge up the words Geraldine had used.

Aleck nodded, clearly not satisfied he had enough information. "Listen darling, I have to rush back to the office for a meeting, but how about I give Gerry a call after I finish work this afternoon and we can talk further about it tonight?"

Aneeka smiled. "Okay, my sweetheart, but I've been thinking of some other plans for this evening, so I hope there's not too much to discuss." She surreptitiously brushed her serviette against his groin.

*

Aleck made good time back, reaching his chambers with ten minutes to spare. He freshened up in the adjoining small washroom before returning to his desk.

He'd left one file on his desk before lunch – he'd spent most of the morning reading up on the case and it interested him, so he was looking forward to meeting his new client and finding out more.

His office was well-lit by natural light, and from the window Aleck could see a neighbouring school oval. If the children were out playing, he sometimes paused to daydream about when his son would be running around on the same school field.

His secretary messaged to confirm that Mr Hartland had arrived, so he rose, walking to the door to welcome him into his office.

Gesturing to the older man to take a seat on the well-upholstered chair opposite his own, Aleck offered him coffee from the espresso machine that sat discreetly on a sofa table near the window.

"How do you like your coffee, Mr Hartland?" Aleck asked.

"Short macchiato, thank you – and please, call me Leon."

They went through the opening dance of pleasantries, feeling each other out as they sipped their coffee.

Leon was a man of small stature, smartly dressed in an older fashion. His face was creased, his hair thin, and he did not look like he took great care of his health. His eyes were watery, giving the impression that his regular partner in life was strong coffee rather than sleep. However, his voice was well-modulated, albeit a little gravelly, and he gave the impression he was an educated man.

"Now then Leon, let me ask you to explain in your own words what brings you here today," requested Aleck.

Displaying no emotion, Leon embarked on a succinct and condensed version of some of the documents that Aleck had read earlier that day.

"I am concerned about the whereabouts and welfare of a citizen known as Claus Proger," he began. "I do not know this person myself, but I speak on behalf of others who know of him either as a colleague, friend or occasional companion. I concede that the information I have been given may not be completely accurate – poor memory, lack of attention at the time, reluctance or fear of getting involved … whatever the reason. Nevertheless, I contend there are people worried about him," said Leon, making a point of looking directly into Aleck's eyes.

Aleck calmly made the obvious remark that he was a solicitor, not a member of law enforcement, so why had Leon come to him? "Would it not be more appropriate to report citizen Proger as a missing person to the constabulary officers?" he added.

Asking Aleck to hear him out before forming any conclusions, Leon resumed his story.

"As you will have read, Proger kept to himself, did as he was instructed, and his behaviour gave no cause for alarm. He worked uncomplainingly in a low-skilled casual position at a small manufacturing firm. His work colleagues described him as quiet and reserved, his employer as conscientious and reliable. His social life appears to have centred around a local pub, where he proved to be a good darts player. The few that know him think it is out of character for him to disappear without a word."

Aleck hadn't heard anything he hadn't read earlier, so he chose to stay silent, waiting for Leon to add to his story.

"No doubt you are wondering how I come to be interested in what has happened to Claus," Leon said matter-of-factly.

"Through a friend of a friend, shall we say, I was told that Claus had shared some information about himself with a barmaid who worked at his local pub. Apparently, the two had become friendly. Claus reportedly told the barmaid that he wouldn't be in for a drink for a few days as he would be undergoing a minor procedure on the coming Friday and that he would then be resting at home for the weekend, before returning to work on the Monday. Neither she nor anyone else has seen him since ... well, going on for around four weeks. What the 'minor procedure' was, the barmaid had not asked, respecting his privacy, and Claus had not divulged it voluntarily."

Pausing, Leon's eyes drifted sideways to the print above the coffee machine; Aleck had chosen it for its vibrant colours and simplicity. Taking this pause as an opportunity to get more coffee, Aleck walked over to the espresso machine and quietly made them both another drink. Leon looked up in surprise and appreciation.

"Well, young man, this could be the start of a beautiful friendship! Thank you." Both men chuckled, each recalling a familiar line from an old movie. Aleck smiled: watching classic movies was one of his and Aneeka's favourite pastimes.

He resumed his seat, allowing Leon to get to the point of his visit.

"What I really want is for you to serve a freedom of information request on the Department of Health to find out what they know of Claus."

Leon smiled ruefully. "I'm confident that you will have done your homework before this afternoon's meeting, so you'll have read the 'Leon Hartland' file. You therefore should understand why I'd prefer not to submit this request myself."

Leon's personal file was the document that Aleck had found particularly interesting earlier in the day. However, apart from acknowledging that he had read the file, he chose not to make any comment on what he had discovered.

Aleck was a good solicitor: preparing and presenting Leon's request would be straightforward. However, a solicitor was not required for such a simple task, and, from what he had read that morning, he felt confident that Leon already knew this. Aleck was both intrigued and puzzled by Leon's real motive. *Why had Leon chosen to come to him, knowing full well that such a request could be made, at much less expense, by a legal clerk?* Instinct told him there was something more going on here.

So again, this time more firmly, Aleck asked Leon why he was asking for his help. The older man did not reply at first, again gazing over at the two cranes in the art print.

With a sigh, he turned back to Aleck. "It's very simple why I chose to approach you. This will be a game of chess, Aleck, where the freedom of information request is just the opening move. When the game becomes more intense, I want you on my side."

Aleck was not satisfied by Leon's response. He knew himself to be competent, and one day he did intend to put his energies into developing his career further, perhaps progressing to barrister level, but that had not yet happened, so he retorted amiably that while he thanked Leon for his faith in him, his flattery was not justifiable.

Knowing there must be more to the story, he pushed for a more enlightening response. "Come on Leon, if we are going to work well together, you need to be open with me."

Leon looked at his timepiece and murmured that he must not take up any more of Aleck's afternoon. Grinning, he told Aleck that he would return in a week's time to see how he had got on and they could talk further then.

"I feel we've achieved all that I'd intended on today's visit – and it's such a nice-looking day that I'm about ready to take a stroll."

Reluctantly, Aleck said no more.

Walking Leon to the door, he shook the older man's hand in farewell. Leon was almost through the door when he turned to him and said: "I knew your father, Aleck. He never betrayed me, and neither will you."

And with that, Mr Leon Hartland was gone.

Aleck returned to his desk and sat down, feeling somewhat stunned. That Leon had known his father came as a complete surprise. Both of Aleck's parents had died, his father three years ago and his mother the year before that. He quite often found himself feeling sad that neither would ever have the joy of seeing their grandchild. He searched his memory but found no recollection of his father ever mentioning a Leon Hartland, and he was certain he'd never met Leon until this afternoon.

Aleck's parents had both been schoolteachers, so perhaps Leon had also been a teacher and that was the connection. However, what had Leon meant by 'he never betrayed me'?

From Leon's file, Aleck knew that as a younger man Leon had experienced some clashes with the Department of Law and Order through his participation in various anti-government demonstrations. Aleck couldn't imagine his quiet, academic, peaceful and law-abiding father taking to the streets to protest against some point of contention with a government program. At most, his father may have written a polite letter to a minister, in which he would have set out his argument using logic and reason. His father was no rebel; he'd saved his passion for supporting his family and his students, and for mathematics, the subject he'd taught for thirty-eight years.

As a teenager, Aleck remembered questioning his father's order of priority between family and mathematics. His father, laughing at his adolescent son, would reply: "Don't be a smart alec, Aleck." His father thought he was being funny and often used the phrase, much to the embarrassment of his teenage son. Yet this 'dad joke' was one of the stories Aleck had lovingly told at his father's funeral.

I wonder if my son will be irritated by the things I say or do?

Aleck sighed, collecting the coffee cups and taking them to the dishwasher in the staff kitchenette. Returning, he dictated a summary of his meeting with Leon and sent a message for his clerk to draw up the freedom of information document, instructing that it should be ready for him to check the next day. Leaving thoughts of Leon Hartland and his father for another time, he turned his attention to the rest of his day.

At 6 pm, just as he was about to leave the office, Aleck remembered he had to ring Gerry. He tried her number but was told that she was unavailable, so he confirmed his contact details and said he would try again the next day.

The evening air was crisp, but the light was clear and bright. Aleck's thoughts turned to food and Aneeka, possibly in that order, and he silently laughed at himself as he wondered whether his wife might have preferred the order to be reversed. With his father's old joke still running through his mind, Aleck set off to walk the kilometre to the underground station and catch his train home.

CHAPTER 4

Leon Hartland had enjoyed meeting Aleck. He liked the younger man.

The physical resemblance between Aleck and his father Colin (at the younger age when Leon had known him, at least) was quite marked. They both had an unruly crop of curly hair, clear blue eyes and a square-set jaw. Aleck was a little shorter perhaps, but he had inherited his father's slim, athletic build. Even their voices were similar, although Leon felt Aleck probably possessed the more light-hearted disposition of the two.

He and Colin had been vaguely aware of each other at university, but they only became properly acquainted during their honours year. They were both completing degrees majoring in mathematics, with Colin specialising in mathematical genetics and Leon in game theory. Although not especially close, they had a friendship of sorts. Both were competitive and eager to outshine the other academically, a rivalry fought in good spirit – with each interested in the progress the other was making with his honours thesis.

Over the course of that year, the two became closer. They would occasionally meet for a chat over a cup of coffee or a crisp lager, and they came to discover that, other than mathematics, they both shared an interest in political reform – the issue of the time.

Ah, those were the days, thought Leon, interrupting his reverie to pour himself a glass of cider, now his preferred tipple over pale lager.

Settling himself comfortably on his sofa, Leon's thoughts drifted back to the days of President Homer. Homer had first come to power as the leader of a socialist party and, following the success of his first term in government, he had been given an overwhelming endorsement for a second term.

Even now, Leon could not decide what had motivated Homer's 'Revised Democracy' manifesto. Perhaps power corrupts, or perhaps Homer had always intended to pursue the policies he'd introduced during his second term.

He did, however, remember how wary people were, with rumours abounding that Revised Democracy would allow the President control of the military, law enforcement, and possibly even the judiciary.

Although both he and Colin had supported the abolition of the old political parties in favour of a more centrist form of government, they, along with other students, had joined in the on-campus protests against the proposal to grant the President the increased and far-reaching powers for which he was canvassing. These, Leon and Colin had argued, would mean the presidency would be akin to a dictatorship: the Government would become an autocracy, and the citizens would be disenfranchised.

We weren't far short of the mark, he thought with a sigh, swallowing a mouthful of cider.

President Homer had responded to the protests by calling for calm and enunciating his plan in a reasonable and caring way, repeatedly pointing out that his record showed he was trustworthy and driven only by an agenda of improving the lot of the people. He had asked the people to give his reforms a chance, making a solemn promise that, should they not bring benefit to the Country, he would stand down from the presidency within two years.

Fat chance that would ever have happened, thought Leon with a cynical snort.

At the time, many people had been reassured by the President's words and willing to give the reforms a chance. Leon and Colin, however, were not so easily convinced.

In the lead-up to the vote, Leon – and, to a lesser extent, Colin – had continued to take part in meetings and marches to express their concern.

He had also joined in public demonstrations outside the university, but Colin had only joined him once that Leon could remember.

Then things had started to get more serious. Journalists were being discouraged from reporting protest events (other than to denounce the participants as activists and troublemakers). This ploy led to a lack of sympathy for the protesters and, quietly, some of the leaders of the protest movement had been briefly detained in custody for alleged unlawful behaviour. Without the leaders, the movement faltered and the number of protestors dwindled.

Despite having no major role in the marches, Leon and Colin had been shocked when they each received a warning about their behaviour from the Dean of the Mathematics Faculty. The unfairness of this had succeeded in bringing the two men closer together and cemented their opposition to the President. Nonetheless, Colin took the advice of the kindly Dean and ceased altogether his involvement in protests, telling Leon that he'd be exercising his democratic right to express his opinion at the ballot box.

The Country had gone to the polls in what would be the last act of old democracy – the last time its citizens would vote. Even today, Leon could recite the details of the outcome with accuracy.

"It was close," the President had announced, his proposals having won endorsement with 42% in favour to 34% against, with 24% informal.

"Bollocks!" Leon couldn't stop himself from yelling, before laughing at himself for allowing the figures to rankle despite the passage of time. He was starting to enjoy this trip down memory lane, helped along by the cider.

He remembered that President Homer, while thanking those who had supported his plans, had fulsomely praised their forward thinking and courage. He also recalled the President's commitment to those who had not given him their vote, promising that he would earn their trust and they would come to see that the reforms were good for the Country. Revised Democracy, or RevDem as it became known, was born.

As far as Leon could remember, life had settled back to normal – for the majority, at least. Citizens were generally content; their standard of living was good, and they quickly came to accept RevDem as the way the Country was governed. The loss of the right to vote seemed to pass by unmourned, much to Leon's consternation. Also unlamented was the extinction of the formal system of political parties.

The citizens, as far as Leon could judge, by and large did not feel unheard. Any matter could be raised with an OCM, it was argued, and any citizen could nominate themselves to become an OCM. OCMs held their positions for an eight-year term, with half reaching their fourth year as the other half reached their eighth, meaning OCM applications were invited every four years – open to all citizens, including the outgoing members themselves. The citizens seemed to accept the way that positions were allocated, after careful consideration by the Heads of the Government Departments. And, while many members were reappointed for a second term, there was always the opportunity for new blood.

That the citizenry was not disaffected, that the Country had advanced – those were facts.

Finishing the remains of his cider, Leon acknowledged that RevDem had worked out better than he'd expected. *Unless you were one of the more marginalised members of the citizenry,* he qualified, the old fire of opposition not completely extinguished.

Take this fellow Claus Proger, he reasoned. *No records, no family coming forward – my hunch is he's an illegal. Makes him an ideal candidate for a government program once identified.*

Having, as yet, no proof to back his hunch, he had declined to share this view with Aleck, but Leon was keen to learn the outcome of the freedom of information application that Aleck was lodging on his behalf.

Noting his thoughts had returned to the present, and mildly castigating himself for wasting so much time in indulgent reverie, Leon raised himself from his sofa to get on with the rest of his day.

By late evening, Leon found his thoughts returning to Colin. Unable to settle to sleep, his mind journeyed back in time. In this fitful, dreamlike state, it was as if he and Colin were the characters in a play he was watching, viewed from the perspective of a detached narrator.

After being awarded their honours degrees, it had been surprising, in view of the acknowledged quality of their research, that neither Leon nor Colin had been offered a scholarship to finance their postgraduate studies. Undeterred, they were able to pick up some casual work in local cafés, which allowed them to continue their studies on a part-time basis.

Leon, in particular, had been somewhat incensed about the lack of a scholarship offer, and he had added this setback to the list of grievances he held against the Government. Not that he needed the scholarship, coming as he did from a wealthy family, but he saw the rejection as politically motivated and said as much to Jacques, one of the regular customers at the café where he worked. Leon had immediately regretted his outburst, knowing it was unwise to express such a view to a virtual stranger, but he'd come to be quite friendly with Jacques and was sure no one else had overheard. He had been relieved when Jacques had just shrugged sympathetically, and no more had been said.

A month or so later, Jacques happened to mention to Leon that he had a birthday coming up. He invited Leon to join him at a local pub, where he was meeting a few of his friends for a birthday drink. Flattered to be included, Leon went along and found he quite enjoyed the company of Jacques and his three friends. As the friendship developed, Leon joined the group quite regularly. The conversations were usually about football, billiards, their jobs and their plans for the future.

One evening, the conversation had turned to politics. Leon was not one to drink to excess, but he had drunk two lagers in quick succession and was feeling warm and sociable. The group seemed to be of a like mind, and Leon felt emboldened to share his opinion – that the vote to introduce RevDem had been rigged. The informal vote had been too high and did not match with the records from some polling stations, he had claimed.

The group had been immediately intrigued, with a couple of them commenting that they'd heard similar rumours. Leon remembered saying, "So, what should we do to expose the President for his unpresidential behaviour?"

It was Jacques who had suggested that Leon write a paper to explain the mathematical reasoning behind his belief that the vote was rigged. Jacques had claimed that he could pass it on to a friend at a news organisation who might be prepared to publish it.

Leon had accepted the challenge and worked with deep thought on the proposed paper. When he went to share his workings, as he often did, with Colin, he remembered being surprised by his friend's reaction. Colin had refused to be involved and seemed worried by Leon's plans to publish his work.

Colin was more pragmatic and grounded than Leon. Perhaps he had sensed that Leon could get himself into territory he might come to regret if he attempted to publish any such critique, whether the argument stood up to scrutiny or not. Leon would not be deterred from pursuing the task, but Colin had made him promise not to publish it under his own name and, reluctantly, Leon had agreed.

It had been another couple of weeks until Leon was completely happy with his work and ready to pass it on to Jacques. Leon had explained that he thought the article, if it was to be published, should be published under an assumed name. Jacques had thought for a moment before nodding in agreement.

"What name?" he had asked Leon.

"I've given the author's name on the paper," replied Leon, and nothing more was said.

Leon had returned to his studies and waited to hear from Jacques, but Jacques did not appear at the café again. From time to time Leon would pop into the pub they used to frequent, but he never came across Jacques, or any of Jacques' friends. He was concerned and hoped Jacques had not got into any trouble over his paper. Early on, Colin had stopped asking Leon if he had heard anything, and he never asked Leon about his chosen nom de plume.

The weeks had turned into months, and soon Colin and Leon were approaching the end of their first postgraduate year. Once again, they applied for scholarships to support their full-time studies – and this time they were optimistic of success, since they had both been called in for an interview. They had practised interviewing each other in order to hone their responses to likely questions, and they'd even discussed what parts of their work they should take to the interview to highlight their potential.

Colin had the first interview. Leon could remember him making a special effort to look smart, iron his shirt and polish his lace-up 'proper' shoes that Leon had never seen him wear. Colin had been excited, optimistic and confident. Leon saw Colin off to the interview, wishing him all the best, and set about preparing for his own interview later that day.

Leon had been reasonably satisfied with his interview. Initially, it had followed the path that he and Colin had predicted, and Leon felt he had delivered his rehearsed responses well. To his surprise, the interview had then gone off on a tangent, the upshot of which was a proposal for Leon to leave the university and transfer to a government institute, where his work would enable him to complete his doctoral thesis while contributing to an interesting and important research program. Leon had felt both flattered and excited about the proposal.

He remembered looking forward to discussing the offer with Colin and wondering whether something similar had been put to him. They had agreed to meet later that afternoon to exchange stories about their interviews.

When Colin arrived, it was immediately obvious that something was wrong. All that Colin would say was that he had been advised that the greatest contribution he could make to the prosperity of the Country lay in the field of education rather than mathematical genetics. He had been told that his scholarship application would be turned down. Consequently, he intended to abandon his postgraduate studies in order to undertake teacher training as advised, and thereafter he planned to apply for a position as a school mathematics teacher.

Leon would never forget Colin's totally unexpected announcement. Colin would indeed make an excellent mathematics teacher, Leon had thought, and he was well aware that mathematics education was a high priority for the Government, but he was shocked by the sudden twist of Colin's fate. Not waiting to find out how Leon's interview had gone, a drained, sober-faced Colin had wished Leon all the best and walked out of his life. Leon had never seen him again.

Years would go by before Leon found out the whole truth of what had happened in Colin's interview. It was only then that he'd realised that Colin had been his greatest friend – the friend who, as he told Aleck so many years later, had never betrayed him.

CHAPTER 5

It was not only to maintain his fitness level that Aleck would rise early from the warmth of his bed to go running, untangling himself from the arms of his still-sleeping wife. The peace and beauty of his chosen running area alongside a nearby stream, with its early morning scents of lilac, hyacinth and lavender, beckoned him like a siren. The glory of the wild rhododendrons that grew in batches between the weeping willows and the field maple trees, intertwined with luscious euphorbias and agapanthus, never failed to delight him, reminding Aleck how fortunate a life he lived.

As the fallen leaves from the camellias and magnolias prostrated themselves at his feet, forming a light carpet over the path on which he ran, Aleck became Zephyrus, an ancient god of wind and air, the one to whom all nature paid homage. With each gentle wave brushing against the stones that lay in its watery path, the little stream would join him as his running companion, murmuring its respectful encouragement.

As the early morning unfolded, the number of people out running started to build, signifying to Aleck that it was time to cast off his imagined persona and resume his life as husband, father-to-be and solicitor of good repute. Besides, as he would whisper to the little stream, "I feel like breakfast."

Having showered, breakfasted and kissed his wife farewell, Aleck caught the train to the Professional District, where his law firm, Oostends, was situated. He greeted several of his familiar travelling companions, but when each settled in to check their devices, Aleck marshalled his thoughts and mentally set up a 'to-do' list for the day. Top of the list would be to follow up on Leon Hartland's request – and also, he reminded himself, recalling Aneeka's parting words, he must call Gerry. He thought of doing so as the train carried him along but, unlike several of his fellow travellers, decided that it was not an appropriate environment for a private voice call.

Within the hour, Aleck was settled comfortably in his office checking the freedom of information request that Erik, his clerk, had prepared for him. Satisfied, as he almost always was with Erik's work, he instructed Erik to deliver the request in person to the Department of Health that morning.

Erik was an earnest and industrious young man who Aleck had worked with for some time. "How long have you been with us, Erik?"

"It must be about five years."

Aleck nodded, and responded as he had many times before. "You know, your work is very thorough Erik, so good in fact that I always feel you're not achieving your full potential. Have you given any more thought to completing a law degree?"

Erik grinned. "Well Aleck, thank you for your faith in me. One day I think I may follow that path, but quite frankly, while I find my job satisfying, as you know I also love my time away from work. Music is still my passion, and I'm not yet ready to give up my evening gigs in order to study. As I admitted to my father just the other day, I know it's looking less and less likely that I'll crack the big time ... but I'm not ready, not yet, to stop trying."

"Well, good luck Erik, just don't leave it too late. Besides, I don't think law and music have to be mutually exclusive," observed Aleck. "Anyway, enough for now, we both have work to do. Let me know how you get on with that FOI, it's rather urgent."

Glancing at his watch, Aleck remembered that he still needed to call Gerry. He thought there was a good chance he could catch her between completing her hospital rounds and starting the morning's consultations. He dialled her number and was pleased when her secretary placed him on hold, promising to see if Miss Geary had returned. Moments later, Gerry arrived on the line.

"Aleck, it's Gerry here. Sorry to have missed your call last night, I had an emergency to attend to but all's good now. What's the problem? Is Aneeka okay?"

"Hi Gerry," replied Aleck. "Everything's fine with Aneeka. However, she mentioned that you had suggested she take part in some research, and I just wanted to be a little clearer about what that entailed."

"Oh, I see," laughed Gerry. "Let me assure you that there's nothing in it that should worry you at all, Aleck. Just a monitoring of statistics really. Aneeka would be part of a control group whose data we want to compare with that of a group with troublesome pregnancies."

She continued. "As you know, families are strongly encouraged to restrict themselves to one offspring these days, so we want the experience to go as well as possible for both baby and mother. All I'm really asking for is permission to share Aneeka's data with a small research team, of which I am part. Data that I collect routinely in any case, as her doctor," Gerry explained in her good-natured way.

Chortling down the phone, she added, "Naturally, Aneeka's name would be suppressed. After all Aleck, I know you're a lawyer so I'm not stupid enough to mess with you!" She guffawed again.

Aleck smiled; he liked this woman, there was no stuffiness or grand dame-ness about her, he thought. Gerry's personality was direct and straightforward writ large (to match her not inconsiderable girth).

"Thanks, Gerry, for reassuring me that it's non-intrusive. Sounds like we get a chance to help others by participating. Of course, it's Aneeka's call whether to participate, but you can both discuss that at her next consultation. Good to talk to you, have a nice day."

"Any time, Aleck. All the best."

Aleck's attention swiftly turned to other matters, with coffee above them all. As he waited for the espresso machine to finish its work, his thoughts briefly centred again on Leon Hartland's connection with his father. If Leon had had a strong friendship with his father, it was odd that his name had never been mentioned, at least as far as Aleck could recall.

His father could still have one surviving cousin, he realised. Charles had been at Colin's funeral, but Aleck had not seen him since that day, and he had no idea whether Charlie was still alive. He made a mental note to try and contact him. *A stab in the dark, but worth a go,* he reasoned.

Aleck opened his next case file and checked his appointments for the rest of the day. His heart sunk a little when he saw Eidish Smythe had booked in to make yet another alteration to her will. She was consumed by the fear that her family was only interested in getting their hands on her money; she kept them in check by regularly getting Aleck to make codicils that removed whoever was out of favour and reinstalled whoever was now back in favour as her beneficiaries. Presuming that would again be the purpose of her visit, Aleck counted up her three previous amendments – all from the past four years. He had even requested a year ago that a doctor attest that Eidish was of sound mind when insisting on such changes to her will. On that occasion, Aleck had tried unsuccessfully to reason with Eidish that her adult children and grandchildren cared more for her welfare than her estate.

As one of the Owlds (the name given to people from Aleck's grandparents' generation), Eidish Smythe had borne four children, a feat virtually unheard of these days. From these children Eidish had four grandchildren, and there was also the likelihood of great-grandchildren in the near future – although, given her advanced years, Eidish would probably only know them briefly, if at all.

After a childhood marred only by a scarcity of fresh food, Eidish had enjoyed a reasonably good life, during which she had seen much change. By and large she had adapted to most of the rapidly evolving technologies, and she had outlived her husband and many of her contemporaries. Why she would want to end her days caught up in the throes of pettiness and unhappiness quite baffled Aleck, but her doctor said she was of sound mind and so he felt he had to follow her wishes regarding the pecking order within her will.

Aleck could only vaguely recall his own grandparents, but he remembered his mother and father talking about how deeply conservative and suspicious of government and change they were, traits that Aleck's school education had helped him come to understand.

Some two generations before the Owlds' time, there had been a period of time known as 'The Disaster', a time in which so much of their planet had been reduced to wasteland – left parched, radioactive and fragmented. Many of the world's countries were thought to have been led by selfish, inward-looking, unscientific and primitive governments, which – through collective neglect, ignorance and aggression – had brought on the catastrophe. Only one country had survived, thanks primarily to its geographic isolation from the rest of the world, as well as its rapid erection of nuclear shields. Aleck, like his contemporaries, knew how fortunate he was to live in it.

Refugees who had survived The Disaster and managed to make it to the Country's borders had been welcomed. Eidish was a granddaughter of one of these survivors, and, by the time she was born, the Country was managing reasonably well given it was the only habitable place that remained on the entire planet.

"Of course, the borders were closed by then," she had previously explained to Aleck. "Any late refugees had to be housed in the arid North due to concern that, by then, those poor Souls would carry contamination and unknown diseases into our Country."

Aleck knew that the descendants of the Souls, also referred to as Souls, who were permitted to trickle into their society, did so only after many years of incredible patience while they waited for their applications to be processed.

A more progressive government – the beginning of the Homer regime – had been elected by the time the children of the Owlds were ready to start families of their own. The Homer Government had introduced a set of recommendations for family planning. Controlling population growth, it argued, was a good and necessary economic measure. It would allow higher standards of living and security; enable greater funds to be diverted into dealing compassionately with the sick, those with social problems and those unable to work; and also allow greater funding for research programs, as well as investments in education, health and the sciences.

While the restrictions on the number of children per family were recommendations rather than laws, both Aleck and Aneeka, like many of their generation, were only children, with their parents agreeing with the Government's argument. For Aleck's generation, however, the 'Only Child' recommendation was a universal given. Aleck understood without question that the child Aneeka was bearing would be their only offspring.

It certainly simplifies who will inherit our currently meagre estate, thought Aleck wryly.

Eidish herself had often told Aleck how very thankful she felt towards the Homer Government, especially once the RevDem reforms were instigated. Wagging her finger at Aleck, she would say: "Look at me now. We Owlds have aged, but we are so well looked after. There's access to affordable medical treatment, and financial security without market risk – that President Homer was a great man, Aleck. He did so much good for our Country, and he trained President Nuewen so she'd continue his good work."

Eidish's generation generally lived longer, healthier lives than their parents, something else she attributed to Homer's reforms. "When you were just a boy, Aleck, your food was plentiful and safe to eat – unlike in my childhood, where soils and grasses often harboured contaminants that made safe food hard to come by. That's another reason to give thanks for the wisdom of President Homer. Ceasing the practice of slaughtering animals for food because of what they may have grazed on sure helped to reduce illness."

Aleck would usually wonder by this stage in their conversations if animal welfare might have been the higher priority, but he kept those thoughts to himself.

Aleck's deliberations about Mrs Smythe and generational changes were interrupted by Erik, who lightly tapped on the open door and strode in, saying, "Thought you would like to know two things." Not waiting for a response, Erik pulled up a chair, turning it around so he sat leaning forward against its back.

"First, I presented the FOI application to the officer at the Department of Health," he said. "As instructed, I took a number and sat down to wait for the receipt. This seemed to take longer than I expected, but after twenty minutes or so my number was called. Which brings me to my second point, and this is the strange bit: instead of being handed the receipt, I was ushered into an interview room and quizzed by two men about why I was making the application."

"I agree, that's very odd," said an intrigued Aleck.

"Well, I explained to them that there wasn't very much I could tell them, since I was just a law clerk following instructions." Erik grinned mischievously at Aleck. "Perhaps another reason why it's good to be at the bottom of the legal pile!"

Aleck laughed. "So, what happened next?"

"They wanted to know whose instructions I was following, and I said the law firm Oostends. Then one of them asked which member of the firm had given me my instructions, so I gave your name Aleck, pointing out to my inquisitor that if he had read the application in the first place rather than hassle me, he would find your name and signature and the firm's name on it. Don't think he appreciated my observation!" laughed Erik.

"By now I was getting a bit irritated myself, so when he asked the name of the client you were representing, I said I didn't know as that was above my pay scale."

"I did ask the two of them who they were, since they hadn't paid me the courtesy of introducing themselves, and also what the fuss was about, but they just said their interview with me was a routine check and that I could go.

"I asked them for the receipt, which they allowed me to snap, and here it is," said Erik, handing Aleck a receipt he'd printed from his phone.

Aleck placed the receipt in Leon Hartland's file, saying to Erik that he would need to contact the department every day until they received a response.

"I think it's important for us to let them know that we won't be fobbed off. First thing tomorrow morning, Erik, and each morning thereafter as necessary, I want you to front up to the department to ask if the application has been processed. Also, please can you send me an official report of what's happened today for the file?"

"Consider it done," said Erik as he turned the chair back to its normal position and left the room.

A new client was waiting for Aleck, so he had no time to ponder the meaning of what had happened. His client, an amiable young businessman, had a short consultation and left armed with advice about acquiring a new property that would allow him to relocate his burgeoning business away from his home. As they shook hands in farewell, Aleck wished the budding entrepreneur well, inviting him to get in touch again if he could be of future help.

Aleck quickly dictated a summary of the entrepreneur's consultation, before heading into a staff meeting. He usually tried to participate and offer suggestions when he could, but today he found himself unable to focus. Mercifully, the meeting was a short one, and after exchanging some banter and pleasantries with his co-workers, Aleck was soon back in his office.

Now for dear old Mrs Smythe, he thought, bracing himself.

It was not until Aleck was on his train home that his thoughts returned to the strangeness of Erik's experience at the Department of Health. He messaged Leon Hartland to arrange to meet him for an update on the curious reception of the FOI application, and before Aleck had reached his stop Leon had replied that he'd be at Aleck's office around 11 am the next day.

Arriving home, not even his adorable Aneeka could take his mind completely off the events of the day.

"You seem very preoccupied, darling, anything the matter?" she asked, as they were eating their evening meal.

"Sorry, sweetheart, bit of an unusual day at the office today. But," he smiled, "very rude of me to bring it home. Distract me by telling me what you did today."

"Oh, Aleck, I can think of a much better way of distracting you," she cheekily replied. "Finish your meal, and then I'll be very happy to share a special dessert with you."

Some glorious time later as he lay peacefully with Aneeka, satiated by their love-making, Aleck remembered that he hadn't told her about his conversation with Gerry. Aneeka seemed pleased that Aleck was comfortable about the research, and she said she would definitely agree to participate at her next appointment.

Rubbing his hand gently over her swollen belly, his eyes filled with love and contentment, Aleck asked, "So, what did my favourite one and three-quarter people do today?"

Aneeka rolled onto her side to face Aleck. "I wonder if it will be so easy for us to get about once we are in separate bodies? Anyway, today I took your son and heir for a walk. We walked along that trail by the stream that you desert me for each morning. It's so pretty and peaceful. No sense of any hustle and bustle from the city around it.

"Maybe we should think of moving out that way once bubs grows into wanting his own room rather than sharing your study. I did notice a smart apartment block not far from your jogging route that might be worth checking out sometime."

"Running route, you mean, not jogging route," interjected Aleck.

Kissing her, he added jokingly, "Keeping my darling satisfied requires a high level of fitness."

"Oh, is that so?" laughed Aneeka as she raised herself, leaning her weight on her elbow and pressing her body tantalisingly against Aleck's. "Then I think you need to prove your case, Solicitor Raine."

Much later, as he tidied up the dishes and the kitchen dining area, Aleck remembered Charlie. He went to his study and, searching through his parents' bits and pieces that he couldn't ever seem to bring himself to discard, he found his mother's address book. In it he found an address and telephone number for his father's cousin. Aleck didn't know if the information would still be correct, assuming Charles was even alive. However, deciding it was too late to try calling right then, Aleck copied the number and added 'Check out Charlie' to his mental to-do list for the next day.

Aneeka was already asleep, so Aleck quickly undressed, joining her in their bed. Once he had read the next chapter of his book, he switched on the alarm, switched off his bedside lamp, snuggled against his wife and quickly joined her in sleep.

CHAPTER 6

The consensus view of various political analysts was that the Country had been governed well since the introduction of Revised Democracy. The absence of an official opposition party (whose sole purpose would be to argue against and attempt to delay, alter or prevent whatever legislation an elected government proposed, regardless of its merit) meant that a government could actually get on and do things. The move to the present system (whereby decisions were not driven by ideology and party mantra but rather the culmination of independent deliberations by the best people in the Country) had ushered in an era of stability and real progress for all.

Now, with The Disaster and its aftermath consigned to history, the one remaining country was all anyone had known. It was only Owlds who could remember, albeit with diminishing clarity, the tales of the catastrophe as told to them by their grandparents. The wastelands of the planet remained far too radioactive, even now, for human life to exist. Robots were used to carry the dead and those consigned to death to these desolate areas, but even these ferrymen had to be cleansed to exacting standards upon their return – or even destroyed. President Nuewen strongly doubted that in her lifetime any happier use of the wastelands would be possible.

Gretel Nuewen was by and large much respected and thought to be a wise, energetic and empathetic leader. She basked in this good will. Being adored was a just reward for dedicating her life to governing her people.

When quizzed by reporters and researchers alike, Gretel would always nominate the investments made in education as underpinning the success of her government, despite the initial scepticism that some of the reforms had received.

She would often elaborate further, recalling that the requirement for at least a second-class honour in final year school mathematics as a prerequisite for entry to university, whatever the intended course of study, had been controversial at first. Those who had argued for more balance in school curricula, believing that the emphasis on mathematics and science had come at the loss of creativity in the arts, had been able to raise their concerns, she would say.

Once Gretel warmed to a theme, whatever that was, she was hard to stop; however, if the topic was education, she had quite a patter.

She would go on to explain that in its public response, the Government had pointed out that the arts were still present in the curricula; that performance arts, sports, and health and fitness programs remained well-funded; that the Government had promised to invest in more public galleries and theatres to encourage citizens to enjoy great works of art and literature; and that it had noted that a mathematically fluent graduate of the education system would be able to make a productive contribution to society, yet be able to follow other interests as a private citizen. Gretel would conclude that the Government's argument had calmed most citizens, and the issue had raised few questions since her government had delivered on its promises.

Some few of the older reporters or researchers listening to her spiel knew that the citizens who had continued to protest had been quickly – and in the more strident cases, forcibly – shut down. However, the education debate remained a good illustration of the way the RevDem Government under President Nuewen operated: research well, make informed decisions, present them to people for comment, make minor adjustments where needed, and close further debate.

Coming from a mathematical and musical background, Gretel had become fascinated by politics some twenty-seven years earlier as a protégé of President Homer, the 'father' of Revised Democracy. She had shared similar viewpoints to him, and he had taught her the art of politics during the ten years she spent as his muse, confidante and, on occasion, lover. It was understood that she was his heir designate from the time he appointed her to the Inner Cabinet. He introduced her to all the right people, encouraged her to set up her own chain of loyal followers, and explained to her all the intricacies, responsibilities and duties of government.

Gretel was a fast learner, excelling in all the lessons she had been given to such an extent that much of the initial reserve and resentment some ministers had felt on her fast-tracked appointment to Cabinet quickly evaporated, respect soon replacing their early impressions.

Destined to lead, she rose quickly in the esteem of her fellow ministers so that seventeen years ago, when President Homer retired, she assumed the highest office of government and became President.

Delicately, she had started to distance herself politically from Homer, yet she had remained a friend until his death a few years into his retirement. Over time, she had gradually built up her own fresh team of younger people who had not worked for Homer, but she continued to maintain contact with those retired ministers, still living, from the former Homer Cabinet.

Her current Cabinet, Gretel believed, contained excellent people. Although several of her ministers were former OCMs, she had exercised her right not to be exclusively restricted to that pool. Her powers of persuasion had encouraged some fine citizens to respond to the greater need and accept her offer of an appointment to the Inner Cabinet. A personal tap on the shoulder did much to foster a sense of mutual loyalty.

As that sentiment filtered through her mind, Gretel thought of Timothy. He was the exception. Despite his excellent management of his current portfolio, he irritated her in ways she could not completely explain to herself. It was more than just his conceit and arrogance – though he did strut about like some vain peacock. His belief that he'd be a future president had to be watched, but it wasn't entirely that either, since presumably many of her ministers carried that same baton in their knapsacks. He had quite the sharp tongue, yet he seemed popular. Perhaps it was his lack of seriousness, his cavalier attitude to life that rubbed her the wrong way.

She had enlarged her Cabinet over the years to include twenty-six ministers. These were from diverse backgrounds, including academics from several fields, medical and social workers, community administrators, lawyers, former Heads of Government Departments, leading figures in business, and even a musician. Most shared her passion for education and recognised the importance of a mathematically competent society.

Gretel was aware of how pragmatic she was: she liked to control situations and did not like surprises. She knew how important it was to manage and massage her ministers as part of the game of politics, and she also knew that the game could be somewhat rough and dirty at times. Everyone had something in their past about which they were not proud, so she had made it a rule to arm herself with such information. She had learnt that being highly intelligent did not rule out forming an incorrect opinion, and nor did professed altruism entirely negate self-interest.

Gretel worked extremely hard; her staff were often amazed that she seemed able to survive on just a few hours' sleep while retaining her mental acuity. She always worked her Cabinet hard too, especially prior to important meetings. In this regard, she was able to soothe the fears of some, stroke the egos of others with a quiet word in confidence, give every appearance of seeking the advice of many, and generally court and counsel those around her in her own charming way to ensure she knew where each of her ministers stood on any important matter requiring a vote.

She had adopted that same approach when canvassing the questions that were put to the Chief Scientist prior to her Cabinet appearance. Gretel's visit to Eva in person had reassured her that Berry would be appropriately briefed and, on the day, Berry had been able to give concise and satisfactory answers to each question posed.

Prior to that Cabinet meeting, Gretel had singled out Timothy as the minister who was most likely to grill Berry beyond her endurance. She had subtly let him know she was aware of a particular fetish he practised, while less subtly explaining her expectations regarding the limits of his questioning. She had confirmed that she was prepared to sack him if he acted against her advice. Under different circumstances, threatening to sack Timothy could have been a dangerous move – but she had been confident that he valued his reputation enough to toe the line.

Under RevDem, if all ministers unanimously so determined, they could oust the sitting president from office and elect, by unanimous agreement, one of their own to be the next president. Timothy posed a small threat, which she had been able to neutralise while also solving her concerns about Berry's Cabinet visit. As Gretel was prone to confide to her nearest and dearest, she would never be removed from office – of that she was very confident.

Berry's appearance before the Inner Cabinet had gone smoothly, the nobbled minister contributing very little to the discussion. Subsequently, her ministers had ensured that the OCMs, and through them the citizens, had heard that the Government of President Gretel Nuewen remained steadfast in its commitment to delivering progress to the Country without harm to its citizens, any rumour to the contrary being as outrageous as it was ludicrous.

Not that she controlled the outcome of every issue. A case in point was currently taking place in that day's Cabinet meeting, though, as this was still in the early stages of discussion, Gretel found herself struggling to focus on her ministers' views.

She had invited the Minister for Planning to present to Cabinet her plans for creating a greater supply of housing. Improvements to health and ageing had seen the population steadily increase, despite the Only Child policy that was strongly advocated. Most people lived in small apartments, which they rented from the Government over the course of their lifetime. Currently, apartment buildings were one, two or, less commonly, three storeys high, but due to the projected future shortage, the Minister for Planning was proposing that the Government permitted greater building heights for future developments.

Gretel was somewhat ambivalent about the issue. Personally, she disliked the idea of towering buildings, but she could see it would be a way to help improve the availability of good-quality housing. She was genuinely interested in the views of her ministers and prepared to be guided by their wisdom, so she made a mental note to review the meeting's minutes at a later stage so she could be sure she hadn't missed anything crucial.

On assuming office, Gretel had moved out of her apartment and into Government House, one of the few grand buildings still in existence. However, Javier, her partner, did not move with her, preferring to stay in their apartment. The two spoke frequently each day and met professionally most days, since Javier held the important official role of the President's Principal Advisor. Gretel tried to spend some part of each day or night with Javier, but work and other commitments sometimes got in the way.

Nonetheless, their personal relationship was rock solid and did not suffer. Their relationship was based on mutual trust, shared ambition and a 'whatever-it-takes' attitude. They had an enduring need for each other, despite their squabbles, differences of opinion and occasional indiscretions, and they were as united now as they had been when their relationship had first formed nearly thirty years ago. If asked, she knew they would both cite their total honesty and openness with each as being the key to the success of their relationship.

Initially Javier had been the driving force of the pair, but it gradually became clear that Gretel was the more ambitious of the two. Acknowledging this, Javier had given Gretel his total support and backing when she had entered politics.

He knew of her occasional dalliances with President Homer, yet he'd swallowed his pride and remained steadfast. In turn, Javier had never concealed his few casual affairs from Gretel and, although piqued, she had accepted these – with one exception. She had been extremely upset and angry when Javier had renewed his romance with

Eva Baritz. Gretel had swiftly issued Javier with an ultimatum to end the affair, or she would end their relationship.

At the time, Javier had been shocked by the intensity of her anger. This had been the low point of their time together, and their relationship had hung on a knife-edge for a short while until Javier had accepted that, for the second and final time in his life, his romantic involvement with Eva was at an end.

Javier and Eva had worked together when they were both quite young. The two had been close, the relationship between them based on friendship, sexual attraction and possibly even love. Javier had never hid this from her.

Leon Hartland had also been part of the team back then. In introspective moments, Javier would often reflect with Gretel on their friendship with Leon: "Strange how we were once so close, yet now we're so far apart."

When Gretel had joined the same research program, the four of them had become good friends. Gradually, however, Javier had become increasingly attracted to the magnetic power he sensed in Gretel, despite the strong feelings he held for Eva. She knew it had been a time of some confusion for him – caught between two people he cared about. Unsurprisingly, Eva had thrown him out when she discovered his infidelity.

It would have been easy for their shared history to have caused a deep rift between them, yet Eva had always had Gretel's backing, professionally at least – and never more so than in recent years, when it had become Gretel's fervent hope that her Government's space program would be able to establish meaningful contact with their sister planet.

The four of them had worked in space research, as part of a team led by Eva. The lure of discovery, the shared curiosity over whether or not their planet was alone or there were other, undamaged worlds like theirs - or like theirs once was - had been among their driving purposes. While she, Javier and Leon had moved on to other things after the first mission had failed, Eva had continued on, forming some amazing theories with enormous potential. The confirmed existence of a sister planet had then offered tantalising prospects.

As President, Gretel harboured the humanitarian desire to warn the peoples of their sister planet, the planet Earth, not to make the same mistakes as those on her own planet had made. Only through the brilliance of Major General Professor Eva Baritz could this be accomplished. So, even though she had at times felt reservations about Eva's methods, Gretel had never wavered in her support for Eva's research.

A frivolous thought struck Gretel as she continued to try and absorb her ministers' views on the housing issue. Javier sometimes teased her about wanting to become the ruler of both planets, their own and Earth, but, if travel between the two planets became possible, maybe there was another way to solve the housing crisis rather than ruin the landscape with high-rise apartments.

She managed to muffle her giggle.

CHAPTER 7

It had been disturbing to receive the news that an enquiry about the civilian Claus Proger had been formally lodged with the Department of Health. Perhaps it had been too heavy-handed to interview the clerk who'd presented the request; after all, he was just the messenger and unable to shed any light on the details, mused Jacques, the Head of Security and Intelligence. Of course, the request could be handled in a way whereby it would eventually be lost in the system, but he was puzzled as to why the request had been made in the first place, even more so when this morning he'd been informed that the clerk had returned to see if the application had been processed.

Who is this Aleck Raine representing? Jacques asked himself, determined to find out more about the solicitor before the day was out.

Jacques sent a message to Javier to alert him of the development, as well as an instruction to Cabut to pass on the news to Professor Baritz.

*

Two messages had arrived with Cabut at around the same time: one regarding an enquiry about their civilian test subject, the other arriving from the President's office, instructing Cabut to pass on to Eva an invitation to dinner at Government House.

"Cabut, you're becoming everyone's dogsbody," Eva had said in an attempt at humour, one not well received judging by Cabut's lack of response. She considered both pieces of news together, knowing that Gretel had chosen to issue the invitation in this manner for two reasons: one, so that Eva would see it as a formality she was expected to undertake; and two, to remind Eva that her work needed to be drawn to a conclusion, sooner rather than later. Sighing, she explained to Cabut that she wanted to be in a position to have her next test case assured before her dinner with Gretel.

Together, they perused the shortlist of potential candidates who could be used to trial the DNA program. Eva did not feel convinced that any were suitable.

There were no prisoners allowed any more – they, like her first human test case, had often been keen to trade off some of their sentence by volunteering to participate in a research program. Nowadays, as Cabut had advised, they were confined to looking towards illegal migrants for volunteers.

As there was only one country remaining on their planet, there were no current immigrants in the true sense of the word. The few immigrants who had survived The Disaster, making it to their shores shortly afterwards, had been welcomed and assimilated long ago; some of their descendants were government ministers.

Eva, like most citizens, had been schooled to know it was not illegal to be an immigrant, but those stragglers who later had tried to enter had been rejected, feared for what contagion they might now bring. In confining these immigrants – known as Souls – to the North, the government of the time felt it had done its best to help them, without compromising the safety of its own citizens. And, to ensure ongoing protection, the border that delineated the rest of the Country from the damaged but not completely desolate north-west pocket (where the Souls and some ancient tribal peoples still managed to survive) became monitored and patrolled.

Today, the word 'migrant' was the official name used to refer to the descendant of any Soul who had ventured south. Those who had patiently undergone the correct procedures were 'legal' migrants; those who had somehow bypassed such tortuous processing were 'illegal' migrants.

The recently deceased citizen had been one of the latter. He had managed to cross the border undetected and to assimilate into the citizenry. His detection had led to an opportunity for him to become a legal migrant by agreeing to join a research group, an offer that Eva had neither any part in nor knowledge of at the time, but a gamble that did not end well for either of them.

Eva couldn't afford another failure, so she felt it prudent to pursue an option other than a Soul. Accordingly, she rejected those on Cabut's shortlist.

No, she thought, *I shall run my other idea past Gerry and see what she thinks.*

*

It was 11 am. *Leon is prompt,* thought Aleck as he welcomed the older man into his office. He quickly outlined Erik's unusual experience at the Department of Health.

"So, fun and games have started then, Aleck," commented Leon, quite jocularly.

"It would appear so. I've instructed Erik to continue checking on the application each day, in order to show that we're serious. However, Leon, you don't seem surprised by the reception of the application, so I think it's time you became more open with me."

"Correct, Aleck. I wanted to test what reaction the application would produce, and I'm quite satisfied actually – although I'm sorry that your clerk had to go through that interview. The FOI request won't be successful, but at least I now know that its lodgement disturbed the powers that be."

"What next then, Leon?"

"Let me give you a little more background, Aleck," Leon said. "The Government's research departments have a habit of testing their programs on the vulnerable and those people they consider invisible. I don't know what they are testing this time, but I feel reasonably certain that Claus Proger was chosen to be, or maybe volunteered to be, one of their experimental guinea pigs. I also suspect that Claus was an illegal migrant, a poor soul in more ways than one considering the way things turned out for him."

Leon sighed, then added, "He fitted the profile of invisibility, except that in his case the authorities slipped up because they didn't know that Claus had a friend that he'd confided in about having a procedure done."

"You mean the barmaid you told me about?"

"Exactly, and that barmaid has a friend who in turn is a friend of mine, and hence I came to know of his disappearance," Leon replied. He went on to observe that Claus seemed to have been a fit and healthy person.

"That fact is also intriguing, Aleck. Quite often, government experiments are conducted on the ill and dying, but not this time. Whatever procedure they're researching now it seems to be important that it can be applied to healthy people."

"You know Aleck, it could be that the research will ultimately lead to great benefit, even you or I may one day be grateful for whatever the process is. But, to my mind, the end does not justify the means. You can call for volunteers to undertake experimental procedures so long as they are fully cognisant of the risks and what is involved, but it is an outrageous infringement of a citizen's right, indeed a criminal action, to experiment on unwitting persons. Do we agree on this point?"

"Certainly, any reasonable person would agree with you," replied Aleck. "But how can you be sure that Claus was a guinea pig and not just the unfortunate victim of a bungled minor procedure? After all, Claus knew he was undergoing some sort of procedure – he told the barmaid as much. Maybe the Department of Health is trying to cover up a mistake made by one of its doctors?"

"You're correct; that could be the case, Aleck. However, would your clerk have been treated so rudely if so? If Claus were a 'normal' patient who was unlucky enough to draw the short straw, there would be no concern about issuing a generic statement that essentially would cover up the mistake. Quite possibly your clerk would have been introduced to some spokesperson trained to handle such a situation, someone who would have been compassionate and caring but in an obfuscating way. No, it's the alarm set off by the FOI request that rules that out and suggests something more sinister. That's why we had to serve the FOI request first."

Realising he hadn't offered Leon coffee, Aleck rose from his chair and walked over to the espresso machine, at the same time asking,

"What is it that you propose next, or have I carried out all that you require from me here?"

Leon waited till Aleck returned with the two coffees, thanking him for remembering his preference for macchiato. It was another beautiful day, and the sun shone brightly through the window. For a few moments, neither spoke as each savoured their drink and basked in the warmth of the light-filled room.

Breaking the silence, Leon asked Aleck to continue sending Erik each day to check on the progress of the FOI request. "That way," he said, "the authorities may think you genuinely expect an answer. They will then continue to string you along, expecting to eventually weary you so much that you finally give up. But, to give up straight away would look suspicious, and they would want to know why."

"Okay," replied Aleck, "but, how do you know this is the way they think – and who exactly are 'they'?"

"That's a long story, Aleck."

Pausing for a few seconds, Leon's face was a mask, but his eyes were focused on something far away, as if wrestling with a thought. He sighed. "I know how they operate because once I was one of them."

Aleck was astounded. Trying to collect his thoughts, Aleck sputtered, "Leon, I've read your file. You seem to have been in conflict with the Government over the years, and now you're telling me that far from being a protestor you were on the Government's side all along? What were you, some sort of double agent?"

"Nothing of the sort," retorted Leon. "When I was younger, I worked in one of the research departments. It took some time before I became more and more aware that those in charge, those I'd considered to be my friends, actually had different values to me. I tried to reason for a more moral approach, but my protests and arguments at the time were ineffectual, and the act of speaking out eventually cost me my research career. Over the years since, it has become somewhat of an ongoing crusade of mine to stand up for and protect the most vulnerable in our society."

Leon paused before adding, "By the way, don't believe all that you read in my file, Aleck – some of it has a resemblance to accuracy, but much of it is the poetic licence of the powers that be."

Curious, Aleck asked Leon how he had supported himself after losing his job. After all, he appeared to possess a sartorial elegance that would require a reasonably good income to sustain. The question appeared to amuse Leon.

"I was transferred to another department: Finance and Treasury. I think they wanted to keep an eye on me while still making good use of my mathematical prowess, immodest as that may sound. Then I inherited my parents' sizeable wealth following their deaths, and I acquired the power of privilege that the possession of a fortune bestows. I now pursue my own interests, ones that have proven very successful. Nevertheless, outfoxing those still trying to keep an eye on me has been an interesting game, and game theory was my original area of expertise," laughed Leon.

"Did you ever teach with my father?" asked Aleck, surprising himself at his own question.

"Regrettably no, Aleck, and for now you've heard enough about my background," replied Leon, a touch of mirth momentarily suffusing his face.

Becoming more serious, Leon cautioned Aleck to say as little as possible about him, should anyone ask. "Remember, Aleck, you never know who people really are sometimes," he warned.

Glancing at his watch, Leon rose from his chair, saying: "Now, it's time for me to leave you to your other clients. Shall we meet again early next week for an update?"

Aleck agreed and ushered Leon to the door, shaking his hand in farewell. He sent a message to his secretary to apologise to his next client that he would be delayed by five minutes and started to record his impressions of the meeting.

Leon had taken charge, Aleck realised, and he was left wondering exactly what Leon expected of him and where things were going.

Puzzling, even a bit of a putdown, thought Aleck as he remembered how initially he'd questioned why Leon had sought the assistance of someone of his 'superior' calibre. *Guess I've been put back in my place. I am just an ordinary solicitor when all's said and done, and that's all Leon wanted – some second-rate lackey who is to continue to chase an FOI request that won't ever eventuate.*

For the first time, Aleck felt angry and found himself resenting Leon Hartland's apparently low opinion of him. Added to which, Aleck had never had any reason to doubt the good intentions of the Government. He began to think that Leon's version of events might be rather far-fetched.

It was not until Aleck was about to leave work that evening that he allowed thoughts of Leon Hartland to re-enter his head. Something about him was strange, and Leon's relationship to his father was still a complete puzzle.

This reminded him that he was intending to try the phone number for cousin Charlie that he'd found in his mother's old address book.

Looking up the number, he pressed its digits and, after a short pause, a female voice answered. Aleck introduced himself, explaining that he was a relative trying to get in touch with Charles Raine.

"Mr Raine doesn't live here anymore," said the voice at the end of the phone.

"Do you by any chance know where he now lives?" asked Aleck.

"Oh gosh, let me think. We moved in here after he'd been moved into care, but for the life of me, I can't remember the name of the place where he went. Lovely old man, I remember he left a beautiful bunch of flowers to welcome us to the house. No, I'm sorry, we didn't keep in touch, always meant to but you know how it is, never got around to it, too busy ... so sorry, but I don't think I can help you. Of course, he may not still be alive ..." she acknowledged, her voice trailing off.

"I've been wondering if he's still alive, too," said Aleck. "Actually, you've given me the idea to check with some of the nearby care homes, so you've been very helpful. Thanks for your time and have a good evening."

Aleck glanced at the time, debating whether to look up aged care homes straight away, but he decided he should be on his way to catch his train, which would already be a later one than usual. He could do the search after dinner at home.

CHAPTER 8

Towards the end of her working day, Eva made a call to her gynaecologist, Miss Geraldine Geary. They had known each other on a patient-doctor basis for some years, and over this time they had developed a friendship of sorts. Eva had been able to offer Gerry some assistance with the statistical analysis of the results from at least two of the research programs Gerry had worked on. Each time, as a token of thanks, Gerry had invited Eva out for drinks; other similar but infrequent catch-ups had followed. Their conversations on such occasions were interesting, often entertaining and comfortably companionable without venturing into much of a personal nature.

"Hello Gerry, Eva here," she said, as Gerry took the call on her private phone.

"Good evening Eva, nice to hear from you. How are you going?" came the booming voice of Gerry.

"Busy, as no doubt you are too, so sorry to interrupt you. Any chance of a quick drink sometime this evening? I've got a favour to ask of you that I'd rather discuss in person."

Gerry responded, "I've got an emergency caesarean; in fact, I'm on my way to scrub and gown up as I speak, but I could do this evening, I think, all being well. How does nine o'clock, Hotel Berchus, sound to you?"

"Sounds fine, really appreciate you fitting me in. See you at nine. Bye for now."

Excellent, thought Eva as she switched off her phone. *I think I can see the final stage of this program drawing to a close.*

Feeling in a good mood, she ambled out of her office to alert Cabut to her plans. She would stay at work until it was time to be driven to the hotel. On the spur of the moment, she said to Cabut: "How about you and I grab something to eat before I have to depart?"

At this invitation, Eva had the great pleasure of seeing the unflappable Cabut, just for the teensiest moment, seem nonplussed. But it was just for a moment. Appearing to collect himself, Cabut replied that he would see to a light meal immediately. "Would there be any objection to a burger?"

Smiling sweetly, Eva said that would be fine. As it turned out, she ate the veggie burger in her office, alone, Cabut having left the room immediately after bringing her the food. Eva idly wondered why Cabut had been so thrown by her simple invitation.

Arriving at Hotel Berchus with time to spare, Eva strolled through the upmarket lobby, admiring, as always, the understated elegance of its cream furnishings set against the polished mahogany timber of the surrounding small tables. The soft lighting and the thick taupe-coloured woollen carpets completed the welcoming scene. She went through to the inviting bar area, which was quietly busy with a throng of people – some enjoying a social drink and downtime after their day at work, others like her with prearranged assignations, and some with nothing much better to do but while away the evening in pleasant surroundings, perhaps with the hope of sharing the time with a new companion.

Ordering a martini and a bowl of olives, Eva sat herself at the bar to await Gerry's arrival.

The wait was short; Gerry arrived soon after her. They exchanged kisses on both cheeks and, following the courtesy of initial greetings, Eva asked Gerry what she would like to drink. Gerry selected a cocktail from the drinks menu and suggested some tapas would be good, too.

"I had a few things to tidy up before I could get away, so I only had time to forage for a snack from the hospital canteen. As you can imagine, I'm still a little peckish," laughed Gerry.

"Me too – I've not had a huge meal either, so a couple of tapas dishes to share is a good idea," said Eva. She indicated their requirements to the bar attendant. "Shall we move over to that table in the corner?"

Settling themselves in the well-padded upright chairs, Eva asked Gerry why it was that hospital canteens rarely seemed to offer healthy options.

"Good question Eva, one that gets asked of the hospital board on a regular basis. The board promises a review, sometimes changing caterers – who maybe add something with a healthy name to the menu but take it off not long after, claiming it doesn't sell. Around in a circle we go, with everyone too busy to really pursue the issue. And, let's be honest, sometimes when things are going badly, a few fried chips are comforting."

They chatted further for some time, enjoying their drinks, the saltiness of their food and each other's company until Eva decided it was time to get to the point of the meeting.

"I guess you're wondering what the favour is that I'm about to ask you," she smiled.

"Indeed, I am curious, but let me say at the start that if I can, then it would give me great pleasure to be able to assist you in some way, Eva. After all, you have helped me so much in the past," replied Gerry.

"Appreciate that very much Gerry, thank you," said Eva, reaching out and touching Gerry's hand. "Now, you understand that I can't go into great detail because the project I'm currently working on is somewhat hush-hush, so what I tell you is strictly confidential, but the gist of the project involves mapping and adjusting DNA."

Before Eva could elaborate, Gerry interrupted to say that it was already possible to obtain a map of the human genome and from it to identify genetic markers to illustrate traits, especially those of familial diseases.

Holding up her hand to prevent Gerry from continuing further, Eva patiently went on, saying: "Our research could open up the potential of being able to replace a section of a damaged part of the DNA, or even, if we are really successful, to be able to predict at birth what is likely to need replacement in later life. You know how the Government likes to plan ahead … so the bean counters would argue this is about positive and sound economic management," she laughed, while noting that Gerry didn't even offer a forced smile in response.

Gerry seized her chance to interrupt again. "I thought you worked in space science, Eva, I never realised that you had medical training."

"What I just described is not part of my space research, Gerry, rather a spin-off from it that I mentioned solely to whet your appetite. You're quite correct, I'm an astrophysicist, not a medical doctor. But you as a doctor must see that if we achieve our goal here, then we scientists will have been of great help to you medicos."

"Absolutely, it could open up amazing possibilities. Though," Gerry added cautiously, "there would have to be strict regulations surrounding its use in order to prevent unethical or even immoral abuses. And, you'd have to be very sure that any editing would not result in the creation of a new problem. How come you got into this? What applications does DNA therapy have in space research?" queried Gerry, seeming quite nonplussed.

"Ah, that's the bit I can't elaborate on, sorry Gerry. Of course, that's also the bit I'm interested in, but I'd be most happy to share appropriate results with you and other medical researchers once I'm satisfied that we've achieved what we need. Which brings me to my request."

Thinking to herself that things had not got off to the best of starts, Eva paused, helping herself to more food and drink and allowing time for Gerry to absorb the situation. Once Gerry resumed partaking of her food and cocktail, Eva judged it was time to continue. Clearing her throat, she put forward the case for her request.

"The simulation experiments have been very successful, but we need to verify we can apply our process to the DNA of a human person. All that we want to test is whether, given a human's DNA, we can adapt a part of it and do so very quickly. The process works on robonauts in simulation studies, but I haven't been able to test enough humans as yet to be able to claim I have statistically valid proof that the process can be successful for actual astronauts."

Since Gerry made no comment, Eva continued. "Now, Gerry, I'm under a bit of pressure to complete my task, but, due to the secrecy surrounding our space program research, we can't call for volunteers. So, in pondering over how we could get the final case studies to complete the research, it occurred to me that if we had a pregnant female then that would give us two in one body: the yet-to-be-born child and the adult mother-to-be."

Gerry seemed to be processing the details; frowning, she asked why Eva hadn't tried out the procedure, whatever it was, on herself and her co-researchers. Eva enigmatically retorted "What makes you think I haven't?" With a trace of exasperation, Eva added that all she was trying to do was accumulate the number of satisfactory test cases required for meeting the statistical bounds for claiming success. "One case more, two would be a bonus – that's all I need."

Gerry asked whether there were risks involved for the case study subjects.

"No riskier than that of an amniocentesis procedure," replied Eva, keeping her expression neutral. She neither had any intention of fully explaining the procedure nor of sharing with Gerry the recent failure of the procedure on the citizen receptor. Forcing a smile, she put forward a compromise position. "In fact, if you could provide me with a sample of amniotic fluid, plus blood samples, then that would almost cover things – except, of course, I would like to be able to interview the mother-to-be myself."

As she often did, Eva inwardly consoled herself with the thought that she was not a bad person. Sometimes one had to be not entirely truthful, even to a friend, and she had already told Gerry there was much she could not discuss with her. Besides, she was desperate; she needed to find a case study, and quickly. She was confident the procedure would work despite its recent failure, so she felt it reasonable to downplay any risks.

"Do you have a current patient you could share from one of your own research programs?" asked Eva. "Someone whose data you've already collected, perhaps?"

Gerry did not immediately answer. Eva resisted the urge to persuade her further, still hoping that Gerry would conclude that she owed her a favour or two.

Eventually, raising her eyes to meet Eva's, Gerry said she did have a patient who was nearing term who might be suitable. She had intended to include this patient in her own research, but she was prepared to donate her to Eva's program. They talked further about Aneeka Raine, Gerry's suggested patient, and as the conversation evolved Eva began to feel confident that Aneeka would be the perfect test subject. Gerry confirmed that, provided Aneeka gave permission, she would pass on the data she had collected for both mother and babe, and then Aneeka could arrange to meet with Eva for further discussion.

Gerry wasn't quite done with querying Eva's intentions, it seemed. "Sorry to press you, Eva, but I take it I have your word that all is as you say it is, so there's no risk to my patient?"

"You have my word on it," she replied.

They finished their respective drinks, but the conversation was not as spontaneous, and Eva was unsurprised when Gerry decided to call it a night. Apologising to Eva and saying she had an early start the next day, Gerry took her leave.

Alone, Eva ordered herself another martini, drinking it slowly, feeling much relieved. She had her case study. Her single-mindedness may have put some strain on her relationship with Gerry, but the end justified the means. For the first time in a long while she found herself feeling a frisson of excitement about the future; even the prospect of her coming dinner with Gretel was no longer such a bugbear.

CHAPTER 9

"Come on Aleck, share with me what's troubling you," Aneeka coaxed. Cuddling up to him, she tenderly stroked his hair.

Aleck gazed at Aneeka, her love and concern for him written all over her face. Aneeka was beautiful, and as he continued his gaze, he found himself slowly starting to relax. He had been curt and dismissive since he'd walked through the door, and yet Aneeka was worried for him rather than annoyed with him. *How did a man like me have the good fortune to find a woman like Aneeka?* he wondered.

Without violating any confidences, Aleck found himself telling Aneeka about Leon Hartland's claimed association with his father, how utterly different to his father Leon was, and how Leon's behaviour had started to worry him. He added that he'd tried to contact Charles, his father's cousin.

"Do you remember him at all, from the funeral perhaps?" he asked her.

Aneeka stopped to think, but she seemed unsure. "Not really, sorry to say, Aleck," she replied.

"I found his phone number in Mum's old address book, so today I gave it a ring. The person who now lives in his apartment told me he'd gone into care, but she couldn't remember the name of the place."

"In that case, let's start searching so we can compile a list of possible places," she responded thoughtfully. "After all," she joked, "I'll be prepared for when we have to put you into care down the track."

Aleck laughed and gave Aneeka a hug. "You are the most adorable person I know," he said.

"Stop it Aleck, we're on a mission, we can't get distracted just yet," Aneeka giggled.

They sat together at Aleck's screen and did a search for aged care homes both in the environ around Charles's old apartment and further afield. Aneeka recorded the name and contact details for each one, despite Aleck sending an email to each home asking whether a Charles Raine was a resident.

They agreed to wait for a response to the emails before proceeding further. This gave them the rest of the evening to spend happily together, now he was back to his usual self. Aneeka, her arms clasped around his shoulders, said teasingly, "What was it you were saying about me being adorable?"

The following day was a work-free day, so Aleck chose not to go for his morning run. They slept till quite late, made love and dozed again, finally choosing to acknowledge the arrival of the new day long after it had dawned. They took brunch outside in their little courtyard (theirs being a ground-floor apartment) and discussed how they would spend the rest of their day. Aneeka was keen to have a closer look at the apartment buildings she had mentioned a few days earlier, and, with the warmth of the day, a walk seemed a good choice. However, first of all Aleck wanted to check out whether there had been any responses from the aged care homes.

While Aneeka tidied away the remnants of their meal, he checked the several replies he had received. Coming to the fifth response, he was rewarded by an email acknowledging that there was a person by the name of Charles Raine in residence. Excitedly, Aleck noted down the address and decided that visiting this home would be the first priority of the day.

They set off for the aged care home, with Aleck driving their small car. They had often debated whether they needed a car at all, given that Aleck caught the train to and from work, as had Aneeka before her maternity leave, so the car was only really used at weekends. But keeping it charged was inexpensive, and Aneeka was now finding it useful during the week for avoiding the strain of carrying heavy loads when she had a lot of shopping to do. Once the baby was born it would no doubt continue to be useful – they had already hired a baby capsule for that reason.

Their destination was only about fifteen kilometres away from their home, and Aleck felt a little guilty that this would be their first visit to the person he hoped would prove to be his father's cousin and not just someone bearing the same name.

Arriving at the home, Aleck parked the car and the two of them went into the reception lobby. There, a cheerful middle-aged man greeted them, directing them to a room on the third floor.

The lobby had seemed pleasant: garden views filled each of its generous windows, and the impression was of a well-kept residence. Holding Aneeka's hand and feeling surprisingly nervous, Aleck guided them to the door of Charles Raine's room. Aleck took a deep breath and knocked on the door. A male voice rasped in response for them to enter, which they did. The moment Aleck looked at the bent, white-haired old man sat in an armchair near the window, he knew he had come to the right place.

"Charles, hello! I'm Aleck, your cousin Colin's son, and this is my wife Aneeka. How very nice to see you again," said Aleck warmly.

"Aleck and Aneeka, well I never! What a lovely surprise to see you both. Forgive me for not standing to greet you but I'm rather unsteady on my feet nowadays. Please pull up a chair close to me so that I can see and hear you well," said Charles, gesturing towards two cane chairs spread around the room.

"Aneeka, my dear, I see congratulations are in order. When is your baby due?"

Although much aged since Colin's funeral, Charles still had his marbles intact and he seemed genuinely delighted to see them. Charles suggested that Aleck make them each a cup of tea, pointing out some cake on the bench alongside the kettle.

Charles's room was a rectangular bedsit, with the bed and a wardrobe against one wall, a tiny kitchenette along part of the opposite wall and a sitting area between the two, in which the three of them were seated. A bathroom opened off the kitchenette. Charles sat in front of a large window that admitted good light and, although tiny, the room was pleasant.

"Funny how you downsize as you get older. I've gone from a two-bedroom apartment to just one room that contains all that I need," commented Charles. "Just one more downsize to go, I suppose," he added, reflectively.

Aleck handed mugs of tea and slices of fruit cake to Aneeka and Charles.

"Do you take milk, Charles?" asked Aleck.

"No, I like it black, thanks Aleck. However, if you would like some milk, I can call downstairs for some to be brought up."

"Both of us are black tea people too, so we're all good," replied Aleck.

As they sipped their tea, they spoke of many things, mostly to do with the family. Charles seemed to be enjoying having company, and Aleck resolved that he would make regular visits in future. Eventually, Aleck asked Charles if he remembered anything about his father's time as a university student.

"Your father was a very clever man, Aleck. Being a few years older than him, our times at university did not overlap, but I do remember that Colin was considered a highly promising mathematician.

"In fact, years after his student days, I once asked your father whether he regretted not doing postgraduate study – as we all had expected he would. His reply was that he had at first been quite bitterly disappointed that he hadn't won a scholarship, but he had come to realise that this was one of the best things that ever happened to him. And when I asked why, he explained that if he'd followed a career in mathematical research then he would never have known the joy that his years of teaching had brought him.

"He said to me: 'Charlie, I was meant to be a teacher, not a researcher; someone was looking after me that day my scholarship application was turned down.' I've always remembered those words," ended Charles.

"Why was his application refused, do you know?" queried Aneeka.

"Not sure, Aneeka, maybe he wasn't as good as the family had thought, although I personally don't believe that. You know in those days the remnants of the cloud of The Disaster were still not far from the minds of those in the Government, so I've always been inclined to think that maybe it was thought he would better serve the Country by becoming a schoolteacher. It was high on the Government's list of priorities that mathematics and sciences be supported in school education, just as it still is, I guess."

"What about his fellow students in mathematics, did any of them go on to postgraduate studies?" queried Aleck, thinking this might be a way to introduce Leon's name into the conversation.

But Charles was either unable to remember or simply never knew if any of Colin's peers had received scholarships. "It stands to reason that some of them must have, I suppose," was the best he could offer in reply.

"Does the name Leon Hartland ring a bell?" tried Aleck once more.

Charles was beginning to tire – something that Aneeka indicated to Aleck by suggesting that it was time for them to leave. Picking up the mugs, Aneeka took them to the kitchenette and started to rinse them, despite Charles saying not to bother as someone would come and do that later.

Aleck chatted a little longer in case Leon's name suddenly rang a bell, but Charles's only response was that he thought he knew the name but really couldn't remember why.

Thanking Charles for the tea and saying they would visit again soon, Aneeka firmly insisted that they had tired Charles enough for one day and that they really had to go. Aleck said how much he'd enjoyed seeing Charles again and that they'd be back another day soon. "Perhaps we could take you out for a drive another time," he suggested.

Each embraced Charles before departing, leaving him to the snooze he clearly was used to at that time of day.

Aleck left his contact details at reception with the man who had first greeted them and asked whether Charles had many visitors. The man, who introduced himself as Ronnie, replied that Charles was more fortunate than some of the other residents because his niece and some of her family visited him most weeks.

As they walked towards the car, Aleck and Aneeka agreed that Charles was a lovely person and they would definitely return in a couple of weeks.

"Remind me where Charles fits on the family tree," said Aneeka.

"My great grandparents had two sons, Rufus and Magnus. Rufus married Antonia and they had one son, Charles; Magnus married Colette and they also had one son – Colin, my father," Aleck explained.

"No-one mentions Charles marrying. Did he have any family?"

"Actually, Charles did marry, but sadly his wife died quite young and without child. I can't remember what the circumstances were, since she died before I was born."

"Oh, in that case does that make you Charles's next of kin?" questioned Aneeka.

"No, I would think not. Charles remained close to his wife's sister and the child from this sister-in-law's marriage, Matilda if I remember correctly, would be his next of kin, I presume. Ronnie just told me that Matilda and her family visit Charles regularly, which I was pleased to hear. You see, once Charles married, he didn't have much to do with our side of the family, he was far more connected to his wife's family. That's why I was surprised to see him at Dad's funeral. Until then I wouldn't have known he was still alive. But now that we've resumed contact, I intend to visit him more often. I really enjoyed seeing him today."

They had reached their car. Aleck switched on his phone out of habit and was surprised to find a message from his firm's Principal partner, Bruce Daniels. On opening the message, he read that he was to ring Daniels as soon as possible regarding an urgent matter. Muttering "work" and excusing himself, Aleck walked into the nearby garden and made the call.

Daniels wasted no time with pleasantries. "Aleck, I've had a query from someone I can't name, but let's say someone of influence and importance. The caller was checking you out, which was not a problem and I handled that fine, but the caller particularly wanted to know who engaged you to serve a recent FOI. I fudged for time, wanting to speak to you first. Is there any problem with this Leon Hartland fellow that I should know about before I get back to inform my caller of his name?"

"Honestly, I'm beginning to wonder who he is myself, even more so now that I've heard from you. There's nothing untoward in my actions; I have served the request as instructed by Mr Hartland, and I continue to follow up on its progress. Hartland said a citizen by the name of Claus Proger had undergone an unspecified procedure, medical I assume, and has not been heard of since. I am puzzled by Hartland choosing me as his solicitor, but I have no other information I can give you."

"Good man, Aleck. I'll pass that on and hope that's the end of it. However, I'd like to see you 10 am Monday in my office. Sorry to disturb you, enjoy the rest of your weekend," said Daniels, and the call ended.

Bemused, Aleck shook his head but decided not to dwell on the call. Returning to Aneeka, he suggested they drive out to the apartments she wanted to see, go for a walk and then head home for dinner. Brunch felt like a long time ago.

CHAPTER 10

Eva had dressed with care for her dinner with Gretel the previous evening. She felt she had looked quite sophisticated and had sensed her appearance may have initially irritated Gretel, who, for once, was looking tired and a little peaky. At first, she had been somewhat taken aback by the unexpected presence of Javier; however, she had quickly recovered her poise and as the evening had wound on, she had relaxed and actually enjoyed seeing him again. Gretel, of course, had controlled the conversation, and she had asked her several work questions that she was able to respond to confidently and without hesitation. In essence, she told Gretel just what she wanted to hear: yes, she had found her research subject; and yes, she expected to complete this stage of her research within the week.

Eva lazed on the designer chair in her apartment, deep in thought. Gretel had shared some exciting developments, notably her decision to allocate greater funding to the current space program. Excellent news in itself, but Gretel's enthusiasm had been even more interesting to witness. Clearly, Gretel was looking to her legacy, staking out how she would be remembered long after she was no longer President.

Maybe Gretel is slowing down and even thinking of retirement, thought Eva, cattily adding, *that would fit with her physical appearance last night.*

Gretel may have been grandstanding, but she had made it clear to Eva that she wanted the space program to be a top priority, claiming that while she still held office, she wanted meaningful contact to be made with planet Earth.

Gretel had reasoned, "We might be reduced to only one habitable and relatively small country, but if we can forewarn Earth then it doesn't have to follow suit."

Historically, the two planets had followed similar patterns to each other. However, despite Earth being the slightly older of the two, their own planet had always progressed more quickly than Earth. Getting ahead had not worked out so well for them in the end though; better to have been in Earth's position, where it might be possible to learn from the planet that had shot ahead.

The discussion had been exciting; indeed, it had taken Eva back to when they had been young, ambitious and starry-eyed. Javier had aged considerably, but there was still something attractive about him. She had accepted long ago that Gretel was meant to be with Javier; they were good for each other, and she could see through the soft, respectful way Gretel spoke to him and her casual tactility towards him that their relationship had stood the test of time.

They'd reminisced about their early attempts to contact the type 1 humans on Earth; how they had worked together to send robots there, even though the robots seemed to have failed at establishing meaningful contact with Earth's people. They knew that the robots had made an attempt to return home, although they'd lost contact with them and had assumed that their spacecrafts had been destroyed in space. They had theorised that they could be trapped in a wormhole, but now Eva suspected that some of the robots at least might still be on their journey home, given the eons of time required to travel against the gravitational wave.

The four of them – Eva, Javier, Gretel and Leon – had been a great team until that failure. The shared impetus that had made their bond so strong had started to break, and so they had begun to drift in different directions. Gretel had taken her lofty ambitions into politics, while the complications of the triangular relationship between herself, Gretel and Javier sent Javier in the same direction, to become Gretel's political advisor. That had left just Eva and Leon in the program. Leon's treacherous leaks had eventually left only Eva struggling to keep the program going, despite severe funding cuts.

The thought of Leon reminded Eva that Javier had revealed that Leon was up to what he had called his 'old tricks': he was behind the

FOI request about the deceased citizen, apparently. How he had known about this was not yet clear, but Javier had said the Security Agency was on the case. Gretel had made no comment in response and Eva had thought better of it.

After an excellent dinner with fine wines, they had adjourned to Gretel's private sitting room within Government House. Eva had never been invited into Gretel's sanctum before, and she was fascinated to see the way Gretel had combined the heavy drapes and selected pieces of antique furniture with comfy sofas piled with cushions and walls adorned with modern abstract art. Over whisky and coffee, Eva had enthusiastically shared her plans for how she hoped to make meaningful contact with their Earth cousins.

"We can get there okay, surfing the gravitational waves so to speak, but it's always been the return journey that's the problem, as you both will recall. But the most recent theory we have worked on gives us a new approach. We now believe we can use black holes as connector tunnels between galaxies. However, as contact with ground staff would be lost and we're still not completely confident what happens in such a tunnel, it's difficult to pre-program a robot to respond to those conditions; after all, ultimately, they are robots, incapable of original thought unless those thoughts have been built into their programming."

Eva remembered catching a glimpse of some unspoken communication between Javier and Gretel, though she hadn't thought much of it at the time. It niggled at her now, though she wasn't sure why.

She'd gone on to explain the need for a human crew member who could think about and adapt to the changing conditions by continually monitoring and instantly adjusting their DNA. This was why her current research was so important, she had reminded them.

Gretel had demurred, saying that she didn't wish to know any actual details. However, she'd reiterated that Eva could rely on her support if the testing procedure were a success.

It had been well past midnight when Eva had taken her leave. *A surprisingly good evening,* she thought, stretching her body out along her chair.

By now, it was Saturday afternoon. The sun was shining, and Eva was not at work. She'd been to the gym in her apartment complex earlier in the day, but she now decided to treat herself to a rare jog out in the fresh air. Changing into her running gear, she logged in a message to tell Cabut of her whereabouts and set off outdoors. The breeze felt good against her skin as she briskly walked towards the path that ran alongside the stream, the one upon which she gazed most mornings.

She ran some distance at a fast pace, counting her usual 'one, two, three, four; one, two, three, four' refrain to spur herself along, repeating its permutations until slowing to a jog after some while. She exchanged nods with others as they passed her, including a young couple. The young woman was heavily pregnant. How different might her life have been had she not lost Nolé and their unborn daughter, she momentarily wondered. Brushing aside such melancholic thoughts as she had been trained to do, Eva set off on the return trip to her apartment.

*

Leon was on his way to rendezvous with Rueben Thiem, the editor of an underground publication – the same person who, after hearing no more from Jacques all those years ago, Leon had approached in the hope of publishing his article about the illegality of the vote for Revised Democracy. To his disappointment, however, Rueben had declined to do so on the grounds that it was difficult to follow, difficult to verify and, at best, it was old news that could serve no real purpose in being published after the event.

Rueben had retained ownership and editorship of the small independent publication, partly as a hobby and partly because he believed any form of democracy should allow a small degree of subversiveness and the expression of sentiments contrary to the orthodoxy of its government. Surprisingly, the Government had tolerated the publication's existence, possibly because it reached only a small audience – or perhaps because it allowed ongoing monitoring of dissenters and their issues with Government policy, Leon judged.

Despite his disappointment over their initial interaction, Leon had found it useful to keep their line of communication open. He had leaked classified information intermittently during the days he had worked on Government-funded programs, and Rueben had accepted these gratefully, publishing what he considered appropriate, with some publications resulting in changes for the better. Leon had no regrets about his role in diverting funding from the space program to the renewable energy program after he'd assisted with making the public aware of the exorbitant costs that had been poured into the failed endeavours of the space program; he'd also rather enjoyed outing the rorts behind the management of funds within the Department of Finance and Treasury, which had resulted in the resignation of the minister responsible.

But there had been information that Rueben had not been prepared to publish. Leon had come to understand that Rueben would always juggle whether to publish against how he thought those in power might react – it explained why only some of the material he'd leaked had been used. However, Leon also respected that Rueben would never reveal who had passed on the confidential documents.

Leon was intending to ask Rueben to run an article he had penned about the disappearance of Claus Proger, calling for anyone with information to come forward. He considered the chances of Rueben agreeing to publish the article were high, since it seemingly contained nothing controversial.

His optimism seemed well-founded: Rueben was interested enough to promise to consider publishing the article after closer reading. They chatted amiably enough for a few minutes then went their separate ways, having spent barely fifteen minutes in each other's company.

They could not be called 'friends', reflected Leon on his journey home, yet he felt there was some sort of bond between them. Rueben was either a very conservative subversive, or else one possessed of the wisdom to know when he could make a difference and when he could not. Leon could only trust that his most recent article would seem reasonably innocuous and therefore be received sympathetically.

Rueben had been Leon's second appointment that afternoon. Earlier, he had spoken with a friend, the much younger Timothy Augustine. Once, Leon had believed greatness beckoned for Timothy, but he was becoming less sure: Timothy's promise seemed to be sliding away. However, Leon reasoned, if Timothy was content to waste his opportunities and his potential, then that was his choice.

Career counselling was not what the two had discussed. Leon had enlisted Timothy's help in confronting Gretel over the Proger case. It was a bold and risky move but, in Leon's estimation, a move worth playing – and, who knew, maybe one with a good outcome not only for Leon but for Timothy's future. *Perhaps I am a career counsellor after all,* Leon had thought afterwards, laughing.

CHAPTER 11

The dawn of the Saturday morning had dutifully awakened Gretel and Javier. They had elected to stay overnight at Government House, given the late hour at which their dinner with Eva had finished. Theirs was not a relationship driven by ardent libido, yet that night they had enjoyed an unhurried intimacy, a tenderness brought on by their closeness and their privileged access to the other's body. Gretel couldn't recall when they had last shared such a perfect, soothing feeling of quietness and togetherness.

With the new day there was no possibility, nor indeed any expectation, of an encore performance of the night before: they had duties to carry out, appointments to meet and the continual responsibilities of government to shoulder.

Over a hasty breakfast, Gretel quizzed Javier about his plans for dealing with Leon. "Javier, dear, I trust none of your agents will draw attention to themselves or claim any authorisation from the Government."

"Of course not, sweetheart. I've placed Jacques in charge, and he is to report only to me. It will be discreet surveillance at first – once we figure out where Leon is. But Gretel, you know we may need to take further action depending on exactly what the intent of the wretched man is."

"We'll face that when and if necessary, Javier. Now, a quick shower for me and I'm off. I'll try my hardest to join you this evening," she said, adding, "thank you, my darling, for staying here last night."

Javier smiled; raising her hand to his lips, he murmured, "Always glad to be of service to my President, ma'am."

*

Javier left Government House shortly after breakfast, returning home in the early evening. Gretel didn't make it back to their apartment that evening – he was unfazed, imagining she'd ended up back at Government House. He was content to watch a movie and have an early night after the excesses of the previous evening.

The next morning, he received a message from Jacques saying that he'd been informed the editor of UndPress had been asked to publish an article about Claus Proger.

Rueben was well-known to Jacques. Despite his role editing a publication that oft-times carried criticism of the Government, Javier knew that Rueben was a cautious man. Without revealing his sources, it was not uncommon for him to check in with Jacques to gauge the severity of any Government reaction to what he was proposing to publish. His decision to publish, or not, usually depended on the level of that severity.

Javier called Jacques to find out more. "The source has to be Leon, don't you agree?" asked Jacques, with little preamble.

Javier thought there was little doubt. "Almost certainly. Transmit the article to me right now so I can read it." The article swiftly appeared. "Okay, Jacques, got it – stay with me while I read it."

He quickly perused the article. "Tell your editor friend that he can go ahead – the Government has no knowledge of the person involved. Then, probe how the article was received. I want to know Leon's current whereabouts before the end of the day – get a watch put on him to see where he goes and who he meets. Good job, Jacques, thanks."

Nearly found you again, Leon, thought Javier.

They'd been friends once, way back in those spacey days. Leon was good with people, and Javier knew that he'd been particularly supportive and kind to Eva during her troubled period, long before Javier had known either of them. Throughout his own relationship with Eva, she had rarely referred to that time in her life, but her shared bond with Leon had always been evident. How odd then that it was Leon who attempted to damage her through the leaks about the space program's failures. Javier had never mentioned it to Gretel, or Eva for that matter, but he had wondered at the time whether Leon had in fact been trying to punish him – punishment meted out for not allowing their own relationship to deepen as Leon had wished.

Javier had already been juggling Gretel and Eva, so the thought of adding Leon to the mix had been altogether too much. Nor was he that way so inclined, although he had been tempted by the novelty of such a new and different experience. Fortunately, however, he had recognised how unkind it would have been to exploit Leon's feelings for the sake of his own curiosity.

Through her 'contacts' (in other words, President Homer), Gretel had managed to get Leon transferred to the Department of Finance and Treasury. He had a brilliant mind, after all, and the Department had benefitted from his expertise. But, years later, having endured the upshot of several more unwelcome leaks, Gretel had decided that enough was enough, so Leon was 'let go'.

Javier had asked operatives in the Security Agency to keep an eye on Leon for a while, partly as a precaution and partly to discreetly provide him with assistance if he should need it. He need not have worried on the latter part, however. Leon had set up an online gambling business, which quickly turned him into an extremely wealthy and influential person. His mathematical training in game theory, his judgement and agility had paid off handsomely, a fact Javier had always acknowledged.

Leon now employed several mathematically versed young people to run his organisation, but few of his employees had ever met Leon in person and none had any idea where Leon lived.

Javier had managed to establish that, at one stage, Leon had moved around a lot, even couch-surfing at times. However, after a while he'd instructed the Agency to stop trying to keep an eye on him. Now that he knew Leon was active again, that decision needed to be reversed. Javier figured that as Leon was now an older and richer man, he would likely have his own home – and he was confident that Jacques would locate it.

Sundays were Javier's rest days – days when, to Gretel's amusement, he liked to tidy the apartment, tend to the plants he kept on the balcony, and bake a cake for afternoon tea.

"Why bother?" Gretel would exclaim. "We employ staff to do those things!"

But Javier persisted. His mother had trained him to share in the housework and to keep his room tidy, and she had also taught him how to cook. He hadn't known his father (and he wasn't altogether certain how well his mother had known his father either, for that matter … but that was his mother's business, not his, he had reasoned from a young age). However, he had adored his unconventional mother, and on Sundays he liked to indulge himself in honouring her memory by baking.

An update message arrived from Jacques to say that Leon had been on foot when he'd met Rueben, so they'd been able to narrow down the area on which to concentrate. He also said he was off to meet the waitress Proger had befriended in the hope she might know Leon.

Javier acknowledged the message and returned to preparing his hummingbird sponge cake. The cake was in the oven by the time Jacques checked in again. This time his message simply said, 'Got him!'

Javier quickly replied: 'My office first thing tomorrow.'

*

Peering through his balcony window, Leon observed the car that was parked a short distance away. It had been there for over an hour, in a parking spot that was rarely used by any of his neighbours, its driver still sat in the car. It was too far away for Leon to get a good view of the driver. Each of the six townhouses in Leon's complex had its own underground garage and there was a car park for visitors at the rear. *Time to get someone to check out the car,* he thought.

He rang the security firm that patrolled the area, requesting that they send someone to speak to the driver of the car, and settled back to watch what would unfold. Five minutes later the security car arrived, and Leon smiled as he saw the car driver flash an identification card at the security officer. "Good old predictable Rueben ... and well done, Javier, it didn't take your folk very long to find me," Leon said to himself. He deleted the security firm's reassuring message as soon as it arrived.

Leon weighed up what to do next. It would be easy to slip away to one of his other residences; after all, he had two others he could relocate to. However, he knew he had done nothing that the Agency could class as wrong: he hadn't handed over any leaked information, the article about Claus Proger was accurate, he had acted only as a concerned citizen by raising the matter of a missing person, and he had made no allegations about why the man was missing. Best of all, he knew for certain now that they were worried that he might know something about whatever their dirty secret was. He decided he would stay put, allow himself to be monitored and see where things went.

Perhaps he could go for a nice walk, sit and read his book in the sunshine and watch the children fly kites in the nearby park: that would allow whoever was on duty to get a bit of exercise. *Then I might get a friend to pick me up and disappear before the security agent can get back to his car. But I'll return in an hour or so.*

Weighing up his plan, Leon thought this all sounded quite fun.

*

Jacques had asked Clovis, a relatively new recruit, to keep watch over Leon's home and to report on Leon's movements.

Noticing Leon emerge into the remains of the day, Clovis followed him from a discreet distance to a park where children played. Leon sat on one of the several benches spread around the park, alternating his attention between the children and the book he was carrying. He made a call on his cell phone and then, seemingly, started to walk back towards his home. However, shortly afterwards, a small late-model grey sedan pulled up at the kerb then took off again, with Leon inside.

Clovis did not have a chance to get a description of the driver, but he did get the car's number. Reporting this immediately to Jacques, he stayed put while Jacques looked it up. The car was registered as belonging to a Frederick Kline, whose address Jacques messaged to Clovis, with instructions to drive there to see if he could locate Leon.

Anything he could learn about Kline would be welcomed, but he was not to reveal himself.

Clovis had little trouble locating the apartment building. It was quite near the university, the area bubbling with groups of students sat outdoors at cafés, drinking coffee, eating snack foods, immersed in lively conversations. After parking his car, Clovis casually strode towards the entrance steps to the foyer of the two-storey building. He checked the names on the building's letterboxes, but he did not see one labelled Frederick Kline. Then again, few were labelled with names in any case. He strolled further along the street, making his way towards where a crowd of people lined the pavement enjoying their Sunday afternoon. It was there that he noticed a group of four men sat outside a café playing cards, Leon being one of the players.

Clovis quickly crossed the road rather than walk straight in front of Leon. He ordered a coffee for himself and sat at a table where he could view Leon and his companions from across the street. Although Leon had his back to him, Clovis managed to surreptitiously take a photo of the three others in the group. Pleased with himself, he sat back and enjoyed his coffee, still watching the card players. He hazarded a guess they were playing Bridge, since one hand would be placed upwards on the table before play began. Clovis observed that when Leon was the dummy he appeared to check his phone, as did the player who was Leon's partner when he was dummy, but this seemed unremarkable.

Why was his boss so interested in this man? he wondered. He seemed to be leading a perfectly normal life for someone who appeared to be of retirement age. Clovis was reminded of his own retired father, who also enjoyed playing cards with his friends – except in his dad's case it was poker, much to his mother's annoyance, since his father would sometimes lose most of his monthly pension during a game.

He realised that it had been quite a while, well over six months, since he had been in contact with his parents. He rationalised that the nature of his job made it difficult to plan too far ahead. Take this weekend as an example, when he had hoped to go fishing with a few of his mates.

Bet the lads have caught a lot of trout, he thought jealously.

The weekend surveillance order had come from Jacques late Friday afternoon, just as he was about to knock off for the day. It was with much regret that he'd messaged his friends to say he couldn't join them after all. However, he did enjoy his job most of the time, despite some boring interludes, and he was grateful for the faith Jacques appeared to place in him.

In truth, Jacques had probably turned Clovis's life around, rescuing him from the quicksand of petty crime after his attempts to pursue a boxing career had faltered. At first, Jacques had only seemed interested in using Clovis's muscle to carry out a few standover missions for him. Clovis had taken care of these discreetly and without asking any questions. He liked to think that Jacques had seen more in him than just the thug he appeared to be, since, before too long, Jacques had invited him to undertake training for a position in an organisation Jacques described as 'a law and order division of an army security agency'.

Clovis had started the training a couple of months earlier and felt he fitted in very well. While the training was physically demanding, it also involved rigour and intelligence, which, to his surprise, Clovis had found appealing. He'd done well in the first stage of the training and was looking forward to completing the course. In the interim, he was required to report to work each day for Jacques and carry out whatever was assigned to him. Since some of this was clerical work, he was glad to escape from that mundaneness and be out on his own, even though it had meant missing the fishing trip.

Noticing the card players appeared to be finishing their game, Clovis ceased his musings, drained his coffee and prepared to follow. The players shook hands and parted, one of them walking with Leon towards the direction of the apartment building in which Frederick Kline was said to reside. Clovis noted Leon's companion was the person who had been sat opposite him in the card game. Perhaps this was Frederick Kline? He would suggest this in his report to Jacques.

As the two men walked, Leon briefly used his phone, and by the time they reached the apartment building a taxi was pulling up. Leon got into the taxi as his companion waved in farewell before continuing towards the apartment building entrance.

As Leon's cab drove off, Clovis moved closer towards the building in the hope of observing which apartment Kline, or whoever he was, would enter. He discreetly videoed the man as he entered his passcode, hoping that later he'd be able to work out the code from the positions of the man's fingers.

Once Leon's companion had disappeared into the building, Clovis ran the short distance to his car while reasoning that Leon would probably be going back to his home. Jacques would not be happy if he lost Leon, but Clovis felt comfortable with his decision to have stayed watching his companion, who might or might not be Kline; after all, the location of the taxi cab could be identified if Leon didn't go straight home.

Clovis returned to Leon's apartment and parked in his earlier spot. He decided he would wait for ten minutes or so before contacting Jacques: he hoped he might observe some movement in the apartment to indicate that Leon had returned. His patience was rewarded as he saw a person, presumably Leon, come to the window and glance outwards before drawing the curtains together. Clovis messaged Jacques, updating him with his report of the afternoon and sending the photos he'd taken. A short reply from Jacques came with the order that Clovis was now off duty until 7 am the next day, when he should return to shadowing Leon's movements. Clovis switched the car's engine on and quietly drove home.

*

As he discreetly watched the car's departure, Leon congratulated himself over the way the day had panned out. *I played well today,* he thought, *and not only at Bridge.*

Attempting to put himself inside Javier's head, Leon speculated about what Javier might be contemplating as his next move. He grinned.

Javier won't get a second move; I've already outplayed him. Timothy will see to that.

CHAPTER 12

The quietness of their Sunday had been disturbed by a late morning phone call from Matilda, Charles Raine's niece. Aneeka had answered the phone and the two women had briefly exchanged pleasantries before she passed the phone to Aleck.

"Hello Matilda, it must be many years since we last spoke. Nice to hear your voice again. Is everything okay with Charles?" enquired Aleck.

"Hi Aleck. Uncle Charles is fine and he did so enjoy seeing both you and Aneeka yesterday. Thanks so much for bringing him some joy. I try to visit most weeks, but it can get very lonely for him, especially now his mobility is not so good. I popped in to see him earlier this morning and he told me all about your visit," said Matilda.

"We both enjoyed the visit too, and now that we know where he is – quite close to us actually – Aneeka and I have promised each other that we will try to call in on him quite regularly." With a little laugh, Aleck added: "Of course, that depends on how well we cope with becoming parents in the very near future. Now, bring me up to date about your life and family, Matilda."

"Fairly ordinary, but a happy life, Aleck. I'm a demographer working in a government department, and I've been married to Mikhail for nearly ten years. We have a five-year-old daughter, Nina, who's the joy of our life, so I can strongly recommend parenthood to you and Aneeka, tiring though it often is. Sadly, Dad didn't live long enough to get to see Nina, but at least my mum, Charles's sister-in-law, was part of Nina's life for her first few years. Mum died over a year ago, around about the time Uncle Charles had to go into care."

"It's a real regret of mine that neither of my parents are still with us, so our child will never know them," said Aleck. "It seems our parents' generation died at relatively young ages. Is that a true observation from your analysis as a demographer, Matilda?"

"No, I wouldn't say that," replied Matilda. "The mean lifespan for our parents' generation is 78.9, a figure Mum managed to exceed, although I'm sorry neither of your parents did."

Warming to her theme, Matilda continued.

"Before our parents, there were our grandparents, the Owlds, and some of them are still alive despite a life expectancy of 72; for the Owlds, that is a significant increase on their parents' life expectancy of 65 years, and their grandparents' too, which was lower still due to the significant impact of The Disaster on both generations. You'll be pleased to know the lifespan average continues to increase: it's 84.2 for our generation Aleck, thanks largely to government initiatives in so many areas."

Aleck said, teasingly, "Sounds like you're a propagandist for the Government as well as a demographer, Matilda."

Matilda laughed. "Forgive me Aleck, if that's what I sound like! But to be fair, we do owe them a lot for making what remains of our planet cleaner and healthier."

Changing the subject, she continued: "Now, it's lovely to speak to you, Aleck, and to share my passion for demographic statistics with you, but the other part of the reason I'm calling is to pass on a message from Charles, an upper-quartile statistic for longevity," she joked. "Uncle Charles asked me to let you know that he does remember someone called Leon Hartland. Just hang on a sec while I find the note I jotted down, at Charles's insistence."

There was a brief pause, and then Matilda's voice returned. "Here it is. Uncle Charles said that at a time when he was asking your father why he didn't complete his research degree and went into teaching instead, Colin had mentioned a university colleague who'd also had his scholarship application turned down. However, this person, Leon someone or other – Charles doesn't remember clearly, but when he woke up this morning he thought the surname could well have been Hartland – anyway, this Leon fellow was invited to join a physics research team, or it could have been astrophysics … Uncle Charles couldn't remember exactly. But he does remember Colin saying somewhat derisively that it was strange that Leon had been allowed to do research when it was his activism that had cost the pair of them their scholarships. Charles said it was out of character for Colin to be bitter. It was short-lived, however, as Colin had quickly gone on to assert that he loved his life as a maths teacher and wouldn't have swapped it for anything. He never again mentioned this Leon fellow to Uncle Charles, as far as he can recall."

Matilda paused to ask Aleck if any of that sounded plausible and whether it was helpful to him. Aleck replied that his father had been such a law-abiding, non-aggressive person that it was difficult to imagine how anyone else's activism could ever impinge on him.

"Maybe Dad was different at university. I don't know about you, Matilda, but I guess I'd have to confess to a few escapades as an undergraduate, usually those involving an excess of cheap red wine. However, what you've told me is really interesting and helpful, so please convey my warm thanks to Charles and tell him we'll see him soon."

After exchanging a few more family reminiscences and wishing each other all the best, with promises of keeping in touch, they concluded the call.

Turning to Aneeka, Aleck shared Charles's recollection, adding that he was beginning to think he didn't know his father as well as he thought he had.

"Yet, it was Dad who would walk home with me after school commitments had finished; Dad who prepared our evening meal – which we ate together, leaving Mum's portion to be reheated on her return home; Dad who would help with my homework, in between marking the work of his own students; and Dad who would play games with me, when time permitted.

"My mother was the one with the greater drive. She'd been appointed school principal when I was quite young, and she was always busy and often absent from home. Sometimes I was fast asleep in my bed before she returned, and I would only see her over breakfast. However, she always made sure that we did something together as a family at the weekend."

Aneeka put a comforting arm around his waist. Appreciating the hug, he added that he still missed his parents, particular with the baby about to be born – even more so today since, if his mother was still around, she could share stories about his father – maybe even explain more about his relationship to Leon.

Aneeka's parents, by contrast, were still alive, but Aneeka was estranged from both of them. Despite Aleck's encouragement to forgive and make up, especially with the baby soon to arrive, Aneeka had remained steadfast in her refusal to mend fences, saying the situation was irretrievable.

How it was that Aneeka was such a loving, fun and well-balanced person never ceased to surprise Aleck. Her parents were self-obsessed and self-indulgent. Both came from really wealthy families, which set them apart as rare, given that the Government had been largely successful at reining in excessive wealth through severe taxation laws.

Aneeka's parents had hired a surrogate mother to carry Aneeka, using the ova from both parents and the sperm from a male friend whose identity had never been revealed to Aneeka. Which of her parents was her biological mother Aneeka did not know for sure either, despite feeling she looked more like the one rather than the other; it's possible she took after the father rather than one of her mothers. Aneeka believed that her parents had decided to have a baby to give them something to show off to their friends, in much the same way they would show off their new designer clothes or latest acquisition. Neither parent had any interest in the job of parenting, and Aneeka had been looked after by a robo-nanny during her first three years. Thereafter, Aneeka liked to claim she looked after herself.

As a teenager, Aneeka had recognised the shallowness of the interest her parents held in her and she had stopped performing for them, abandoning any hope of being included in their affections. Their pretty, sweet child had morphed into a moody and resentful teenager, and before too much longer she had become estranged from her parents. Years later, after she met Aleck, she refused to invite either parent to their wedding. Aleck had never met Ann or Kay, and Aneeka rarely mentioned them: it was as if they too, like his own parents, had died.

Moved by his recollections, Aleck gave his adored wife a big hug and patted her swollen belly. "You, my darling, are the best thing that ever happened to me," he murmured.

Aneeka grinned mischievously. "Matilda should ring more often if that's the effect she has on you. Now, I recall her saying parenthood can be very tiring, so maybe we should make the most of the time left and have a little lie down. What do you think, Aleck?" And, taking Aleck's hand, she started leading him towards their bedroom.

Later that day, while they sat outside enjoying a lunch of green salad and trout served with chunks of fresh bread, Aneeka reminded Aleck of her appointment with Geraldine the next day. "Blast, I'd forgotten that," he said. "I'm sorry, sweetheart, but I have to see Bruce Daniels tomorrow morning so I'm not going to be able to come this time."

"That's a shame, Geraldine will be disappointed not to see you," Aneeka replied. She continued more cheerily: "It's not a problem, I'll tell you all about it tomorrow evening. Now, if you've had enough to eat, let's go somewhere for a drive. Maybe past the lovely old homestead where you and your parents once lived?"

*

It had been a very busy weekend for Gretel. She had spent Saturday meeting with interested parties keen to make changes to the planning statutes, followed by meetings with some individual ministers to canvass ideas about the proposed alterations to the building code. Then there had been lunch with the heads of three of the larger charities, all keen to lobby the Government for additional funds. In the afternoon she had paid short visits to several neighbourhoods to admire and applaud the initiatives being taken to set up communal vegetable gardens, instigate programs to protect the environment and reduce waste, and offer educational short courses for those who needed to be retrained for alternative work possibilities.

In the evening, she had hosted an educational symposium where the key speakers presented differing but well-thought-through ideas for strengthening the education system. In her own presentation to the assembled experts, Gretel was sympathetic to the idea of a broader curriculum and particularly interested in the proposal that the study of literature should become compulsory. However, she had stressed very firmly that under no circumstances could she ever envisage being convinced to reduce the Government's insistence on the compulsory study of mathematics and science. The dinner that followed had offered some good opportunities for networking, and as dinner hadn't finished until late, Gretel again stayed overnight at Government House.

Her Sunday morning had been spent catching up on paperwork and meeting with some of her personal staff. In the afternoon, she presented awards to citizens who had displayed commendable courage under adversity; gave another speech about the importance of maintaining first-class auxiliary services, lavishing praise on the members of the fire, ambulance and constabulary services for their first-responder roles to emergencies; and attended a 'greet and mingle' event to encourage citizens to volunteer to assist where they could in special programs, such as those brightening the lives of the remaining Owlds or others who were lonely or incapacitated.

On returning to her office, Gretel's plans to spend Sunday evening quietly at home with Javier were stymied by a request from Timothy, the Minister for Roads and Transport, who wanted to speak to her urgently.

It was through her continued contact with the former Homer ministers that Timothy's name had first become known to Gretel. She had learnt through these former ministers that Timothy was a descendant of President Homer through Homer's sister's lineage. Timothy, it seemed, had been raised with the expectation that he would come to emulate the greatness of his ancestor: that is, he believed it was his destiny.

Good government is not about creating dynasties, Gretel thought, recalling her reticence in welcoming Timothy to the Inner Cabinet. She had demurred at the time, only promising the old ministers, of whom she was very fond, that the most she was prepared to do would be to ask her most trusted Heads of Departments to consider Timothy's case and that she, and these Homer ministers, would respect their judgement.

We know how well that went. I should have trusted my own instincts.

The Heads of Departments had been adamant in their support for Timothy as someone who, given guidance and opportunity, would come to bring honour to the Government. Gretel couldn't see it herself at the time and she didn't see it now, but she had accepted their advice, and so Timothy had accepted her offer to join the Inner Cabinet, relinquishing his university position in economics.

That he was clever, Gretel recognised immediately. He was an independent thinker too, but so far there were few signs of a future leader in evidence, although he was a popular and competent minister. It seemed to Gretel that Timothy was more intent on becoming an undermining figure rather than a future leader.

However, she did acknowledge that Timothy had never, not even once, tried to use his many-times-removed relationship to President Homer to his own advantage. This she had always found puzzling. *Perhaps he feels the relationship is so tenuous that not even he can claim any close connection?* she reflected. *Or, more likely, he feels the comparison between himself and his much-loved ancestor will not be one that reflects well on him.*

Twenty minutes later, the youngish, awkwardly slim and somewhat self-important minister arrived at her office.

Timothy started by apologising for interrupting her day of leisure. Gretel let that pass without comment, but she soon became very attentive. Timothy was saying that he had come to warn her that there was something disturbing and possibly underhand going on at the Department of Health. Gretel abruptly interrupted him, suggesting that since Timothy was not the minister in charge of health, what gave him the right to be speaking on any such issue, adding acerbically, "Have you thought to raise this concern with Grigor, the actual minister?"

Unfazed, Timothy countered, "True, Gretel, I'm not the health minister, but that does not stop people coming to me with concerns. I am well-regarded by the citizens, as you are aware."

Conceited little upstart, thought Gretel. Timothy continued.

"The matter I raise is not strictly a matter for the health minister, as you will understand if you'd give me a chance to say my piece." Gretel maintained her silence; Timothy ploughed ahead.

"A request for information about a missing citizen is being stonewalled by the Department of Health. I put it to you, Madam President, that you know about this and the reasons why."

At this, Gretel decided he really was being too insolent. "Are you threatening me or accusing me of inappropriate behaviour, Timothy?"

Timothy threw his arms up in the air theatrically, sighing for effect, before calmly continuing to speak.

"No Gretel, or at least not yet. I'm here as a loyal member of your Inner Cabinet simply to warn you that it may come to light that you have participated in hushing up the disappearance, in strange circumstances, of this citizen. At this stage, I'm on your side. I'm trying to alert you to the fact that something serious may be about to break that will damage the Government, and possibly you personally."

"So, what is this breaking information, Timothy?" she demanded imperiously.

"My informant, who will remain unnamed, tells me that this citizen has been an unfortunate victim of a failed experiment conducted by one of the Government's research departments. The informant says it is possible to produce evidence to substantiate this claim."

"That sounds totally fanciful and far-fetched, Timothy. How reliable is your informant, and how could this person have such knowledge? Which research department is alleged to be involved?" parried Gretel.

"I cannot tell you much else, but I have total confidence in my informant, Gretel. I am here today following correct protocol by alerting you to this looming problem. I continue to give you my full support, especially as you claim ignorance of this matter. However, I should tell you, Gretel, that if it is proven that you have sanctioned some despicable experiment and cover-up, then my support will be withdrawn."

Controlling her anger over his sanctimonious utterings, she curtly responded: "Your support is noted, minister. I shall ask that the matter be investigated, but I think your informant may have an alternative agenda behind his or her claim. If so, this would make you appear rather gullible at best, or part of a plot to remove me from office at worst. What say you to that?"

"I don't deny that I am ambitious Gretel, but I'm not stupid. I am young; forgive me, you are not. In the goodness of time, you will choose to retire. When that happens, it may well be that I will stand as a candidate for the presidency; however, I assume that time may still be several years away. I am aware that you find either my views or my person somewhat irritating at times but, nevertheless, I suggest you accept me at face value. I am reporting to you as a member of your Cabinet, alerting you to a potentially significant problem. That is what should be expected from someone who at this point in time remains loyal to you."

"Have you shared these preposterous allegations with anyone else in my Cabinet, Timothy?"

"No-one else in your Cabinet, I assure you. However, clearly that will change if my information can be substantiated."

Frowning, Gretel brought their meeting to an end. "Then we shall leave it here until enquiries have been made. Accepting your actions at face value as you claim, I acknowledge the 'heads up'. Let me reiterate that I have neither involvement in, nor knowledge of, what you claim. Nonetheless, I shall ask that the matter be investigated."

With a penetrating and steely eyed glare, Gretel sternly concluded, "You must understand that, in my opinion, this will almost certainly prove to be baseless rumour-mongering. In that event, there will be another meeting between you and I – one in which we shall be discussing your future."

With that, Timothy departed.

Gretel, who had in any case been intending to go home before Timothy had arrived, quickly gathered up her belongings and also departed, feeling she urgently needed to speak in private with Javier.

*

Timothy lingered, watching discreetly from a distance until he observed Gretel's car depart. He took out a cell phone – not his usual one, this one reserved for only the most private of calls – and pressed a pre-set number.

Leon answered with the one-word query, "Well?" to which Timothy replied, "Bait laid, reaction as you predicted, and Gretel has just driven off at some speed."

"Good work," said Leon.

*

Leon snapped his phone shut, ending the call to return to his card game. He smiled at his Bridge partner and said, "Game on."

CHAPTER 13

Gretel composed herself as she was driven home. *It's important to remain calm and act logically,* she counselled herself. She felt certain that Timothy had come to hear something about Eva in relation to the disappearance of that citizen. *What was his name again? Ah yes, Proger, Claus Proger. Who is he – or rather, was he? Why has he created such interest when he's supposed to have been security screened?*

She had not authorised any experimentation, and she had already told Eva she didn't want to hear any details about her work. So, who could know, since she, the President, did not know exactly what Eva's research involved? Eva was unlikely to have let anything slip, Javier was out of the question, but did Eva say there had been someone else overseeing the procedure? She messaged Cabut to send her a list of any such persons or anyone who had nursed Claus Proger after his unexpectedly poor reaction to the procedure.

Arriving home not exactly in good spirits (save for at least feeling in control once more), Gretel changed into more casual clothes and joined Javier at the table outside on the patio. Over tea and cake – delicious of course, Javier was an excellent cook – she summarised her visit from Timothy. They discussed her position and how she should be seen to react.

The daylight was starting to fade when Gretel broke the discussion. She went inside to draw the blinds and switch on a lamp. Pouring two glasses of wine and settling on the couch, she was soon joined by Javier who had formed some potential courses of action.

Firstly, he felt he personally should summon Timothy to a meeting so that Timothy could explain his claims and actions to Javier himself, as the President's Principal Advisor. This would show that Gretel was looking into Timothy's allegation as she had promised, and it might yield something more than Timothy had told Gretel. He cautioned Gretel to stay on civil terms with the man, as he shared Gretel's wariness about Timothy's genuineness of motive. Gretel nodded in acquiescence.

Javier briefed Gretel about the publication of Leon's article calling for anyone who knew the citizen to come forward. Jacques would ensure that any response to the article would be shared with the Security Agency. Background checks and, if necessary, interviews could be conducted with any responders, as well as checks on the very short list of names Cabut had promptly provided Gretel in response to her earlier request. Soothingly, Javier surmised that these actions would allow Gretel to report back in confidence to Timothy that extensive investigations had been carried out, likely without any real concern being unearthed, which should be the end of it.

"Although it's not up to me, maybe it also should be the end of Timothy's ministerial career," Javier quietly suggested. Once again, Gretel nodded her head in agreement.

Javier then reflected that, rather than continue to obfuscate, it might be wiser to release some sort of response about the Proger enquiry to the law firm acting for Leon. As she began to agree, he added: "Leon's movements are being monitored. Maybe it's time to interview him, even set in action the possibility of accusing Leon of being involved in the citizen's disappearance, perhaps?" Gretel again nodded, though less decisively.

Javier went on to say that it was looking increasingly likely that Eva may have made a misjudgement, an error or spoken unguardedly. Taking Gretel's hand, Javier said softly, "If there were some unfortunate findings uncovered in Eva's actions, then you might have only one recourse – and that would be to throw Eva to the wolves." This time, Gretel did not nod.

Gretel was a great believer that bedtime was for sleeping, not for lying awake and allowing the trials of the day to run around in her head, causing unnecessary waves of worry over hypothetical events. What would be would be, tomorrow would come, and often enough the new dawn tended to usher in a sense of certainty about the best action to take: a good night's sleep was the genesis of good decision-making. Accordingly, she and Javier ceased their deliberations and settled down for an uneventful Sunday evening: an omelette followed by another piece of hummingbird sponge cake, eaten while watching a movie that Javier had downloaded earlier. An early bedtime then beckoned.

*

Eva had enjoyed what for her was quite a domesticated Sunday. She had purchased some hellebores from a garden nursery that was quite close to her apartment building. The little flowers peeked shyly out at her from their position on a table that would normally catch some morning sun. These little green treasures seemed so demure, refined and elegant to Eva – her favourite plant, despite several other contenders for her affection. As usual, Eva's maid had Sundays off, so Eva enjoyed a day of not-so-healthy snacks and an unbalanced combination of leftovers. Her evening meal consisted of a toasted cheese and tomato sandwich and a piece of chocolate, both washed down with a glass of cider as she watched a program from the History channel. Early to bed, she read two chapters of the historical romance she allowed herself to read only on Sunday nights, then switched the lights off, her alarm set. An early start would be required the next day.

*

Aleck and Aneeka were enjoying a tasty meal of pumpkin ravioli doused with a simple sage sauce, embellished with a dash of tzatziki and a sprinkle of pine nuts. They chatted about the changes they'd noted had been made to Aleck's childhood home following their drive past earlier in the afternoon. Aleck said he felt virtually no affinity with the place anymore as it was so changed. The surrounding area was more densely housed, and the old field where Aleck and his father had played cricket together had been replaced by apartment blocks.

"I wonder if our child will have a similar experience?" Aleck pondered. "In twenty years' time, will he come to visit his ageing parents and feel the area has changed so much from the way he remembered it as a child?"

"That's called progress," Aneeka said. "At least you envisage him coming to visit us. By the way, have we come to an agreement about his name, my darling?"

"I still like the idea of Mack," argued Aleck. "It's got an A and a K from both his parents, and a C and an M after his grandparents. I know you didn't think much of it at first, but has it grown on you at all?"

"Humph," responded Aneeka.

"Is that a suggestion for a name darling, or are you just being disparaging?" quipped Aleck.

"Seriously, Aleck, do you really think Mack sounds okay? I can see you calling to our young child at bedtime: 'Mack, it's time to hit the sack!' I get where you're coming from and I quite like the letter selection; however, my preference remains Cameron," she said.

"Humph. You get three letters, A, N and E, while I only pass on two: A and E."

"Wrong, Aleck. Let me help you with the spelling of your own name. You also have a C in your name. You have an A, an E and a C, I have an A, an N and an E, your father has a C, an O and an N, and your mother has an E, an M, an R and an A. Perfect suggestion, thank you Aneeka," she laughed, congratulating herself.

"Oh well, I guess when I'm taking a photo I could ask, 'is the camera on, Cameron?'" he teased.

"When was the last time you used a camera, Aleck? I'm willing to predict Cameron will not know what one is," quickly shot back Aneeka.

"Humph," grumbled Aleck, once again. Then, more generously, he gave Aneeka a hug and whispered, "Clever clogs Aneeka. By George, I think you've got it for this Raine. Would Cameron Mack Raine be a possibility?" he ended, hope in his voice.

"Let's keep it simple, Aleck. Cameron Raine it is, except you could use Mack as a nickname until your son is able to speak, at which stage I strongly predict he will forbid you to do so. Now, tomorrow is a busy day for us both so I'm going to read in bed for a little before lights out. Hope you join me soon," she invited.

*

While many people enjoyed an early night on a Sunday, Leon was an exception to the rule. He was working through data so he could issue plans for the next three days, aiming to do so before midnight struck. It needed to be available early the next morning for his clicker employees to publish the odds to offer as he directed. Sunday evening was always a busy working time for him: it was when he carried out the mathematical analysis of the results from the previous week's games and absorbed these into the long-term stochastic process on which he based his decision-making.

Timothy had rung again, although Leon had chosen not to answer the call, being both pressed for time and predicting it would be more a social call than anything urgent.

Leon knew Timothy well; they had been quite close, and Timothy believed they still were. He had been Leon's protégé and, for a brief period, his lover. Leon had harboured (perhaps still did harbour?) a long-term scheme to assist Timothy into the presidency. However, Timothy's recent lack of discretion had started to rankle, and Leon was still weighing up whether he might have to consider supporting another potential candidate. The Minister for Energy and the Environment seemed to possess a visionary yet sensible purpose – perhaps he should be offering his support to him.

Leon understood very clearly that there needed to be a change of leadership – a change to someone who would protect, not feign ignorance of, or turn a blind eye to, the human rights abuses he believed were taking place on the periphery of government research programs.

He had known Gretel well back in the days they had worked together, and he supported and applauded much of what she had achieved during her presidency. But now, maybe it was time for her to pass the baton to the next generation, to retire while she was still ahead.

Leon had always recognised that governing and politics form part of a game – one that ends in a loss, not a zero-sum game. When Gretel had stymied Timothy's intentions to ask the probing questions of the Chief Scientist that he and Leon had discussed, Leon had realised Gretel's time was up; however, he was feeling less confident about testing his hypothesis that Timothy should be the one to replace him.

*

Timothy was not in bed yet – he was seeking company. Having not received a reply from Leon, he had called his friend Frederick.

He had met Freddy through Leon, but since then Freddy and Timothy had become close, relegating the ageing Leon to being Freddy's Bridge partner.

Taking his call, Freddy invited him over to his apartment, an offer Timothy was pleased to accept.

When he arrived, Freddy listened patiently as Timothy spoke of his plans and motivations.

Timothy knew his family's expectation, and he intended to fulfil that destiny one day, but, as he explained to Freddy: "I want to be selected on the strength of my own qualities, not those of my uncle many times removed. And, should I be so honoured as to be appointed president, then and only then will I acknowledge my relationship with the revered President Homer.

"Plus," he added, "I want to live freely, to enjoy my youthful years unencumbered by too much responsibility before I adopt a more serious demeanour. The presidency is my future, not my today."

That Freddy understood helped strengthen their relationship. And the pair went to some effort to revel in the self-indulgence Timothy desired before he would be willing to cast off his youthful excesses. Only when he was ready, Timothy claimed, would he cease altogether his drug play – that 'fetish', a surprisingly prudish Gretel had called it, which she thought she held over his head.

As he and Freddy continued to drink, snort coke, and wax and wane on life and matters of common interest, Timothy had laughed that he couldn't deny that his one or two acts of Gretel-undermining were sweet payback for her indifference. Gretel knew of his family connection, and he was miffed that she hadn't taken him under her wing as his forebear had done for her. Far from grooming him, teaching him the art of politics, she had done very little aside from offering him a couple of assistant minister positions, and later the Roads and Transport portfolio. It was left to Freddy to point out that those roles were excellent training in themselves.

Although Freddy had no great personal desire to enter politics, he was interested in the subject from an intellectual point of view. An aesthete, Freddy considered himself to be a playwright and artist, albeit one that was waiting to be discovered; equally, Timothy considered himself a future president, albeit one that was waiting to be recognised. When he assumed that office, it was Timothy's intention to promote the arts, with possibly Freddy as the minister responsible for that portfolio. In Timothy's opinion, creativity would be vital for the future success of the Country, and it was his intention to foster this in the education system.

All that lay ahead. For now, the two were happy to boast to each other about how important they would become, and it would be fair to say each enjoyed the other's company extremely. As their moods rose higher in direct proportion to their consumption of alcohol and other drugs, the preamble dance around sexual moves gained pace, and it wasn't long before Timothy made his way to bed – although sleep, it would have to be said, was not at the top of his immediate intentions.

CHAPTER 14

Eva woke before her alarm. She showered and took her small breakfast out to her balcony, observing, as she so often did, the joggers already in motion along the path that ran beside the stream. Superficially at least, these were her breakfast companions, although Eva rarely speculated on what the life stories of these people might be; whether citizens Green and Nice-Abs were a couple, for instance, simply held no interest for her. She finished her slice of toast and went to get dressed.

Her car arrived to take her to the office, and soon Eva was greeting Cabut with a "good morning." *Whatever time does he arrive?* she wondered, concluding for the umpteenth time that his apartment must be nearby.

This was an important day for her. Today she would meet the pregnant woman, her final test case, the one who would validate the procedure. The meeting was scheduled for 10.45 am. As promised, Gerry had sent Eva samples of the mother's blood and the amniotic fluid surrounding the baby, and Eva had already arranged for the DNA to be extracted and to undergo sequencing. Although this was a lengthy procedure, a partial map for a relatively small selection of genes and diseases could now be carried out relatively quickly, albeit at some cost to the budget – but cost was not something Eva ever concerned herself with. Awaiting her perusal, the laboratory results already lay on her desk, placed there earlier by Cabut.

Comparing the two sets of data, Eva noticed the mother-to-be was having a baby boy. However, she also carried a mutation in the BRCA2 gene, indicating an increased risk of developing breast cancer at some later stage in her life. There was no sign of this on the baby's report.

Good, thought Eva. *Maybe that could be a topic for discussion with the mother and certainly something to pass on to Gerry. Maybe Gerry will feel more grateful towards me.*

She also noticed a difference between mother and baby in the gene ABCC11, but this, unlike the BRCA genes (1 and 2), was not mentioned on her chart nominating association with potential cancer. Perhaps it was part of a sex-related chromosome, which would explain why mother and son differed. Consulting her computer again, however, Eva found it was not the case.

"Okay," she said to herself, "let's see if we can identify it, because this could be just what we need."

It wasn't possible to have a genome chart for every type of disease. So far, researchers had only been able to produce the few that Eva already had in her possession. She thought it worth querying for more on this gene, so she messaged through to the head of the laboratory, asking for any information about it and stipulating she needed a response urgently.

Half an hour later, she was informed that the gene ABCC11 affected the type of ear wax – some ear waxes were wet and could form into small balls, while others were dry and flaky. She also discovered that the gene may be linked to body odour, but there was no link to any of the diseases that had been mapped to date.

Excellent! thought Eva. *I can work with this.*

Then she became more sober. The realisation, despite its unlikelihood, that if the chromosome was damaged in an unusual way it might mutate to form a neo-chromosome, gave Eva a salutary reminder that she needed to carry out her procedure with great care, as neo-chromosomes were thought to be linked to some rare forms of cancer.

Not that she was interested in either medical implications or applications. For Eva, it was all about testing whether it was possible to use her 'cut and paste' editing procedure on part of a chromosome and then have this process reversed. Over the course of the past several weeks, she had made considerable simplifications and adjustments to the procedure, ones she hadn't earlier even envisaged, all to reduce the chance of shattering the chromosome to almost negligible. The failure with the last civilian receptor would not be repeated: she had run out of time to risk losing another case study.

*

Aneeka arrived for her appointment with Geraldine, who greeted her cheerfully. To Aneeka's intense irritation, Geraldine's first comment was, "Aleck not with us today?" Only after she had explained Aleck's reason for non-attendance did her obstetrician ask how Aneeka – the actual patient – was feeling.

The consultation was brief but reassuring. All was continuing to go well, and the antenatal visits would now be on a twice-weekly basis. Then Geraldine turned to the research program, explaining there had been a change of emphasis. A colleague would be taking over the main role of conducting the research.

"I want to thank you again, Aneeka, for volunteering to participate in this research. It is only with the help of people like you that we move forward to achieving better health outcomes for all. Now, I need you to confirm your participation formally by signing this form. Do take your time to read through it first."

Aneeka did a quick scan of the single page form and signed.

"I have shared my collected data about you and your baby with my colleague, and, if you wish, that can be the end of your involvement; we would still be grateful to you for allowing your medical records to be used for research purposes."

Geraldine paused, but Aneeka had already decided she was happy to participate further.

"In that case, I'll now send you to meet Professor Eva Baritz, who has arranged her availability in the expectation of seeing you in about ten minutes' time."

Handing Aneeka the referral form, Geraldine gave her the directions to the professor's room.

"Professor Baritz is on the third floor. Take the lift from here, turn to the right when you exit the lift, and follow along that corridor till you reach her office. It's the fourth one on the left. You can't miss it, but just ask someone to direct you if you get lost."

If I can't miss it, then why should I get lost? thought Aneeka. Dismissing her irritability, she figured she had just enough time for a quick bathroom visit before going to meet Geraldine's colleague, Professor Eva Baritz.

*

Eva opened the door to greet Aneeka in person. For just a millisecond she was taken aback, as she realised she was greeting the mother-to-be she had passed on her run on Saturday. Collecting herself and noting that Aneeka had shown no signs of recognition, Eva introduced herself as Professor Baritz.

After shaking hands, Aneeka sat down on the chair nearest to the door. Eva chose to pull up a chair next to Aneeka rather than face her more formally across her desk. She took the referral form and asked courteously if she could call Aneeka by her first name, before inviting Aneeka to call her Eva.

"Thank you so much for giving me some of your time today, Aneeka. I can see you must not be far off term now. How have you enjoyed being pregnant?" Eva enquired conversationally.

Aneeka replied that it had been a fascinating experience so far, that she'd been very fortunate to have enjoyed good health throughout, and that she was looking forward to the birth of her baby.

"Bet you must be looking forward to seeing your feet once again and getting back into normal clothes too," laughed Eva.

The two chatted quite casually for a few more minutes about the ups and downs surrounding pregnancy, and Eva was pleased to see that Aneeka seemed to be relaxing in her company.

"Now Aneeka, let me explain a little of what I do," she eventually said, judging it was time to get down to business. "First, I need to make it quite clear that I am not a medical doctor, just a simple research scientist really." Eva smiled. "I have been working on what's called genome sequencing, which Gerry may have explained to you. Ultimately, my team and I hope to develop a simple procedure whereby we can use someone's blood sample to detect if that person has, or is likely to have in later life, a serious illness such as diabetes, cancer and so on. And, once identified, we want to be able to prevent some of these diseases from occurring by being able to edit the chromosome that has the defect.

"My examples are in the medical field, but we're hoping there may be other applications too," she added.

Eva sensed that Aneeka was interested to understand her research further, so she suggested that Aneeka might like to visit the laboratory with her in the future, if she so wished.

"Gerry sent me a sample of your blood, Aneeka, and a sample of the amniotic fluid that surrounds your baby," she said, pausing to check that Aneeka was aware of this. When Aneeka confirmed that she was, Eva continued.

"We're working on that now, and we've made some progress that I would love to discuss with you, as you seem genuinely interested in the research. Nothing to worry about, I hasten to add," she said with a warm smile, leaning forward to lightly touch Aneeka's arm.

"However, I'm wondering how you would feel about donating a little more blood. Our work is definitely progressing, but we are still in the exploratory stages and the more samples we have to work with the better. How do you feel about that?"

Aneeka did not hesitate. "You are most welcome – just leave me enough blood to be getting on with, please!" They both laughed.

"That's great, Aneeka, I hope you don't think we're vampires." They laughed again, companionably.

Eva was pleased that her humility and her charm offensive were having the desired effect on the young woman. She decided to seize the opportunity to go straight to the next stage while her subject was feeling so cooperative. Gerry need never know.

"What interests me the most in my research is to be able to isolate a particular gene in an instant of time. Imagine the applications of that, Aneeka. We could directly carry out a repair to a damaged area in a non-intrusive way. Mutations that lead to cancer and so on could be immediately reversed if picked up early enough. I believe we have devised something simple and painless to do just that. It has worked in laboratory tests and now we are trying it out on a range of humans, in your case as a pregnant female sample. There's no danger to you involved, only to my reputation if it doesn't succeed." She laughed reassuringly.

"The procedure I'm using to extract what I need should only take a few minutes. Are you up to this now, or would you prefer to wait till another time – or would you prefer not to participate at all?" asked Eva.

Aneeka questioned whether the procedure could put her baby at any risk, and when Eva reassured her again that there was no danger whatsoever to either her or her baby, Aneeka agreed to proceed – on the proviso that none of the procedure could be carried out on the baby.

"Just to be cautious, and fair to Cameron-to-be, who is not in a position to voice his opinion," Aneeka said.

"Ah, so you know you are having a boy. This showed up when we tested the amniotic sample Gerry provided, but I wasn't going to tell you. Not everyone likes to know the sex before the baby is born," observed Eva.

"What else did you find out Eva, anything I should know?" queried Aneeka.

"I think you can be very confident that you are carrying a healthy little boy," smiled Eva, making an instant decision not to reveal details of the BRCA2 gene finding in Aneeka's sequencing that she had identified earlier in the morning. She also decided in that instant not to surreptitiously attempt to carry out the procedure on the baby as she had intended, a decision she could interrogate herself over at another time.

"The gene I've chosen to look at is the ABCC11. It plays a role in the type of ear wax we produce (Eva having earlier decided this was somehow nicer than body odour). The sample I'm taking needs only to be minutely tiny so it's not going to disturb your body or the baby's. There are two stages to the procedure, and at the end of each stage a drop of your blood will be analysed. Do you have any questions before we get started?"

*

Aneeka had found Eva's outline of her research, brief though it was, really interesting, and she had listened with great attention. *What a clever and admirable person this Eva is,* she thought, and she felt really pleased that she would in some small way be contributing to her research.

Eva asked her to hold out her hand when she was ready to get started. Eva placed a small circular device on her middle finger, adding what looked like a thimble to cover the top of her finger. Eva explained that these objects were linked to her laptop, and she was checking to ensure that both receivers were registering her data correctly. She then placed Aneeka's hand so that it was resting comfortably on a small cushion.

"Right, we're ready to go, Aneeka, if that's okay with you. This little device is programmed to locate the gene I mentioned, and it will send the sample data I need straight to my computer. You will feel a pinprick as the device is activated, and that will be followed by another as it switches off in about three seconds. Then the thimble-like device will send the first blood sample analysis. Does that sound okay?"

Aneeka nodded.

"Great. Try hard not to move your hand until I say so."

Managing not to jerk her hand as she felt the first prick on her skin, Aneeka sat quietly through the first stage of the process – until a very slight sting signified the connector had switched off. Aneeka then felt a tiny prick of her finger as her blood sample information was transmitted. When Eva asked how she was doing, she was able to say that she was doing fine.

"Good, Aneeka, you're an excellent research study, I wish they were all like you. Now if you're ready, we'll continue on to the second stage."

Aneeka agreed she was ready.

The second stage seemed to Aneeka to be no different from the first, perhaps just faster. Wriggling her hand and fingers once Eva had removed the circular device and thimble, Aneeka thought about how smooth and efficient the process had been.

"That's all there is to it, Aneeka. I can't tell you how grateful I am to you and those like you who are participating in this research. Thank you very much. There should be nothing to have upset you or your baby, but I guess you can never be too careful so, just in case, I would recommend that you take it easy for the rest of the day."

Grinning, Eva held out a jar of lollies, saying, "Would you care for a small sweet as a tiny reward?"

As she chose a green-coloured candy, Aneeka felt almost sorry her time with Eva was over. She said, with some amazement, "That seemed so easy, Eva. I take it that the programming of the device you placed on my hand is your creation? And, that you didn't actually draw my blood out, just somehow sent its characteristics immediately to your computer?"

"That's pretty well the gist of it, Aneeka. Have you a technology background? You seem to have followed all that we've talked about and have a good understanding of the process," marvelled Eva.

Aneeka explained that her background was in engineering and public administration, but nevertheless she was fascinated by Eva's research and would love to hear of the advances it would lead to once Eva had completed her work.

Eva smiled, seeming to be delighted by Aneeka's words. She invited Aneeka to get in touch once the baby had been born, assuming she had enough time and energy to come over to visit the laboratory. In turn, Aneeka volunteered that if she could be of further use to Eva's research then she would be keen to participate.

They warmly shook hands in farewell, and a happy Aneeka set off to catch her train home. Once on the train, Aneeka reflected on how impressive the smartly dressed professor had been. She was also struck by how fit and attractive she'd appeared to be, despite seeming to be quite a bit older than her.

She messaged Aleck to say all had gone exceedingly well and that she couldn't wait to tell him all about it that evening.

*

After Aneeka had left, Eva messaged Cabut to organise a car to collect her in half an hour's time. Before she completed packing up, she also thought to email Gerry with the news that Aneeka was carrying a mutation in the BRCA2 gene, stating that this had not been discussed with Aneeka. She knew that this would be appreciated by Gerry.

Eva was looking forward to analysing the data she had taken from Aneeka.

The procedure was not as she had described it to Aneeka, although fortunately Aneeka hadn't realised this. She had made an incision in Aneeka's ABCC11 gene, a cut too small for the human eye to see, and she had pasted in the alternative version of the gene she'd been able to extract from the baby's amniotic fluid. The first blood sample should show this change when she sequenced its DNA. The second stage of the procedure should have undone the gene editing, restoring Aneeka's gene to its original status, and the second blood test should be able to confirm that this had happened.

Her mind raced ahead – if this worked, someone travelling through space would be able to perform a similar simple cut-and-paste edit of their genes. Edits that could extend lives under adverse conditions, not just ones that fiddled with ear wax: if edits could be made successfully to this gene, then surely they could be made to any others on any chromosome.

Eva grinned. "Planet Earth, prepare to receive us – we're getting closer," she said to herself.

CHAPTER 15

Shortly before Aleck's meeting with Bruce Daniels on Monday morning, Erik tapped at his open office door and, not waiting to be invited in, he entered, a big smile lighting up his face as he waved a document in his hand.

"You won't believe it Aleck, we have a response to the FOI!" he exclaimed. "There I was, waiting patiently for my number to be called so that I could go up to the counter to be told yet again that there was nothing for me, when, blow me down, over walks one of the heavies I'd had the dubious pleasure of being interviewed by on my first visit. This klutz says to me that he hoped what he was giving me would satisfy the curiosity of Solicitor Raine and that he also hoped he would not see me ever again.

"Ta da! Here it is, Aleck," said Erik as he handed over the document.

It was a short and concise statement acknowledging that a Claus Proger had been admitted to the hospital as a precautionary measure following a routine vasectomy procedure. The stay was overnight only, with the citizen being discharged the following morning. However, at the time of his release, Proger had complained of a migraine. He was given a pain relief tablet and allowed to rest in the ward for a little longer. When next checked later that morning, he was found dead in the chair in which he had been resting. An autopsy report showed he had suffered a brain aneurysm that was considered to be due to natural causes, and unrelated to the vasectomy procedure. As there was no record of next of kin given, and neither any visitors nor any enquiries about his welfare, the hospital had later arranged for the disposal of the body.

The statement ended with regret for the passing of the citizen, while reiterating that hospital management had complete confidence that the deceased had received due care from its staff and would vehemently reject any suggestion to the contrary.

"All very interesting; it seems they think that we intend to bring a suit against the hospital for negligence," commented Aleck, feeling quite gratified that persistence had been rewarded with this unexpected breakthrough.

Leon hadn't raised the possibility of a lawsuit as his intention, but Aleck acknowledged that his intentions weren't at all clear.

Thanking Erik for his tenacity and efforts, Aleck placed the document at the top of the pile of papers he was taking with him to show Bruce. Together, he and Erik left his office, one to head off to a meeting, the other to make himself a cup of coffee.

Bruce greeted Aleck warmly. He was a jovial character who enjoyed his outdoor sports, especially yachting, but he was someone who didn't like the boat to be rocked.

"Now, tell me all about this man Hartland, Aleck. Bit of a leftie, is he?" asked Bruce.

Aleck relayed his interactions with Leon so far, sticking to the facts and refraining from commenting on Bruce's observation, saying only that he found Leon's motives both unclear and puzzling. "However, perhaps the update I've just received will bring matters to a close," said Aleck, passing the document to Bruce.

He waited patiently while the senior partner perused the FOI response.

"Is that what Hartland has been implying, do you think, that the hospital staff have been negligent in their handling of the patient and have tried to hush up his death?" queried Bruce.

"Possibly," shrugged Aleck. "It will be interesting to see how he reacts once he learns the details of the FOI response." He hastened to add, "I've only just received the document, so I'll be contacting him immediately after we're finished here."

Bruce paused for a moment before responding, carefully choosing his words. "I would advise that you give Hartland a copy of the document and then you make it clear to him that you have carried out his wishes and that, as far as you and this firm are concerned, the matter is concluded."

"Why do you think it best to drop the case?" queried Aleck, who was curious to understand Bruce's reasoning and yet had been coming around to that same thought.

"Let's just say that a chap at my yacht club knows a chap who works for a minister, and he happened to tell me in good faith that the firm's name would not be advanced by dealing with the likes of this Hartland fellow. Said he was an old revolutionary with a record of trying to undermine government institutions and processes. Very important, Aleck, that we maintain our reputation for integrity."

"I'll keep you up to date with how Mr Hartland reacts," was all that Aleck said in response as he took his leave of Bruce Daniels.

Aleck thought that the best way for a law firm to garner a reputation for integrity was to be seen to act in good faith and to achieve justice for its clients. He'd never been particularly fond of Bruce – if pressed, he would even have described him as a bit of a dickhead – but the fellow knew which way the wind blew, and it was rare for him to give unsolicited advice.

"Maybe he's right," Aleck thought. "The sooner we part company with Leon Hartland, the better."

Pausing on his way back to his own office, Aleck asked the receptionist to call Leon to tell him there had been a development and to ask him to come in when convenient.

He was back at his desk when he read a message from Aneeka, sent after her research visit. Feeling relieved that all had gone so well, he promised himself he'd get home early to hear about her day.

Not long afterwards, there was another tap on his door as Erik again entered the room.

"More news, boss," he smiled, as he showed Aleck the article published that day on the UndPress site.

Aleck quickly read the short piece about Claus Proger and the appeal for anyone who had information about his whereabouts to contact the editor. "That has to be the work of our Mr Hartland," said Aleck.

"My thoughts exactly," concurred Erik, who went on to say that he had obtained the contact details of Rueben Thiem, the editor of UndPress, should Aleck wish him to make contact.

"Good work, Erik, but I think that's beyond our current brief – so keep the details, but we won't do anything until I've seen Leon."

"As you wish," said Erik, and he departed.

Aleck had a number of other cases and clients to deal with and the day was passing quickly and productively, leaving Aleck feeling confident he'd be able to catch the early train home. A call mid-afternoon from Leon halted his absorption in his work.

"Mondays are not good days for me Aleck, so I apologise for not ringing you earlier. What is the new development you referred to in your message?"

"I'd prefer to discuss that with you in person, Leon. Can you come in tomorrow morning? Anytime, I'll work around you," replied Aleck.

"I'm already on my way now, Aleck. I hope you don't mind and that you can squeeze me in. Your secretary said you might have 'a window', to quote her expression."

Without waiting for Aleck to respond, Leon added, "My driver reckons we're fifteen minutes away. See you very soon."

"Damn the man and his impertinence," Aleck said out loud. In that moment of anger, any lingering doubts about following Bruce Daniels' advice were swept away. Calming himself, he stepped outside to gently chastise the receptionist, telling her to buzz him upon Leon's arrival, but to tell Leon that he would have to wait for another ten minutes before Aleck could see him.

Eventually, Aleck deigned to see Leon. He greeted the older man pleasantly and professionally. After initial formalities and the serving of coffee, the two men got down to the reason for Leon's visit. Aleck gave Leon a copy of the response to the FOI request and waited silently while Leon read its contents.

As he finished reading, Leon looked up, beaming at Aleck.

"Round one to us, Aleck," he said. "Whoever put this together surely did not think this would be the end of the matter. They have admitted the existence and the death of the citizen in their hospital, yet have the gall to think we'd accept that they bear no responsibility."

"I agree that they sound defensive; however, perhaps what they say is exactly what happened," said Aleck in response. Taking a breath, he went on.

"Which brings me to suggest to you, Leon, that our work here is done. Your brief was for us to serve the FOI papers, and it would seem we have carried out your wishes."

Leon eyed Aleck shrewdly for a moment, before saying, "Come now, Aleck, this is just the beginning of the game."

Aleck replied, "If that is the case, then now is the time to be more open with what you are really wanting to achieve."

Speaking quite crisply, Leon responded: "Has someone been warning you against dealing with me, Aleck?"

Aleck admitted that one of the senior partners in the firm had suggested that their task was complete now that the response to the FOI had been issued.

"And what about you, Aleck – do you agree with your senior partner?"

"I think he has a point … and without greater transparency from you, I'm inclined to support his view. For example, Leon, an article about Claus Proger has been published in UndPress this morning. Now I assume you either wrote the article or commissioned it, yet at no time have you mentioned that intention to me. It is also on record that you have anti-government views, so your actions could be interpreted as troublemaking. This firm has its reputation to protect: we are not happy to associate with dissidents."

A slight smile crossed Leon's lips, and he murmured, "Javier has been particularly busy these last couple of days." However, before Aleck could make sense of this, Leon continued.

"Some of what you say is true, Aleck, though I don't resile from my past. Yes, I did write the article for UndPress, and for two reasons: firstly, to see if it brought forward anyone who could add to what little is known about Proger, and secondly, to see if it would provoke any reaction from the Government. On the second point, I see that it has, which strengthens my belief that something abnormal happened to Proger."

"In which case," expostulated Aleck, "why are you not working with law enforcement or even a detective agency if you prefer cloak-and-dagger goings-on? Why come to us, a well-respected, somewhat conservative law firm?"

Walking back from the window to stand by his chair, Leon said, "I can see your dilemma Aleck. Let's change our approach." He smiled, and added, "Thank you for your services, Solicitor Raine. I am grateful to you for your thoroughness and expertise in carrying through my wishes, and I shall settle my account as soon as I leave you."

With that, Leon shook Aleck's hand – but instead of walking to the door to depart, he guided Aleck over to the window, one arm lightly wrapped around Aleck's shoulders. Together they stood momentarily in silence, both seemingly noting the cricket match in action on the nearby oval. Then Leon spoke.

"Now that I'm no longer your client, I'd be pleased if you would join me for lunch the day after tomorrow, Aleck. There is much I'd like to tell you, but on a private basis. Consider it as a meeting with someone who is a family friend."

Aleck hesitated, then responded that while he would be interested to learn more about Leon's relationship with his father, he did not think it wise to continue their association.

"Okay, Aleck, let's make it lunch on Sunday so that it is strictly in your own time. I'll not take no for an answer.

"Oh, just to be clear, I mean lunch with both you and your wife, so a social occasion of sorts and a family one too – after all, I am Aneeka's biological father. For now, good day to you."

Leaving a stunned Aleck to take in what he had just said, Leon waved goodbye and departed.

Who is this man, what is it he's about? Aleck wondered. *Yet another theatrical farewell, with yet another bombshell as he departs. First it was about my father, now it's about my wife. What next?*

Aleck's head was spinning. Aneeka claimed she had no knowledge of her father. Was Leon lying? And if he was, how did he know the manner of Aneeka's conception? If he was telling the truth, should he tell Aneeka? How would she react?

Aleck did not think lunch for the three of them was a good idea at all. He thought it would be best to leave things be. He didn't want to upset Aneeka at this particular time.

These thoughts crowded his brain, giving him a headache and making further work too difficult. He would go home, he decided. Besides, he had intended to leave early and it was already late afternoon. Quickly looking to see which cases he would be dealing with the next day, Aleck packed the relevant papers in his briefcase, planning to look over them that evening. He tidied his desk and rang the receptionist to say he was not feeling well and was going home. As he was leaving, he remembered to ask the receptionist to message Bruce Daniels to confirm that Mr Hartland had settled his account, bringing his relationship with the firm to a close.

By the time Aleck arrived home he was feeling calmer, although his head was still throbbing. He had come to the definite decision not to say anything directly about Leon to Aneeka, for now at least.

Aneeka was thrilled to have Aleck home earlier than usual. She excitedly related to him all that she had been involved with that day. She clearly had been most impressed with Professor Baritz.

"And how was your day, Aleck?"

"Just another day," he replied wearily. "Maybe I'm getting a cold, because I've got a bit of a headache. Do we have any headache tablets?"

Aneeka shook her head, saying she was pretty sure they didn't. But then she added, "I know, why don't we go for a walk together and call in at the pharmacy to get some? The fresh air will do you good, Aleck."

So, together they set off on their walk, Aneeka still bubbly as she chatted about her day, with Aleck half listening and half considering whether to subtly probe Aneeka's memory about any information to do with her biological father.

"You know, Aneeka, I've been thinking that you're right – Cameron would be a good name for Mack."

Aneeka squeezed his hand with pleasure. "I knew you'd make the right decision. I hope Cameron is good at decision-making, just like his dad!"

"I wonder what other traits are developing in Mack's little body? What genes he'll inherit from each of us, and those of our ancestors?" pondered Aleck. "That professor of yours could have lots to tell us."

Aneeka nodded. "You're right, Eva seems really clever to me. Did I mention that she has invited me to visit her at work once Cameron is born? That might give me an opportunity to learn more about genetics from her."

"Wouldn't that be fascinating! You'd like that, Aneeka," said Aleck.

Taking a deep breath, he pushed on. "You know, Mack could inherit some genes from your parents' sperm donor. Do you wish now, for Mack's sake, that you knew him, or knew a little more about him?"

Aneeka frowned. "That thought hasn't ever occurred to me, Aleck. I don't really know what to feel about that. Maybe we should know something about whoever he was, just to be able to rule out anything nasty that might affect Cameron's future health. Although, come to think of it, Eva did say the tests she ran showed that Cameron looked very healthy, so maybe it's not an issue. I'll ask her when I next see her."

"Sounds like Eva is becoming your new best friend, the way you refer to her," chortled Aleck, deciding to drop the subject now that they had reached the pharmacy.

CHAPTER 16

Javier sat opposite Timothy, Gretel's Minister for Roads and Transport, listening to the self-important younger man repeat almost word for word what Gretel had claimed he had said to her. *Well-rehearsed little speech,* thought Javier.

As he had when questioned by Gretel, Timothy had stonewalled about the source of his information. Javier decided to try a different tack and involve Timothy as an equal in trying to solve an apparent mystery.

"In your opinion, who do you think this citizen Claus Proger was?"

Timothy seemed quite pleased to be asked for his opinion, which he willingly shared with Javier.

"I've checked the immigration records, but there's nothing on him. I think he managed to get here from the North and either continued to evade detection, or else the records on him have since been destroyed. Not that I have any proof, mind you, of either possibility, so you understand this is pure speculation on my part," he stressed.

Continuing on, he expanded his theory: "It was probably just sheer chance that he came to the attention of whoever is behind this sad business. That person saw the opportunity to try out something experimental on someone who was known to few others. I don't think for one second that he was meant to die … but, unfortunately, the experiment seems to have gone awry, costing this unlucky sod his life."

Javier looked at Timothy with greater respect. What he postulated was quite probably close to the truth, although Javier knew that the Department of Immigration did indeed hold embargoed records about the citizen.

"Very interesting theory, Timothy, I follow what you're saying," said Javier. "Let's assume for the moment that your thinking is correct.

Is it your own theory or that of whosoever tipped you off in the first place?"

Timothy paused to consider the question before replying. "It's probably a bit of both, to be fair. I've added my own thoughts to the situation. My informant would probably argue that Proger was targeted rather than simply in the wrong place at the wrong time. I should clarify that I'm not claiming there is a policy targeting new migrants, legal or illegal; there are so few nowadays that waiting for one to arrive to experiment on hardly seems plausible."

"Okay, let's return to the identity of your informer. Another theory is that there has been no experimentation at all: that Proger, if indeed he existed, died from natural causes or some explainable illness or, alternatively, may still be alive but for reasons unknown has chosen to disappear. Under any of these hypotheses, your informer could be using you to bring disrepute to the Government. Maybe the informant is a disaffected citizen; maybe at some time that person feels that he, or she, did not get fair treatment by the Department of Health, or some other scenario. Isn't something along those lines possible, Timothy?"

"My source seems credible to me, Javier. I am a minister in the Inner Cabinet, which means at least two things: one, that I am considered intelligent, so it's unlikely I would be easily fooled by a disaffected citizen; and two, that I hold high allegiance to the Government in which I serve, so it is not in my interest to help undermine it."

"You are indeed an intelligent and highly regarded member of the Government, Timothy, there's no question about that. However, we must explore all angles on this matter, so excuse me for having to say this, but there is another hypothesis I must put to you.

"Maybe there is no informant – and whether there is a citizen called Claus Proger or not is irrelevant. Instead, it is you yourself raising these allegations with a view to discredit the Government, positioning yourself to run for its presidency."

Timothy chortled.

"Funny how you and the President both consider I'm after her job. I should feel flattered, I suppose. When the time comes, I hope Gretel will support my candidacy. However, as I've already made clear to her, I've more to learn before I will be presidential material. Further, if I wanted to undermine Gretel, I would be speaking to my colleagues, not to her. I give you my word, Javier – there is an informant, and his allegations have substance."

A silence descended between the two, while Javier thought about his next action. He thanked Timothy for answering his questions and apologised if any had seemed impertinent.

Holding eye contact with Timothy, Javier continued. "I believe you when you say you do have a male informant. Would this informant be Leon Hartland?"

For the briefest of instants, Javier's well-trained eye discerned a momentary reaction from Timothy, but then it was gone. Timothy smoothly replied that he had already made it clear that he would not reveal the name of the informant.

"Do you know, or know of, Leon Hartland?" asked Javier, to which Timothy smiled, replying that the name had a certain familiarity.

"No marks for that question, Javier. As I'm sure you well know, Leon and I have been friends in the past. However, I can assure you that we have not met recently, nor for some time."

"In that case, minister, I have to ask you to hand over your phone so that I can check whether there has been any recent contact between the two of you."

In response to this demand, Timothy said he was not obliged to comply, and that he felt insulted by Javier treating him as if he had done something wrong.

"I have acted in good faith by alerting Gretel to the situation and I have cooperated fully with you throughout our discussions this morning. As a minister, I expect more courteous treatment from you, Javier."

"Minister, you do understand that I can access your phone records. I was being courteous by asking for your phone, to avoid having to request such access," Javier responded quietly.

Timothy maintained his indignant act for some minutes, delivering a lashing of invective at Javier before succumbing to the request. Javier took the phone with him out of the room, returning some minutes later to say all was in order as he gave the device back to Timothy.

"I know you're just doing your job Javier, so no hard feelings," was Timothy's soothing response on the return of his property. "Now, I must do my work too and get to a subcommittee meeting for which I'm already running late. Please keep me in the loop over this matter we've been discussing, Javier." And with that, Timothy departed.

Javier checked the updates on Leon's movements from Clovis and messaged Jacques to ask if there'd been any response to the UndPress article.

'Not so far,' messaged Jacques in reply.

*

Leon was feeling rather disappointed by his visit to see Aleck. He understood that Aleck had been placed under pressure to end their professional interaction, so he was not especially surprised by this. However, Aleck's reluctance to continue a social relationship had hit Leon harder than he would have thought.

He was growing fond of Colin's son. He had not intended to reveal his relationship to Aneeka, and he regretted his rashness, recognising that he had overplayed his hand. He knew his impulsive action would have further disconcerted Aleck, making it more likely that he would decline his offer of lunch on the weekend.

Brightening briefly, he reasoned, *Then again, maybe Aleck will want to know more about someone who could be considered the grandfather of his child-to-be.*

His rising spirits were quickly doused. *Will Aleck tell Aneeka about me? Might she be curious to meet me? Nah, not a chance,* he thought, dismissing each possibility.

He had hovered in the background during Aneeka's early childhood before summarily being told he was not part of the equation and his presence was neither appropriate nor wanted by Ann and her wife. He had never completely complied with their request, however; he'd watched over Aneeka from a discreet distance as she grew from childhood to young adulthood.

Unbeknownst to Aneeka or her parents, he had smoothed over some situations where Aneeka was short on funds after the estrangement, her parents having cut her allowance in the hope of forcing her to return home to them and their control. Aneeka had never seemed to question what she must have assumed was her good luck in finding places to live at rents well below median prices, or of being offered reductions on the costs of some attractive clothing said to be on special for that day only … she remained unaware that her luck was due to Leon financing the price differences rather than the universe smiling on her.

Although he could not say he knew her well, Leon liked what he had observed in Aneeka. He admired that she had stood up to her controlling parents. And, if he were honest with himself, he would truly welcome a relationship with her and her soon-to-be child – his grandchild.

He and Ann had known each other from childhood. As adults, they were aware of an expectation that they should marry each other, as much to protect the fortunes of both families as from a wish for their mutual happiness. It was strange then that both he and Ann had been attracted to same-sex partners, despite their fondness for each other. It made good financial sense that the two families should join together, and there had been a time when they had contemplated marrying for convenience. However, honesty had prevailed, especially when Kay appeared on the scene, and, although disappointed, both families had accepted the situation.

Regrettably, neither Leon's nor Ann's parents were still alive when they planned to have Aneeka. Had they lived to see her, Leon felt sure that Aneeka's younger life would have been enriched through their love and goodness, and that they would have insisted he be allowed a visible part in her childhood.

Leon's reverie was broken by the intercom announcing the arrival of a visitor, a most unexpected one. Pulling himself together, he went to greet his guest.

"Welcome to my humble home, Javier. I take it you are on your own. Please do come in."

"Thank you, Leon – and yes, this is an unofficial visit. I am not accompanied."

After limited niceties and with the offer of coffee declined, Javier and Leon settled into two deep armchairs, facing each other.

"It's been some time since we last met," commented Javier.

"Indeed," acknowledged Leon. "Although you have had your man monitoring my movements these past few days. Why is that, Javier? Is that the way you treat all your old friends before you pay them a visit?"

Ignoring Leon's mockery, Javier opened the discussion. "Our mutual friend, the Minister for Roads and Transport, has made some serious allegations that need to be investigated. I assume you are the source of the message and the minister is simply the messenger. Why not come to me directly, Leon?"

"Protocol, dear boy. Don't you remember that you warned me to stay away from matters pertaining to the Government? I can hardly turn up at your office."

"I have a vivid memory of the directive you were given last time you sought to interfere in government issues, as well as an excellent memory of the clearly explained implications of what would happen should you choose to ignore that directive. Up until recently, you appear to have been abiding by our past agreement. I am very saddened that you have chosen to start playing your undermining games again."

"Naturally, I deny I am playing games with you Javier, and – as our conversation today is off the record – you have no grounds for claiming I am meddling in government business. I'm confident Timothy has acted honourably and not implicated me in whatever allegations he has made," smiled Leon.

"Correct, of course, and as I've already said, this conversation is unofficial. However, whether this becomes more serious depends on you, Leon. What is it that has caused you to put yourself so at risk? Tell me what you know."

"My guess is that having heard Timothy out, you know about as much as I know. There's some unethical experimentation going on within a government department. Timothy doesn't know which one, because I haven't told him, but ..." Leon paused, before leaning towards Javier, his face full of concern.

"It's obvious which department, Javier. She's doing bad things again, only this time they are very bad things. How many more citizens like Claus Proger are going to lose their lives to Eva's madness? The Government cannot keep covering up for her."

"Well, here's the thing Leon, and I'm being straight with you. I don't accept that Eva is involved in something bad. You know we keep her under surveillance, and there's been no recent cause for alarm or concern. In fact, Gretel and I had dinner with her recently, and we were so pleased to see her well and acting like her old self. That brain of hers is still firing. She was easily brighter than the three of us put together – and still is, I would suggest."

Leon made no response, so Javier continued, but not before making it very clear to Leon that he would completely deny what he was saying if he was to act dishonourably and repeat any part of their conversation.

"I can tell you in confidence that the space program that we all once worked on has actually made very good progress under Eva's directive. In fact, something big may soon be announced. Eva is working in space aeronautics, she's working with artificial intelligence, and so she cannot possibly be experimenting on citizens in her spare time just to amuse herself, especially without anyone noticing. In short, if indeed something has happened to this citizen over whom you're so concerned, it's impossible to see how it could be linked to Eva."

Javier was an accomplished liar, able to blend a mix of truths and untruths, noted Leon. His character assessment was swiftly interrupted by a question from Javier.

"By the way, how do you know of this Claus Proger?"

Leon repeated the summary of the circumstances he had previously described to Aleck – those that had led to his awareness of the citizen's disappearance.

"I assume you know the rest of the story, Javier. You know that I asked a solicitor to act on my behalf to lodge an FOI application. The fact that this caused ripples at the Department of Health made it likely that something was being covered up. By means I won't reveal, I obtained a copy of Proger's papers from the Department of Immigration, just days before they were embargoed. By the way, if you don't mind me saying, there was some sloppy work in both departments that you should attend to, Javier. Then again, perhaps you've already done so now that you've been on my trail, but I digress.

"I assume my good friend Rueben checked in with Jacques or another contact in the Security Agency, as he's always been prone to doing, so you know about the article in UndPress. I've had no response as yet, have you?" Leon asked, one eyebrow raised quizzically.

Javier smiled briefly but made no comment, other than to ask Leon to continue.

"The report of Proger's interview with the Department of Immigration was more than interesting to read. Newly arrived, no known relatives, shy and retiring person and so on. Newly arrived? Certainly less than accurate, eh, Javier? He was an illegal, wasn't he? Newly detected more like."

Javier declined to comment.

Looking up at Javier, Leon questioned him as to when the last time was that he had heard such a description as that recorded in Proger's papers. Javier merely shrugged his shoulders.

"Let me prod your memory, Javier. Several years ago, a newly arrived young woman appeared, who was also described as shy and retiring, with no known contacts and no relatives other than the five-month-old infant child who accompanied her. Shall we remind ourselves how that ended? Ah, yes; the infant disappeared, snatched from her pram. Snatched from her pram by Eva. Do you remember that?"

Javier looked irritated. "Of course I remember, but Eva did not harm that child – as you well know, Leon. We were able to rescue the baby and return her to her mother. Eva was in a fragile state and was looking for someone to love, someone to replace the baby she lost. Do you want to talk about that, Leon?" snapped Javier.

"I don't need you or anyone else to remind me of the harm I've caused Eva. I have accused myself every day of my life since the accident," he said quietly, pausing momentarily before continuing.

"My point is that Eva knew how to find the 'little people', the people that very few would know and whose disappearances would go unremarked. Just like the time, about five years ago, when another citizen died, this one a newly released prisoner whose family had turned their backs on him. The prisoner found it very difficult to reassimilate so he duly reoffended, this time seriously, and found himself with years of incarceration stretching before him. A sad case, and a poor advertisement for the Department of Social Affairs, as I said publicly at the time.

"I still claim that Eva had a part in his death, although I know he was drug-riddled and goodness knows what else when she took him on. He died days after she experimented on him in some way, and it's no use denying it Javier. We argued this one over and over at the time, and you effectively banned me from making further speculation that, in your words, 'was attempting to undermine government processes'. This is where we started today's discussion, for goodness' sake."

"Let's not rake all that up again, Leon. Eva has been monitored ever since then, as I promised you at the time. And I'll remind you again that it was not an admission on our part that you were correct; it was simply the agreement we brokered so you would stay out of any further meddling in government issues.

"I cannot see how she could have taken on this latest citizen without someone immediately reporting it to me," argued Javier.

"Surely you can see the thread linking all three cases, Javier? That's why, in my opinion, Eva is indeed involved in the case of citizen Proger," maintained Leon.

Javier ignored Leon's comment. "I understand that the FOI application has been processed Leon, and the response has been conveyed to your solicitor. I've seen the document and, sure, maybe there was a stuff-up by some medic or other, but the statement puts an end to your wish to read more into Proger's unfortunate death than is rational."

Leon's silence led Javier to add an observation he found curious.

"While we're being open with each other, I'd be interested to know what influenced you to engage a top law firm like Oostends to handle your case. I know the firm has become uncomfortable dealing with you."

"It was not the law firm Oostends that I was attracted to, but rather one of its solicitors, Aleck Raine – an up-and-coming young man with great potential."

"One from your coterie of young men, Leon?" queried Javier sardonically.

"Certainly not, Javier. Aleck is a happily married man whose wife is expecting their first child any day now," he replied sternly.

"I apologise. Cannot say I have heard of Solicitor Raine, although the name sounds somewhat familiar," commented Javier.

"It ought to sound familiar to you, Javier. Aleck is the son of my university friend Colin Raine. You remember Colin, don't you? He had his application for a postgraduate scholarship turned down despite his outstanding academic record, and someone – perhaps it was you – recommended that he pursue a career in teaching rather than pursuing mathematical research."

Javier paused briefly before responding. "I can't imagine I had much clout in decision-making in those days Leon, so you can't hang that one on me. How did his career work out?"

"Perhaps you should have been a career counsellor, Javier, because after he recovered from the initial shock of rejection, Colin never stopped being grateful for the advice and the direction his life took. He loved being a mathematics teacher."

"So, no hard feelings over that at least, Leon," replied Javier, seeming to shrug aside Leon's sarcasm. "But, getting back to the purpose of my unofficial visit to you today, I strongly suggest you accept the FOI information at face value. I, in return, promise to recheck

Eva's movements, despite not believing that she has had a relapse as you claim. Why don't you pay her a visit to assess her mental state for yourself? She might be pleased to see you, and I would be pleased to hear your assessment."

The visit reached its end. As he was being ushered to the door, Javier asked Leon, quizzically, "How serious are you in supporting Timothy's candidacy for the role of president, should Gretel retire?"

"Possibly no longer as serious as I once was – ambivalent, at best – but Timothy doesn't suspect this," offered Leon, candidly.

CHAPTER 17

Eva was feeling both elated and relieved. The tests she had trialled on the pregnant woman had validated her gene editing program. She could move on to her real purpose, launching a discovery mission to their sister planet, Earth. "Finally!" she sighed, a sense of release and excitement fusing through her.

The test case woman – Aneeka, that was her name – she had seemed nice, thought Eva. She had been quite genuine when she'd invited Aneeka to visit her research department. *What surprise and pride this Aneeka will feel when she learns she has been instrumental in allowing the space program to continue!*

The success of the testing meant that Eva did not feel the need to castigate herself for choosing not to apply the tests to Aneeka's foetus; she remained content that she had not.

However, the thought of the baby did provoke that little voice in her head – the one that would ask from time to time whether her own baby might have been saved had the technology existed all those years ago. *But it didn't,* she told herself firmly. *Nothing can bring her back; accept that and move on.*

She did, however, allow herself to briefly indulge in thinking about how proud her father would have been to see his little Eva enable the first meaningful contact with Earth. He had whetted her interest in the theories of the day: the big bang and the multiplicity of universes. Why, even as an early adult, the newly graduated Eva had still believed that there were multiple versions of herself, each also newly graduated, just as her father had taught her. Later, however, her own work led to some adjustments to such theories.

Eva was aware there were those who persisted in believing in the existence of their doppelgangers. *Is it comforting to do so?* she wondered, remembering that terrible time in her own life when, having lost her adored Nolé and her unborn baby, she had found some comfort in that theory. Somewhere, in another universe, another Eva had made a different choice – the 'sliding door' option, whereby Nolé and she would not get into that car and therefore there would be no accident. *Logic can be overridden in times of extreme distress,* she thought sadly.

As a scientist, she supported theories relating to the creation of the universes and the beginning of time as a dimension, in keeping with prior theories. Her own findings were consistent with the theory that life evolved from the same starting blocks, and that human form could only be sustained on one planet in each universe – as in the Goldilocks principle, first described to her by her father. However, as life forms developed, choices became possible, allowing game theory to be applied. Because of this, different rates of development in different universes would occur and, as increasingly intelligent forms of life evolved, the playing of the game of life would begin to differ substantially.

The multiplicity of universes did not mean an infinity of exact Eva replicas after all, she had concluded. There could be an infinite number of differing Evas, so different as to not be recognisable as bearing any relationship to each other, their only point in common being that they had evolved from the same few initial cells.

Her theory was partly borne out by the limited information that had been collected about planet Earth when the first robotic missions took place. Geographically, the planet was considered to be quite like their own (or what their own had been before The Disaster). Physically, the people were larger but with a similar physiology, though mentally they appeared to be less advanced. These type 1 humans didn't seem to be aware of the hexagonal nested packing of universes; they didn't seem to understand the role of the fourth dimension either, let alone envisage higher dimensions. To be fair, however, she acknowledged that Earth may have evolved much further since those first missions. Still, it surprised her that the type 1 humans did not appear to have attempted to visit the type 2 humans on Eva's planet.

The existence of an omnipresent destiny-controlling god of some sort played no role in Eva's scientific analysis, nor for that matter any role in the conduct of affairs in the Country. She understood that on Earth this was not the case and saw this as another sign of the earthlings' primitiveness – when something could not be explained rationally, a god had been introduced to fill the void.

Perhaps by now the peoples of planet Earth had come to realise that mathematics was the only 'god'; all could be, or would be, explainable through mathematical analysis.

Eva was excited about finding out more about Earth with the prospect of the upcoming space launch. She knew how important the project was to Gretel, and she believed in what Gretel said about their responsibility to warn the rulers of Earth to make different decisions from those their own leaders had taken (or failed to take). And perhaps there would be things they could learn from planet Earth in turn, who knew – it was quite exhilarating to imagine a new world opening up, to no longer be just one small country all alone on their damaged planet.

Other universes also intrigued Eva. Her planet was more advanced than Earth, but were there more advanced beings on the Goldilocks planets in other universes? She assumed so, but the fact that she could only hypothesise was only a minor frustration to her. She was realistic enough to accept that addressing this would be the work of those who came after her: she would have to be content with paving their way.

Throwing off her musings, Eva returned to her work. She finished preparing her document and forwarded it to Cabut for action. In it she had listed the scientists she particularly wanted to be involved in the end stages of the space program. She was also requesting additional government funding for the final training of the human astronauts and seeking a minister to be assigned to the project – one with vision, a scientific background, clout and influence.

This latest version of the space program had been a work in progress for nigh on eleven years: two spacecrafts had been built in readiness, several astronauts had completed the initial training, and the additional training phase required for the two astronauts selected for the mission would not take a great deal of extra time. Had Eva been quicker to solve the puzzle of how to enable human astronauts to survive transportation through black hole tunnels, the mission might have been accomplished some five years ago, as originally intended.

The optimal conditions for the spacecraft to escape the pull of their own solar system only occurred every few years. As they were shortly heading towards that position, Eva had warned that for the mission to proceed that year, they would need to work to a very tight timeline. In her document she had stressed that the Government's support and cooperation was critical. She assumed that no-one would want to see a further delay.

*

The personal assistant to President Gretel Nuewen tapped lightly on the open door to her office at Government House. "Cabut suggests you should see this," he said, handing over Eva's document before withdrawing from the room as quietly as he had entered.

Gretel was mightily relieved to read that Eva's research into her 'problem' had come to an end and that Eva was now satisfied all was in order to proceed with the space launch.

She noted the list of names Eva had provided, and she circled those new to the team as they needed to be security checked.

On the matter of the choice of the special minister with responsibility for the space program, she procrastinated. Should it be the former Minister for Science (currently the Minister for Education), a conscientious person of good repute who would benefit from the accolades of a successful launch? Or, should the launch not be successful, would it be better to give it to someone like Timothy, whose reputation would be trashed as a consequence? Recognising her decision lay with her degree of confidence in the success of Eva's mission, she resolved not to make a hasty appointment. She wrote in the margin 'to be determined' and then forwarded the document to Finance and Treasury for advice on funding.

Gretel also sent a confidential memo to Cabut seeking his assessment of the likelihood of the space mission's success. She needed to gauge whether the project could really be ready to activate in the short timeframe Eva was proposing. It could be delayed if needs be, however unwelcome such a decision might be for her personally.

On assuming the presidency of the Country, the only surviving land mass able to allow human habitation, the idea of warning others had begun to strengthen in Gretel's mind. As Eva's research moved closer towards inventing a procedure that could allow a human to return home safely from a mission to Earth, Gretel dared to hope that such an achievement would be possible during her presidency.

But Gretel was realistic and familiar with Eva's chequered history, as well as unavoidably entangled in its later chapters (though not part of its beginning, her knowledge gained firsthand or by report).

After the accident all those years ago, before Gretel knew her, Eva had undergone therapy; she had been damaged in her soul, unable to bear further children, lost without her Nolé and subject to aberrant behaviour. She recovered physically, however, and her academic and intellectual powers were still acute. The doctors had decided to keep her working and researching, which Gretel believed had proven to be a good decision, despite the subsequent failure of the first space mission. After Gretel entered political life, there had been a brief reversal when Eva had kidnapped that baby, but, with luck more than anything else, the baby had been returned to her mother unharmed and the matter hushed up. Eva had become re-absorbed in her theories, but a further unfortunate incident caused some to believe that she should be classified as criminally insane.

She had been moved to a secure apartment, where she was microchipped and her movements were monitored – a form of institutionalism, but one that allowed Eva to believe she still functioned normally. It was the best Gretel could do for her. Cabut, donated by the Security Agency, was assigned to watch over her, and this Gretel largely believed to have been successful, although she herself still harboured some anxiety, unrelated to Eva, about the use of Cabut.

And now there'd been another incident.

Maybe it was wrong of me to ignore the loss of that unfortunate citizen, Gretel thought. But, in her defence, she argued that Cabut had not sounded any alarm over what was going on. So she decided, as did Javier, that the citizen's death had simply been an unfortunate accident, not a result of Eva's 'procedure'. Gretel recalled Eva's remorse, not for the citizen himself, but for an outcome that was both unexpected and a setback, one meaning another test case needed to be found before the space mission could become a reality.

How Leon had come to hear of the failed test case was not clear, but his intention to stir up trouble was most unwelcome. Yet, oddly, Javier had been quite calm about Leon since he had spoken at length to him the day before. Gretel did not know, nor want to know, the details of their conversation, but she had been reassured by Javier's equanimity. She was thrilled to read Eva's assertion that the second test case had been successful. It was hard to contain her excitement now that the mission looked to be viable.

Gretel knew she was coming to the end of her presidency, not because of the likes of Timothy, but because she was exhausted. She promised herself she'd resign sooner rather than later. If Eva's mission turned out to be a success, that would be the time to go – to leave on a high, having accomplished one of her most cherished and altruistic aims. She would go down in history and long be remembered for the success of the space mission – it would be her legacy.

That decided her. She would choose Bethany, the Minister for Education, to be the special minister responsible for the mission.

Feeling a spring in her step, Gretel popped out to her assistant, asking him to make an appointment for Bethany to see her later that afternoon. "And get on Finance and Treasury's back to hurry up, please, I want the financial estimates before I meet with Bethany. Thanks a lot."

She returned to her office before another thought came to her mind. She asked her assistant to free up a couple of hours in her diary the next day and to ensure that she would be undisturbed during that time. She wanted to get started on writing the most important speech she would ever give – the one that would be delivered to the leaders of planet Earth warning them of their peril and offering her hindsight advice on how to avoid it becoming

CHAPTER 18

The phone pinged. Leon answered. "Hello Aleck, nice of you to call."

"Hello Leon, I'm ringing you about two things. First, we, that is Aneeka and I, will not be joining you for lunch this Sunday. Second, I will, however, accept your original invitation to join you for lunch either tomorrow or the next day, whichever suits you, if you are still agreeable."

"Excellent, Aleck, although I'm most disappointed not to be meeting with Aneeka. Any reason why not, that you're willing to share?"

There was a brief pause before Aleck replied. "I don't know how to explain to Aneeka your connection with her or whether I should keep that information to myself; I don't know whether to argue our son's right to know his gene pool; plus, I'm not even clear what exactly your connection with my father was. In short, Leon, I am feeling strangely confused, and I want to discuss this with you, man to man, and hopefully sort out a few things first."

"That's a good start Aleck, I appreciate your honesty. Let's meet at midday-ish tomorrow at the Ensemble Café near your office. Do you know where that is?"

"Yes, yes, I know it well. Till tomorrow then." Aleck ended the call.

Leon pondered how strange the last couple of days had been. First, he had been surprised by the relatively cordial meeting he had had with Javier and astonished by Javier's suggestion that he should visit Eva. And now, Aleck was not only prepared to lunch with him but he seemed genuinely anxious to do so. "Gosh, next thing you know, Gretel will be inviting me to dine at Government House," he chuckled to himself.

Leon reasoned it was time to lay more of his cards on the table for Aleck. He was quite genuine in his wish to get to know Aneeka; Ann and Kay had been cruel and wrong to lock him out of her life.

*

Aleck had mentally wrestled with what best to do about Leon and Aneeka. He felt both Aneeka and Mack had either an obligation or a right to know more about their genetic inheritance. But how to broach the subject with Aneeka had eluded him.

He was feeling a little relieved that he had instigated some action following Leon's casual acknowledgement of his relationship to Aneeka, and his head hadn't stopped aching despite the tablets he'd continued to take. Aneeka was convinced he had picked up some sort of virus and was coming down with an illness; she was keeping her distance from him in order to lessen the risk of becoming infected herself.

To appease Aneeka, Aleck had visited his local doctor that morning, something he rarely did. The doctor had said there did not appear to be anything physically wrong with him and had counselled that anxiety was not uncommon for those facing parenthood. He was advised to keep up the tablets and to return should the headaches continue. Tomorrow, he promised himself, he would resume his early morning exercise routine, sort out Leon's connections with both sides of his immediate family, and move on with his life.

He rose from his chair to usher in his next client. "Good afternoon, Mrs Smythe. You're looking well. Please come in." As he took her arm and guided her towards the desk, he added, "I have the latest version of your will ready for you to sign. Now, can I get you a tea or coffee before we go through the document?"

*

Timothy was feeling out of sorts as he returned from the Cabinet meeting to his relatively small office that looked out over the car park. He didn't begrudge his colleague, the Minister for Family and Community Services, the success with which that minister's proposals had been greeted by most of the Cabinet members. Evan had worked on those plans for some time, and they were generous and effective proposals. The Treasurer had been the least enthusiastic of those present, but then she often was when it came to allocating funding: Timothy always got the impression that she seemed to view it as a payment from her own personal account.

It wasn't Evan who had affected his mood, it was Gretel. She had barely acknowledged his presence and had cut short his speech, despite it being largely supportive of Evan's proposals. Admittedly, she had seemed distracted and he thought she'd been trying to rush through the meeting.

Neither Gretel nor Javier had made any further contact with him following his revelations, a standoff that both disappointed and puzzled him. Now he'd heard that Bethany had been summoned to Gretel's office. Something was up, he could smell it, and he was not part of whatever that something was. Poor return for his loyalty in alerting Gretel of his information; poor judgement cast by Leon, who had overruled him and insisted he not leak the information to other ministers. And why had he not heard from Leon since reporting back to him about his meetings with the President and her Principal Advisor?

Perhaps it was time for him to take matters into his own hands.

Picking up his jacket, Timothy left his office to re-join his colleagues, who were having a drink with Evan to congratulate him on his worthy proposals.

"Any idea why Bethany's before the boss?" he lightly enquired of the Minister for Fisheries. When he received the reply that the minister was unaware that Bethany was meeting with Gretel, Timothy mused, as if to himself, "I wonder if it's connected to that matter Gretel is trying to keep hushed up?" Before the minister could respond, Timothy moved on to join another group and repeat his performance.

*

Bethany was thrilled with Gretel's offer of involvement in the space mission. She would continue in her education portfolio, but she would step back to allow her assistant minister to take over many of her duties and assume greater responsibility for the next few weeks or so. Bethany was very happy to endorse her junior colleague and welcomed the experience it would give him.

Until the plans for the launch were released to the Cabinet, Bethany was sworn to secrecy, an undertaking she gave without any hesitation. Thanks to her time as Minister for Science, Bethany had a good understanding of the magnitude of what the mission might achieve. She could also recall the pain and disappointment of failure, which had beset so many of their scientific plans. She listened attentively and admiringly as Gretel gave a little lecture to explain the challenges and what, for her, would be the major purpose of the program. Gretel was prone to little lectures; some ministers ridiculed her for this behind her back, but not Bethany.

"I know that as scientists we feel a sense of great achievement in being in a position to undertake such a launch. This would not be possible without the detailed knowledge we now possess about harnessing gravity waves and the necessary conditions that must exist for a rocket to escape not only the attraction forces of our own planet, but those of the other planets in our galaxy. Then there are the conditions likely to be faced by those on board the spacecraft, which we now know so much more about. Recent research has given us further knowledge about how to adapt to these conditions, which is so essential for the safe return of our brave explorers."

Bethany nodded in agreement and knew she would have to study hard to learn of the new discoveries made since her time as science minister.

"No matter how exciting this all is, for me the major purpose is to make meaningful contact with our human cousins who live on the planet Earth, which is in the Milky Way galaxy in a universe parallel to ours." Gretel went on to elaborate on the warning she would give those cousins.

Bethany heard her out before hesitantly speaking. "Don't the things that happen in our world either repeat themselves in other worlds, or might they already have happened in other worlds? Wasn't that part of the parallel universes theory?"

"Ah, Bethany, you have a lot of homework to do. You need to read and absorb Professor Baritz's more recent work, preferably before your first space program meeting, so that you are up to date with current thinking."

Bethany was greatly surprised to hear Professor Baritz's name mentioned, and she couldn't stop herself from commenting. "I didn't realise Professor Baritz would still be involved. Wasn't she ill? I thought someone else would be leading the program by now ..." Her voice trailed off as she stopped herself from alluding to Eva's age, realising Gretel was probably much the same age.

"Professor Baritz is central to the success of this program. Her work is outstanding and her health good, to my knowledge," retorted Gretel, rather acerbically. Bethany got the message and refrained from further comment. Their meeting ended on a better note shortly afterwards, with a shared sense of excitement about what was soon to take place.

*

Timothy arranged to 'just happen to be' in a corridor not far from the Minister for Education's office when Bethany returned. He greeted her conversationally by observing that the proposals Evan had presented for the aged care of the Owlds seemed very well-prepared and asking if she agreed with that view. Bethany replied, not rudely but nevertheless dismissively, that she agreed with him but could not stop to chat. Timothy could see, however, that she was very chuffed about whatever had taken place during her meeting with Gretel.

Bethany is definitely not in charge of a department that has carried out nefarious experimentation, he thought. *Although, isn't experimentation what educationists do ... they keep wanting change, being prepared to discard older but often well-tried approaches in favour of experimenting with new and yet-to-be-tested theories?* He returned to his office with as many questions as answers.

CHAPTER 19

Returning home from work, Aleck felt that some weight had been lifted from his shoulders. He was getting back in charge of his emotions. Why, even his headache of the past few days was subdued, something for which he was grateful.

Aneeka seemed pleased to see that he had recovered his energy. "I'm so glad to have my darling Aleck back in the house; that grumpy, tired and ill-looking version was a bit of a pain," she said.

Together they prepared a light meal of green salad with tomatoes and herbs freshly picked from their own small garden. They ate the salad with spinach rolls left over from the day before. Aleck had a small whisky with water, Aneeka restricting herself to just the water. They chattered about this and that and nothing in particular, content to just enjoy being together as they ate. Eventually, they cleared the table and cleaned the few dishes themselves, Aleck rinsing and Aneeka drying.

"Isn't tomorrow your Service day?" asked Aneeka, as she came to the last item. "How about we have lunch together?"

"Oh, sorry darling, you're right, it is my Service day but I've arranged to have lunch with a former client," he replied. "It's the only time I can fit him in, and it will have to be a short lunch so I can get to the school for my afternoon session."

Taking a breath, he added: "It's that Leon Hartland fellow I told you about, the one who knew my father. Did you ever know him at all?"

Aneeka gave him an odd look. "Why in heaven's name would I know him? What a strange question, Aleck."

Aneeka cheerfully continued chatting, observing that Service days were such an important privilege for the employed as well as for the people they helped.

It was part of the Right to Work legislation that every fully employed person was required to spend at least half a day, usually a whole day, in the service of a charity, institution, youth detention centre or similar, roughly once a month. Aleck knew that Aneeka had found her service work in aged care to be something she valued, and she was looking forward to returning to the home to introduce Cameron to the residents during her maternity leave.

Aleck agreed with Aneeka's sentiments, saying that it was one of the Government's better decisions. He was currently working with a couple of young teenagers, helping them with their studies and hoping that through his encouragement and advice, they might develop greater confidence and self-esteem. The Country didn't have a huge problem, but unemployment, lack of skills, apathy and low self-esteem still caused some young folk to lose their way.

They continued talking as they moved into their sitting area. Aneeka stretched out on the sofa, her head resting in Aleck's lap, Aleck's hand resting on her taut stomach.

"Let's go visit Charles this coming weekend, Aleck," Aneeka suggested. "It might be the last chance we get before Cameron is born."

"Good idea, darling," agreed Aleck.

The evening slipped by quickly. Aleck was moved to observe how strange time could be. He described to Aneeka how, for him, that morning had gone slowly, yet one of his clients, an Owld, had said to him that for her a week went by just like a day used to. There was a perspective view to time; time never felt the same to each person.

"We've been waiting to welcome our little Cameron for nearly nine months, but looking back from today's perspective, it has taken so little time for him to grow. How quickly will our time with him flash by, I wonder?"

"Let's just learn to live in the moment, Aleck, and give thanks for every precious one of them," counselled Aneeka. "It's been such a lovely and peaceful evening, thank you my darling. Now, given you intend to resume jogging tomorrow morning, I suggest we have an early night. I'm feeling a bit tired in any case, although I've still enough energy for a little gentle exercise before we go to sleep, if you're up to it," she grinned invitingly.

Aleck was brushing his teeth when he heard the ringtone of the phone he'd left in the sitting room. Aneeka called out that she'd answer it and by the time she returned, Aleck was sat on the edge of the bed ready to climb in. He smiled as she came through the door, but he saw immediately that something was wrong.

Her eyes were welling with tears. "That was Matilda, Aleck. She's still on the line waiting to speak to you. It's about Charles. I'm so sorry, but he's gone."

She gave him a hug as she passed the phone over to him and waited quietly, sat beside him, as he and Matilda spoke. Once the conversation came to an end, the two of them stayed seated on the edge of the bed, surprised and full of sadness at the news that Charles had died. Aleck relayed the news that Charles had had a severe stroke and he had not responded to the efforts made by paramedics, who arrived shortly after they were called. Charles was pronounced dead on arrival at the hospital. Matilda had been told that he would not have suffered.

Holding each other close, stroking each other's arms and back, they attempted to console each other. Eventually, they climbed into bed proper and fell into an exhausted but troubled sleep, waking early the next morning with neither feeling rested. Aleck postponed his morning run but decided he would proceed with the rest of the day as planned. Matilda would send a message during the day about funeral arrangements.

They had a light breakfast, sitting close together at the kitchen table, then Aleck showered and dressed. Aneeka remained in her nightwear, having agreed with Aleck that she would go back to bed and rest once he left for work. Both of them were feeling light-headed due to sorrow and lack of sleep. Aleck slipped the remainder of the headache tablets into his bag, leaving a couple behind at Aneeka's request in case she might feel the need for them.

*

Aneeka had not known Charles well, nor for long, but she had liked him very much and was filled with remorse that they had not visited him again before he died. The issue of living with regrets after it was too late for them to be rectified had troubled her as deeply as the shock of losing Charles. Both thoughts had swirled round and round in her head for much of the night.

Aleck was gathering his things, getting ready to leave for work. Looking up at him, her kind, considerate and now saddened husband, Aneeka cautiously and slowly said, "Aleck, I don't want to find myself in the situation one day where I am filled with regret over decisions I've made that are too late to overturn. Give me a little time but, after Charles's funeral, I would like to talk more seriously with you about Cameron's lineage and his right to know any of his grandparents still living."

Aleck went to her and, clasping her shoulders, he sobbed into the nape of her neck. "You are the most wonderful person I have ever known," he said between sobs. "Thank you."

Wiping his eyes, he kissed her, took her hand and led her back to bed. "Let's get you tucked in again so you can sleep." He drew the curtains in the bedroom, plumped up the pillows and ensured Aneeka had the doona covering her. Kissing her again, he whispered: "Goodbye my darling, sleep well. I'll see you this evening," and then he left the room, closing the door softly behind him.

*

The weather was looking promising. Strange how some families were in mourning while others would be happy, praising the beauty of the coming day. *I guess you can do both,* thought Aleck.

The station was quite crowded. Aleck and his fellow passengers awaited the approach of the train. Everything would appear as normal to a detached spectator, yet how many of the lives of his fellow travellers were anything but normal this day, he wondered. At some stage, death would visit them all. And one day, death would inevitably select Aleck for a personal visit.

He shrugged off his morose thoughts. He certainly expected, or hoped, to live longer than his parents had. Feeling he was about to start grieving anew for his parents as well as Charles, Aleck took control of his emotions by taking out a work document and studying it.

He arrived at work in a brighter frame of mind. He chose not to mention Charles's death to his colleagues; he would do so when he knew which day he would be taking off for the funeral. He spent the morning on case work and preparing related documents, and he posted a message to say he would be out of the office for the rest of the day as it was his Service day. Aleck felt no need to mention he would be having lunch with a former client, especially as that client was Leon Hartland.

CHAPTER 20

Arriving in good time at the Ensemble Café, Aleck was, as always, welcomed by Felix. "Is your lovely wife joining you today?" he enquired.

"Not today, unfortunately," replied Aleck. "Today I'm meeting with a Mr Hartland, who may have reserved a table?"

"Ah, excellent, you are a friend of Leon's. Please come this way," and Felix led Aleck to a table towards the back of the café, where it was less crowded.

After asking how Aneeka was, Felix enquired if Aleck would care for a drink while he waited for Leon to arrive. Aleck said he could do with a long black, so Felix left him to carry out his request.

It was Ivana who brought him the coffee, and she wanted to know how Aneeka's pregnancy was progressing – was she well, how big was she, did she find it difficult to sleep, were her ankles swelling, and so on – causing Aleck to laugh and assure her that Aneeka was in excellent condition. The baby was due in just over a week, and everything was coming along very satisfactorily. He listened attentively as Ivana described her own pregnancy, even though he had heard the stories before.

Ivana was in full flow when she was interrupted by the arrival of Leon, escorted by Felix. Aleck was intrigued to notice that Ivana greeted Leon as an old friend, each exchanging kisses on both sides of the other's cheeks. She was only torn away by Felix pointing out that there were other customers waiting for service.

Aleck stood to shake hands with Leon. Once they were both seated, they shared some good-natured laughs at Felix and Ivana's expense, until Leon suggested they order and then they could talk more seriously. After perusing the menu, Aleck was ready to order but when Felix returned, Leon asked Felix to surprise them by bringing whatever he recommended from the day's menu. Felix smiled and headed to the kitchen.

"Is that okay with you, Aleck?" Aleck felt quite happy with the arrangement; after all, he was the guest and Leon was paying. Leon smiled. "Now for wine; any requests, Aleck? We should probably see what Felix rustles up for us before we choose."

Aleck still felt below par and had taken another headache tablet prior to leaving the office, so he replied that he had a slight headache and would prefer water, though he stressed that shouldn't stop Leon from ordering something stronger.

Leon looked keenly at Aleck for a moment and asked if he was prone to tension headaches. "You seemed rather tense the last time I saw you," Leon observed. Aleck decided to explain that he'd had little sleep.

"Did you know my father's cousin Charles?" he asked.

Leon said he thought they may have met way back when he was still a student. Aleck explained that Charles had died the previous day and that neither he nor Aneeka had slept particularly well, having just received the news. Leon offered his condolences and said he was grateful that Aleck had kept their luncheon appointment, but he would have understood if he'd cancelled.

The mood was lightened by Felix bringing each of them a baked rainbow trout garnished with almonds and served with green salad and potato frites. Without asking, he had also brought them both a glass of white wine.

"Thank you, Felix, this looks delicious. However, I hadn't yet chosen any wine," grumbled Leon.

"This is the wine you should drink with this fish," insisted Felix. "And Leon, you well know that your doctor has told you that one glass is sufficient," he scolded with a smile. Felix brought them some extra water before he walked away.

Aleck was most amused. Grinning at Leon, he said, "I think my headache is going away."

As they started to eat, it was Aleck who broached the purpose for their meeting. "I'd first like to learn more about your relationship with my father, and what it was that caused you to say he hadn't let you down."

Leon nodded, and he began to relate the history he shared with Colin, Aleck's father. He explained that they were friendly rivals as mathematics students, each vying to surpass the other.

"Today I would concede that Colin had the edge on me, but I knew how to sell myself better than he did," acknowledged Leon.

"For me, but not your father, politics was also an interest. Colin was quite conservative in some ways and liberal in others. He had a strong sense of justice and believed in the protection of individual freedoms, but he wasn't politically active at all, whereas I was fascinated by the 'politics of politics', the great game of life, and I started to become a minor activist. Unfortunately for your father, on the one and only time that I recall him joining me at an off-campus protest march, he was photographed and called before the faculty's Dean for a sharp dressing down."

For a few minutes nothing more was said as the two men tucked into their trout. Then Aleck asked whether that incident was the reason his father's scholarship application had been turned down.

"Not entirely. The far more serious black mark was his refusal to denounce me – that's what lost him the scholarship," replied Leon.

Aleck took a small sip of his wine and waited for Leon to continue. Leon seemed in no hurry, but after drinking half a glass of the Chablis he eventually spoke once again.

"After the Homer Government claimed its RevDem proposals had been sanctioned, I became convinced the vote had been rigged. Long story, but I tried to publish an article purporting to prove this. Colin refused to get involved, but he did urge me not to use my own name on the article."

Leon paused to extract a stray fish bone stuck between his teeth, before elaborating.

"The sods who interviewed him for the scholarship were more interested in talking about my so-called subversive article than Colin's qualifications for a scholarship. He was given a copy of my paper and questioned at length over its authorship. It was put to him that he and I had collaborated on the article."

By now, Aleck had finished his meal. He waited with veiled impatience for Leon to do the same. Finally, Leon pushed his plate away and, wiping his lips with his serviette, he completed his story.

"Now Aleck, I'd taken your father's advice and not used my name. The paper claimed it was jointly written by 'Harold Lanten' and 'Elon Carini', but I'd been too smart by far, too full of conceit at my own supposed cleverness in choosing those names. Can you see why?"

"Neither name means anything to me," Aleck shrugged. "Are they mathematicians, perhaps?"

Leon chortled. "Sorry Aleck, you're not quite as quick on the uptake as your father; hint, they're anagrams."

Aleck pondered this, and eventually noted that while Elon was an anagram of Leon, Carini was certainly not a rearrangement of Hartland.

"I can see we'll be here all day at this rate," said Leon, not unkindly. "Look at Harold Lanten. That's an anagram of Leon Hartland. Your dad would have seen that straight away."

Aleck was beginning to feel he was back at school being chastised over his inability to see the meaning in a poem the class was studying, but he made no comment. Leon expounded further.

"In reading the article, Colin would have also recognised that my proof was an extension of the work of a respected mathematician, Professor Nolé Thraldan. We were both quite taken by him, even though his work was not in Colin's field. Very sadly, the professor died in an accident some years later."

Felix arrived to clear their plates and to ask what they wanted to drink with the cheese platter he was about to bring them. Opting for a long black and a macchiato, they both complimented Felix, telling him the trout had been perfect. When the cheese arrived, Leon picked up where he'd left off.

"Now, where was I? About to put forward what I think happened in the interview. I imagine your father said to the authorities that they had no grounds for accusing either of us of writing the paper, pointing out that the article could just as conceivably be the joint work of a Professor Thraldan and a Dr Leonardo Arinci. My guess is he pointed out that Harold Lanten was also an anagram of Nolé Thraldan, and Carini rearranges to Arinci – and, as you yourself observed, Aleck, Leon is an anagram of Elon. He may have added that Dr Leonardo Arinci was often called Leon rather than Leonardo."

Leon paused while Aleck digested his claim.

"Your father was very shaken after his interview and told me very little about what had happened. I pieced together a few things, and that is how I think he would have responded. Your mother said that he didn't discuss much with her, even years later, but she agreed with what I thought."

"You knew my mother?" Aleck interrupted.

"I met her a couple of times, just to ask how Colin was getting on. He wanted nothing to do with me, so it was only through her that I was able to find out that he was doing well and was very happy in his teaching career," replied Leon. "Once I was reassured about that, I let them be.

"By the way, Aleck, your father didn't lie to protect me; he didn't say I wasn't the author, he simply pointed out there were other feasible anagrams of the given letters possible, and so the authorities shouldn't be jumping to conclusions that could be false."

Leon helped himself to an ample slice of the red cheddar. "So, now you see what I meant when I said your father never let me down, Aleck. He knew I was the author, but his quick-thinking and logical mind enabled him not to have to admit that."

Something about Leon's description of events still bothered Aleck.

"What you've told me still doesn't really explain why Dad didn't get his scholarship," he said, challenging Leon.

"To explain that, I have to admit to something well-meant but utterly stupid, something I strongly regret doing," said Leon candidly.

"Dr Arinci was unknown to me; fortunately for my sake, your father knew of him. I should never have been such a smart arse in adding 'Elon Carini' as co-author. You've probably realised by now that Colin Raine is an anagram of that name. At the time I thought I was so clever in acknowledging the support your father had given me without using his actual name. Likewise, I knew that Nolé Thraldan was both an anagram of my name and the fictitious name I gave on the paper. My attempt to acknowledge both Nolé and Colin for their support was too clever by half, and it lost me your father's friendship."

Aleck saw no reason to admit to Leon that his tired brain had not unravelled the anagrams. He let Leon continue.

"You see, Aleck, the people interviewing your father had already concluded that your father and I were the authors because of the anagrams and the record of us participating in the demonstration. I don't think they'd even thought of the alternative interpretations till your dad pointed them out. It was too late by then; they'd already decided neither of us would be getting a scholarship."

Aleck looked perplexed. "Why wasn't Dad offered a similar chance as you to work in a government department?" he asked.

The two men savoured their coffees in brief silence before Leon responded.

"I've entertained a few theories about that. These days I think I believe that it was just unfortunate timing. There was no great interest in Colin's field back then, but there was a need for enthusiastic, highly skilled mathematicians in education. Not that I think the authorities ever expected Colin to remain in the classroom for so much of his career. More likely, they may have expected him to rise to director level," he mused.

"By contrast, in my field of 'expertise', there was then a growing interest in its applications. It probably helped that Professor Thraldan worked in the same field and put in a good word for me. Then again, I do believe the authorities wanted a reason to curb my growing nuisance value, and I suspect that they were angry with Colin when he wouldn't cooperate by denouncing me. Bringing me 'inside the tent', so to speak, meant they could at least keep an eye on me."

Aleck was feeling a mixture of responses to this news, of which pride in his father, and sadness for him, were the strongest. "Thank you for your honesty in telling me all this."

Leon looked at his watch. "That's taken longer than I expected, Aleck. I suspect you must have to rush off now, and we haven't even started talking about my connection to Aneeka."

Aleck confirmed that he did have to go. However, he quickly shared that Aneeka had just that morning had a change of heart and agreed that their son should know something of his grandparents.

"I haven't yet mentioned who you are in connection to her, but I'm feeling more confident that we, as well as Aneeka's parents, are going to be able to work this out together. Next time we meet, I'm sure Aneeka will want to join us." Leon beamed at his words.

Felix escorted the two men to the door, and Ivana waved farewell to them both. "I trust you gentlemen enjoyed your lunch?" enquired Felix. "Very much," they both replied.

The two men shook hands, Aleck thanking Leon again for the lunch and promising to be back in touch before too long. "Although it might have to wait till after the baby is born," he said.

"You have a good obstetrician for my grandson, I trust?"

"The best – Geraldine Geary."

"Oh good, I hear she has an excellent reputation," remarked Leon, as he set off along the sidewalk, leaving Aleck to wonder how familiar with gynaecologists and obstetricians Leon could possibly be.

Although he was very tired, Aleck was grateful that his headache had subsided. He hailed a taxicab and set off for the school. The afternoon ahead helping two highly unmotivated youths would be worthwhile, or at least he felt so. It was hard to tell with his students.

Today was no different. As always, they tried to distract him from the work he was trying to explain to them, asking him personal questions, this time about his school days, most of which he deflected as he attempted to keep his charges focused on their studies.

"I suppose you were always clever and hardworking, Aleck," said Nathaniel, in a tone that suggested Aleck was both a loser and a nerd. Taking the statement as a question rather than a statement of fact, Aleck jested that he had chosen his parents well and they had helped him with his work and kept him motivated.

"Are you implying Nath's parents are no good?" interjected Sammi. "Well yer wrong, Mr fancy lawyer, Nath's parents are important people."

Deciding for once to accept the bait, Aleck closed the screen they were working from and asked courteously what their parents did for a living. The young men looked pleased. Plus, there were only fifteen minutes left in the session, so he figured that they'd try to stretch their answers out to cover that time, so there'd be no more x's and y's for the rest of the day.

Aleck was surprised to learn that Nathaniel's mother was a CEO at one of the large banks and his father was an architect. He didn't ask their surnames – you weren't supposed to get too familiar with the students in the correction system – but he thought it likely he might know them through his law firm. Instead, he observed that his parents had been very busy people too, but they still had supervised, and ensured he'd done, his homework, plus they had known where he was at any time.

"Didn't your parents try to do that?" he asked Nathaniel carefully, to which Nathaniel scoffed, "They never had time for me, they just assumed I'd behave proper."

"Properly," corrected Aleck, which had the unwanted effect of closing down Nathaniel's short musings about his upbringing.

Aleck switched his focus to Sammi. "And what about your parents Sammi, did they try to help you with your school work?"

"Nah, they soon got sick of that once they realised that I had no brains."

"Course you've got brains," admonished Nathaniel. "They just didn't like that you wanted to be an actor. You were supposed to go into medicine like they did."

Turning to Aleck, Nathaniel explained that Sammi's mother was a dental nurse and his father was an osteopath.

"So, both of you come from families that value education. What was it about school that you both rejected?" Aleck asked.

"It's so boring," the two youths replied in unison.

Sammi elaborated: "You're forever sitting tests of some sort that only tell you how bad you are, never do you get tested on what you know or get praised for what you know. It's far more interesting to skip the test classes and just take off and smoke a joint somewhere nice."

"Trouble is," Sammi continued, "sooner or later you get caught with the joint or get caught shagging one of your classmates … and then you get labelled a troublemaker, parents called in to the school, and before long you get expelled and your parents are ashamed and so it just spirals downwards …"

"Yeah," said Nathaniel, picking up the thread. "The Ps feel really bad cos you've made them look like failures as parents – they're pissed off, other kids are warned by their parents not to have anything to do with you. You feel an outcast, a pariah or whatever the word is. Me and Sammi are lucky cos we're tough and we've got each other for support. The ones who get thrown out of home are the ones you feel sorry for; homeless drifters can soon find themselves in deep shit."

With a smirk, he added: "Fortunately Aleck, we chose our parents well and, disappointed though they may be, they haven't thrown us out."

Aleck laughed, refraining from commenting on the unsuitable language Nathaniel had used. Instead, he spoke to both young men with much earnestness.

"Between the three of us we are going to get you through the system. You two are going to catch up on your studies: I am absolutely determined about that. I'm going to help as much as I possibly can, then once you complete your education, you're going to make a difference so that people like my soon-to-be-born son see schools as encouraging and nurturing places, places that value all aspects of education."

He went on to promise the two young men that once his son was born, he'd bring the baby in to meet them, adding optimistically that he might even have a little more time to spend helping them with their studies once he was on paternity leave.

"Remember, you're both still entitled to five more years out of the sixteen years of free education to which every citizen is entitled. You're going to finish secondary and then you will have three years' tertiary to use at drama school or wherever you wish."

He sighed. "Okay, I'll get down from my soapbox because, like you, I'm well aware we've gone over time; but boys, we're going to see this through together."

Aleck attempted a high-five, but his students had already turned their backs and were heading to the door.

Sammi whispered, "He's a bit of a dork," and Nathaniel nodded. However, Aleck had a feeling that something important had just happened, and the two boys knew that.

And, possibly for the first time, Aleck understood why his father had loved his life as a teacher.

CHAPTER 21

His service commitments completed, it was time for Aleck to quickly dash back to his chambers before heading home. He switched his phone on to find there were three messages from Aneeka. The first said she'd just woken up, the second said she'd showered and dressed but was still feeling a bit seedy, but it was the third message that startled Aleck. Aneeka said she was feeling giddy and nauseous and asked if he could please come home ASAP. There were no more messages and no reply to the call he immediately made, so he left a voice message saying he was on his way.

Cancelling all thought of returning to work, Aleck ran the entire way to the closest station. Although this one was not on his line, he could change to his branch after two stops and, given how busy the traffic was starting to become, he reasoned this would be quicker than hailing a taxicab. Even so, the journey seemed to take a long time and Aleck was worried that Aneeka was not answering his calls. Maybe she'd fallen asleep again – he hoped that was the explanation.

He arrived home as fast as he could, quite out of breath, half expecting Aneeka to greet him.

She didn't.

On bursting into their bedroom, he found Aneeka, fully clothed, lying on her side on their bed, a small puddle of vomit mixed with tinges of blood on the sheets. She didn't respond to him, and a check of her pulse gave only a faint response. Distraught, he immediately phoned for paramedic assistance, following their instructions to keep her lying on her side.

In less than ten minutes, the paramedics arrived and quickly assessed that her condition was serious and she needed to go to hospital straight away. On the short journey, siren blaring, Aleck had the foresight to ring Gerry. While she wasn't available, he left a message that Aneeka had taken ill and was on her way to hospital and could she come to her as soon as possible.

The rest of the journey and Aneeka's admittance to hospital were a bit of a blur. He was asked to stay in the waiting room while the medics attended to Aneeka.

There seemed to be a lot of staff coming and going in and out of Aneeka's room, but no-one spoke to him, even though he rose from his seat each time someone emerged. He was feeling shaky, worried and puzzled. Aneeka had always been so well … what had happened to change this so suddenly?

He was greatly relieved when he saw Gerry arrive. She spoke to him very briefly, then calmly strode towards Aneeka's room and disappeared.

Aleck had lost awareness of time, but maybe fifteen minutes later Aneeka was wheeled from the room. She had a mask over her face helping her to breathe, and a number of other connections and attachments that hooked her up to some expert medical machinery. A grim-faced Gerry spoke to Aleck as they passed. "We're taking her to intensive care. I'll talk to you after we've finished there, but we may have to do an emergency caesarean section."

Aleck felt so helpless. A kind nurse brought him a cup of tea and patted his shoulder soothingly, reassuring him that his wife was in good care. Questions kept whirling through his mind. He started blaming himself: he shouldn't have left Aneeka in the morning, neither had slept well, both were upset over Charles's death. Why hadn't he called in sick? Then common sense kicked in to some extent, and he acknowledged that Aneeka had been tired but not ill that morning, that she was always well and that there had been no warning signs that she was becoming ill.

But what was this illness? Was she just exhausted? Had something gone wrong with the baby? His mind went on and on, around and around in circles, tormenting him with questions that he could not answer.

Get a grip, he told himself. *If you work yourself into such a tizzy then you'll not be of much help to Aneeka. She must have picked up some sort of virus, and the lack of sleep has allowed it to get a hold on her immune system. Surely some rest and antibiotics will see her regain her strength.*

Then he remembered that Gerry had said she might do an emergency caesarean. That would probably help because Aneeka's body would not have to keep feeding Mack. She was close to full term anyway, so the baby should be okay.

Aleck drank his tea, feeling a little calmer. One day he and Aneeka would share a laugh with Mack – oops, Cameron – about the drama of the day leading up to his birth, he felt sure of it.

About half an hour later, Gerry, dressed in her theatre scrubs, appeared at his side. She pulled a chair over, close to his. "Aleck, the news is not good. Aneeka's body is shutting down and so far, we haven't found the cause. We have her on life support, but right now I cannot say to you whether she will recover. I'm so very sorry to have to tell you this."

She paused to allow her words to sink in, then continued. "I think, and my colleagues agree, that it is now essential to operate to save the baby. Do you give us permission to do so?"

"Will Aneeka survive the operation?" asked an ashen Aleck.

Gently, Gerry replied, "The operation gives the baby a chance of survival. Whether we operate or not, Aneeka's survival is not looking promising. She is being kept alive in the hope we can identify what's wrong and then treat the condition. By some miracle, she may pick up of her own accord – that's been known to happen; however, I am so saddened and troubled to tell you her condition is critical. We think we can save the baby, but we cannot operate without your permission. If you agree, you need to sign this form." She passed him a pen and the two-page document, pointing to the section where his signature was required. Aleck sobbed as he signed.

The kind nurse returned and asked if there was somebody she could call to join him for support. Aleck shook his head, barely able to speak, aware of what a tightly entwined unit he and Aneeka had become. They had friends, but there was really no-one he felt he wanted with him. He couldn't imagine life without Aneeka. The feeling he was trapped in a bad dream persisted. He'd wake up soon, and Aneeka would be fast asleep in bed with him and their happy normal life would go on. But a growing dread was entering his whole being, telling him this nightmare was no dream, it was real, he was living it. Never again would he feel the embrace of his beautiful wife, never sit listening to her talk about her day, never walk with her hand in hand, never hear the sound of her laughter nor feel the warmth of her smile, never watch her brush her shiny brown hair ... how could he go on without her? With his head in his hands, Aleck wept uncontrollably.

Gerry was back at Aleck's side. She took his hand and told him his son had been delivered. She told him that the baby had been placed in an incubator under neo-natal care, a precaution they took for all babies delivered by caesarean section or that were born before full term.

"I'll arrange for someone to take you to the nursery so you can see him through the window," she said. Aleck noticed that Gerry then hesitated, as if trying to choose her words. "You won't be able to hold him until we see how he gets on overnight," was all that she ended up saying.

"And Aneeka?" asked Aleck.

"No change following the operation, which is a small plus, but she's still critical. I can arrange for permission for you to see her if you wish. You'll need to be gowned up."

"Okay," was all Aleck could say.

A little later, a different nurse, a male one, collected Aleck and took him to the window of the neo-natal ward. The nurse pointed out the incubator in which baby Cameron lay. Aleck felt a surge of wonder and tenderness sweep through his body. *Hello little man,* he thought to himself. *Welcome to life.*

He noticed tubing attached to the small bundle that was his son, but the four other premature babies in the ward were similarly hooked up. One of these other little people was moving a tiny hand as if in protest that he, or she, was still in a confined space despite having been released from their mother. For the first time since coming home to find Aneeka gravely ill, a brief smile momentarily formed on Aleck's lips.

When he was ready, Aleck indicated to the nurse that he now would like to be taken to see his wife. The nurse showed him into a preparation room, where Aleck scrubbed up and donned the clothing and mask that the nurse issued him. He was then taken a short distance to intensive care, where Aneeka lay motionless, except for the slight rising and falling of her chest as a machine kept her breathing. Her eyes were closed, and she didn't respond to the sound of Aleck's muffled voice that softly crackled with emotion.

He sat alongside her bed, quite close to her head, holding her hand with his gloved hand. He whispered to her how much he loved her. He told her he'd just come from viewing Cameron, using the name he would always use from then on. He described what he'd seen in the nursery. He told her that he needed her, that Cameron needed her and that she must get well soon. After a while he fell silent and just sat gazing at the face of his beloved wife. Yesterday she was her usual bright self; now, just one day later, she was unresponsive. He couldn't stop the tears that yet again consumed him.

The nurse reappeared and, with quiet authority, told Aleck that he needed to leave Aneeka for a while. Gerry had called in another specialist to examine her, who would speak to Aleck afterwards.

The nurse led Aleck to a nearby small waiting room, where he waited for the specialist to appear.

When he arrived, the doctor introduced himself as Professor Kupka and offered his commiserations. He told Aleck that in his opinion there was no chance that Aneeka would pull through, and she was only being kept alive by machines. He sympathised with the predicament but counselled Aleck that he should consider turning off those machines.

"Perhaps you might care to sleep in your wife's room this evening by way of goodbye and then have the machines switched off tomorrow," the Professor tactfully suggested.

Unable to speak, Aleck slowly nodded his head.

He and Aneeka had discussed a long time ago that while euthanasia was not a legal option, neither wished to be kept alive should they have a stroke or meet some other misfortune that left them incapacitated. It had been such an abstract scenario at the time; yet now, here, he was about to carry out her wishes.

As he moved towards the room in which Aneeka lay, Professor Kupka added one more stipulation – as he and Dr Geary were still not yet agreed on what caused Aneeka's body to shut down, he insisted that Aleck continue to wear the protective clothing he had been given.

Aleck said he thought that hardly mattered anymore since he no longer cared what happened to himself. It was only when Professor Kupka reminded him that he now had a child to care for that he agreed to do as requested.

Aleck entered the room to spend one last night with his wife.

CHAPTER 22

The first meeting of the reconvened space program group had gone well, and Eva was feeling quite pleased. There were many calculations that needed to be carried out to plan and check the optimal pathways for the spacecraft, and these would preoccupy her for some time. She was looking forward to the task: it was exactly the type of work she enjoyed.

She was pleased by the enthusiasm shown by Bethany, Gretel's new ministerial appointment to the program, and she had asked Cabut to send a note of thanks to Gretel for her cooperation.

She was hoping the selection process to choose the two astronauts would be finalised very soon as well. While she wasn't directly involved, she was anxious to start the explanations and training for their travel through the connector tunnels. If her calculations could find the way, she was hoping to bring forward the date of the launch; in her own mind, she had reduced the time by half the originally suggested three months.

Cabut interrupted her thoughts with a message to call Geraldine Geary urgently. Cabut was unable to shed any light on why the request was urgent.

Picking up a phone, Eva rang Gerry, who answered immediately.

"Hello Eva, thank you for getting back to me so quickly," she said. Skipping the niceties, Gerry went straight on. "I have bad news. I've lost one of my patients. Aneeka Raine died this morning."

At first Eva was puzzled about why Gerry would be ringing to tell her this. *Has Gerry been negligent in her duties; is she looking to me for support and advice?* Eva replied that she was sorry to hear of Gerry's loss, although she was sure Gerry would have done all in her power to prevent the death and so shouldn't blame herself.

With some exasperation, Gerry interrupted Eva's flow. "You remember her, Eva, you met her quite recently – she participated in your latest research program. Surely you must remember her?"

Eva realised that Gerry was referring to the heavily pregnant woman who had helped her with the testing procedure. She felt a little saddened at the realisation and responded more genuinely. She explained that she did recall Aneeka now, and she was most sorry to hear of her death.

"She seemed to be a very nice person and appeared to be in good health, apart from carrying a mutation in the BRCA2 gene. I'm sure you remember that I told you about that, Gerry. That wouldn't have caused her death at this early stage, so what did? Did she get an infection or pick up some sort of vicious virus?"

"This is partly why I'm ringing you, Eva. So far, we cannot seem to identify what caused her body to shut down. I need to ask you an off-the-record question, one from left-field, but first let me explain the background."

Eva listened carefully as Gerry continued.

"Both Aneeka and her husband Aleck attended their appointments with me together. It always seemed to me that Aneeka was a bit on edge, somewhat guarded or withdrawn, and it was Aleck who came across as the dominant partner. I thought nothing of this until now, and indeed I had thought Aleck quite charming. He did not come to the last appointment – which seems odd when I look back on it, although I didn't think anything of it at the time."

Pausing momentarily to take a deep breath, Gerry said: "Awful though it is to say it out loud, I am now wondering whether Aleck was an abusive and domineering partner."

Gerry continued speaking without waiting for any comment from Eva.

"Had they argued prior to Aneeka's last appointment, and that's why he didn't come? Did Aneeka's decision – and it was her decision – to participate in your research without Aleck being there to 'be in charge' and to 'monitor her behaviour' … did that lead to greater abuse from Aleck? Was he a control freak who punished her if she showed any signs of independence? Might he have done something or administered something to her that could have led to her death, even if her death was not his intended outcome?"

Ceasing her monologue, Gerry addressed Eva directly.

"Tell me your opinion Eva, did Aneeka seem unhappy? What was your impression of her state of mind when you saw her? Would you say there's any chance that she may have been a victim of domestic violence?" implored Gerry.

Eva contemplated the situation in silence for a few seconds, before replying.

"I don't think I'm in any position to be able to give an opinion, Gerry. Aneeka was with me for about an hour: she seemed lively, intelligent, interested in the research and pleased to be involved. I don't remember her mentioning her husband, and she certainly didn't give any indication that she was at all fearful about something. Gerry, I can't add anything to support your theory, or otherwise; I only met her once, and I've had no contact with her since that one session – not that I would have expected to, I might add."

"I wonder if Aleck resented that she obviously got on well with you?" pondered Gerry. "It sounds like she was much more at ease with you than she ever was with me. Honestly Eva, this death has really shocked me – and I can't understand why I can't find what was wrong with her. I even called in Kupka, but he seems none the wiser too. Anyway, I expect you're busy and I'm sorry to have taken up your time. We'll catch up for a drink sometime again soon. Bye for now."

Eva thought it was a sad turn of events, and she was sorry to hear how rattled Gerry sounded. Nevertheless, it was time for her to move on: there were pressing issues facing her and her team of experts.

*

Matilda found it very odd that she had not heard back from Aleck. She had left a message for him with Charles's funeral details. She'd also asked him, as the only relative she knew on Charles's side of the family, if he would deliver one of the eulogies. She herself would give the other. Charles's funeral was drawing close, and she would have appreciated discussing some of the details with him.

She was starting to feel worried. Over breakfast the following day, she and Mikhail resolved that she should call at Aleck's home after she finished work that afternoon.

However, on checking her messages during her lunch break that day, Matilda was relieved to see there was at last a message from Aleck. Her crossness with him evaporated the moment she read his words. She read and re-read his short message, which explained that Aneeka had died that morning, having been delivered of a son the previous evening.

Matilda fought back her tears, feeling desperately sorry for Aleck. She had not known Aneeka well, but she had liked her, and she felt life had been very cruel to her. From Aleck's message, Matilda assumed that Aneeka had died in childbirth, which she knew to be an uncommon event – the maternal mortality rate was 0.048 per 1000 women.

This tragedy coming so soon after Charles's death was too much. She decided to take the rest of the day off. Perhaps she could prepare some food to take over to Aleck later that afternoon.

Matilda sent Aleck a message of sympathy, and she sent Mikhail a message to tell him the sad news before leaving work for the day.

*

After he had regained his composure and been to view his son, who was being kept under observation, an exhausted Aleck accepted an offer from the hospital administrator to arrange for his transport home. Once there, he collapsed on the bed, not bothering to change the sheets soiled by Aneeka's vomit, and he cried himself to a troubled sleep.

When he woke up later, it was as if he was learning anew of Aneeka's death. *It can't be true!* part of him shrieked, although he knew that it was.

Slowly, he took himself off to shower and to put on some clean clothes. He was about to strip the bed when Matilda rang to say she was at his front door with some food. Opening the door to let her in, the two hugged, each dissolving into tears. Matilda made them both a cup of black tea, and they sat quietly as Aleck explained what had happened.

When Matilda took her leave, telling Aleck that the casserole she had brought only needed reheating, she promised to return the next day to see how he was feeling. Aleck felt grateful to her for her kindness.

As Matilda drove away, a delivery van pulled up. The driver handed him flowers sent in sympathy on behalf of the Oostends law firm. Aleck put the beautiful white lilies with their strong perfume in the largest vase he could find and placed the vase in the sitting room. He sat staring at the lilies for some time, his mind a blank. Eventually he started to come out of his trance-like state as the thought struck him that until the results of the autopsy were released, he could not make funeral arrangements for Aneeka.

That thought reminded him that he had not asked Matilda about Charles's funeral. Flicking through his phone, he retrieved her messages. He was about to reply to her to convey that under the circumstances he would not be delivering the eulogy and that his attendance would be dependent on how Cameron was faring, when a voice in his head (that he recognised as his father's) spoke to him about the importance of fulfilling his commitments. He felt he would be letting his father down should he decline this one chance to speak of his father's cousin. Colin would expect nothing less of him. Besides which, the pragmatic side of his mother would reason that Cameron was yet to be released into his care; nothing more could be done for Aneeka at this stage, he was on compassionate leave from work, and he therefore had the opportunity to do something constructive by preparing a tribute to Charles.

Aleck delivered his tribute at the morning service for Charles, after an evening in which he had put together his childhood memories of Charles, the respect and love his parents had held for Cousin Charlie, and the instant regard and affection Aneeka felt towards Charles when they met. He was surprised but unembarrassed by the tears that rolled down his face as he spoke.

Matilda had spoken lovingly of her uncle and the important part he had played in her life, sharing family anecdotes, the more amusing of which generated gentle laughter, evoking similar cherished memories from the small congregation gathered to mourn Charles's passing. The music that accompanied the short service was beautiful, and it was felt by all present that Charles would have approved of the proceedings.

After the service, Aleck was touched by the number of people, many unknown to him, who expressed their condolences for his loss of Aneeka.

He left the wake early to return to the hospital to see Cameron. He realised with a little shame that his grief for Aneeka and Charles had somewhat overshadowed his thoughts about his newborn son.

CHAPTER 23

Aleck gazed in wonder at his son, who slept peacefully in his incubator. Wondering when he would be able to hold him, Aleck went in search of the ward's enquiries desk. The health professional on duty explained that Cameron was likely to remain in the hospital under observation until he started to gain weight and reach that of a newborn babe. He had lost a little of his birth weight, but apparently this was not unusual. Provided Aleck wore protective clothing, she would be happy to allow him to enter the ward to see his son up close.

Soon, Aleck found himself standing motionless next to Cameron's incubator, looking tenderly upon his son. For those brief minutes, he was able to forget the tragedy of recent events; he was filled with a love so keen it almost hurt.

Aleck longed to hold Cameron in his arms, but that would have to wait till the wee one was more developed. Cameron's eyes were shut and he was firmly swaddled with some sort of protective beanie over his head, so Aleck was unable to tell the colour of his eyes or his hair. Though he was allowed to stay for just a few minutes, the nurse told him that he could visit each day for a similar brief period, if he wished.

After he changed back into his street clothes, Aleck went off to enquire whether Gerry or Professor Kupka was available to see him, only to be told they were in conference. He was welcome to wait, but it could be over an hour before they would be free.

He decided to wait and to use the time to resolve an issue he couldn't avoid: informing Aneeka's parents of her death. Aleck had no contact details for them; actually, he didn't know if they were alive or not. If alive, he wanted to pay them the courtesy of delivering the sad news himself in person, rather than risk them reading about Aneeka's death by chance on social media.

He had been mulling over whether or not Leon would know of their current whereabouts, given that he had been close to at least one of Aneeka's mothers. There was also the birth of their grandchild that Aleck felt the three of them, Ann, Kay and Leon, had a right to know about, particularly since Aneeka had been starting to come around to that very idea. For a moment, Aleck was overcome with emotion as he recognised that Cameron would never know his mother in person. He made a silent vow to himself that he would keep the memory of Aneeka alive throughout Cameron's childhood.

Taking himself out into the garden that surrounded one part of the hospital, Aleck made his call to Leon. He told the older man what he could of Aneeka's death, of Cameron's birth and then of his wish to let Aneeka's mothers know of both events. From the tremor in Leon's voice, Aleck could tell he was shocked and very saddened by the news. Leon said he knew where Ann and Kay lived, explaining that it was in a geriatric centre for dementia patients. "Neither would be capable of comprehending the news," he said quietly, adding that, if Aleck insisted, he would take him to them, but he suggested that any such visit would be futile.

Leon then asked if he could join Aleck at the hospital in order to see his grandson for the first time. Pleased by the request, Aleck told Leon he could view Cameron through the nursery window any time Leon wished, but he might not be able to join him that day as he would be meeting with Aneeka's doctors.

Aleck was ushered to a seat in a room in which Gerry and Professor Kupka both sat awaiting him. After exchanging solicitous sentiments, they informed him that the autopsy suggested Aneeka had died from a subarachnoid haemorrhage. They were of the opinion that Aneeka had ingested something that had brought on the bleeding in her brain and caused the extraordinary shutdown of her vital organs.

"Almost like a reaction to arsenic poisoning, except there were no traces of arsenic detected in her body," explained Gerry.

"The last thing I want to do is to add to the misery of your loss, Aleck, but as a lawyer you will understand that we need to ask you some questions in order to eliminate any suspicion that you, as the husband, contributed, unwittingly or otherwise, to her death."

Aleck was astounded by the implication behind Gerry's words, but he recognised the necessity of this interview. He calmly refuted the suggestion that he and Aneeka had recently quarrelled; with pursed lips, he vehemently denied that he was a controlling and abusive partner; and, finally, he exploded with anger at the suggestion that he had harmed her by surreptitiously feeding her some type of chemical.

"Now you are just being ridiculous and offensive, Gerry. I loved Aneeka and would never, ever have harmed her," he stressed, tears welling in his eyes.

Professor Kupka, who had been silent until that moment, finally spoke, crisply and authoritatively.

"Asking you those horrible questions was also very unpleasant for Dr Geary; please bear that in mind, Mr Raine," he noted, adding that the alternative would have been to allow law enforcement to do the asking.

He continued, matter-of-factly: "We are struggling here. Is there an outbreak of some sinister virus that has public health implications, or is there some hitherto unknown drug in circulation? Does whatever killed your wife have implications for the lives and wellbeing of our entire community, including in particular that of your son? Could the death be explained in terms of domestic violence? These are among many of the questions we have had to face. I think now we can look beyond the domestic violence option, just as Dr Geary predicted, but we seek your continued cooperation as we try to identify what happened to your wife," he said.

Aleck nodded to confirm his willingness to continue, despite his distress.

"It would help us if you could write a statement explaining what you and Mrs Raine did during the last week of her life: where you went, what you both ate, what she ate but you didn't … add in anything else that occurs to you, no matter how small or insignificant it may seem," the professor requested.

Gerry added gently, "You don't need to do it this instant, Aleck. We want you to go home and compile everything you can think of into a document. Send it to me when you're ready, and perhaps we can meet again at 11 am tomorrow to review your summary."

Professor Kupka's comment about the potential implications for Cameron greatly worried Aleck. He took himself back to the ward window and gazed in, his sight transfixed on the little bundle in the incubator. There was no sign of Leon, so eventually Aleck wandered off to catch the train home. The train was crowded, which reminded Aleck of the first time he had set eyes on Aneeka.

The train had been crowded that day, too. Back then a slim, good-looking young woman had got into the same carriage as him. The carriage had been full, so the girl had sat on the floor, her legs crossed under her, balancing her phone on one knee. She had earphones hooked up to the phone, and she was reading from small slips of paper. Aleck had presumed she was preparing for an exam that the train was carrying her towards. From time to time, she would look up something on the tablet she was carrying in her backpack. Aleck couldn't make out what subject the girl was studying, because the handwriting on her notes was so poor. They had alighted from the train at the same stop, and the girl's jacket had fallen to the ground. Aleck had picked it up for her and they'd started walking together, both heading towards the university. And that had been the start of the most beautiful relationship. Aleck always said he'd fallen for her the instant she'd so unselfconsciously sat on the floor of the train. If he hadn't felt so sad, the thought that Aneeka's handwriting had never improved since might have brought a smile to his face.

*

Leon had been to view his grandson – not that he could make out his features, but one of the nursing staff had pointed out his incubator. Seeing the infant gave him a feeling he was at a loss to describe. Pride, perhaps – pride that some of his genes would live on through the tiny baby, but a great sadness, too. He had lost his chance to get to know his biological daughter.

As he walked away from the neo-natal ward, it occurred to Leon that he should take the opportunity to have a brief word with the staff who had cared for Claus Proger. He'd been meaning to do so for a while now, but the urgency had dissipated after Javier had assured him of the semi-authenticity of the statement the Department of Health had released to Aleck. *What a very long time ago that seems – is it even important anymore?* he reflected. Despite those thoughts, Leon was nothing if not thorough, knowing he should check for himself.

Approaching the admissions desk, he concocted a story – that he wanted to thank in person the staff who had cared for his friend. He gave the approximate date of admission and spelt the name, but there was no record of such a person being admitted in the past six months.

"That's rather odd," said Leon. "He had a vasectomy procedure. Can you search for him through that?" The health professional tried that route, again without success. A little embarrassed, he suggested that Leon try the relevant ward directly, giving him directions.

Leon wasn't entirely surprised the citizen's name had not registered: either he'd never been officially admitted or his name had been expunged from the records, he guessed. It did make him wonder whether Javier had been entirely honest with him. Maybe even semi-authentic honesty was beyond Javier.

When he reached the ward, he again tried the same story. When that proved a dead-end, he politely asked the nurse if she could look up the names of the staff on duty over that weekend, which she was able to do. However, she seemed hesitant about giving Leon any names, since there was no record of such a patient.

"How about starting with any of them who are on duty right now?" said Leon who was trying not to show his exasperation.

A nurse and an orderly appeared, and the duty nurse suggested he ask them if they remembered his friend. When they both shook their heads over the name, Leon added that his friend had died during that weekend.

The orderly reacted. Yes, he remembered that a patient had died that weekend because he was the one who'd found him dead. He hadn't had anything to do with the guy until he'd been sent to escort him downstairs so he could be released. He'd been told that the patient had complained of a headache prior to being discharged, so he'd been given a headache tablet and told to rest for a while before going home. The orderly said it had been a big shock to then find the patient dead in his chair.

Leon introduced himself to the orderly and thanked him for being with his friend. "Would you have a little time to talk to me about what you remember?" asked Leon.

"Well, I guess so; I'm just signing off from my shift now, so I could give you a couple of minutes," said the orderly, introducing himself as Josef.

"How about I shout you a drink, Josef, just to say thanks," suggested Leon, and Josef said that would be nice, although he couldn't stay too long. They settled on beer for one and cider for the other at the bar across the road from the hospital.

"What happened after you found Claus?" asked Leon.

"Well, it was clear that he was dead, poor chap. I immediately called for help and a nurse came straight away. Then – actually, I don't really know what happened next. A doctor arrived and took charge and told me to leave things to him, so I did. I asked about the patient the next day, but nobody seemed to know who I was talking about except the nurse who had come to my aid. She said to me that the patient must have been someone important, because a government official had taken charge of the body. Was your friend high up in the Government?"

"No, not at all … he was just one of us. Do you recall the hospital carrying out any investigation into his death?" asked Leon.

"I suppose they did, not that I would know anything about it. The hospital administrators normally expect the doctor in charge to investigate any unexpected deaths."

Leon felt he wasn't getting much useful information from Josef. He was about to finish his drink and make his excuses to leave, when Josef added: "Take yesterday, for example – some poor pregnant woman died from causes unknown, and the doctors involved have been in a right old flap investigating ever since. Actually, come to think of it, it's a bit odd that most of us have heard of her death, yet no-one apart from me and the nurse seem to know about your friend's death."

Signalling to the bartender for another round of drinks, Leon casually asked Josef what had happened the day before, and Josef was happy to talk about what he knew. Assuming Josef was speaking of Aneeka, Leon listened quietly to what the orderly had to say and was interested to hear that Miss Geary had called Professor Kupka in for a second opinion. He knew that Kupka was considered a leading figure in the medical world. With sadness, he thought that not even the best practitioners had been able to save Aneeka.

Although he knew the answer, Leon asked Josef what had happened to the baby. Josef confirmed that the baby had been delivered while the mother was still alive – he had been one of the orderlies who had wheeled the patient to theatre. Whether it was the effect of his second beer or not, Josef was quite forthcoming, and he surprised Leon by reflecting that the mother had had the same look in her eyes as had Leon's friend, Claus. When pressed, he was unable to describe quite what that look was – something "not of this world" was the best he could offer.

Leon remained in the bar long after Josef had taken his leave. He was struggling with what Josef had meant by the 'same look'. *Surely not, surely there can't be any connection,* he thought, downplaying Josef's claim as fanciful, simply an embellishment brought on by the man having had two beers in quick succession. But the words continued to gnaw and grate. Eventually, desperately hoping to dismiss the niggling doubt once and for all, he rang Aleck to ask him the two questions pulsing through his mind. By the end of their short conversation, although he did not say as much to Aleck, Leon's worst suspicions had been confirmed.

Eva had unwittingly evened up the score. Long ago, his actions had caused her daughter's death – and now Eva's actions had caused his daughter's death. He was sure of it.

CHAPTER 24

Timothy was feeling unloved. He had heard nothing more from Leon or Gretel; he hadn't even heard from Javier since their meeting. However, he *had* heard that Gretel intended to appoint Bethany to a plum position – some science committee or space science program, wasn't it? The rumours varied. He wondered if Gretel had considered him for the role. Not that he really wanted it right now ... but that wasn't the point. He'd demonstrated loyalty by privately alerting Gretel to the concerns over that citizen, so it was perfectly reasonable to expect that he should have first right of refusal. Besides, she should know better: she'd be sorry one day that she hadn't treated him more respectfully.

Feeling unloved and overlooked didn't entirely encompass all that he was feeling. A creeping change was occurring within him, one that was hard to describe and not ready to be received: a growing awareness that it was time to start casting away his self-indulgent excesses. He wondered about the driving force of this change: was it Leon turning his back and ignoring him; Leon's dismissiveness, imagined or real?

Freddy hadn't exactly been sympathetic to his anguish either, telling him it was called 'growing up'. "You're reaching the stage of needing to behave less like an indulged puppy and more like the leader you will become when you cease shying away from your destiny," Freddy had said in a burst of frankness.

"But that doesn't mean we have to be serious types all the time, my dear friend," he had added, which had soothed him temporarily.

Recently, they had enjoyed some earnest discussions about his future political career, his political manifesto and what he actually wanted for the Country. He was coming around to Freddy's view that his strengths and superiority outweighed his comparative youth and inexperience. After all, he was an excellent economist, and what the

Country needed was strong economic leadership and vision. He could provide that; he could make a difference.

Gretel had been good, but now she was getting tired and worn out. Timothy speculated that before too long she'd be announcing her retirement. Some small-scale undermining of Gretel to help push her towards that retirement seemed in order: some covert criticisms about her becoming ineffectual, for starters.

Informally, Timothy had started some counting of numbers. There was minor support for him to take over the presidency at some unspecified time in the future, but he was a long, long way from having the numbers to justify mounting a challenge.

However, his budding better self was beginning to needle him, suggesting that a challenge may not be the way to gain the presidency; better that he had a succession plan in place to activate when Gretel retired – better too if that plan contained altruistic aims designed to bring benefit to the Country and its citizens, not just aims to advance his own career.

Timothy really was feeling conflicted – he half wished these bouts of benevolent introspection would stop nibbling away at him and go away.

And there was Leon to consider. Timothy was particularly troubled about him. Without Leon's support and financial backing, any attempt to attain the highest office would be likely to fail. Leon was one of the richest people in the Country, and he wielded considerable power and influence. Timothy had often wondered why Leon had never stood for the presidency himself. He also struggled to understand Leon's relationship with Javier: at times this appeared fraught, yet Leon seemed to be 'in the know'.

Why is he ignoring me? Timothy asked himself yet again. He took out the phone he used for calling Leon and tried it for the fourth time that day.

To his surprise, Leon answered.

"Hello Timothy, it's good that you've called. I think you should know that the Government is about to be plunged into a crisis that may see the President choose retirement sooner rather than later. Whether you judge this as opening up opportunities for yourself, I leave to you."

Timothy was taken aback by this sudden development, but he quickly recovered himself. "Should I decide to advance my cause, can I assume I would do so with your backing and good will?"

"As of right now, the presidency is not vacant, Timothy. When, or if, it becomes so, then I will think carefully about the candidate that I would like to support. Now, I must go as I have something urgent to complete," replied Leon, ending the brief call.

Timothy was a bit nonplussed and annoyed that Leon hadn't anointed him straight away. *Leon can be very autocratic and superior sometimes,* he thought, *a result of always having been well-off, no doubt.* When he became president, he would ensure that those with outrageous fortunes were forced to share more of their wealth through a revision of the taxation system.

And what did he mean about a looming crisis? Did he mean that issue I warned Gretel about? It would really help if he had paid me the courtesy of explaining, he thought, irritated.

However, as he calmed down, Timothy acknowledged that Leon sometimes acted in strange ways, and perhaps he had been very deliberate in not being more forthcoming.

He had decided on his course of action. He would let it be known to many of his colleagues, in confidence of course, that they were on the brink of crisis – and when they pressed him for more, he could simply say that he wasn't able to share that information just yet … and that perhaps he'd already said too much, but he knew he could trust them.

That should ensure the news spreads like wild fire – and it will be interesting to hear the rumours as they circulate, smirked Timothy, his mood lightening, the fledgling signs of his better self once more suppressed.

*

Leon was drafting a report for Professor Kupka. It explained that Professor Eva Baritz had conducted an experimental procedure on Aneeka Raine that he believed had caused an unintended reaction, leading to her death a few days later. The symptoms were similar to those of a Claus Proger, someone on whom Professor Baritz had previously carried out a procedure, and one who had also died from complications after a few days. In both cases, each person had suffered stroke-like deaths.

Leon intended to share his report with Javier, but only after he was sure Kupka had received his copy.

Completing the document, Leon transmitted it and sat in quiet contemplation, awaiting a signal from Professor Kupka. He did not have to wait for long.

Next, he messaged Javier to say he had to see him urgently: only then did he send Javier a copy of the report. Javier responded almost immediately, telling Leon a car was on its way to bring him to his office.

Leon picked up his hat and stepped outside his home to calmly wait for the car. He felt a sense of sad resignation, as if it were an inevitability that he would one day reach this point.

It did not take the driver long to arrive at Leon's home. He got out of the car, politely introduced himself as Clovis, and held a rear passenger seat door open for Leon.

"I see you had no trouble finding the place," quipped Leon. "At least today you won't have to spend your time cooped up in the car watching my movements." Clovis smiled back at him. The two men talked quite conversationally during the short drive to Javier's office.

A grim-faced Javier ushered Leon into his office, indicating with a sweep of his hand where Leon should sit.

Still standing, Javier scathingly asked: "Why didn't you consult with me before you contacted Kupka?"

"Because you would have stopped me," replied Leon. "I decided to strike first and face the consequences afterwards."

"Very selfish – though, in that regard, typical of you, I think we could both say," snapped Javier. "In the event that your claims against Eva are upheld, you should have allowed the Government to drive the case. But, no, you have to big-note yourself and be seen as the one in power, the quasi-hero. Where do you think this places Gretel? As

President she has backed Eva, supported her work and very recently given the go-ahead to her major project, soon to be announced to Cabinet. Now we have to spin into damage control, all thanks to your selfishness and longstanding preoccupation over Eva."

"It's time to stop spinning, Javier," interrupted Leon quietly. "Please calm down, sit down and listen to me very carefully."

The two men held each other's gaze for some seconds until, reluctantly, Javier resumed his seat. Only then did Leon continue.

Predicting that eventually questions, if not charges of some sort, were almost certain to be asked of or laid against Eva, Leon explained that he had decided that the details surrounding the long-ago car accident that led to Nolé's death and the loss of Eva's unborn daughter should be revealed as part of the defence case to assist Eva. He stressed to Javier he would not be implicating him or Gretel in being aware of that knowledge. But, he argued, by confessing to his part in the accident, he would be publicly accepting some responsibility for Eva's mental state and, as a consequence, her subsequent behaviour. Acknowledging she had a form of ongoing mental illness or mental distress arising from that accident would allow her to be viewed more sympathetically.

Javier looked furious; he was clearly not mollified by Leon's words. "You've expended so much blasted time and energy pursuing her, digging up as much dirt and innuendo as you can; now, when things are starting to bite, you rush to me, pleading that together we plan how to protect Eva from your trumped-up charges. It drives me to total distraction. Make up your mind, man, for goodness' sake. On which sodding side do you stand? Are you her protector or her foe, for crying out loud? This is not a frigging game."

Unmoved by Javier's intensity, Leon waited for him to collect himself before replying.

"We've had this out before, Javier; my position has not changed. I care for Eva, as do you. However, the irreparable damage that I've caused her makes it my life-long responsibility both to protect her and to stop, if not prevent, some of the excesses she pursues. These cannot be mutually exclusive.

"My argument, as it always has been, is with the Government, which turns a blind eye to the means yet shares the end successes of Eva's achievements as reflected glory. It is the Government that is her foe, and I her protector."

There was silence between the two – the silence of an age-old debate upon which they never would agree.

Leon eventually broke the impasse, attempting to ease the tension between them.

Looking up at Javier, he reflected on Gretel's position.

"I disagree that Gretel is necessarily tainted by association. The Government's employment and backing of Eva has been professional. Eva does have an outstanding intellect and her work has been of great value. It is a crisis, but it is still possible for Gretel to be seen as handling this crisis well."

Digressing, Leon added an opinion about Gretel's position. "Gretel will have to resign one day, but she doesn't have to resign in disgrace. Once this is all behind us, I suggest Gretel takes that opportunity to move on – something that I sense, as you must do too, Javier, will not be an unwelcome prospect for her."

Javier made no comment, so Leon continued with a personal reflection.

"As for me, I was long ago cleared of any responsibility for the accident, but the burden of shame I shall carry with me always. I'll just have to continue to cope with that," he ended.

Without showing any reaction, Javier moved the subject on.

"Okay, let's for a moment assume the Proger case can be handled. What about the Raine woman? It would require an unreasonable stretch of forbearance to accept no-one in government raised an eyebrow about the work Eva was continuing to do, despite the loss of Proger."

There was a long pause before Leon responded. "Isn't that what actually happened?" He sighed. "I've tried to help you, Javier, but I'm too involved with Aneeka's case to be able to offer any advice here."

Javier looked puzzled. "I know you've become pals with her husband and you told me he's Colin's son, but why do you seem so invested in this case?"

"Let me fill you in Javier, as clearly not even your Security team, led by Jacques I assume, has cottoned on to this," said Leon dryly. He explained his biological relationship to Aneeka.

Javier seemed to be genuinely surprised. "So, justice has already been done, eh Leon? An eye for an eye, a tooth for a tooth, a daughter for a daughter?"

"Cruel words, Javier, but true ones," was all Leon could think to say in reply.

Javier immediately apologised; Leon believed that he genuinely regretted his callous comment. Javier certainly looked wretched enough as he apologised, and Leon recalled momentarily a time when they shared a deeper bond. Their relationship was a complicated one: they were longstanding fellow travellers, at one time friends, at some times foes.

Seeming to recover himself, Javier took charge. "Now, this is the way I think we should proceed from here," he began, and he and Leon continued their conversation at length: rationally, cooperatively and with common purpose.

*

Leon's visit to Government House did not go unnoticed: Timothy's view of the car park from his office was often useful. He'd spotted Leon alighting from a government car.

Game on, he thought. Was this the moment when Leon would exert his influence and insist Gretel announce her retirement in order to make way for new blood: that is, for himself? Perhaps he should draft a statement of his intention to stand as a candidate for the presidency, an announcement that he would be ready to make as soon as Gretel made hers.

Timothy kept a strategic watch over the car park, which was later rewarded by the sight of Javier shaking Leon's hand and helping him back into the car. He was even more delighted to see Javier head in the direction of the President's suite as the car moved off. It was only then that it struck him how like an old man Leon had looked.

*

Javier made two calls, the first to Jacques, the second to Cabut to ask if Eva was in her office. Answering in the affirmative, Cabut asked if Javier wished to speak with her. Declining, Javier carefully enunciated his instructions. "Keep Eva occupied tomorrow; make sure she meets with no-one until after the Cleaners have been."

CHAPTER 25

After a fitful evening, Aleck was on his way to his morning appointment with the two doctors. As requested, he had sent his recollections to Gerry, glad to have done something tangible despite feeling it would be of little help.

He was beset by worries. When would Aneeka's body be released? When could her funeral be held? When could Cameron come home? How would he cope as a single father? Who would look after the baby while he was at work? All these questions and more kept running through his mind. He felt helpless, weighed down by questions to which he had no answers and the need to plan ahead without knowing how. He realised he'd have to take an extended break from work, but what would he do after that? With these thoughts whirling through his mind, he disembarked from the train and walked towards the hospital.

Greeting Gerry and Professor Kupka, he neither minded nor was curious as to what they might tell him. In some ways it no longer mattered what had caused Aneeka's death, since nothing could undo the fact that she was no more. However, he felt a shiver down his spine when he noticed that Gerry appeared to have been weeping. The thought that Cameron, too, may have died struck him like a hammer banging an anvil.

He could hardly breathe as Gerry opened their meeting with the words, "There's something we have to tell you about Cameron."

Inwardly, Aleck screamed, *No, no, no, not him as well.* Outwardly, he tried to appear calm and attentive. "Go on," was all he managed to say, his voice barely audible.

Gerry explained that Cameron should survive, but there was more than a 90% chance that he would have some brain damage. Whatever had killed his mother had seeped through to him also, but in a diluted form. The extent of the damage would only be understood as he developed. He was likely to remain in hospital for some time, she had added.

"But he'll live, is that what you're saying?"

"Yes, we believe so. However, he will carry a disability, the extent of which we are not in a position to be sure about yet," replied Gerry.

Aleck tried to absorb this new setback. And then, his brain seemed to switch back on and he almost smiled.

I can cope with this, no matter how severe the disability. The important thing is he will live, and through him some of Aneeka will live on.

For what was almost becoming a daily ritual, Aleck allowed tears to flow down his face without embarrassment, while Gerry tried to mop up her own tears.

Once they had managed to regain some composure, Professor Kupka spoke. He assured Aleck that Cameron would receive the best medical treatment possible, adding that if the brain damage wasn't particularly severe, there was every hope that Cameron could lead a relatively normal life.

Quietly, Kupka continued: "Thank you for your thorough statement recollecting all that your wife did and ate in the days leading up to her death. That information was very helpful and leads me to ask if you can recall any further details, in particular, about the time your wife spent as a volunteer in Professor Baritz's research program? Did she later complain of a headache, for instance?"

Aleck paused to think hard. He couldn't remember Aneeka mentioning she had a headache. In fact, she had seemed very upbeat about her involvement in whatever the program was.

"No, definitely not," he replied.

Elaborating, Aleck commented that Aneeka hadn't slept well the night they were told of Charles's death but it was he, not Aneeka, who had taken a tablet for a headache, and he'd taken more of them the next day.

This recollection sparked his memory: he recalled that as he was leaving for work, Aneeka had asked him to leave behind a couple of the tablets, which he had done.

"Whether Aneeka had one, both or indeed neither of those tablets, I have no idea," he said, adding that he hadn't given it any thought because that was the day he returned home to find her unconscious.

Professor Kupka nodded. "This may be important, Mr Raine. We'd like you to check when you go home whether the headache tablets you left for Mrs Raine are still there. Do you remember what brand they were?"

"Just regular tablets we bought from the local pharmacy," shrugged Aleck. Searching his pockets in case he still had the bottle, he promised to get that information to them. Puzzled, he observed: "Surely it can't be the tablets, since I definitely had some of them and I experienced no unintended after-effects."

"We must check everything, Mr Raine," was all that Professor Kupka would say in reply. "Remind me, how many days after your wife's session with Professor Baritz did you hear of the death of your, was it your uncle?"

"My father's cousin, actually," corrected Aleck, while trying to recall the events of those last few days with Aneeka.

"On the evening of the day Aneeka met with Professor Baritz, we went for a walk – and that's when we purchased the tablets from the pharmacy, because I had a headache. I think I'm right that Charles died two evenings later."

"So, if she took any tablets it would have been on the third day after her session?"

Aleck nodded.

Noticing the quick glance the two doctors exchanged, Aleck said: "Does that help at all? And, if so, why?"

"It certainly does, thank you Mr Raine. It ties in with a theory we're exploring. By the way, do you happen to know a Leon Hartland?" asked Professor Kupka.

Flummoxed, Aleck said, "Yes, it so happens I do. What's he got to do with this?"

"We're currently following a line of enquiry suggested to us by Dr Hartland."

"Dr Hartland, that's the first time I've heard him addressed as such. Perhaps we're not talking about the same person?" suggested Aleck.

"Oh, I think we are, Aleck," said Gerry, not waiting for Professor Kupka to respond. Glancing at her watch, she apologised. "For now, we'll have to let that go by – we need to wind up this meeting."

Rising from her seat, Gerry warmly shook Aleck's hand, reminding him to let them know about the tablets he had left for Aneeka as soon as possible.

*

Gerry felt subdued as she watched Aleck leave. As he also rose to depart, Professor Kupka said gently, "Geraldine, I'm sorry to say it sounds like Dr Hartland may be correct."

"It certainly does," she replied sadly.

"Try not to take this personally, Geraldine – you bear no professional responsibility."

"Just a moral one," she responded with a deep sigh.

*

Aleck headed to the neo-natal ward after his meeting with the two doctors. As he looked upon his tiny son, he made a promise to himself that he would devote his life to looking after him. "We will prevail, Cameron," he whispered.

On the journey home, Aleck's mind was clearer than it had been on the trip to the hospital. He knew that he was on the verge of framing the future direction of his life and, although still so very sad, he felt ready and able to face this.

As soon as he arrived home, he sent Gerry and Professor Kupka the name of the headache tablet that he, and now very probably, Aneeka, had taken, confirming that of the two tablets he had left for Aneeka, only one remained. He also confirmed the chemicals listed on the back of the bottle in case they needed further details.

*

Eva had been surprised to be informed by Cabut that both of her anticipated meetings that morning had been cancelled 'due to unforeseen circumstances'. In particular, she had been looking forward to speaking with Bethany in her capacity as the government minister appointed to the Space Program Council. She also thought it odd that the chief of astronaut training had not paid her the courtesy of explaining why he'd had to cancel at such short notice; she hoped that there had been no negative developments in the astronaut selection process.

Never mind, she thought, recognising the cancellations would give her the opportunity to respond to the rather tedious request for a full description of what had happened during the procedure conducted on that pregnant woman – the one who had sadly died not so long afterwards, she reminded herself.

Although she had heard Gerry speak of him, Eva did not know Professor Kupka personally. As the one of higher rank, she was a little put out not to be treated with greater respect by him. She most certainly was not answerable to him, and up to now she had not bothered to reply. However, she reasoned, Kupka was a colleague of Gerry's, and if his plan was to censor Gerry over the woman's death, then now would be as good a time as any to do what she could to thwart his intentions.

Naturally, she could give only an outline of the procedure, its full scope being top secret and not for general release. She would, however, be able to accurately list any medications 'given or recommended' (to quote the professor's words) – there were none, just 'rest' recommended – and she intended to add a few comments about the high regard and respect she held for Gerry's professionalism as well.

As she completed the task, Eva became annoyed that some technological hitch was preventing her from sending her reply to Professor Kupka. It then dawned on her that she hadn't received any messages all morning, either. Cabut had informed her about the cancellation of her meetings.

Technological problems were extremely rare, so she stepped out of her office to alert Cabut. His opinion was that the problem, whatever it was, must be restricted to her office, as all was working as normal for him. He promised to get technical support in to deal with the issue and suggested that Eva try sending her document to him through the internal network and he would forward it on.

*

Javier noted Eva's response to Professor Kupka, which Cabut had helpfully shared. He had other concerns, however. Javier was sending Cabut a large confidential file. This file, marked top secret, contained all the relevant information about each of Gretel's twenty-six Cabinet ministers. Cabut's task was to process this data and scientifically select the three ministers, in rank order, that possessed the greatest presidential potential.

Javier knew that Cabut was used to handling such sensitive information. He had relied on Cabut's analyses a number of times and had every confidence that the names he would select would be chosen dispassionately, logically and without any personal bias. Cabut made excellent decisions, it always seemed. *But then he would, wouldn't he,* he smiled to himself.

The smile was brief, for today was not a day for smiling. He and Gretel had discussed the situation around Eva and Gretel's presidency long into the previous night, by the end of which they no longer felt troubled by Leon's involvement in the investigation of Aneeka's death. Gretel had confirmed she was ready to consider retiring, although not until the space mission had launched.

Following the resignation of a president, it was customary for there to be a hiatus during which to appoint a successor. This was followed by a further induction phase, which the outgoing president was heavily involved with. Javier had suggested launching the space mission during the handover process. The instigating president handing the baton to the president who would oversee the mission's successful completion would be excellent symbolism for both Gretel and the new president.

All that remained was to delay the consequences of any case against Eva until Eva's role in the space mission had been completed. This would allow Gretel to announce her resignation without any connection to Eva's wrongdoings. But quite how to do this was not yet clear.

*

Gretel was comfortable with the strategy she had devised with Javier the night before. However, she harboured an additional major concern, one that she had not yet raised with him.

Eva's testing had been declared successful, her procedure had been validated, and the upcoming space mission had already been set in motion and was about to be announced to Cabinet. But – and it was a big 'but' – the successful test case had subsequently died, so could Eva's results still be considered to have validated her procedure?

Perhaps the death was unrelated: Eva certainly seemed to be of that view. Gretel sure hoped that was the case, because right now she couldn't bear to face the alternative. *Let's first see what the doctors have to say – or, more importantly, the coroner, if it comes to that,* she counselled herself. *Maybe I'm worrying unnecessarily.*

CHAPTER 26

Leon had been invited to a short tele-meeting with Professor Kupka and Geraldine Geary. They explained to Leon that, due to the additional information provided by Aleck concerning a headache tablet Aneeka had taken, they now had no choice: the matter had to go before the Hospital Board. Leon supported their decision and volunteered to inform the President's Principal Advisor and, through him, the President, that a government employee, Eva Baritz, would be expected to participate in the coronial proceedings that would follow. The two medical doctors also confirmed that Aneeka's body would soon be able to be released to Aleck by the coroner.

Leon took it upon himself to update Javier and Aleck in person, which was why he soon found himself being driven away from Javier's office yet again and towards Aleck's home, with Clovis driving him.

Leon and Clovis were getting to know each other quite well. They chatted amicably as they travelled towards Aleck's home, with Leon asking about Clovis's parents. Clovis spoke of his father's passion for poker, thinking this might be of interest to Leon; Leon shared that he also played the game, but he preferred Bridge.

"And, what about your mother?" enquired Leon.

"Mum's not that keen on poker," laughed Clovis. "She reckons Dad's just throwing his money away. Mum likes to potter about in her garden, and she doesn't mind a flutter on the nags. But mostly, she hangs out with her buddies, talking and drinking tea, it seems to me."

"Sounds like a good life, I'm with your mum," joked Leon.

Leon was careful not to ask Clovis anything too personal. He wanted to portray himself to Clovis as an old retired person content with amusing himself with hobbies, no different to Clovis's parents and many others of their generation. Whether Clovis might become useful was unclear, but Leon was not one to miss an opportunity.

Arriving at Aleck's, Leon thanked Clovis for the lift, politely suggesting that unless he had orders to the contrary, he'd be able to make his own way home. A little embarrassed, Clovis said he would have to double check, but he couldn't see why his boss would object. Leon shrugged, adding "I'll leave that up to you and Javier." He noted Clovis's brief hesitation, deducing that Javier was not the person Clovis considered to be his boss.

Interesting, he thought as he smilingly waved goodbye.

It was the first time Leon had been to Aleck and Aneeka's home. With considerable sadness, Leon recalled how he had hoped to be welcomed to their home by them both one day. He gave Aleck a hug and accepted the offer of coffee.

The kitchen was quite small, but it let in lots of light despite the shade offered by the large liquid amber tree in the garden. The room was furnished simply but tastefully, and Leon felt it was 'homely'. He could not help observing that it was also untidy, with dishes piled up near the sink and various odds and ends on the table and elsewhere.

Aleck rearranged the table's clutter to create space for both men to sit down. He placed an already opened packet of biscuits on the table, indicating that Leon should help himself. Then, his voice calm, his eyes filled with sad resignation, Aleck quietly told Leon about the probable brain damage Cameron had incurred.

After a short pause, Leon reached out and patted Aleck's arm.

He said how sorry he was to learn of Cameron's likely disability and immediately offered his help.

"As you may be aware, I'm a wealthy person, and I want you to know that I will help you in any way possible with whatever financial support you may need to look after Cameron," said Leon, very sincerely.

"Thank you, Leon, I appreciate your generous offer and the sentiment behind it. Actually, I've been doing some deep thinking about Cameron's future since I was told about his condition and, strangely,

I'd welcome the opportunity to run these thoughts by you. No offence intended Leon, but I use the word 'strangely' because I still don't feel I really know you. However, I do accept that you are genuine in your interest in Cameron's welfare and that you have a right to be involved in his life."

Leon made no reply and waited for Aleck to go on.

Firstly, Aleck told him about the pleasure he felt in spending his regular Service days with students whose education had suffered, not ever anticipating that he, himself, would have a son whose own education could be compromised. Then, he explained that he now planned to retrain to become a teacher, one specialising in the education of students who were outside the mainstream: juvenile offenders and those with special needs, like Cameron.

Aleck went on to observe he'd need to employ someone to help with Cameron initially but, as a teacher, his hours away from home would be less than if he remained working as a solicitor. He noted that he would have no income while he underwent teacher training, and he again expressed his gratitude to Leon for his offer of financial help, but said he hoped to be able to get by on his savings.

Aleck paused. Leon had to admit that he hadn't anticipated the direction Aleck was planning to take.

He cautioned Aleck against making any firm decisions right now. It was such a traumatic time for him, and he suggested that there may be some benefit in maintaining his current position and not rushing into things. Cameron was still in hospital, unlikely to be discharged for a few weeks at least, and it was not yet clear how much damage he had suffered: he might be able to lead a normal life after all.

Leon also took the opportunity to explain that he'd been charged with confirming to Aleck that Aneeka's body would very soon be released to him.

"Why were you asked to tell me this?" asked Aleck. "Does that mean the doctors are now certain they have identified the cause of her death? Was it a reaction to the chemicals in the headache tablet?"

"It hasn't been proven, but the procedure Aneeka underwent with Professor Baritz may have had the regrettable side-effect of altering how her body reacted to one of the ingredients in the headache tablet.

"Professor Baritz would not have been aware that this complication could occur," stressed Leon, wondering to himself why he was defending Eva's 'procedure'.

Aleck did not comment. After some moments of silence between the two, he asked Leon if he was a medical doctor, having been referred to as Dr Hartland by Professor Kupka.

Leon smiled slightly. "I got to complete my PhD in mathematics a long time ago – unlike your father, I'm sorry to say. However, it's interesting that you are now thinking of following almost in his footsteps and becoming a teacher," Leon said, switching the conversation away from himself.

Aleck was not to be sidetracked. "If you're not a medical doctor, why would you be discussing Aneeka's death with the doctors investigating it? There's something about you Leon that I don't understand, and never have, but I can't put my finger on what that is," he said with a trace of a smile. "It's not only that you are Aneeka's father; I have this feeling there's more to you than even that, stunning though that bit of information was to learn."

Leon gave a short, subdued chortle.

"I once worked with Eva Baritz and, thanks to her, I had the opportunity to complete my doctorate. At one stage we, together with her partner Nolé, were quite close. After Nolé unfortunately was killed in a car accident, I, and later a couple of other friends, tried to support Eva through a tough period in her life. Eventually, the circle of friends broke up as people moved on to other roles, and I too moved on, losing personal contact with Eva. However, from a distance I've kept abreast of her research. Hearing Aneeka had been in contact with Eva allowed me to offer an insight into the type of research in which Eva involves herself. I thought Kupka and Geary ought to be aware of her background, that's all."

"Gerry and this Eva Baritz are colleagues," interjected Aleck. "Gerry allowed Aneeka to participate in her research. She told me it was routine, not some ground-breaking research full of risk," he said with rancour.

"Eva told Geraldine it was routine because she believed it was, and she continues to stand by that claim," said Leon, in their defence. "I don't believe that Geraldine had any reason to doubt her, but, believe me Aleck, she feels really bad about this now. It seems to have been just some awful, awful fluke that the headache tablet had that effect on Aneeka, its ingestion coming too soon after the procedure."

"This Eva needs to be held accountable, not that it will bring Aneeka back. I really don't care what happens to her," contended Aleck, looking away with tears in his eyes.

"I don't believe for a moment that Eva set out to deliberately harm Aneeka, but the fact is she likely did – and for that she will be held accountable, sooner or later. She'll be called before the coroner, as will Geraldine, as a matter of course, and we'll see what happens after that," reflected Leon.

Aleck merely shrugged his shoulders and said no more. A silence descended upon them. Aleck broke the mood by speculating that he should be entitled, on behalf of Cameron, to seek compensation from Eva or the Government.

He sat upright, appearing energised by the idea.

"That would be my best way of ensuring Cameron has all the care he needs. I'll become a teacher, but we'll manage without having to empty my savings or ask you for financial backing because the professor's professional insurance should cover this.

"Do you know which government department Professor Baritz works for, Leon?" he asked.

"I believe she was working for one of the Government's scientific research departments," said Leon carefully. "Why don't you just for now concentrate on organising Aneeka's funeral and return to this train of thought once that emotionally draining event is behind you. Can I offer my help with the preparations? It would mean a lot to me to do so."

Aleck nodded, and together the two men set to drawing up a list of what needed to be arranged and who would take responsibility for each aspect of the funeral.

*

Eva was becoming increasingly frustrated by Cabut's lack of success at fixing her technical problems. Two technicians had arrived an hour or so earlier, but Eva didn't know what they'd done because, at Cabut's insistence, she had left the two techs to their own devices. Whatever they had done hadn't worked, because here she was, back in her office, and still nothing seemed to be working.

"For heaven's sake," she cursed out loud. "What century are we living in? Have we suddenly been thrust backwards in time?"

Storming out of the room, she railed at Cabut that she needed the situation to be fixed.

As always, Cabut was calm and unruffled in his response. He said he would contact the Head of the Technical Division to request an urgent reassessment. In the meantime, he suggested Eva calm down and try once more to see if things were working. "Perhaps it just takes a bit of time to settle down," he had added unscientifically. And that indeed did seem to be the case, because when she tried once more, Eva found her devices were operating normally.

*

Cabut sent a message to the Head of the Technical Division to confirm that the task of 'cleansing' Eva's files had been completed. As instructed by Javier, he had removed all records of the two previous unsuccessful tests but left in the references to Aneeka's tests being conducted successfully, almost as Eva had written them. Everything was ready for the Hospital Board officials to arrive and seize Eva's files.

*

Before Eva could get back into the flow of her work, she found herself being escorted from her office. She was outraged by the intrusion and vigorously protested against being placed under what she saw as 'house arrest'. She was told that she would be returned to her apartment and placed 'on leave' for the duration of the inquiry into Aneeka Raine's death. Her eyes searched in vain for Cabut, trusting that he would notify someone to come to her aid. However, he was nowhere to be seen.

On arriving at her apartment, Eva contacted Stewart Weisman, her lawyer, who agreed to come to see her at around six that evening. He advised she spend the intervening hours preparing a statement of the facts, from her perspective, surrounding her interactions with Aneeka.

Stewart was explaining the legal process that pertained to her case. In the Country, justice was usually administered after careful consideration by a sole judge (or a panel of three judges, if the case was particularly serious or complex). Trial by jury had long ago been discarded, seen to be flawed due to the lack of legal training or experience required by the juries of old. But Eva was not about to face trial. She was reassured to realise that despite her initial outrage, the requirement for her to appear before the coroner was actually a routine procedure followed whenever an unexpected or unexplained death had occurred.

Both Gerry (as Aneeka's obstetrician) and Eva would be interviewed. Only if the coroner then determined there was a case against one or both women would the matter be further investigated.

Stewart reiterated that she was not on trial at this juncture, even though information had been seized from her files pertaining to Aneeka and she had also been temporarily placed on leave. No case ever went before a judge unless, or until, there was a solid case against an accused person.

Stewart's words were soothing to Eva. She had never been required to follow such 'reportable death' procedures before. She really couldn't see that Aneeka's death had anything to do with the procedure she'd undergone.

Nevertheless, as Eva resignedly concluded, even though she believed that Aneeka's death was unrelated to her research, she had no option but to follow the normal hospital procedure.

*

Stewart was pleased to see Eva become less agitated and less angry. Together they discussed the types of questions she was likely to be asked and her responses, although Eva had remained unforthcoming about the nature of the research she had been conducting.

His parting advice to Eva was for her to be very guarded in what she had to say, and to answer the questions put to her briefly and confidently without unnecessary elaboration.

As he came away from Eva's apartment, Stewart felt quite comfortable about the likely outcome for Eva. It was always difficult for a coroner to bring down a finding of misconduct against a medical doctor or researcher, despite having the power to seize records to prevent evidence tampering.

This was good for his current client, he reasoned, placing Eva in the role of the researcher, but less so for a few of his past clients who had lost family members as a result of alleged misdiagnoses or other inept practices. The best he'd been able to achieve for these clients was a private financial settlement with the practitioner's insurance company. This would usually discreetly cover the situation, leaving the practitioner to resume practice (or not, as the case may be). In Stewart's experience, it was the most devoted practitioners who were their own harshest critics, accepting responsibility with regret despite no adverse finding from the coroner and the ongoing endorsement of the Hospital Board. He wondered how Eva would decide to move forward after the case concluded.

CHAPTER 27

When Eva presented herself at the coroner's office, her timing coincided awkwardly with Gerry emerging from the interview room. The two women made eye contact but neither spoke to the other. Eva observed that Gerry did not appear to be accompanied by anyone, not even a lawyer.

Stewart arrived, and they were ushered into the interview room. The coroner asked the types of questions Stewart had prepared her to expect, and Stewart sat in silence as Eva gave the same answers she had either given him or she had allowed him to tweak the previous evening.

The procedure was not medical; Aneeka had volunteered to participate in a scientifically valid research program, having been recommended by her obstetrician as being in excellent health and keen to participate. The procedure was simple and straightforward and Aneeka had been unaffected by it, leaving in the same excellent state of health in which she had arrived.

Eva could not explain her stroke-like death, said to be caused by a reaction to a common headache tablet ingredient. And no, she did not believe this could have happened as a result of the minor procedure, but she felt saddened by the young woman's death, nevertheless.

When pressed on the nature of the procedure, Eva said she was unable to comment due to the Secrecy Act that she had signed. The procedure itself was simple, but the research program was top secret. Any questions relating to the research program should be referred to the Government.

The interview was short. However, just as it appeared to be drawing to a close, the coroner introduced a new case – one involving a Claus Proger, whose death appeared to be not dissimilar to Aneeka's.

Eva stared straight ahead, saying she knew no-one of that name.

"Who is this person, and what are you alleging is his connection to me?" she asked, just as she had been instructed to reply. But not by Stewart this time; instead, she had been further advised by a person she had not spoken to in many years – Leon.

Eva had taken the call from Leon late the night before. She'd noted that his voice was a little gravelly these days, but she'd still recognised it instantly. She had listened intently to his curt instructions during the brief call, not doubting his advice for a moment. She had not attempted to prolong the conversation by asking questions, and she'd immediately expunged all traces of the call, as Leon had instructed.

The interview concluded. After the coroner had left the room, Eva and Stewart reviewed her answers. "I don't believe you have anything to be concerned about," Stewart said. "It would seem to me you'll be back at work very soon and no case will go forward to the Judiciary."

Stewart paused, levelling his eyes on Eva's. "Unless there's more to this than you're sharing with me. What did you make of the questions about this Claus Proger? Do you really not know him?"

Eva held his gaze and repeated that she had no idea who Claus Proger was. Stewart seemed to believe her, and with that they both gathered their papers and left the room.

As they descended the steps leading out to the street, Stewart asked if Eva would like a coffee; however, not wishing to be further quizzed, and besides her car was waiting, she thanked him but declined the offer.

*

As the editor of UndPress, Rueben was kept informed of most comings and goings at the Judiciary Department by a well-rewarded lackey. Mostly this was money expended for little return, but on occasion it offered him some interesting intelligence.

As he reviewed the latest on that morning's activities, Rueben recognised Stewart's name but thought little of the name of Stewart's client.

Perhaps she is being interviewed over some civil matter? mused Rueben. There was a lot of that these days. Citizens who crossed a road at an unregulated spot seemed to be this month's target. Rueben planned to write an article about the increasing number of fines being handed out for very minor offences; however, he hadn't started this yet, partly because he was unsure of his own position on the matter.

One the one hand, he could argue that maybe the Government was right to try to correct the behaviour of these minor offenders in order to protect them; and, after all, the funds raised from the fines were being redirected into community projects. On the other hand, should the Government act as an 'overbearing quasi-parent' by reprimanding its citizens for not crossing the road at a designated crossing? A similar argument could perhaps be applied to fining citizens for exceeding the allowable number of plastic bags permitted per household or for failing to recycle enough of their waste.

He was also guilty of taking the easy way at times, despite recognising the sense behind the rulings. Perhaps the article he should be writing was one querying the legitimacy of the way the Government hovered over every aspect of its citizens' lives.

It was at this juncture of his internal debate that Rueben recalled the name Eva Baritz.

Isn't she the Government's leading astrophysicist? he thought, shrugging his shoulders. *Maybe I can work her into my article, demonstrate that no-one is above the law, however trivial that law, that kind of thing.* He could include a photo of the scientist – she was quite striking in appearance, as he recalled, so that could add to the appeal of the article. *Just as well the Government is yet to monitor this citizen's base thoughts,* he laughingly derided himself.

He messaged his contact to try and find out some details about why Eva Baritz had attended an interview. He didn't know Stewart Weisman personally, but he might try contacting him for a comment once he knew more about what Stewart's client had supposedly been up to.

*

Javier put the phone down with some relief. He had just spoken to a representative from the coroner's office who'd told him that at this stage there was insufficient evidence to consider laying any charge of malpractice against Professor Baritz. Her files supported all that the professor had claimed in her interview. The case would not proceed to the Judicial Courts, thereby allowing Professor Baritz to resume her duties. The officer also confirmed that the deceased's body had been officially released.

The officer had stated, however, that the coroner's official findings would be delayed until the nature of the professor's research became less opaque. The coroner would be seeking cooperation from the Government on this matter.

When pushed, the officer had told Javier, off the record, that if the Government felt it could not cooperate and disclose that information, then the coroner was likely to hand down a narrative verdict. This was because the deceased's participation in that research was alleged to be linked to her death by two eminent doctors, one of whom was the highly respected Professor Kupka.

Becoming quite loquacious, the officer had shared that Professor Kupka had also alleged there had been a previous death from that research. However, as Professor Baritz's files contained no reference to that matter, and she herself had been convincing in her denial of such an event, that case would almost certainly not proceed without something more substantial coming to light.

Good, thought Javier. *We managed to stay a step ahead.*

The officer had also noted that Professor Baritz had said she was saddened by what had happened and offered her condolences to the deceased's family. She had already reviewed her research and found no connection with the death. However, she had volunteered to re-review her research once more, and the officer had concluded that this would have given added impetus for her speedy return to work.

That's exactly the reason for not letting her return to work straight away, thought Javier. *If she tries to re-read the Proger and Raine cases, she'll discover the file tampering. We'll keep her on leave for a couple of days to give Cabut plenty of time to get his technicians back to restore the original files. After that, she'll likely be more interested in the space preparations than in going over old cases. Maybe Gretel can come up with a way of adding urgency to focus on the program ahead.*

Quite satisfied with the turn of events, Javier let Gretel's office know that the coroner would not be implicating either Baritz or Geary in the pregnant woman's death. However, the President would have to field a call from the coroner, one which he suggested she should handball to the Minister for Health.

He then notified Cabut that Eva would be returning to work after an additional day's leave, by which time her files needed to have been restored.

As an afterthought, he added he was keen to receive Cabut's response on 'that other matter'.

*

Bethany entered Gretel's office, immediately sensing that she was happy and excited about something.

Gretel is a strange person in some ways, thought Bethany as she sat in silence, patiently waiting while Gretel made tea for them both. You could never be sure what was going on in Gretel's mind. Some days she was very curt and gave only the briefest of acknowledgements when she passed her colleagues in the corridor, while on other days she would beam widely and treat her colleagues as if they had really brightened her day, simply by being present. She had to acknowledge that Gretel was a good president, however. She really did seem to care for the welfare of the Country's citizens.

Was Timothy right – is she really on the point of resigning? she wondered.

Bethany's mind focused as Gretel handed her a cup of tea in a porcelain teacup with a matching saucer.

"Green tea is said to be very good for one's health," said Gretel. "But do we believe this because it is marketed to us that way? Where are the controlled experiments to support such a claim?"

"If you have doubts, why do you drink it?"

"I drink it because I like the taste, I like the way it looks when served in good porcelain, and maybe I'm hedging my opinion on its claimed health benefits; they could be correct – but if not, no harm done," laughed Gretel.

Emboldened by Gretel's good mood, Bethany observed that Gretel had taken a stand against false advertising and over-excessive advertising, so if she wanted evidence to back the claim that green tea was good for you, why had she not used her legislation to bring the tea companies to task?

"Oh, Bethany," Gretel laughed. "Everything is about juggling and balance. By giving a little leeway in the not-very-important areas, you act as a small government, choosing not to interfere in the lives of its citizens." She took a sip of her tea, warming to her lecture topic.

"When you see a company make unsubstantiated claims about something serious, such as the quality of its fishery products – those obtained from an ocean that independent scientific tests tell us still contains traces of contaminants harmful to us – then that's the time for the Government to step in and force the company to cease its sales. But, importantly, at the same time we also bring the company, together with its workers, into the discussion. We include and reassign them in monitoring the situation and in finding the solution to cleaning up the ocean. Then the company can get back to selling its products. This is a big government move – acting to protect the lives of its citizens by providing a resolution that encourages the so-called 'bad guys' to help solve the problem, rather than become the problem."

Gretel giggled. "However, this is not why I wanted to see you, Bethany. What you and I are about to do, quite soon, is to address our citizens to announce the imminent launch of our space mission. We shall present to them our confidence that we have the capability to reach Earth and return home safely, and we shall explain *why* such a mission is important. I also want to refer to some of the side benefits, more immediate to improving our control and treatment of disease, that have been made possible through our space research."

Bethany felt as enthusiastic as Gretel at this news, and together the two spent nearly an hour in discussion until Gretel apologised that she was already late for an appointment and they'd have to wrap things up. They agreed to meet again in a couple of days.

It was only as Bethany was walking back to her own office, her mind buzzing with suggestions and excitement, that it occurred to her to think it odd that Professor Baritz had neither been present nor spoken of by Gretel. Shrugging off the thought, she reached her office.

CHAPTER 28

Aleck had wanted Cameron to be at the short funeral service – to hold him in his arms as he farewelled his beloved wife, and Cameron his mother. However, the medical advice he'd received strongly recommended against the idea, even for a short time and even with a nurse present. Cameron was holding his own and making progress but in no way was the tiny baby ready for release from care, Aleck had been sternly advised.

He found himself feeling grateful to Leon, who had taken on the task of acting as his secretary. It was Leon who had made the necessary bookings, hired the funeral director and the person who would conduct the service, organised the refreshments to be served after the service, and, in consultation with Aleck, notified all the people who might wish to attend. He had even made sure Aleck had a clean suit to wear.

The service was to be held in the same small building in which Aleck and Aneeka had exchanged their wedding vows. The building dated back many centuries and was one of the few ancient structures still standing. It was a site often used for community celebrations and times of mourning, thereby maintaining a link with the practices of the long-distant past. Once known as a church, the ancient peoples had gathered there to celebrate their religious beliefs.

That people had at one time worshipped various gods was taught as a part of history in the school curriculum. It served to remind the citizens that despite the comfort that these god-beliefs gave to some, the lack of rationality on the part of their ancestors had led to shocking wars and atrocities in the defence or the support of their particular god-belief. Today, thankfully, no-one could imagine worshipping some deity, let alone killing in that deity's name. Mathematics and science explained the workings of their universe, and the Government did not encourage any faith practice – other than to adopt from the Quakers the maxim that each human being was of unique worth.

However, some of the music of those times had been passed down through the ages, and Aleck was debating whether or not to include an ancient hymn in the service. In the end he decided not to: the music was beautiful, but the words weren't quite appropriate. He settled, instead, on some old classics of yesteryear: 'To Althea from Prison' by Fairport Convention for the gathering music, 'Dance Me to the End of Love' by Leonard Cohen to be sung as part of the service, and 'Nimrod' from Edward Elgar's Enigma Variations for the recessional. The celebrant would read the third verse of Thomas Moore's 'Farewell! But whenever you welcome the hour' since Aleck and Aneeka had both enjoyed that particular piece of poetry, and, of course, Aleck would deliver the eulogy. He had almost completed writing this, finding the experience emotionally draining and yet cathartic.

Making himself a cup of tea, Aleck carried it out into the small garden to drink while completing his words. He and Aneeka had often sat outside together, enjoying the light and the colour of their blooms, always promising that they would pay greater attention to caring for the garden (and rarely carrying out that promise). Despite its lack of attention, the little garden did its best to look cheerfully neglected; it was a comforting place.

*

It had been very strange to hear Eva's voice again, mused Leon as he sat out in his courtyard, taking in the sunshine. He'd carried out his part of the agreement with Javier to conceal any incriminating evidence that could be held against Eva. It was the logical course of action, and Leon was a very logical person; so, he was surprised at how difficult it had been for him to quell an emotional reaction that Eva should be held publicly responsible for the actions that had led to the death of his birth daughter.

He felt cross and uncomfortable with himself. He'd lived his life as a player of a game, a player who would make rational decisions at every turn, anticipating and covering any move of the other player or players by choosing the pathways with the greatest probability of success for him or his cause. He understood why Javier felt that he should be the one to make the call to Eva. Nevertheless, it had been a very difficult call to make.

A breeze rippled through the air, causing a small leaf to land in Leon's lap and another at his feet. As he bent to pick these up, Leon's mind was taken back to another sunny day.

Nolé was driving the coupé, with Leon squashed in the small back seat, holding a picnic basket packed full of goodies for their lunch and admiring the way Eva's hair rippled in the breeze as they drove along.

Halcyon days.

Leon had enormous regard and respect for Nolé, and he had been flattered that this esteemed mathematician had taken him under his wing. He had learnt so much from the older man and had been overjoyed that their professional relationship had developed into a friendship close enough to include Leon in Nolé and Eva's social life.

They had lunched on sandwiches washed down with copious glasses of wine, nibbled on cheeses and grapes washed down with more wine, laughed, argued and acted the fool in their inebriated states, and had a marvellous time before falling asleep, their bodies spread out on the soft grass. Sometime later it had started to rain, not heavily but enough to wake them from their drunken slumber. Although Eva had drunk the least (in fact, she'd been quite restrained), they'd decided that Leon was in the best shape of the three to drive them home. Nolé had insisted that he'd sit in the back seat nursing the now-empty wicker basket.

And so they had set off merrily, Leon enjoying the drive. The roof was now up to keep out the showers, but the fresh air that wafted in through the driver's open window had kept the cabin comfortable and unstuffy. Leon remembered that he and Nolé were discussing how to apply the 'prisoner's dilemma' to trade policies, and he'd taken his eye off the road briefly to look in the rear vision mirror at Nolé as he spoke. In that instant, the car had skidded on some loose gravel as they crossed a bridge over a river. Leon – probably because of his unfamiliarity with the car (many cars had been driverless by then), but possibly too because he still had some alcohol in his system – had applied the brakes and overcorrected. The car had hit the railing at a speed that carried it through the railing and over the edge into the water below.

Leon had hit his head on the dashboard as the car landed in the relatively shallow water. For a second or so he was out of it, but then groggily he'd come to. He hadn't been able to get the door open, but he had been able to climb out through the window. He'd rushed through the water around to the passenger door, managing to open it and to drag a semi-conscious Eva out. He'd pulled her over to the side of the river then returned to rescue Nolé, who was trapped, unconscious, in the back seat.

By this time, Nolé's head was under the water that had already entered the back of the car as it started sinking. Leon had worked furiously, trying to drag him up into air and over to the front seat. With superhuman effort he had finally succeeded in doing so, but his Herculean task had taken too long – Leon had realised then that Nolé was not going to survive. After dragging him to the riverbank, he'd applied CPR – but to no avail. Leon had contacted the emergency services before resuming his work on Nolé until the paramedics arrived and took over.

They had been taken to hospital. Nolé had not shown any response, so he had been rushed straight into the emergency ward.

Eva had also been admitted to the hospital.

After a thorough examination, Leon was told he had no serious injuries. All he could do was wait to hear how his friends were.

The sombre face of the approaching doctor told Leon what he'd already suspected: Nolé could not be revived, and he had been pronounced dead.

Leon remembered how he had wept for his friend.

Later, there had been further bad news to endure. Another doctor had told Leon that Eva's head injuries would require monitoring, but those were not life-threatening. However, she was very sorry to have to tell Leon that Eva had lost her baby. The complete surprise shown on

Leon's face caused the doctor to apologise. Did he not know Eva was three months pregnant?

Leon's blood alcohol reading had been 0.035, below the 0.05 level that would have seen him held responsible for the incident. Had the accident occurred in later years (when the Government had reduced the allowable reading to below 0.03), he would have been charged. Leon didn't need a reading: in his own mind, he would always hold himself responsible.

The death of Nolé had been shocking, the loss to the mathematical community inestimable; the death of Eva and Nolé's unborn child had been incredibly sad. The damage to Eva's mental wellbeing would have ongoing implications that would continue to cast a shadow over Leon for the rest of his life.

Remembering it all as he flicked the two leaves back onto the garden, Leon felt glad he'd warned Eva after all.

CHAPTER 29

Although Gretel was enjoying her light meal with Javier, she was more focused on their conversation than savouring the piquancy of the pancake filling. They had a lot to discuss: firstly, exactly when she was going to announce the space mission; and secondly, how soon after that event might she announce her retirement.

She also wanted to discuss who might take over the presidency. She was tending to favour Bethany; after all, she would be sharing in the kudos surrounding the space mission. On her own (quite long) list there was also Arjab, the Minister for Jobs, Pensions and Industrial Relations; Evan, the Minister for Family and Community Services; Hannah, the Minister for Planning; and she hadn't ruled out Stefano either, the youngish Minister for Energy and the Environment.

"You know, Javier, I've been so blessed with the people I have worked with in government. There are so many that rightfully could claim to be ready to stand for the presidency. Maybe it would be simpler to draw up a list of those less suitable for the task!"

Javier laughed. "It's strange that I haven't received Cabut's list," he commented. "Personally, I think it will be a contest between Evan, Bethany and Grigor, who's done a good job in Health and who may be owed a favour depending on how this business with the coroner plays out. And don't dismiss Timothy. He won't be on our lists, but he will almost certainly campaign for the position."

"I think his colleagues will recognise that he is driven by his self-serving interests rather than more altruistic ones," said Gretel dryly.

"Agreed," replied Javier. "Now, getting back to the timeline, my advice is you declare you have two significant announcements to make, and you make them both together in your broadcast to the citizens.

"First, elaborate on the major initiative of the space mission and involve Bethany as you've already planned, especially if she becomes our preferred candidate. Then, announce that you wish to share with all citizens that you have requested that your Inner Cabinet activates the start of the process for considering who should succeed you as president, since it is your intention to retire in due course. You announce this now in order to give plenty of time to carefully select your replacement. Stress that for the time being you will continue, as you have always done, to devote yourself to the service of your country and its citizens, and that citizens can be assured that the Government's activities will proceed as usual," outlined Javier.

"And, as a further suggestion, what do you think of the idea of publicly inviting any citizen who wishes to express an opinion to make it known to their OCM representative, who will, as always, collect and pass on such comment?"

"I think I would use the word 'remind' rather than 'invite'," replied Gretel thoughtfully. "In broad terms, the rest sounds a good start to work on, thank you darling – although I wonder whether the space mission might run the risk of being overshadowed by news of my retirement? Maybe it's more prudent to stagger the two announcements. Let's allow things to run around our heads for a little longer before we make any firm decisions."

Javier shrugged, and Gretel continued.

"There is something else we have to face, and that is what to do about Eva. Given the current cloud over her, I don't think it's wise for her to join me to announce the mission, do you?"

Javier nodded in agreement, adding that they also needed to decide what to do about Eva in the long term.

"I know, darling, it's such a worry. I'd like to think we could announce her early retirement once the mission has launched and the capsule has moved beyond our universe. I'm keen to avoid having to take my successor too much into our confidence about her mental fragility."

Javier suggested that perhaps Leon could be called on to help with Eva. The mention of Leon quite surprised Gretel. She had total confidence in Javier's ability to find solutions to awkward problems, but, as he did not elaborate further, she decided not to pursue the subject.

They moved on to dessert, a light meringue roulade filled with a raspberry cream laced with a trace of brandy. Gretel asked Javier what the effect of her decision to retire would likely hold for him. Javier grinned, that roguish, boyish grin of his that she so loved.

"Madam President, you know I exist only to serve you, my lady," he said, as Gretel giggled.

"So, I will join you in retirement, and we can sail away – just like the Owl and the Pussy-cat," he added.

Then, more seriously, Javier added that although he was not sure he was ready to completely retire, the incoming president was likely to appoint his or her own choice for his position, so his time in government circles was coming to an end. He explained that he saw this as an opportunity to do something quite different from his current role, but he hadn't really given much thought to what that might be.

"I think you are making the right decision my Gretel petal, for both of us. I could always become a chef, given all my experience feeding you over these last many years," he joked.

*

An unusually sullen and preoccupied Timothy was dining in a private room with a group of friends, impervious to the chatter swirling around him.

He was still feeling left out of the loop. No further message from Leon – *had he in some way offended the older man?* No word from Gretel either, not even any gossip from her staff. But something was happening, because Bethany was like a bitch on heat.

He'd been busy dropping hints that Gretel may be under some pressure and could be considering resignation, but he'd had limited success. While people were initially keen to gossip, they soon lost interest when he couldn't add further fuel to stoke the rumour. No-one seemed especially keen to discuss potential front runners for the presidency, and Timothy continued to be a bit miffed that few raised his name without a nudge from him.

To add to his woes, his plans for forcibly acquiring land to expand the road networks were not being received well by the citizens, as more than one OCM had pointed out. The citizens who lived in the affected areas were becoming bolder and lobbying their representatives in protest.

Things are going downhill when the citizens feel they know better than an Inner Cabinet minister; good government procedures should not be allowed to be disputed, he vented silently, claiming this as a failure on the part of the President. *Who knows where this could lead if she doesn't come down harder on the ill-informed commentary of the citizenry?* he grumbled, although he knew he was being priggish and unreasonable. And, in that revelatory moment, Timothy acknowledged to himself that any failure was actually more his own making, not that of the President or the affected citizens; he needed to listen more, to lift his game. He promised his developing better half that he'd try harder.

His thoughts were interrupted by one of his companions asking curiously, "Do tell, Timothy, what's occupying your mind so much that you're not giving us the benefit of your witty repartee?"

"My apologies, chaps and chapesses. Yes, I am a bit distracted. Work pressures, you know how it is. Something big about to happen, but sorry – can't share quite yet. Here, let me get the next round and I promise to relax once I've had my next Mickey Slim – and you all know I do like my Mickeys to be slim."

Banging their spoons, those at the table roared: "Welcome back!"

He headed to the bar and gave the bartender the list of drinks required. As he started to make his way back to the private room, his device pinged. Reading the message lifted his spirits enormously. It was from Gretel's office, urging all ministers to make every effort to attend the upcoming Cabinet meeting. There wasn't usually such a reminder. Ministers were simply expected to attend, unless there were extenuating circumstances that Gretel was aware of anyway. So, something was happening.

With fresh energy, Timothy re-joined his friends, promising to 'lighten up'.

*

Rueben's takeaway noodles had been washed down by an ale as he sat at his desk, the sole person still at the office. It was his wife's book club evening, and as it was her turn to host the gathering, Rueben was in no hurry to go home.

That sad fact was true for other evenings, which did not escape Rueben's mind. His marriage had deteriorated into tolerated co-existence, with little of joint interest that he shared with his wife. They had simply grown apart. *Such is life,* he thought, dismissing any further contemplation of his marital arrangements.

What was absorbing him right now was the new information he'd received about Professor Baritz. Her interview with the coroner had not involved some minor infringement after all.

Rueben was an astute person, usually with an excellent nose for what was going on. In his mind he was beginning to join some dots. The Government had been uncomfortable about the article he'd published about that citizen for Leon. Could Professor Baritz have had some connection with the citizen?

He hadn't heard from Leon for a while, but he knew he was not someone to give up on a cause when his wind was up. Perhaps he'd give him a call to sound him out on his hunch. Acting on that thought straightaway, he rang Leon on the number he had for him. There was no answer, so he left a message for Leon to call him back.

Undeterred, Rueben considered how else he could confirm the link between the professor and the missing citizen. He could try the professor's solicitor now he had a better idea of what to ask, or perhaps Jacques could help him out if that failed. He rang the contact number for Stewart Weisman, not expecting an answer out of working hours but intending to leave a message. To his surprise, a male voice answered.

"Weisman speaking."

Rapidly collecting his thoughts together, Rueben explained who he was and that he was interested in Professor Baritz's appearance at the coroner's office.

"Could the solicitor make a comment for the press on how his client's interview went?"

There was a pause at the other end before Stewart replied. "My client and the coroner had a productive meeting, ending with complete satisfaction on both sides."

"Were the proceedings to investigate a misconduct charge against a colleague of your client, or even your client herself?" persisted Rueben.

"There have been no charges made against my client; she was lending her expertise to an inquiry of interest to the Judiciary," replied Stewart in an even tone.

Deciding to place all his bets on his hunch and sensing the lawyer was on the point of disconnecting the call, Rueben managed to squeeze in one more question.

"Can you confirm that inquiry was about a Claus Proger?" he asked.

"I know of no such person. Now I must say goodbye," said Stewart in his calm lawyer voice, ending the call.

Looks like I'm wrong again and there's nothing much of interest here, dammit, thought Rueben. *She won't be my headline for tomorrow's paper. I'd better continue with the opposition to the proposed road network expansion.*

He set to work to finish compiling his broadsheet for the next day, not bothering to call Jacques.

CHAPTER 30

Aleck was surprised at how composed he had managed to be at Aneeka's funeral. He had wanted the service to honour her, for her to be at the centre of everyone's thoughts. He had delivered his eulogy without incident, managing to quell the few tremors in his voice and to hold his tears till the end as Aneeka's casket took its last journey.

He was surprised by the number of people who were there. Many of them he didn't know, or didn't remember, but they came to pay their respects, telling him they'd been at school or university or yoga class with Aneeka, or they knew her in a myriad of other ways. A large number of Aleck's colleagues attended, in addition to Aneeka's former workmates, and he was moved by Bruce Daniels' sympathy and his kind offer to discuss at another time how best to balance Aleck's work commitments with caring for Cameron. Aleck also appreciated the presence and support of Matilda and Mikhail who, by now, he had come to consider close family. Also, although she did not stay for the refreshments, he was touched that Gerry had attended the service.

Emotionally exhausted as he was, Aleck chose not to return home after the wake but to travel to the hospital to visit his son. He found himself talking to his little man, processing his emotions by debriefing him on the day's proceedings. He promised Cameron again that he would do his utmost to keep Aneeka's memory alive so that he would come to know his mother through his father's stories.

Finally, Aleck returned home. There he found a number of items laid out for him, including the Book of Remembrances that many of the mourners had signed, a vase filled with a few of the flowers that weren't taken in the hearse with the casket, and several plates filled with leftover food from the wake. A deep gratitude towards Leon flooded through Aleck's soul. He'd been so thoughtful and supportive. Aleck messaged

Leon to invite him to join him that evening to share some of the leftovers between them. He finally felt an acceptance of, and an appreciation for, his father's old friend.

*

Eva's life had returned to its normal routine. Her car picked her up in the morning, taking her to the Departments where she greeted Cabut each day, on duty as always. As she entered her office on her first day back, she wondered if Cabut had remained sat at his station over the days of her absence but, knowing Cabut was not one for chit-chat, she kept that thought to herself.

Cabut had placed a neat list of tasks on her desk, the first of which was to contact Bethany Cresswell, the minister seconded to her by the President. Wondering whether a problem had developed in her absence, Eva immediately phoned the minister's office, identifying herself and asking to speak to Minister Cresswell.

Bethany enthusiastically greeted Eva, telling her she had great news but would have to be brief right now because she was shortly due at a meeting.

"Eva, the President has approved the launch date and is about to announce the mission to the Cabinet. Then she intends to address the citizens so that they can share in the excitement. I'm sorry this is the first you've heard of this development, but I was told you were on leave and unable to be contacted when I tried to arrange a meeting with you earlier."

Not waiting for Eva to respond, Bethany quickly continued that she wanted Eva to provide briefing notes for the address. "I'm not sure whether it's just Gretel speaking or whether you or I may be called on to say something."

Eva expressed her delight and enthusiasm, promising to send briefing notes to her that very day, and she scheduled a meeting with Bethany for a few days' time. She then let the minister get back to the world of government business.

She reordered Cabut's task list, postponing for the time being the instruction to contact her lawyer, Stewart Weisman. Eva was back in charge of her domain.

*

Knowing Eva had returned to work, Stewart was a little annoyed that she hadn't yet returned his call, despite his insistence to her personal assistant that she needed to do so. He had arrived at work early that morning to conduct a search for Claus Proger. His searches so far had turned up very little. He couldn't find any birth records; then, on wondering whether the person was a migrant, he found he couldn't identify any record of his admission either. There were no health records, employment records or financial records.

He was beginning to believe there was no such person until, intriguingly, his search did yield two hits: one was in UndPress, where Stewart read of a request for information about a citizen named Claus Proger, and the other was in a list of winners of a darts competition at a small hotel, dated before the UndPress article. *It would seem there is, or was, such a person, but it's hard to imagine any connection with Eva,* he reasoned. *That is, unless she also plays darts!* The thought caused him to laugh out loud.

Stewart put in a call to Rueben, who answered rather groggily, it being quite early in Rueben's day. He explained that he'd been intrigued by his question about Claus Proger, so he'd looked into his background and found Rueben's article.

Rueben told him that he hadn't written the Proger article, it had been a paid advertisement. When Stewart pressed Rueben on who had paid for it, Rueben sighed. Grudgingly, he made the point that had he, Rueben, written the article he would not be willing to reveal his source; however, as this had been a commercial transaction, he could confirm that Stewart would find the author easily through UndPress's public records.

"However, I'll save you the trouble of searching. It was Leon Hartland who paid for the article to be published. Maybe you know him?" said Rueben.

"Not personally, although I do know of him," replied Stewart. "Odd that he would be enquiring about this Proger person. Were there any responses?"

"Yes, there were a few – not many, but a few, nevertheless. Whether they helped Leon with his cause or not I cannot say, and, as you will understand, I cannot release the responses to you because they're Leon's property," said Rueben.

Stewart thanked Rueben, adding that he appreciated his help and wouldn't forget it. As he ended the call, he wondered what that help might cost him in the future when Rueben was looking for a source.

Stewart reflected on what little he knew of Leon. He knew he'd been born into a rich family and that he had substantially increased his already considerable wealth through his online betting businesses; he also knew Leon was a person of considerable influence. However, he had never met him.

Work beckoned, so he had to put the matter aside for the time being, but Stewart promised himself that when Eva finally got around to contacting him, he would ask her what connection, if any, she had with Leon Hartland.

*

The Government's ministers had been speculating about why the President had reminded them to be present at that morning's meeting. Timothy was enjoying the greater deference being shown towards him and his apparent insight, particularly given how peeved he had felt on seeing the front-page piece in UndPress about the opposition to his plans to extend the road system.

Gradually, the ministers found their way to the meeting room and settled themselves in their usual seats around the elliptical table that filled much of the room. It was a bit like a school assembly with assigned seats, and woe betide any young member of staff who sat on the first available seat only to have to sheepishly vacate it when a senior colleague arrived to claim it as their own.

Glancing around, Timothy noticed that there was no sign of Bethany. For a moment, he feared that Gretel was about to announce her appointment as 'heir designate'. His fear was further heightened by Bethany arriving with the President.

The meeting proceeded as normal. Timothy was called upon to elaborate on his roads plan. He answered questions directed at him openly, clearly explaining the reasoning behind his decisions. In acknowledging the concerns of those citizens whose lands would be possessed, he gave some details of the compensation packages that were being developed. He assured his colleagues that he was confident that homes would be found for each person, albeit with some in adjoining areas. His colleagues seemed calmed by his response and impressed by his level of detail, both sentiments that appeared to be shared by the President.

Finally, they reached the last matter on the agenda, an address from the President herself.

Gretel described the space mission, and Bethany added some observations from the perspective of her role in the mission. There was a general buzz of enthusiasm around the room. The ministers passed an informal but unanimous vote of approval, commending the President on her initiative. It was only after Gretel added that she and Bethany would be addressing the citizens so they could share in the excitement that Timothy felt a little pang of jealousy. He quickly subdued his reaction, feeling quite a genuine admiration for what Gretel was about to achieve. Besides, he consoled himself, since no announcement of pending retirement had been made, there was still time for him to overshadow Bethany as Gretel's favourite.

In a good frame of mind, he joined his colleagues for the celebratory finger food lunch that Gretel had provided.

CHAPTER 31

Eva cordially greeted the two astronauts chosen for the space mission, introducing herself as Professor Baritz and inviting them to call her Eva. In turn, each astronaut followed suit, introducing themselves as Sebastian ("call me Seb") and Tanzi ("call me Tanzi"), which broke the ice as all three smiled.

It would be part of Eva's duties to ensure that both Tanzi and Seb were crystal clear about their responsibilities on the mission. Today would be an outline only: the technical aspects to be taught in later sessions, subject to the astronauts' progress.

They would both be launched into space, monitored by Eva and the ground personnel. However, as they approached the extremities of their galaxy, Seb was to be fired in a smaller capsule from the main spacecraft. It was critical that this stage of the mission went exactly as planned. In order for the capsule to pass through to the adjacent universe and the galaxy containing the planet Earth, it would enter and tunnel through the black hole that served as a connecting passage between the two universes.

Eva's work in astronomy and astrophysics had culminated in her belief that in the multiverse, each universe was spawned through a black hole, the process being ongoing. She used the analogy that a black hole was in a sense equivalent to the birth canal of a human being – no black hole meant that a particular universe would be barren.

Since each universe contained a myriad of galaxies, even the smallest of errors could land Seb in a galaxy other than the Milky Way (where he would find the Goldilocks planet Earth). Seb could also experience other challenges carrying significant risk, ones that would be exacerbated by the loss of communication with ground control once he entered the black hole. It was hoped that communication could be maintained through Tanzi on the mother craft. She would continue to travel along the extreme edges of their own galaxy for a year, maintaining contact with ground control at the Space Centre base and, if all went well, re-establishing contact with Seb as his craft exited the black hole and travelled towards Earth.

Both astronauts were already familiar with this scenario. They were showing much bravery, the level of bravery shown by previous renowned explorers who had opened up new frontiers. Eva acknowledged this to them both.

What they, Seb especially, were keen to learn about now was how Eva planned to use the dark energy of the black hole to their advantage. She explained how precise the trajectory of Seb's entry into the medium must be – that it must coincide with the peak of the amplitude of the wave motion of the energy so that he could gain sufficient momentum to rise to the next peak, and so on.

"But don't worry about those details, because that's what we back home will be ensuring," she said. "However, once you're in that hole, Seb, it will be up to you to carry through what you will be trained to do in the coming weeks in order to survive as you ride the energy wave. There will be no possibility of help or double-checking with anyone at all during that dangerous passage: your training must carry you through. One tiny miscalculation and that's the end of you, the craft and the mission."

"You can rely on me to absorb all that you are about to train me to do, Major General Professor," remarked Seb formally. "This mission is exactly why I have trained as an astronaut, and I'm both excited and honoured to be chosen for it."

"Good, that's why the pair of you were chosen. We will be relying on you both."

Eva went on to say that Tanzi would also be trained to navigate the portal as a back-up should for some unforeseen reason there be a need to switch roles at the last minute. She added that another reason was for Tanzi's own safety, since for her to be able to pick up any communication from Seb once he was safely through to the next galaxy, her craft needed to be as close to the asymptotic edge as possible.

"It is something I believe we can manage, but, again, if something unforeseen occurs, Tanzi's craft could be sucked down another hole on the edge. If that were to happen, I am not confident that Tanzi's training would be of much help unless she is able to get the trajectory angle of entrance right, something difficult to do when you're falling in by accident rather than by design," Eva matter-of-factly observed.

Tanzi assured Eva that she was prepared to take the risk and that she would learn thoroughly everything that Eva was planning to teach her. She added that, like Seb, she was thrilled to be involved and honoured to have been chosen.

"However," Tanzi continued, "I am curious how you will monitor Seb's body to withstand the energy forces while he negotiates his way through the black hole tunnel."

"That's a good question, Tanzi," said Eva. "That problem has occupied my time and research for so many years. In fact, only recently did I finally come up with the last part of the solution. I'll be teaching you how to alter your DNA sequencing back and forth with a simple keystroke, which will adjust and reverse your needs as you progress through the tunnel."

Eva elaborated. "It's been a very exciting breakthrough, the antithesis of much of what constitutes current research, with its focus on the transition from robotic form to human-like appearance. The reverse transition from human to a robotic state has been less examined, prior to my research."

With a trace of not so much pride as a sense of accomplishment, Eva added, "I believe I have conceived the way a human can switch to a temporary robotic state in order to sustain life in extreme conditions, yet be able to reverse that process and resume a normal human state once the adverse event has passed."

Looking at her two students, she smiled. "And so, our mission became viable."

Then, as an afterthought, Eva asked: "By the way, do either of you suffer from headaches?" When both said they did not, Eva nodded, then added: "And, although they are not just headaches, I assume neither of you suffer from migraines? Real migraines, I mean."

Again, the pair assured her they did not, looking questioningly at her. Eva shrugged and said she was simply checking because her research had indicated a very small correlation between her process and some headache medications. "Non-causal relationship, however," she emphasised.

Quickly moving on, Eva said, "Okay, let's visit the lab where the training process will take place."

Opening the door to usher the pair out to the passageway, she invited Tanzi and Seb to follow her, pausing to introduce Cabut. There was an awkward moment as both astronauts outstretched an arm, intending to shake Cabut's hand, but Cabut's hands remained resolutely on his keyboard.

As the three of them moved on, Eva whispered, "Cabut suffers from an alexithymia disorder," repeating a suggestion that Gerry, who had never met Cabut, had once casually proffered, based on Eva's description. That, as Eva momentarily remembered, was at a time when she and Gerry were able to happily socialise and speak drolly of their private secretaries.

After showing Seb and Tanzi around the lab, Eva returned to her office, alone. She would meet with the astronauts, now her students, the following day to get stuck into the serious maths. Right now, however, she needed to prepare the briefing for Minister Cresswell, then ring Stewart Weisman.

When she finally did get to call Stewart, they had a brief conversation in which Stewart told her that at this stage she was not required for further interviews regarding her handling of the pregnant woman's case.

"The death is to be recorded as due to unforeseen natural causes, with no suggestion of fault on anyone's part," Stewart said.

Eva expressed her thanks to her lawyer and presumed that would be the end of the conversation. However, she was surprised when he asked her if she was a friend of Leon Hartland. Choosing to dismiss his recent brief contact, Eva merely confirmed that there was a connection between them. She explained that some long time ago they had been colleagues, friends even, but that they had lost touch.

*

Stewart ended his call from Eva feeling that he might be barking up the wrong tree. It was a bit odd that Eva hadn't asked why he had raised Leon's name. Still, Eva was a bit odd herself in some ways. As the question didn't affect her directly, perhaps she just wasn't curious.

Stewart decided not to try to contact Leon and to consider that Eva's case was now closed.

*

Leon and Aleck were polishing off the last of the leftovers. It was Leon's second visit to Aleck's house since Aneeka's funeral. They'd been reminiscing, exchanging further thoughts over aspects of the funeral service, looking through more family photos Aleck had dug out of a cupboard, crying, laughing and talking about Cameron's future.

Leon had made an offer to unofficially 'adopt' them both, which Aleck thought was a form of kindness until he realised Leon was semi-serious. Leon explained that it was something he'd been thinking about ever since the news of Aneeka's death had reached him. His offer was that the three of them would share a home, a large one, where Leon would have separate quarters but be available to look after and care for Cameron. In short, he wanted to treat Aleck as a de facto son and Cameron as his own grandson.

He reminded Aleck that he was obscenely wealthy, so there were no financial concerns about the offer; it would also cover ongoing medical costs and nursing staff at the home, if required. Aleck could continue his work as a solicitor, and, in due course, take time off to study to become a barrister. Leon would be at home for Cameron; his own work, if such it be called, able to be conducted at times that suited him.

"There would be no need for you to change careers just so your working hours as a teacher would give you more time at home, Aleck. Besides, you surely must remember how busy both your parents were as teachers; you might well find you have more time to yourself as a barrister!"

Aleck was very touched by Leon's offer, and of course he could see a number of advantages, but he knew he could never accept such a proposal.

Not wanting to hurt Leon's feelings, he prevaricated by saying that much depended on how disabled Cameron would be, which was not known, as yet.

"I like you Leon, I'm not sure I did at first, but now I think you are a truly decent person. I'm glad you're my son's grandfather. I can accept generosity from you for Cameron, but less so for myself. Let's talk some more about your suggestion after I've had more time to consider it. For now, I don't rule out either rejecting or accepting your proposal, let's just see how things go …" Aleck shrugged as his voice trailed off.

One thing was not hypothetical – he was firm about changing careers. He wanted Leon to realise that his plan to become a teacher was not entirely due to Cameron's situation. He had been increasingly feeling a desire to become a teacher, just like his parents.

"Let me show you something that's helped me reach that decision," Aleck said, thumbing through some of the sympathy cards he'd received. Finding the one he wanted, he showed Leon the message he'd received from his two Service students.

It read: 'To Alik very sorry u have lost your wife from Nath and Sammi', the signatures of the two scrawled under the message.

Leon smiled, commenting that the two young men clearly needed a teacher but at least their hearts were in the right place.

"Okay, Aleck, I do understand. Nevertheless, I want you to understand that it's not only important to me to help Cameron; if I can help you at this critical time in your life as well, then I'll feel I have gone some way towards discharging the debt I owe your father. Did you know that he was detained in custody because of me?"

"Absolutely not!" said Aleck, somewhat taken aback.

"Then indulge me by letting me tell you the one remaining part of the story about your father that I haven't shared. When I finish, you might understand why I want to look after both you and Cameron." He then began to fill in some gaps in what had already been a long story.

"I told you once that your father never let me down, but I've never fully explained what I meant by that cryptic remark. For a while after I completed my doctoral thesis, I became somewhat of a thorn in the side of the Government. This created interesting relationships, shall we say. I uncovered some less than ethical happenings within certain government departments, but, as I was wealthy and a generous donor to some government schemes, there remained a desire to keep me on side. Still, it seems that some in the Government had decided I needed to be taught a lesson.

Pausing to look up at Aleck, Leon observed: "This is what happens in RevDem. It's all very well to argue that without an opposition and an electoral cycle to distract the sitting government, it can get on and do good works and develop long-term plans. But it's exactly the existence of these checks that keeps governments honest and prevents those in them from forgetting why they're in office in the first place. There is too little accountability these days."

Disputing this, Aleck was quick to respond. "People can have a say, especially through the OCMs, and every talented citizen has a chance, should they be interested, in being offered the opportunity to serve in the Government."

"That's exactly what they want you to believe, Aleck. The President has too much power in being able to choose those who are brought into the Government as ministers. Surround yourself with your cronies and you're hardly likely to find them disagreeing with you. In some ways we're lucky that President Nuewen is a decent enough sort of person, driven by a desire to make life better for the average citizen. Even so, she turns a blind eye to the operations that target any nonconformist citizen who starts to become argumentative, and when she goes, who's to say what type of person will become president? Certainly, the people won't have a say in it."

When Aleck did not respond, Leon gave a laugh and apologised for his soapbox address. Picking up the threads, he returned to his tale.

"There is a person called Jacques, he's worked for both the Homer and Nuewen governments, and he's been brought in to 're-educate' some of the Country's citizens. Indeed, at one time I mistook Jacques to be a friend, long before I became aware that creating that feeling in me was part of his psychological expertise. While I haven't seen Jacques since that unfortunate incident, he knew that your father and I had been friends, and of course he knew that Colin had protected me. In his vindictive way he reasoned that if I knew Colin was being detained to punish me, then I would back down on my so-called interference in the workings of the Government."

"Are you saying that my father was arrested?" interjected a puzzled Aleck. "I have no recollection of that."

"Yes," murmured Leon. "Twice, in fact."

Aleck shook his head – he didn't remember anything like that happening, unless it had happened before he was born.

"Do you remember your father going away on a school camping trip, Aleck?" asked Leon gently.

Aleck admitted that he did, commenting that while some of the students might have felt they were being held there against their wishes, a school camp could hardly qualify as detainment. And then he realised where Leon was going with this.

"There was no school camp – that was just what your parents told you to explain your father's absence," Leon explained.

After a stunned silence, Aleck asked what kind of mistreatment his father would have endured.

"I don't believe he suffered any physical harm, but I can only say what your mother told me," said Leon. "The school had been told Colin was on leave due to illness and that he was receiving treatment. Of course, there was no illness. She told me Colin spoke each day to a person called Jacques, but otherwise he was left to his own devices. He'd even joked that he'd used the time to catch up on his preparations and corrections and had the luxury of doing some reading."

"What did he talk to Jacques about?"

"According to your mother, they often had a normal conversation – but your father was wary of him, sensing there was something remote about him, despite him seeming to be pleasant. Jacques told your father that he was being held in custody to punish me, not because he himself had done anything wrong. Colin was also told that he could gain early release if he could give an example of any dishonest behaviour on my part. Despite not knowing how long he was to be held for, Colin had said there were only good things that he could say of me."

"How did this Jacques fellow respond to that?" asked Aleck.

"Colin told your mother that Jacques had merely smiled. He was released a couple of days later and told to maintain the story that he had been ill."

"What happened the second time?"

"I gather that it was fairly similar, except Colin saw less of Jacques. However, he briefly met someone called Cabut, whom he found to be rather strange – very cold and almost robotic in demeanour."

"Did you ever meet me?" asked Aleck out of curiosity.

"I knew your mother Elmira well enough to know Colin was a lucky man to have found such a strong, supportive and kind partner as her. As for you, no, I did not have that pleasure, but I'm sure you were quite delightful," laughed Leon.

"Why did the incarcerations cease?" asked Aleck, returning to the story.

"The Government and I came to an agreed compromise," was all that Leon volunteered.

"Did you speak to my father about his arrests?"

"It was your father's wish that we continue our separate ways, as I've said before. He insisted that I was to have no contact with him. Until I came to you for professional help, I kept to that bargain."

"And Jacques? What happened to him?"

"Very interesting question, Aleck. He's managed to avoid direct contact with me ever since that time when I thought he was befriending me. But I've set it as a high priority to find him, and I'm getting closer. Have you noticed the driver who's been bringing me over here of late? I'm pretty sure Clovis is working for Jacques."

Digressing a little, Leon observed: "Clovis is quite an interesting character. On the one hand he fits the type Jacques likes to have around – minor criminal record, nondescript background, not very well-educated, good at following orders. However, I think I see more in him. He's been a rebellious adolescent, but his family has solid values and he is intelligent."

Smiling at Aleck, he laughed. "With a teacher like you Aleck, he could flourish. I like Clovis, and I'm cultivating our relationship, not only because I think it will lead me to be able to confront Jacques one day, but also because I'd like Clovis to work for me," Leon confided.

"Maybe there's a bit of a teacher in you too, wanting to bring out the best in Clovis," acknowledged Aleck, adding thoughtfully, "You're full of causes, Leon."

"I am," replied Leon, "but a teacher I definitely am not." He laughed. "Now, it's been a long day and it's time I left and traded your company for that of Clovis."

"Thank you for everything you have done to get me through these last several days, Leon, and for your company and honesty this evening," he said, walking Leon to the door and warmly embracing him as the older man took his leave. "I'll be in touch."

CHAPTER 32

Eva was feeling unsettled. Stewart's call had reminded her of Aneeka's death, which, combined with the impact of meeting her students in person – such young, intelligent, impressively brave human beings – had made her feel unexpectedly emotional.

She had dismissed Aneeka's death as unrelated to her research, yet why had she quizzed Seb and Tanzi about their experience of headaches? She was certain, completely certain, that the procedure had been validated by her tests, but what about the headache tablet Aneeka had taken several days later? Was it possible that the tablet's ingredients could have caused such a severe adverse reaction as a result of the procedure?

She had no wish for any harm to occur to her astronauts, both for their own sakes and, above all, for the fate of the mission. What could she do? Time was of the essence; she had no time left to investigate the effects of the ingredients of the headache tablets after completing the procedure. She couldn't even run a test on a chimpanzee (and even if she could, those beautiful animals were not readily available) – and besides, she'd used up her goodwill with their keepers a long time ago.

There was a simple way to deal with this, she eventually concluded, but it would need presidential backing. The first aid equipment for the astronauts on the space mission must contain no headache tablets – only natural therapies should be provided for treating ailments such as headaches and motion sickness. B-complex vitamin supplements and the likes. Also, as some headache medications contained caffeine, including the brand Aneeka had used, herbal teas and decaffeinated coffee should replace the more usual range of teas and coffees. As the drinks would be carried in dehydrated form, the astronauts might not even notice the taste difference.

A full inventory would need to be reviewed for both of the spacecraft. She would need to order the ground crew to check, assess and replace anything containing any of the pharmaceuticals identified in the tablet Aneeka had taken. Accordingly, she sent her recommendations to Gretel for official approval.

*

Gretel had been pleased with the genuine level of excitement about the space mission expressed by her Cabinet ministers. She was also grateful that Javier had reconsidered the timing of her resignation – his rationale being that both announcements were a cause to celebrate her presidency, so she should enjoy each singly.

She had decided to announce her pending retirement after the successful launch of the spacecraft. This meant she could also time her departure from office to coincide with Eva's enforced retirement, there being little Eva could do for at least a year once the capsule had left the mothership.

After the thrill of her Cabinet announcement and the enthusiastic discussions over lunch, Gretel found it hard to settle. However, she was pleased to be distracted by a request from Eva asking her to authorise a 'no drugs' policy on board the spacecraft. She thought it was an excellent insurance policy, one she was happy, indeed relieved, to endorse.

She left the office early so she could dine with Javier at his preferred hour.

"Hello darling, dinner smells lovely. What have you prepared for this evening?" she said, kissing him lightly.

"'Wait and see' pie, my petal," replied Javier as he rolled out some pastry. "Should be ready in forty-five minutes."

"In that case, I'll take a quick shower before joining you," said Gretel as she disappeared through to the bathroom.

She showered and changed into a kaftan dress of subdued but multiple colours. With her wet hair tousled rather than straightened into its usual immaculate bob, she felt happy and relaxed. Javier smiled appreciatively on her return.

Gretel poured them each a glass of white wine and proposed a toast. "To the success of the space mission."

Thanking Javier again for his advice and saying she couldn't imagine life without him, she kissed him again, this time on the lips. Javier grinned invitingly. "The pie still needs twenty-five minutes in the oven," he said, taking Gretel's hand and leading her towards their bedroom.

Later, as they were finishing their dinner with cheese, walnuts and quince, Gretel again raised the issue of what to do about Eva.

"We've agreed that she should be retired around the same time as I retire; we can't expect my successor to be as tolerant of her behaviour as we have been, nor would I want my legacy to be damaged by having to explain certain cover-ups." Javier nodded his agreement.

"But what's Eva going to do? She has no interests beyond her work, she has no friends left … she can't just stay in her apartment doing nothing," continued Gretel.

"Mm, you're right about the friends. After this last episode, she'll have lost Geraldine as a friend – the one remaining person she socialised with," agreed Javier.

"So, here's what I've been thinking, Javier. Before I retire, what if I appoint her as an emeritus professor of mathematics at the university? She can have her own office, and maybe she could supervise doctorate candidates, or perhaps tutor a little. As part of her package, perhaps we could promise her a driver, one that could monitor her movements …"

Javier stopped her at that point. "All our attempts to monitor Eva have failed to prevent, shall we say, some regrettable incidents. Are you seriously proposing that we allow promising young students to be around her? Even if she stays well, she's not likely to care about any hardship a student might be facing. Pastoral care would not be her long suit."

"She'd only be helping and teaching them mathematics, for goodness' sake! What harm can come from that?" replied Gretel defensively, adding that stricter tabs on Eva could be achieved by Javier asking that special contact of his to provide more thorough surveillance.

"My 'special contact', as you put it, does not operate cheaply. We'll no longer be able to pay for his services through the Government's finances once you depart, so I don't see how we can use him."

There was a brief silence, which she broke by saying, somewhat petulantly, "I know who'll pay: Leon! After all, if he hadn't crashed that car, killing Nolé and leaving Eva with brain and psychological damage, not forgetting no longer pregnant, we wouldn't have had to carry this burden as a government for all these years. So there, Javier, I've come to agree with what you've alluded to before. Leon could pay."

She was surprised, however, when Javier chose to ignore her endorsement, opting instead to present another suggestion. He suggested that, if they were looking for an unusual solution, he'd been pondering whether there was any way to include Eva on the spacecraft. Before she could respond, he launched into his rationale.

"Hear me out, Gretel. Firstly, my hunch is Eva would be keen. Secondly, however, we will have to recalibrate the mission if we expect the main craft to carry an extra person, and that would delay the start of the mission. Thirdly, perhaps only Eva can direct the ground control but, against that, surely, she could monitor the mission from within rather than beyond. Fourthly, and finally, it is Eva's theory that black holes are the tunnels, the connectors, between universes. Why not let her be the one to test that theory?"

Gretel stared at Javier in silence for a time, after which she merely said, "I don't think that's a likely plan, my sweet; the march of time is on neither of our sides." She then excused herself, explaining she had work to do on her address to the citizens. She headed to her study, leaving Javier to tidy up after their meal.

*

An energised Eva woke early and slipped down to the apartment block's gym for her morning exercise. She'd been a little remiss in her recent attendance, but she settled back into her usual routine quite comfortably. Returning to her apartment, she took a quick shower and dressed carefully for the day ahead.

Looking at herself in her full-length mirror, she felt pleased with the reflected image: skin still taut apart from a few crinkle lines about her eyes, breasts firm, posture excellent. Maybe she was a little tubby around the stomach, but it was nothing that could spoil the way her dress hung on her. Stepping into her high heels, she noted with satisfaction how slim her ankles still were. *Wearing glamourous shoes really lifts one's spirits,* she mused, thinking half seriously that wearing designer shoes should be made compulsory for those about to teach mathematics. She mentally listed the mathematical aspects she needed to cover during her sessions with Tanzi and Seb that day.

Finishing her favourite breakfast – half a grapefruit followed by two slices of toast with two cups of black tea – she checked the mirror one last time before heading outside to, for once, wait for her car to arrive rather than having to be summoned.

When she arrived at the office, she noted her to-do list in its correct position on her desk, she and Cabut having resumed their challenge to each other. She sat quietly reading over the notes that she planned to teach the astronauts until Cabut messaged her to say they'd arrived. The best part of her day was about to start. She set off to the lecture room armed with both her notes and her enthusiasm.

*

Aleck had decided to return to work on a part-time basis. He'd really come full circle in his opinion of Bruce Daniels. The man had stepped up to the plate when needed, displaying tact, empathy and understanding, much to Aleck's complete surprise. Now, Bruce was listening carefully without interruption as Aleck explained that he intended to resign once he had gained approval to enter teacher training and was able to bring Cameron home. Given his intentions, Aleck asked Bruce if he would prefer for him to resign immediately, as the firm had already allowed him considerable leave on full pay.

Bruce did not immediately reply. When he did speak, he said the firm would respect Aleck's wishes, and if he was determined to pursue another career, then Aleck could depart at the time of his choosing and he would go with the firm's blessing and best wishes. Bruce added that while he remained in charge, there would always be a position for him at Oostends should Aleck later find that he might have made a mistake by switching careers.

With some emotion, Aleck stood and gripped Bruce's hand, warmly thanking him for his support and expressing just how much Bruce's generous words meant to him.

Bruce also seemed to be overcome with emotion, and he quickly replied, "Okay Raine, back to work. We want to squeeze as much as we can out of you before you go." They both laughed, and Aleck returned to his own office.

Aleck spent the rest of the day attending to the work pile that had accumulated. His colleagues had been very supportive, but there was still so much for him to catch up on. Progress was also slow because people kept popping by to see how he was doing and to ask after Cameron.

Cecily came right up to Aleck's desk and theatrically slammed Eidish Smythe's file on it, exclaiming how very glad she was to be able to wash her hands of it now that Aleck had returned. Then she grinned, said it was good to see him and literally skipped out of the room. Aleck laughed, the sound becoming less strange to his ears. *Is it disloyal to Aneeka to laugh so soon after her funeral?* he wondered, but quickly squashed the thought. He knew Aneeka wouldn't want him to be miserable every minute of the day.

By the end of the day, Aleck had found a chance to fill in an application for admittance to teacher training, specialising in students with special needs. As he pressed the send key, he reflected upon the goodness of his legal colleagues. He'd been happy as a lawyer, but he felt quite certain that changing career was the right decision.

Outside, early evening had fallen. People were walking with purpose as they wended their ways back home to their families. Aleck, too, was off to see his family: he was going to call at the hospital to see Cameron before catching a late train. Matilda had left him with plenty of food that he could quickly reheat once he finally made it home.

*

Eva had been impressed, and relieved, that Seb and Tanzi had so quickly absorbed all that she had presented to them during their long classes that day. *The Government should feel pleased with the success of the mathematics and science education programs,* she mused.

Their abilities had been recognised as far back as their school days, when they had been encouraged to undertake appropriate programs to maximise their development and interest in the sciences. They had excelled and revelled in their later university studies, both becoming captivated by the space frontier and by mathematics. Eva saw in her two astronauts the same mindset that had drawn her towards mathematics all those years ago – an appreciation for the perfection of analytical argument, curiosity, challenge, the beauty of new discoveries, and admiration for the achievements and life stories of all those who had gone before them.

As she contentedly dealt with the correspondence and administrivia that had built up during the day, Eva felt no rush to return to her apartment. In fact, she thought it would be very nice to celebrate the end of an excellent day with dinner out somewhere. Normally she would message Gerry to see if she could join her, but Eva had sensed a change in Gerry since the Raine case and so she decided she'd be better off leaving her alone for a while. She could try to cajole Cabut into joining her, but he never seemed to respond well to such suggestions.

No, Cabut be blowed, she'd stay at the office till late, make the finishing touches to the material she planned to teach the next day, send any afterthoughts to Bethany for Gretel's speech to the citizenry, and only then go home. *And if Cabut can't, or won't, go home until after I leave? Well, that's his problem.*

*

Leon was enjoying a late afternoon coffee break with Clovis. The more time he spent in the company of the younger man, the more convinced he was that beneath Clovis's tough and rough exterior there lay the heart of an essentially good person. In fact, Leon felt he could trust Clovis more than he trusted Timothy, who continued to leave phone messages for him that so far he'd not felt like returning.

Leon had two purposes in mind for this meeting with Clovis. He intended to offer Clovis a job as his driver, and he hoped to find out what Clovis knew about his current employer. He was convinced that Clovis was employed by Jacques, someone that Javier always steadfastly refused to discuss.

Leon broached the subject of employment first. "Do you enjoy your work, Clovis? Does your employer treat you well?"

Clovis grinned and replied cheekily. "Of course I enjoy my job, Leon. All I have to do is follow you around and report back to my boss on your movements!"

"Should I be worried that your boss might want you to cause me harm in some way?" asked Leon, smiling as he spoke.

Clovis looked more serious. "I don't think I'm ever likely to cause you physical harm, Leon."

Continuing to smile, Leon said he was relieved to hear that. "In that case, young Clovis, I cannot see the advantage of you working for your boss – you might as well be working for me. How would you feel about joining my staff, initially as my driver, but with the prospect of greater opportunities in due course?"

Clovis looked at Leon, a little puzzled. "Why do you want me to work for you?"

"Why? Because I see a lot of good qualities in you. You're an intelligent, perceptive and decent person – that is, if you dig deep enough," laughed Leon. "I drive very little myself, but I like cars and I like being driven, preferably by someone I know and trust. I think you could be that person. I pay well, I expect loyalty and discretion, and I'm non-judgemental. I expect the same of anyone I employ."

"What do you mean when you say there'll be greater opportunities in the future?" Clovis enquired.

"Ah, I'm glad you asked and interested that you did," said Leon. "Eventually, I'll want someone to be the overall manager of my business interests. As of course you know, one of my interests is in sports betting, and I employ a number of very clever people to assist me. But very clever people can sometimes be very single-minded. I want someone capable of handling diversity. I have several other interests and responsibilities, not all of which currently have an overseer. Then, too, I have family commitments, and there will come a time when they need to be more organised. I'm not getting any younger, so 'they' say – and I want someone who can be across many of my interests and keep tabs on what's going on and report back to me."

Looking Clovis in the eye, Leon made his offer.

"Those are possible incentives for the future, should things work out and I judge you can give me total loyalty. Right now, I need a driver at my beck and call."

"What would you pay me to be your driver, and what hours would you expect of me?"

"First, tell me about your current employer and what your conditions are like now," replied Leon.

Clovis explained that, although he was on call, he really just had to be outside Leon's place by seven in the morning and to follow him throughout the day until seven at night.

"To be honest, the job was pretty boring until you decided to treat me as if I was your personal taxi. My boss was pleased about that and pleased to hear where we went each day. He pays me the standard wage. However, he has hinted that my responsibilities could be expanded and that would mean more pay."

"What's your boss's name? Is he a good bloke?" enquired Leon, trying to sound casual.

"He said to call him Jacques, but to be honest I've only met him in person once, which was when he offered me the job. I often just leave a message for him, as he doesn't always answer the calls I make to report the day's events. Seems an okay sort of person to me, however," said Clovis, shrugging his shoulders.

"Well, I would offer you 10% over the standard wage to be my driver. If the job develops further, we can negotiate an increase in your salary. What do you say?"

"When would this offer take effect? I have to give Mr Jacques a week's notice, and I'm not so sure he'll be happy for me to go to work for the person I'm supposed to be keeping an eye on."

"I see your point," agreed Leon. "If you were to give me his contact details, then perhaps I could speak to Mr Jacques on your behalf to smooth things over for you."

Clovis frowned and was silent for a little bit. Then he said that it wouldn't be right for him to hand over the personal data of Mr Jacques. Leon realised he'd pushed Clovis too far, too fast. Backtracking, Leon said he quite understood and that it had been thoughtless and selfish of him to put Clovis in that position.

"Perhaps we'd better continue as we are for now." Clovis nodded in agreement.

"Can we treat this entire conversation as confidential, so you don't report it back to your boss?" queried Leon. Clovis agreed that might be for the best.

"Excellent. Now, nature calls. Can I get you another coffee on my return?" he asked Clovis.

As he made his way towards the amenities block, Leon felt partially pleased. His hunch that Clovis's boss was Jacques had been spot-on. However, he was no closer to knowing where to find his old adversary's whereabouts. Leon was going to have to play this game in a smarter way.

CHAPTER 33

Gretel was ready to make her speech. She silently ran through it as others fussed over her hair and makeup. She'd chosen to wear a navy-blue dress with some light beading on the bodice. Her silver necklace and matching earrings added further lightness. As her hairstyle took shape, the image reflecting back at her in the mirror looked suitably presidential without being severe or over the top. *Goodness, it's amazing what expertly applied makeup can do to take the years off!* She normally didn't bother much with makeup, but she thought she might in future.

Bethany arrived, dressed in a pale-blue frock with matching jacket. She looked good too, but not so much so that she would overshadow Gretel. It was Bethany's role to nod her head in agreement at the appropriate points in Gretel's speech, to smile when Gretel smiled, and to look straight ahead without movement so as not to distract the viewer from listening to what Gretel was saying.

They were escorted to the reception room at Government House. Javier was there, waiting for them. He complimented them both on their appearance, then leaned forward to lightly kiss Gretel on her cheek, murmuring that Madam President looked especially beautiful.

The introductory music began to play. Gretel checked the teleprompter, as a voiceover announced, "Here is a message from the President."

"Good evening, my fellow citizens," said Gretel in her calm and evenly modulated voice.

"It is not often that I have the opportunity to address you, but I have an exciting and special announcement to share with you all.

"We form but a small country, the only inhabitable one remaining on our planet, not that I need remind you of our history." Gretel smiled. She knew Bethany would also be smiling beside her.

"Despite The Disaster that befell our forebears, we have together made this country a fair and just place, one where all citizens have access to excellent educational programs, where all citizens have employment opportunities and expectations of healthy lives, and where our collective innovation, expertise and care for one another has resulted in outstanding progress and a sense of community.

"Led by our best scientific brains and overseen by Minister Bethany Cresswell, I am both proud and delighted to announce that we will shortly be launching a space mission, with the aim of making direct contact with our closest sister planet, the planet Earth, in an adjacent universe. We are convinced that we possess the knowledge and expertise required to sustain this mission over the coming two or so years, and we are therefore confident of its success.

"Far from being a little country, we shall become an active leader of the universe, able to share our advances in so many areas with our counterparts on Earth. At home, we can anticipate massive spin-offs from the research developments that have given us the expertise to conduct such an ambitious mission. In particular, the health applications that will follow are quite astounding. That we have the vision, the confidence, the knowledge and the audacity to conduct such an undertaking is a strong reflection of the strength and quality of our educational system, a system that has produced the marvellous scientists and mathematicians who will lead the mission.

"For me personally, however, this mission will allow us to advise our contemporaries on planet Earth how to avoid their own, yet to happen but coming, Disaster. Carrying out this act of humanity will be one of the proudest moments of my life as your president.

"Finally, my fellow citizens, I leave you with this thought. Within just a few years we may all be able to anticipate being able to travel to Earth and back. Our own small world will expand as we learn to travel far and wide to visit our Earth cousins, and, who knows, maybe even meet our doppelgangers on Earth.

"It has been a pleasure to share this exciting development with you, and I wish you all a good evening."

The small audience in the reception room applauded warmly as Gretel completed her speech. It was good, short and not too packed with confusing detail, but she was still offering enough information to give people a sense of excitement and anticipation.

*

Eva watched Gretel's speech, surprised by its brevity. She noticed that Gretel didn't mention her name, but Eva was not particularly bothered by the snub: she had no interest in being lauded by the citizenry. What had disappointed her was the lack of information about the research that had enabled the mission to become a reality. Surely the citizens would have been interested – and what an excellent opportunity Gretel had missed to promote the magnificence of mathematics and astrophysics to future students. Eva was also disappointed that Bethany, as the Minister for Education, had not seized on this. *Why did I waste time writing material for her when so little of it was included?* she thought indignantly.

*

Rueben was less than fulsome in his praise over the level of detail in the speech, although he was hopeful that a soon-to-come press release from the Government might contain enough information to add bulk to the leading story he was writing. He intended to publish the speech in full, but he might have to search for snippets from other platforms to complete the article for the next day's edition. He was more pleased about the opportunity for follow-up articles: what the reaction to the announcement was from various citizens and who the 'best scientific brains' were – these experts certainly didn't make an appearance in the President's address. He decided to send a message to Minister Cresswell's office to request further information and an interview so he could pursue these points further.

*

Leon's reactions were mixed. He did feel excitement about the space mission; he felt Gretel's speech had been well-delivered and appropriate in content, and he accepted at face value that her desire to interact with and help the citizens of planet Earth was genuine. His qualms centred around the morality. He was very sure Eva was central to the space program and that it had been the purpose of her research for years. Whatever it was that she was testing and that resulted in the deaths of Aneeka and citizen Proger, it had to be the critical final piece she'd needed for the space mission to get the green light. And that meant, he deduced, that since Gretel had not mentioned Eva by name, then Gretel must be well aware that Eva had stepped over the line separating moral actions from immoral ones. Ultimately, this made Gretel complicit in the deaths of Aneeka and Proger. *What is more moral, saving compatriots on planet Earth by sacrificing two – and who knows, maybe more – of your own citizens, or protecting your own citizens by leaving their Earthling compatriots to blunder along a path known to be doomed?* he brooded.

Leon's night's rest had been somewhat fitful, and he awoke to find his mind still grappling with the thought that had disturbed him overnight – Aneeka died so that others might be warned to avert destruction.

Would it have helped Aleck to know of Aneeka's role? he asked himself anew. *Might it be of some comfort to know that fact? What if she'd donated a kidney yet suffered complications in the procedure that led to her death? It might then be of some comfort to know another lived.*

What if she'd dived into a swimming pool to save a young child who'd fallen in, yet both she and the child drowned?

He sighed. It knew it would be a tragedy for the two families, yet it might be of some comfort to know that she had tried to save someone else.

However, Leon recognised that in both scenarios it would have been Aneeka who had made the decision, considered or instantaneous, to undertake the risk.

Had she been told the real reason behind Eva's research and chosen to take the risk anyway, then Aneeka's actions could be considered noble perhaps, more likely foolish, but either way it would have been her choice.

Participating in a trial under the impression held by both volunteer and supervisor that it was non-harmful, only to find it was lethal, yet that knowledge was subsequently used to save millions of others ... was that a tragic accident or culpable behaviour on the part of the person responsible?

Leon concluded that the ends did not justify the means nor provide any comfort to those left to grieve. The days of human sacrifice belonged to ancient history.

CHAPTER 34

Gretel rolled over and snuggled against Javier, allowing herself to stay warm and cosy for an extra half hour longer than usual. It was nice to lie there, half asleep, half awake, recalling that the majority of the postings and messages she had read late into the previous evening had been overwhelmingly positive. The immediate reaction from the citizens had been excitement and support for the mission.

The extra half hour sped by and it was soon time for Gretel to drag herself out of bed and into the shower, leaving Javier to continue to doze. *No time for a morning jog,* she thought, so after a quick breakfast and a final check of her appearance, she called her driver.

When she arrived at the office, her staff greeted her with a round of applause, which she received with a smile. Most of the ministers had already sent their congratulations the previous evening. Bethany had left her a congratulations card, which Gretel placed on her desk. Bethany had also added a note to say that UndPress had requested an interview with her, and she was interested in Gretel's opinion about whether to grant this. Gretel was happy to give Bethany the permission to go ahead.

Wanting to capitalise on the good support from the citizens, Gretel saw the opportunity to settle the ongoing disagreements over the new roads plan. Accordingly, she asked to see Timothy as her first appointment of the day. She intended to ask him to put out a statement to allay the concerns that some citizens continued to raise with the OCMs. There was a Cabinet meeting scheduled for the next day, which would give Timothy time to prepare a statement for review and approval by the Cabinet.

On being shown into Gretel's office, the first comment Timothy made was to congratulate her on her vision, her humanity and her dignified address to the citizenry. Gretel was surprised and quite chuffed, since Timothy sounded genuine in his praise.

They quickly got down to business, and, before Gretel could make her request, Timothy surprised her again by confirming that he had a plan ready to present to Cabinet. She was even more surprised to discover that his plan was fair, just and well thought through. It was her turn to congratulate him.

"How do you suggest we share the news with the concerned citizens?" asked Gretel, steeling herself for an exchange of cross words between them, as she had no intention of allowing Timothy to formally address the citizens. However, Timothy had yet another surprise for her.

"I'm sure you will agree, Gretel, that it is unsuitable for the Government to make another address to the citizens, especially so soon after your landmark speech. We want them to be reassured we have their best interests at heart, but a sudden rush of broadcasts is not the Government's style."

Timothy laughed lightly and continued. "What I'm proposing is something really old-fashioned. I suggest we employ twenty or so students who, working with me and my team, would hand-deliver an individual personalised letter to each citizen in the targeted area. The letter would contain a written message describing our plan and its benefits, thanking those who have raised concerns and explaining how we intend to ensure that no citizen is disadvantaged by our actions. The letter could be signed by both you as president and me as the minister responsible. Copies of the letter can also be displayed in public areas such as libraries, local cafés, sports clubs and so on, with a copy posted online so that anyone can read its contents, regardless of where they live and whether they are impacted by the proposal or not. If you are agreeable, I would also like to make myself accessible for informal discussion at the shopping precinct the weekend following the letter drop."

Gretel was unable to hide her growing respect for Timothy, as she said: "That all seems to be most appropriate, well done. I'll leave it all in your capable hands."

She stood and ushered Timothy to the door, warmly shaking his hand as he departed. *Timothy may be a weasel, but he's a very clever one,* she thought, reflecting on how nice it felt to have something genuinely praiseworthy to say to him.

*

Rueben shook Bethany's hand in greeting. She had allocated a generous amount of time for him to ask his questions.

He started the interview by expressing an interest in Bethany herself, and how she came to be appointed as Special Minister to the space mission. She modestly linked her former position as Minister for Science with her capable performance as the Minister for Education, then sashayed back to what he assumed was the official line that the space mission was the result of a strong mathematical education system combined with the strong interest in astrophysics possessed by the scientists in charge. Bethany allowed him to photograph her at her desk and agreed to the photo being published with the article, one she said she was looking forward to reading.

Rueben then asked her about the problems that had needed to be overcome before the mission could become viable. In addressing the question, Bethany explained that the breakthrough that made the mission a possibility, rather than just a dream, was the realisation that a black hole could enable a connection between the two galaxies in the adjacent universes in which the two planets, their own and Earth, lay.

"Aren't these very dangerous parts of space from which nothing can escape?" queried Rueben.

"That certainly has been the past thinking, Mr Thiem. However, now we have learnt to listen to them." Bethany laughed, though Rueben was puzzled.

"They 'hum'," she elaborated. "By analysing this sound, the scientists can tell a number of things. For example, the sound can tell us if two black holes are about to implode in on each other – in which case we go nowhere near them!" She gave a little laugh, and Rueben smiled to encourage her to continue.

"However, if the hum is of a particular frequency and amplitude, then our scientists believe that provides us with the opportunity to enter and passage through the dark matter. Of course, how we enter and so on is awfully complex, and it's above my pay scale to try to explain it," said Bethany apologetically.

Rueben was growing increasingly curious. "How can our astronauts cope with the gravitational forces or whatever they are, as they tunnel through this connection to the adjoining universe?"

"Yes, that's a very good question. Finding the answer to that question has held up the space mission for more than five years. It's only been quite recently that our best brains have found a way and so enabled the space mission to become a reality. Oh, and I should explain, only one astronaut is passing through this conduit; the other will continue to orbit around the edges of our galaxy so as to be there for the return of the first astronaut, who will make the return journey after contact has been made with Earth. Actually, that detail was released in the press notes last night, wasn't it?"

Rueben nodded – he did remember that detail. "Is it permissible to know the names of the two cosmonauts? If all goes successfully, they'll be our country's heroes."

"What we've decided, in consultation with the two citizens and their families, is not to release their details until a later time," replied Bethany, adding with a gentle laugh that they should be referred to as astronauts, not cosmonauts (or robonauts, for that matter). Rueben was unfazed by the gentle rebuke, although he made a mental note to come back to the notion of robonauts.

"What about the names of the scientists, your 'best brains', who solved these problems? I don't think they were mentioned in the press release either."

"I think I can answer that one because she was going to be present for the announcement, but circumstances prevented that. Our so-named 'best brain' is an outstanding mathematician and astrophysicist of superior rank in the armed forces, Major General Professor Eva Baritz. She and her team have driven this project for some years."

On hearing the minister's words, the neurons in Rueben's brain started tingling. Baritz was the name of Stewart Weisman's client, the one very recently interviewed at the coroner's office. Surely it was too much of a coincidence to hear the name come up twice in such a short time?

"What is the solution that Major General Professor Baritz came up with?"

Bethany shook her head and said she wasn't willing to try to explain it because her understanding was not good enough. "However, I understand that it is a game-changing breakthrough that will have lots and lots of side benefits and applications for the lives and wellbeing of our citizens."

Rueben nodded, deciding to move on for now. "So, why not just send robonauts?"

"The mission is in part a humanitarian one, so it was thought that it would convey our message more effectively if the type 1 humans on Earth received our message from type 2 humans, not AI bots," explained Bethany.

Rueben could see that Bethany was moving to wind up the interview so he played along, thanking her for her generous time and wishing her every success with the mission. As he took his leave, he asked if there would be any objection to him requesting an interview with the Major General Professor.

Bethany laughed and said it was unlikely that Professor Baritz would be interested, but he could always try, adding it was not appropriate for her to hand out the professor's contact numbers.

Rueben started out the long walk towards his next appointment, one with his doctor, appreciating the opportunity to ponder the interview in the sunshine. He'd liked the minister; she'd been open and helpful, and she was obviously very excited about the space mission. That was one good story he would be able to put together nicely. But his journalistic instincts told him there was another story still lingering for him to sniff out: the one about Eva Baritz.

The last time she had intrigued him, he'd imagined there may have been a connection with the citizen Proger. Well, that hadn't worked out.

However, now, allowing his imagination to rove, he wondered whether the reason Professor Baritz had been called in for her interview was linked to her finding the solution to how an astronaut could survive the passage through the black hole. It was a long shot, he acknowledged, but he'd long learnt to back his intuition.

Then again, he now knew that 'the professional matter' at the heart of the professor's interview had centred around the death of a mother-to-be, so, to be fair, she may have simply been giving advice as her lawyer had asserted.

But now, when he thought about it, he remembered she wasn't a medical doctor; she was an astrophysicist, focused only on the space mission. There had to be a connection.

Rueben always enjoyed these internal debates. Allowing his mind to ramble freely was not only an indulgence, it was often productive (and an excellent quality in a journalist, he believed). On this occasion it led to a lateral thought.

What if there's a connection between the death of that unfortunate mother-to-be, the disappearance of citizen Proger, and the solution to the 'astronaut survival problem'? he wondered.

Suddenly, that didn't sound so crazy after all.

By the time he reached the health clinic, he had determined that his first actions would be to make two calls: one to Leon Hartland, and one off-the-record call to Stewart Weisman.

CHAPTER 35

Aleck greeted his next client warmly. "Mrs Smythe, do come on in. It is nice to see you again," he said as he ushered her towards a chair. Once comfortably seated, Eidish Smythe opened by asking how Aleck and the baby were, expressing her sincere condolences. Aleck thanked her and said they were coping. Then, switching the topic, he asked what issue had brought her to him that day.

"Well, I'm relieved to have you back, Aleck. That silly young thing who stood in for you has overcharged me, and I want you to fix that up." Before Aleck could reply, she added, "I also want you to go over the work she did. I've already spotted a sentence ending with a preposition, so no doubt it's full of lots more errors."

Aleck smiled inwardly, resisting the temptation to point out to Mrs Smythe that she had just ended one of her own sentences with a preposition.

"Mrs Smythe, you didn't need to come all this way because of a potential grammar mistake. You know you can always ring me, and we can go over things on the phone. I'll check there are no grammatical errors for you, but bear in mind that grammar has become more relaxed these days. It's quite acceptable for a sentence to end with a preposition.

"Let's move on to your more serious concern. Why do you think you've been overcharged?"

Mrs Smythe produced a piece of paper with a figure written on it.

"See, the bill's for 288ada, yet you always charge me 260ada. So, I'm not going to pay it."

Aleck looked at the paper, then laughed. "Oh dear, Mrs Smythe, your eyesight has let you down. This scribbled note says 233, not 288 cardanos. Did Cecily write this down for you?"

He patiently explained that Cecily was a junior member of the firm, so her rates were lower than his own, despite her work being excellent.

"When you get the official statement, you'll see more clearly that it says 233ada not 288ada." Aleck smiled kindly at Mrs Smythe.

"Now, is there anything else for today?"

As Mrs Smythe had no other business, Aleck helped her to her feet and slowly walked her out into the foyer. He asked the receptionist to organise transport to take Mrs Smythe home. Wishing her all the best, he returned to his next task, but not before leaving a voice message for his colleague Cecily about the incident, ending with the observation: "Now that she knows you offer a cheaper rate, my guess is you're going to see a lot more of her. Congratulations!"

*

Leon was returning a missed call from Rueben. He listened in silence as the journalist told him what he had learned from Bethany about Eva. "So, why are you telling me this?" queried Leon when Rueben finished speaking.

"I'm telling you because my hunch is there is a connection between the professor, the space mission and the disappearance of that citizen, Proger – the one you were concerned about."

"But what do you want from me?" said Leon flatly.

Rueben sounded impatient. "Well, let's start with some sort of reaction from you, and I'd like to know if you think there's a connection."

"This is off the record, Rueben. My 'reaction' is you are almost certainly correct, but you are in dangerous territory if you intend to publish your claim – and I don't know how you'll acquire the evidence you need before you can go public. Why don't you check with your government contact? My hunch is your friend will have you closed down rather than allow you to write what may well be a true story."

"You don't sound surprised about this, Leon. Had you already reached the same conclusion? Are you prepared to tell me what you know – off the record?"

"I did come to suspect something, but I only finally recognised what might have happened after I listened to the news about the space mission. My suspicion has little by way of supporting proof, so there's nothing I can offer you."

Rueben persevered, to Leon's irritation. "Why is it that you have been a thorn in the Government's side on so many matters over the years, always quick to raise your concerns and to fight for justice, but you suddenly don't want to get involved in this matter, even though it may be a criminal case?"

"Let's put it down to old age and feeling tired. In my defence, ask yourself this Rueben: what would you achieve by exposing what has happened? The space program has huge potential. One citizen may have been sacrificed to save millions on our sister planet. Does that not vindicate the action?" He knew his words sounded hollow, but he now had a responsibility to protect Eva, no matter how much pain her actions had caused.

"I never thought I would ever hear you speak that way Leon; I'm gobsmacked. And, just for the record, I think two citizens may have been sacrificed, not one."

"Sadly, you're probably correct about that too, Rueben. Let me say this to you: forget about targeting the actions of any one individual. If you're going to go all out on this, you should aim to champion a change to our system of government. If you're prepared to take on that battle, then you can count me in."

Not responding to Leon's challenge, Rueben asked if Leon would at least consider coming to a meeting with one or two others to discuss things further. Leon paused briefly before agreeing to accept the invitation. As an afterthought, he cautioned Rueben that he needed to be very discreet and should assume his actions were being monitored – though he realised that Rueben probably assumed as much anyway.

*

Stewart had noticed Rueben's message, but he didn't call him back until the end of his busy working day. He greeted Rueben quite warmly and asked him what was on his mind, anticipating the journalist needed some legal advice himself and was about to call in the favour owed him. He was therefore quite surprised when Rueben said he was calling about Eva. Immediately, Stewart confirmed that as Eva was one of his clients, there was nothing on or off the record he could say to Rueben.

"Did you know that Professor Baritz is the brains behind the space mission the President announced yesterday?" pressed Rueben.

"Is she indeed! Well, good on her, there's no doubting her ability."

"I'm writing some articles on the space mission," persevered Rueben. "Earlier today I spoke with the minister responsible, and that's how I know about the professor's pivotal role. The minister was happy for me to contact her as part of my story, but unwilling to hand out her contact details. So, I'm turning to you, Stewart, in the hope you can provide me with a means of contacting Professor Baritz."

Stewart gave a short laugh and said that he doubted Eva would be at all interested in speaking to a journalist.

"She's not like the rest of us, Rueben; she kind of lives on 'another planet', if you'll forgive my little joke. Nor would she appreciate me handing out her contact details. The best I can do for you is this: send me a short list of questions, and I'll forward them to Eva. If, and I doubt she will, but if she responds, then I'll send her reply on to you. How does that sound?"

Rueben agreed that was better than nothing and accepted Stewart's proposal, which Stewart felt was more than generous. It didn't stop Rueben squeezing in one final question, however. "By the way, you and I had discussed the citizen Proger and whether Professor Baritz knew him. Is there anything additional to add from the last time we spoke of this?"

"She said she didn't know him, it's as simple as that," said Stewart dismissively, and he ended the call.

*

Gretel and Javier were enjoying a celebratory glass of champagne upon her second consecutive early return home, the night sky not yet fully dark. The bubbly sweetness combined well with the zucchini frittata Javier had prepared.

"Mission, tick," said Gretel. "Now, I think it's time for you to share the list of recommended presidential candidates with me, my darling. I'm ready for this. What names did Cabut's analytical processes produce?"

Javier went to his study to collect the list he'd printed out.

"Let's test you," he grinned, as he returned to the table. "How many names are listed?"

Gretel thought for a moment before replying. "Three, of course" she said.

"Correct, one point to you my dear."

"Next question. What is the gender composition?"

"Two male, one female, no transgender," asserted Gretel.

Javier paused for a moment, as if waiting for a ruling from the judges. "Yes! Correct again. You nearly caught us out on that transgender suggestion, but the judges have confirmed the contestant is correct. Let's hear it for our president, audience," and Javier gave a round of applause.

"You loveable idiot," laughed Gretel.

"Now for our contestant's third and final question. It's a tough one, audience. Are you ready, Gretel?"

"I'm ready," she giggled.

"Name the contenders in the correct order."

"Okay, let me talk this through. The female is Bethany Cresswell, one of the males is Timothy Augustine and the other is Arjab Mansur; the order is Timothy third, Arjab second and Bethany first."

Javier pretended to be studying the list.

"Drumroll!" he announced, beating his hands on the table. "Alas, the answer given is incorrect. But thank you for playing. Give her a big clap, audience."

"Come on sweetheart, tell me the correct answer," implored Gretel.

"Patience, petal," teased Javier, holding the sheet of paper out of her reach as she beat on his chest.

"Madam President, please resume your seat," commanded Javier teasingly, but once the two of them were seated again, Javier's mood became more serious.

"This is the ranking from Cabut's analysis. Bethany in third place, Shinzo Nagita in second place, and Timothy in first place. What do you make of that, Gretel? No Arjab or Evan, no Grigor or Stefano, no Hannah but Shinzo's in and, to cap it off, Timothy in first place!"

Javier seemed quite surprised by Gretel's nonchalant acceptance that maybe Cabut had got it right. She acknowledged that she'd always known Timothy to be very capable and occasionally she'd wondered if the reason why he was offside so often was due to boredom and the lack of challenge in his role. She explained the way he'd reminded her of his strengths earlier that day. "I saw him this morning over the roads business and was surprisingly impressed by his handling of the situation, so much so I've given him carte blanche to go ahead with his plans."

"Then, later on in the day, Bethany reported back to me on the press conference she'd held, and it did cross my mind that, lovely person though she is, she is too obliging. I found myself questioning whether she is tough enough to make decisions that may not always be popular," remarked Gretel.

She agreed that she was surprised that Shinzo had made the list. "As my minister for the digital economy and technological advancement, he's kept a low profile – although he's certainly competent, I'll grant him that," she acknowledged.

"As for the others, I can accept that they are not ready to be president just yet. However, they are effective networkers, efficient and intelligent. They might keep Timothy on his toes," she concluded, before asking Javier what he had thought of the recommendations.

"What do I think? Well, initially I found it difficult to accept that Timothy should be placed as first choice. But it's been festering away in my mind for a few days now, and I find that I have become more reconciled to the idea than ever I imagined I would be. He's ambitious, quite ruthless and extremely capable, qualities that, ultimately, are good for the role. However, I'm yet to detect a genuine desire in him to improve the lives of our citizens, and I think he'll find you a hard act to follow, especially in that regard. As for the surprise nomination of Shinzo, maybe the nature of his portfolio acted in his favour."

"So, that's what I think. It makes me hope you're not in too much of a rush to hand the baton on, however," he added with a momentary frown.

"Oh, let me add one more thing that will amuse you, Gretel," he smirked. "I think Cabut is developing a sense of humour."

"Good heavens, darling, how could that be!" she exclaimed with a laugh.

"Pass me my glasses, and I'll read out the last line on his recommendation paper. It says, and I quote: 'As instructed, the above recommendations have been chosen only from the current members of the Inner Cabinet. Should this restriction be removed, then there is another candidate who is the superior in every test applied to the selection. The name of that candidate is Cabut.' The paper is then signed by Cabut in his usual way."

They both chuckled.

CHAPTER 36

Stewart reviewed Rueben's list of questions for Eva. They all seemed reasonable and possibly of interest to the citizens in light of the announcement of the space mission. He forwarded Eva the list, adding a few comments of his own as well as a brief explanation about Rueben's request for an interview.

Stewart felt he'd gone as far as was appropriate to assist Rueben. He doubted that Eva would have the time or inclination to grant an interview, but perhaps there was some chance she would consider answering Rueben's questions.

He thought back to their conversation about Eva the day before. He had found Rueben's ongoing interest in the dart-playing citizen a little disturbing; however, he had to admit he was also feeling a little uneasy about Eva's firm denial of any knowledge of Claus Proger.

*

Rueben woke up unusually early, especially given the hour at which he'd finally collapsed in bed the night before. He'd finished his article on Minister Cresswell, hoping she would be pleased and flattered by it. Then he'd started searching for information about another possible victim of the space mission – a pregnant woman. He'd discovered that her name was Aneeka Martenez, a health and safety engineering officer married to an Aleck Raine, a lawyer at Oostends. Many expressions of sympathy had been posted online and, as he'd read them, Rueben had felt the sadness her unexpected death had generated. She must have been near to term, since there were references to her baby, a boy, alive but in intensive care. He hadn't been able to confirm if the baby was still alive, however.

He allowed his wife's acerbic comments about her surprise in seeing him up so early float over his head, poured himself some strong black coffee, grabbed a pastry and started reading the news on his device, but it wasn't long before he decided to seek the peace of his office.

He soon found himself weighing up whether it was fair to contact Aleck Raine, the bereaved husband. Rejecting the thought as too intrusive at this point in time, he searched the public records of births and deaths and found the birth notice for a Cameron Raine. Happily, there was no corresponding notice in the death section – although he did note the recent death of an older man, Charles Raine.

The baby had been registered as the son of Aneeka and Aleck Raine, and examining the birth certificate further gave him the name of Geraldine Geary, the doctor present at the birth. Miss Geary offered some chance of a lead, though he knew it was unlikely that a doctor would discuss a patient publicly. Both Aleck's and Geraldine's signatures confirmed the birth, with the tragic word 'deceased' placed where the signature of the mother would normally be.

Rueben was about to close the site when his eyes drifted to the foot of the document and rested on the name of the informant who had submitted the document registering the birth. Cameron's birth had been notified for registration by one Leon Hartland, no relationship given. *Where does Leon fit into the picture?* he asked himself, completely flummoxed.

*

Gretel had watched Timothy keenly as he presented his proposal at the Cabinet meeting. There were no dissenting voices, so the proposal was carried easily. Maybe her hunch that his seeming immaturity resulted from boredom had been correct. Now that he had a challenging project to oversee, the best of Timothy seemed to be on display. She was beginning to understand what the former Homer ministers had seen in him.

She had been very pleased by the reception she'd received at the start of the meeting. Her colleagues had been fulsome in their praise of her leadership. Bethany had also been congratulated for her efforts in coordinating the mission. Some ministers had asked for greater detail, and Bethany had handled this quite well. Eva's pivotal role had been openly acknowledged, and if there was a lack of clarity in Bethany's explanations about Eva's ground-breaking work, this was forgiven and accepted as perfectly understandable; after all, as one minister remarked while others tittered, who amongst them were experts in astrophysics?

Gretel had leapt on that remark. Linking the interest in the mission to interest in such subjects as astrophysics and other mathematically based disciplines, she had pointed out that future ministers might well need to be experts in such fields. The suitably chastened ministers were rescued from their discomfiture by Timothy, who defused the situation by querying how the mission was to be financed. Gretel had asked the Treasurer to explain how the funding had been established several years ago and how it had been managed ever since. Timothy had seemed satisfied by that explanation, as had the rest of her Cabinet.

During the buffet lunch that followed the meeting, Gretel found a quiet moment to ask Timothy if he was interested in expanding his responsibilities. Without waiting for him to respond, she said she was thinking of splitting the Department of Finance and Treasury and asked if he might give some thought to adding some of that to his load. She didn't wait for his reply; she just moved on to greet the next minister as she worked the room.

*

Eva and her two protégés were enjoying a short luncheon break. Cabut had organised the finger food – ribbon sandwiches, leek tartlets and spicy dolmades, together with a platter of fresh fruit and another with cheeses and crackers. At her insistence, Cabut had provided plenty of decaffeinated coffee, herbal tea and water to wash things down, although only the water seemed popular with her students.

It irritated Eva that Cabut would never join these functions: it would have been useful to have someone else to help maintain the conversation. *Very selfish of him, he ought to try harder to overcome his disorder; he's such a strange one, still so lacking in social skills,* she thought, far from the first time.

Taking the opportunity to excuse herself, Eva wandered off to check her messages. There, out of the corner of her eye, she noticed Cabut some distance away, seemingly practising how to shake someone's hand. *How very odd!* she thought. However, she was quickly distracted by a message from Stewart.

She read his message without much interest and glanced through the accompanying set of questions. On the spur of the moment, however, she turned heel and returned to the lunch table, having decided that she'd ask Seb and Tanzi to contribute to the answers during the remainder of their lunch break.

Eva was satisfied with their responses, so just prior to resuming the class, she sent Stewart her reply: 'No to interview; answers to questions attached.'

*

Rueben had located Geraldine Geary's clinic (she also had rooms at the hospital, he'd noted). He explained to her receptionist that he was a journalist writing an article about Aneeka Raine, and he was seeking a comment from Miss Geary about Cameron Raine's progress. He took a seat in the waiting room, feeling somewhat conspicuous and out of place, and so he decided that he wouldn't wait too long. Fortunately, it wasn't long before the receptionist came over to tell him that Miss Geary was too busy to see him but, in any case, she was not the baby's doctor. He should refer to Professor Kupka for an update on the baby's progress.

Rueben searched for more on Professor Kupka and discovered that he was currently at his practice office within the hospital. Regretting that he hadn't gone there in the first place, he decided to toddle over. *All this walking must be doing me good,* he thought, as he put one foot in front of the other and traversed the two kilometres to the hospital, aided by the moving pathway.

He was directed to the second floor, so he elected to take the elevator and found himself greeting another receptionist, again asking if the professor could give him a few minutes of his time. The receptionist went away, returning to say Professor Kupka could only spare three minutes between appointments in half an hour's time. Rueben accepted and wandered off to the food bar he'd noticed on the ground floor, keenly looking forward to a drink and something to eat.

Sugar and energy levels restored, he returned to the reception and was soon ushered into Professor Kupka's consultation room. His first observation was that he couldn't help but find it strange that such a prim and proper looking fellow was in charge of paediatrics. Getting straight to the point, Rueben explained that he was a journalist following up on both the unexplained death of Aneeka Raine and the welfare of her baby. "Are you able to offer any comment for our readers on Aneeka Raine's death, as well as the latest on Cameron Raine's condition?"

Kupka replied crisply that the death was not unexplained. The unfortunate citizen had died from complications due to a stroke. What was not as clear, however, was why she'd had the stroke, but it appeared to be related to a migraine the patient had suffered.

"People sometimes underestimate the severity and the impact of migraines, tending to think of them as just headaches, which they are not," he said, adding that the baby was making progress.

Pleased to hear some positive news about the baby, Rueben decided on the spur of the moment to take a gamble.

Telling the doctor that he was in receipt of information that the space mission only recently became viable due to research conducted by a Professor Baritz, who he knew the deceased had been in contact with, he asked: "What is your comment about the possibility that her death was related to that research?"

There was a pause as Professor Kupka looked keenly at Rueben. Then he spoke with a tired voice. "I take it you know that Professor Baritz was called before the coroner and that her claim of no negligence was upheld? If you have further incriminating information, you should be speaking to the Justice, not me."

Rueben reached the point of his visit, issuing the same invitation to Kupka as he had to Leon.

The doctor raised his head and replied without hesitation. "Yes, I would be prepared to attend a private meeting to discuss some new information." Then, apologising that he had no more time available, he handed Rueben a business card with his contact details and ushered him out of the room.

*

Aleck had a late afternoon appointment with Professor Kupka to check on Cameron's progress. He was thrilled to hear that Cameron was starting to gain weight and his prognosis was improving. Professor Kupka told him that if all continued to go well, Cameron might be able to be discharged from hospital within a week or so, although he would need to be brought in for ongoing checks and monitoring. Aleck was even happier when Professor Kupka went on to say that at this stage the brain injury might not be as severe as first feared.

"He's a good little fighter, your son," Kupka said with a rare smile. "His impairment will make him slow by comparison with the norm, but he'll still be capable of learning and acquiring skills that should enable him to have a good life."

"That's encouraging," said Aleck. "However, he'll need special education services, I assume?"

"That's the situation as of now, Mr Raine, but I need to qualify that by two facts: one being that his current progress is better than I would have predicted a week ago; and, secondly, the rapid and ongoing developments in gene therapy research make it reasonable to hold out great hope of considerable improvement, maybe even a cure, in the not-too-distant future."

"What would gene therapy involve, Professor?" queried Aleck.

"Ultimately, one day we would hope to be able to repair damaged DNA with a simple procedure," the Professor replied.

Aleck thought for a moment before looking at Professor Kupka in some puzzlement. "You know, that's the sort of thing that Aneeka said she was helping Professor Baritz to work towards. Is that the case, am I remembering correctly, is that the professor's field of work?"

"In a way, I suppose yes, but she's not in the medical field, and I really don't know anything about her research," shrugged Professor Kupka. "Forgive me Mr Raine, but now that you mention your wife, it reminds me that I had a visit from a journalist earlier today, asking a few questions about how she died. Do you know about this?"

"No, I've never been approached by anyone. What's the angle, why the interest?"

Professor Kupka looked thoughtful. "It seemed to me that the journalist was investigating whether there was any link between the research behind the space mission and your wife's death."

He raised his hand to prevent him from interjecting and continued.

"He said he knew that Professor Baritz was involved in research for the space mission. Now, Mr Raine, he did not say *how* he knew that, but it wouldn't be surprising to learn that Professor Baritz has been involved in research for the space mission. However, it's a very big leap to suggest, as he seemed to be alleging, that there is a connection between your wife's death and that research.

"As you know, at the Hospital Board's direction, the coroner held a routine enquiry into Mrs Raine's death. Its finding was that there was nothing suspicious about her death. I said to the journalist that if he did have any new information then he should take it to the Justice.

"I now need to ask you a question, Mr Raine. The journalist may be a crank. Nevertheless, I found what he said to be interesting enough to agree to meet with him again at another time to learn the basis for his conjecture. My question to you is, are you comfortable with that?"

Aleck really didn't know what to think. Nothing was going to bring Aneeka back. Still, if someone's actions were responsible for her death, then that should not go unchallenged. So he replied carefully, noting that he was okay about things but would appreciate being kept in the loop.

With that, the two men shook hands and Aleck departed, heading for Cameron's ward.

Seeing Cameron had cheered Aleck greatly, and he couldn't wait to take him home. It had been wonderful to find out that he didn't have much longer to wait. As he took a seat on the train home, he started compiling a list of things he needed to do in readiness for Cameron's homecoming. He and Aneeka had already decided that the study would be turned into a nursery, and they had started to purchase some baby essentials. Aleck realised he needed to check exactly what he already had and figure out what else he needed.

His application for special education teacher training had been received, and he'd been invited to attend an interview. Assuming that went well and he was accepted, Aleck would be able to enrol in the course – which started in four weeks' time. He had decided to do the training on a part-time basis, even though it would take him longer to gain his teaching qualification. It had been Bruce Daniels' suggestion that Aleck continue to work part-time at Oostends to fit around his study. *How much I misjudged him,* thought Aleck, yet again.

One major item that he knew needed to be on his to-do list was employing a nurse to help take care of Cameron. He had decided to accept, in part, Leon's offer of help with Cameron's care – so that between him, Leon and the yet-to-be-employed nurse, someone would always be with Cameron. In an emergency, Matilda could be called in at short notice, too. There were some evening classes he'd have to attend; Aleck reasoned that at those times, if he were available, Leon could look after Cameron and possibly stay overnight as well.

Aleck had immediately concluded that he couldn't accept Leon's generous offer of financial support. He would manage somehow – and besides, he'd have his part-time salary from Oostends until he started teaching. However, he was happy to accept Leon's offer of support with childcare as a grandparent, and Aleck wanted to encourage Leon to build a relationship with his grandson.

The thought of Leon, and how good he had been when Aleck had been at his lowest, caused Aleck to message the older man, asking if he was free for lunch any day soon. By the time Aleck arrived home, Leon had replied, "Ensemble Café, midday tomorrow?" which Aleck confirmed would be perfect.

Aleck was excited at the thought of telling Leon that Cameron was coming home soon. The lunch would also give him the opportunity to see what Leon thought of the tale of the journalist and the two professors.

*

Rueben joined his wife for dinner. She observed that he seemed very happy with himself, but when she asked where he'd been all day, Rueben evaded the question and buried his attention in checking his messages.

"Put it away while you're at the table, Rueb. You're so rarely here for dinner that the least you can do is talk to me. Why not start by telling me about your day?"

He looked up at her and, seeing she was serious, pocketed his phone. "You tell me about your day, instead," he said encouragingly. And while she spoke, he allowed his thoughts to retrace the day.

He figured it would be best to capture the interest of Kupka and Leon and have that meeting soon. *Is there anyone else I should invite?* he wondered.

His thoughts were interrupted by his wife glaring at him crossly. "You've nowt heard a word I've said, have you? I don't know why you bother to be here or why I bother to stay." He raised an eyebrow as she placed her food on a tray, carried it over to the sofa and switched on an entertainment channel.

He sighed quietly, but he had nothing he could bring himself to say, despite knowing he should share his recent medical diagnosis with her. As soon as he'd finished his meal, he told her that he had to go back to the office. There had once been affection in their marriage, but, sadly, he had to acknowledge they had drifted apart, perhaps irretrievably.

CHAPTER 37

On arriving at the Ensemble Café, Aleck was greeted warmly but quietly by Felix, and Ivana went out of her way to come over and give him a big hug, asking, with concern, how he was coping. They had both attended Aneeka's funeral service, and this was the first time they had seen Aleck since. When Aleck told them both he had resumed work and was looking forward to welcoming Cameron home soon, they insisted that he must bring him in to meet them.

Ivana, in her kind way, said that if she could help at all she'd be very pleased to do so. Felix cut in and joked that they could do with another kitchen hand. "You just drop him off and we'll set him to work," he jested. The three of them laughed, gently.

Leon arrived and, making his presence known, he joined in the banter, taking Ivana's hand and theatrically kissing it while teasing Felix by asking how a peasant such as he had acquired such a beautiful wife. Ivana flushed with pleasure, demurring that hard work and age had robbed her of her beauty long ago.

Aleck appreciated everyone's efforts to make him comfortable, and he enjoyed the laughter. Eventually, he asked Felix to kindly show them to a table, adding that they mustn't keep Ivana out of their kitchen as he was hungry.

They chose their orders quickly: rigatoni with lightly roasted Brussels sprouts for Aleck and the leek pie with vegetables for Leon. Once they'd settled on a glass of the house red each, Aleck broke the good news about Cameron, which Leon seemed thrilled to hear. Aleck then relayed the decisions he'd made; to his credit, Leon took these in his stride, saying that he would fit in with whatever Aleck thought best. He did, however, reiterate that Aleck should always remember that he would be there for him and Cameron. Leon added with some emotion that he couldn't thank Aleck enough for planning to include him in Cameron's life.

They chatted amiably as they devoured their food, before ordering a brownie slice to go with their coffees. Only then did Aleck mention Kupka's visit from the journalist, one who seemed to be speculating whether Aneeka's death could be related to the research Professor Baritz had undertaken in relation to the space mission.

"Do you think that's rather odd and somewhat disturbing?" Aleck asked Leon.

It was as if a screen had suddenly been lowered over Leon's facial features. Gone was the amiable, smiling face, the kind eyes with their twinkle of humour; instead, Aleck saw a hardness in him, a façade of steel. Aleck almost struggled to recognise his lunch companion.

When Leon eventually spoke, it was with a brusque assertiveness.

"For a clever person, Kupka has been rather indiscreet; I hope he hasn't shared this information with anyone else. The journalist, one Rueben Thiem, is most likely correct. He and I have spoken of this. I'm sorry you've found out this way, I did not want you involved."

Aleck felt bewildered that Leon knew so much. However, he replied quite evenly that he wanted to be a part of the conversation, repeating his earlier words to Professor Kupka that while nothing would bring Aneeka back, justice needed to be done. The doctor had promised to keep Aleck informed; he hoped that Leon would pay him the same courtesy.

"Professor Kupka plans to attend a meeting with the journalist. Do you intend to join them?" he asked Leon.

With a sigh, Leon acknowledged that he did.

"Perhaps I could accompany you?" suggested Aleck.

"Maybe, maybe not …"

In a softer voice, more like the Leon Aleck knew, or thought he knew, Leon continued.

"I'm sorry you've learnt this before we have more than circumstantial evidence. There are officials high up in the Government who would act to suppress any leaks about alleged unethical behaviour behind their precious space program. We must be sure we can prove our assertions before they're aware that we're on to them. Rueben is acting surprisingly bravely by taking things as far as he has. Let me speak to him once more before I decide whether I can risk you becoming involved."

Aleck nodded his assent. The convivial mood now broken, little more was said as they quickly drained their coffee cups and prepared to part. Having farewelled Felix and Ivana, remembering to compliment them on the quality of the meal, Aleck shook Leon's hand and they went their separate ways.

*

Leon walked over to a nearby parked car and tapped on its side window. Clovis lowered it and grinned at Leon, asking if he'd enjoyed his lunch.

"How about driving me home and saving me the cab charge?" proposed Leon, to which Clovis replied, "Consider me at your service."

Once he'd settled in the front seat, Leon said lunch had been delicious and enquired whether Clovis had ever eaten at the Ensemble Café. Clovis shook his head, saying that he was more a pub-grub eater than a fancy café diner.

"In that case, how would you like to join me the next time I eat at the Ensemble – my treat, of course?"

"You're a strange bastard, if you don't mind me saying," laughed Clovis. "I'm not sure what my boss would say about that."

"Perhaps he'd praise you for keeping such a close eye on me that you can report on not only my movements but also what I eat," teased Leon, adding that if the boss gave Clovis a bonus for being so dedicated, perhaps he'd let Clovis pay for the meal after all.

"Ha-ha, very funny," grinned Clovis.

As Clovis drove, they chatted about sport and the teams they followed. It happened that their respective teams were playing against each other that evening, and so each talked up the chances of their team winning, with Clovis asking if Leon wanted to make a small wager on the outcome.

"You do know that sports betting is part of my business?" Leon laughed uproariously. "But, hey, don't let me stop you betting against me and giving me your money."

Clovis seemed to only be dimly aware of the details of Leon's business pursuits, and he listened curiously as Leon explained how his businesses operated. The time passed quickly, and they soon arrived at Leon's home. Before alighting, Leon asked Clovis if he'd had second thoughts about the offer to become Leon's driver, to which Clovis had simply said, "Not really."

Getting out of the car, Leon thanked Clovis for the lift and quipped that he'd wear him down eventually; the offer remained open.

Leon went straight to his desk drawer to rummage around and locate a particular phone, from which he called Rueben. The conversation was short and to the point. He suggested that the two of them meet that evening at a hotel within walking distance of Leon's home, arriving half an hour apart. He hoped Clovis would have gone off duty by then but, nevertheless, he would leave his lights and music on, depart from the back gate, and walk to the hotel.

*

The classes Eva had been conducting were coming to an end. She was most pleased with the quick uptake and responsiveness of her two students; she felt confident they would follow procedures calmly and correctly. They were all excited about what lay ahead, although mindful of the dangers, known and unknown, that the two astronauts might face. In lots of ways Eva envied them the experience they were about to have, noting that, had she been half her current age, she might have been making the journey herself. This was a sobering and odd reflection; it was one of the first times Eva had thought of herself as ageing, despite her trimness of figure and level of fitness.

What lies ahead? she wondered as she bid Tanzi and Seb adieu, passing them on now to the team in charge of overseeing the launch. She would be present at the launch, of course, but its control would be handled largely by the robotechs. She would also be around to monitor the spacecraft's position and progress as it navigated its way towards the ends of their galaxy, although, strictly speaking, she would only be essential if something went wrong with the bots, which was highly unlikely – and would almost certainly mean a disastrous end to the mission. Similarly, steering along the gravitational waves and getting the timing and trajectory absolutely right for entry into the black hole would be left to the robotechs, which had been programmed according to the results of her research. The two astronauts would be in constant communication, where possible, with the robotechs – which meant they would also be in regular communication with her. Eva knew she would be more of an observer to these intense events – she was the composer, watching her work play out.

Reaching her office, she turned back to thank Cabut for his organisational efforts during her lectures. How nice it would have been to ask if he too were experiencing a sense of let-down now that the mission would soon be largely beyond their control. Alas, revealing and sharing one's inner feelings, indeed any feelings, was not an act Cabut had ever shown any inclination towards – and now was no different. Making no response to her 'thank you', Cabut merely replied that the President's office would like Eva to get in touch when convenient. He then returned to his screen.

Eva sat down at her desk, telling herself to stop becoming maudlin and to get on with things. She rang Gretel's personal assistant and was surprised when Gretel answered. Gretel wanted to know how close the mission was to confirming a launch date.

Eva gave the required information, and then she found herself – much to her own surprise – telling Gretel what she might have revealed about her feelings to Cabut (had he been more encouraging). Gretel surprised her further by sounding quite sympathetic and understanding, so she started to elaborate before Gretel interrupted her flow, saying: "Save the rest till you join us, Javier and I, at home for a quick meal this evening. In fact, come straight away, I'm just about to leave in any case." Eva agreed she'd do just that.

Ordering her car to be brought round, she packed her bag, said good evening to Cabut and departed. Normally she would have gone home first to spruce herself up, especially if she was seeing Gretel, but she found she didn't really care what she looked like for once. She decided to go directly to Javier's apartment.

Javier came out to meet her, and he ushered her inside his home.

Gretel greeted her with a kiss on each cheek, and she handed her one of the two glasses of champagne she was holding.

"Congratulations Eva, your dream is about to become a reality," she said.

"To Eva," joined in Javier, as the three of them sat down.

The meal was informal, leftovers really, but delicious all the same. They all agreed that curry tasted even better the next day. The conversation was relaxed. Gretel asked Eva about her plans for after the launch of the mission, to which she replied that she'd still be monitoring the progress of the astronauts until such time as communication was lost, and she had not thought beyond that yet.

"Do you wish you were on board?" asked Javier casually.

Eva replied that she did in lots of ways, and she candidly admitted that she had considered the possibility. However, her strength was in the research that made the mission possible, and for the sake of the success of the mission she had realised she had to dismiss the idea, leaving the responsibility to the properly trained astronauts. "There's no room for tourists," she joked.

Dessert was a variation of a bread and butter pudding with a selection of fresh fruits and walnuts, following which Javier poured them each a small brandy.

Eva gently swirled her brandy balloon, breathing in the aroma of the liquid. Gretel had moved the conversation on to Eva's future role, post space mission, observing that it was important for Eva to keep busy and stay occupied. Before Eva could share her own reflections on her future role, Gretel asked how Eva would feel about the Government appointing her as an Emeritus Professor of Mathematics at the university.

"There would be an expectation that you would supervise a small number of students taking their doctorates and give some lectures for interested staff and able students from time to time. But apart from that, what you would make of the role would largely be up to you. Perhaps you might like to offer advice to those on educational boards, to address the ways in which participation in mathematics and the sciences can continue to be strengthened."

"So, you want me to retire?" she interjected, surprised.

"No, I want you to be occupied – and you said yourself earlier that you were experiencing a let-down feeling now that your central role in the space mission will start to lessen," replied Gretel. "Eva, dear, I'm not expecting you to say yes or no right now, I'm just throwing the idea into the mix."

In response, Eva noted that Gretel probably shouldn't take her low spirits earlier in the evening as meaning anything important.

"But I do, Eva, because I think you will become increasingly unhappy when you lose control of running the space program. Nor can I imagine you twiddling your thumbs for two years while you wait to hear the astronaut has made it to planet Earth and is on his way back.

"Just promise me you'll give it some thought, and we'll talk about it again at a later time," Gretel added. Eva shrugged non-committally, but she smiled and nodded in agreement.

Clearly, Javier had more to say about Gretel and Eva's exchange. He told Eva that he supported Gretel's suggestion, cautioning her not to delay her consideration of the idea for too long. "After all, we can't assume that Gretel will be president forever," he joked.

Eva paused to look closely at him and then at Gretel.

"Are you both in the throes of planning new futures for yourselves?" she enquired, one eyebrow raised quizzically.

"We should all look to the future," responded Gretel. "None of us can expect to go on forever, that is unless you can come up with an anti-ageing solution," she laughed, before continuing more seriously.

"Javier is making a good point, Eva. Someday there will be another president and a different government in power, we have to be realistic about that. When that happens, it will be quite likely that I'll not be in any position to influence support for you. The new broom may well have his or her own people to promote, and you could be forced into retirement to make way for one of those."

Adopting presidential gravitas, Gretel continued.

"As a measure of my gratitude, respect and reward for your outstanding service to this country, particularly in regard to the space mission, and not forgetting our shared history and past friendship, I want to ensure you are well set up before any change of government occurs. If you accept the university appointment, it will keep your mind active during the space wait; you won't be relinquishing your interest in that program."

Gretel then returned to her own situation.

"The successful launch of the space program might, or might not, be a good time for me to step down; you know, go out on a high and be forever remembered with gratitude, rather than stay too long and face the humiliation of being forced out of office," she said. "Hence, I urge you to think seriously about the offer." Gretel added an apology for getting on her soapbox and monopolising the discussion.

Javier proposed another toast. "To our futures," he said. Eva took a sip of brandy, before Javier reminded them of their shared history.

"Remember those early days when we all, we three and Leon, dreamt of making major breakthroughs? We worked hard, loved, laughed and were happy. Do you consider that life after that got better, or not?"

It took a moment for Eva or Gretel to respond, but Gretel answered first.

"Better, definitely, both career-wise and personally," she said. "That training set me up to realise what was really important to me – politics and government, rather than mathematics alone. I remember those days with much fondness, but I feel I was then yet to develop fully as a person and as a leader.

"How about you, Eva?" asked Gretel.

She said it was hard to compare life then and now, since the sadness of Nolé's loss marked the passage between the two stages, both as an upper bound of the first stage and as a lower bound to the second stage. Career-wise, however, she, like Gretel, would select the second stage.

"How about you, Javier?" she asked in turn.

Javier topped up his brandy balloon before responding.

"Interesting that you both looked at the question from the same two angles: career and personal. I suppose that's quite a reasonable approach, so I'll try to do the same. Let's first consider my career. I have far greater diversity and responsibilities nowadays, but I am largely anonymous, or, if known, I am feared by some. My career is dependent on that of my companion. It is not my job that brings me the greatest pleasure. Hence I would disagree with you both and say that I consider my working life was better in the earlier rather than the later period."

He paused to quaff some more brandy. Eva noticed Gretel quietly sealing the brandy bottle, shifting it closer to herself.

"Now, to personal fulfilment," opined Javier. "In those early days, life was blissfully indulgent, and I shall treasure certain memories of those times forever. However, my emotional life was, shall we say, complicated, and I know I caused unhappiness to each of you," he said, bowing to both Gretel and Eva. "And to Leon," he added, at which point Gretel stood and said perhaps it was time they called it a night.

"No, Gretel, don't try to interrupt me, I'm not done yet," remonstrated Javier, and he waited for Gretel to sit down again before he continued.

"I had two – and an unfulfilled third – great loves in my early life. They left me confused and distressed by the sadness I inflicted on each person. Comparing those days with today, where the two loves of my life are Gretel and cooking, I am so fortunate that Gretel stood by me. No man could ask for a better companion in every sense of that word. So, to conclude, ladies, I would say my personal fulfilment is deeper and more steadfast in the later stage of my life."

Gretel and Eva applauded in approval, each lightly planting a kiss on one of his cheeks.

"Beautifully argued," murmured Eva, as she rummaged in her bag for her phone so she could summon her car. "Thank you for an excellent meal, maestro chef – and for a charming evening. And thank you, Gretel, for your proposal – it has considerable appeal, but let me get back to you once I have fully digested it."

CHAPTER 38

Leon was pretty sure his meeting with Rueben the previous evening had gone unnoticed. They hadn't spent a lot of time together, but it had been long enough for Leon to realise that Rueben's claim of new information was not as revealing or damning as he'd hoped. However, the case against Eva and, through her, the Government, was building.

When Rueben had confirmed that he hadn't run the story by Jacques and nor would he, Leon had been intrigued. He'd questioned why the normally cautious journalist was taking risks with such a story, but he'd been shocked and very saddened by Rueben's reply. Rueben had explained, matter-of-factly, that it was due to his recent diagnosis of terminal pancreatic cancer.

Rueben wouldn't hear of any commiseration, instead saying that the prognosis had given him a feeling of freedom to write a story that would reveal the unsavoury machinations of the current government. All too often he had toned down pieces or not published them, but here was his chance to leave his mark – his last chance, perhaps. Professor Baritz and her employer, the Government, should be brought to account for the actions that had cost ordinary, seemingly unimportant citizens their lives, he had said with some passion.

Leon felt deep respect for the dying man.

He found himself sharing his own conflict, that of being caught between a duty of care towards Eva and a desire to achieve justice for Aneeka, she being his biological daughter. Rueben had listened quietly, nodding his head and stroking his chin thoughtfully.

Suppressing lingering emotion, they had discussed their next move, Leon explaining that Jacques had him under observation so he would have to be careful. The canny Jacques would be alerted should he become aware that Leon and Rueben were meeting together. They had agreed that they needed to act quickly and with support from a diversity of citizens. The overall plan was to build the argument, take it to the citizenry through publication, confront the Government, and present their case before the Judicial Courts.

Rueben, Leon, Professor Kupka, Aleck (whose attendance Leon had now accepted) – and maybe others that Leon or Rueben would have to confirm – needed to meet as soon as possible. Leon had agreed to organise the time and place, and it was this thought that he was mulling over as he ate his breakfast.

He was cross with himself that he hadn't as yet been able to win Clovis over. The man was rough but decent, the antithesis of his boss. *Would it help Clovis to change sides if he found out that the suave Jacques was totally untrustworthy?* Leon wondered. If he could win over Clovis, they could all meet at Leon's home. A simple plan, but not so simple to achieve without Clovis in his camp.

Taking care, as always, with his choice of device, he called Aleck to thank him for lunch the previous day, and soon found himself sharing his dilemma over a suitable venue. At first Aleck couldn't think of a solution, but Aleck rang the number back ten minutes later to offer a suggestion.

He'd learnt from Matilda the previous evening that the new owner of Charles Raine's small apartment in the aged care home was due to take possession quite soon. Meantime, Matilda was packing up the last of Charles's belongings and still had the keys.

"What if we meet at the apartment? People come and go all the time as they visit friends and family, so any observer, should there be one, would not assume that all the visitors are meeting together," reasoned Aleck.

"Great suggestion, it sounds perfect! Thank you very much, and thank Matilda, too," said a relieved Leon. "Send me the address. We'll speak again this evening, I'll call you."

However, it wasn't long before Leon realised he had another question for Aleck. He left a message, asking him to ring him again when he got the chance. Eventually, Aleck had returned the call.

"What's the matter?" he asked.

"We need formal statements from Proger's barmaid friend, and one from your clerk, too, over his initial treatment when presenting the FOI application. Can you get someone in your office to help?"

"Funnily enough, I've been thinking something along those lines myself," replied Aleck. "We should have legal representation, but as I'm the plaintiff in Aneeka's case, I don't think I should act as our group's legal advisor. Anyway, getting back to your query, I'll get my clerk to get the statement from the barmaid; just send me her details.

"By the way," Aleck continued, "I've also been wondering whether to speak to Bruce about the possibility of him acting for me in the litigation, but I'm mindful that some government minister warned him through a friend of his not to have anything to do with you. Bruce has become a friend, but …" Aleck's voice trailed off.

"Can you find out who that minister was? Make up some pretext of wanting to speak to a minister regarding concern over Aneeka's death?" he suggested, curious.

"I'll give it a go, but I don't know if that will get anywhere," responded Aleck. He added, almost as if it were an afterthought, "Would it be okay for Erik to come to the meeting as interim legal support? He's competent, and I trust him implicitly."

Leon couldn't think of any reason why not. "Okay, go ahead. We'll hold the meeting tomorrow evening. I'll come to you, then we'll go together. Clovis will think I'm planning to move into the care home!" With a chuckle, Leon ended the call.

*

Aleck spoke in private to Erik, telling him in the strictest confidence of the likelihood that both Aneeka and the citizen Proger had been the victims of an experimental procedure. Erik was appalled and agreed to help with the case in any way he could. He was due to play in a gig the next evening, but he offered to claim illness and get a friend to fill in for him so he could attend the meeting. He promised to trace the barmaid for Aleck and get her statement as soon as he finished work that day. Aleck thanked him and the two shook hands, agreeing to keep the matter highly confidential for now.

Later that afternoon, Aleck approached Bruce Daniels. He put to him that although Professor Baritz, a government employee, had been cleared of any negligence in relation to Aneeka's death, he was wondering whether a case for compensation from the Government could be mounted on behalf of Cameron. Continuing before Bruce could respond, Aleck raised the possibility of informally sounding out Bruce's contact within the Government to see if there had ever been a precedent for such a case. Since Bruce at first did not recall having such a contact, Aleck had to remind him of the time that some minister had warned Bruce, through a friend of a friend, to stay clear of Leon Hartland.

"Oh, Jockey's friend's friend, I remember. Sorry Aleck, Jockey never said who the minister was, although I guess I could ask him as a favour to check back with his contact. Seems unnecessary, however."

Aleck was disappointed, so he changed tactics and asked if would Bruce consider acting for Cameron if he did go ahead with such a case. Bruce said his first thought was that it would be difficult to win such a case, but he was prepared to give it further consideration before being more definite in his advice. And, of course, he would represent Cameron if there was a chance of success.

"By the way Aleck, I can't help but say that I've noticed you haven't taken Jockey's advice to stay clear of Hartland. The pair of you seem quite close."

"It's quite strange the way things change, you know Bruce. Just a few weeks ago I would never have counted either you or Leon as among my 'friends'. Now, following Aneeka's death, I have completely revised my opinions, and I consider both of you such wonderful, compassionate and supportive people that I am proud to call you my friends."

Bruce seemed genuinely touched, even turning away momentarily to clear his throat. Turning back, he simply said: "Thank you Aleck, I appreciate your words very much."

Aleck returned to his office, glad that he'd been able to tell Bruce of his regard for him, but less than satisfied that he'd been unable to find out the name of the minister.

*

Leon and Rueben had spoken on and off throughout the day. Recognising that it was Rueben's conscience and morality that had set things in motion, Leon repressed his natural desire to take the lead; instead, he conferred with and deferred to his seriously ill fellow conspirator. However, he was relieved that Rueben had accepted the suggestion to meet in Charles's apartment. He had also been agreeable to widening the list of attendees. By the end of the afternoon, they had agreed that the meeting would include Rueben, Leon, Aleck and Erik, Professor Kupka (and Geraldine Geary, at Kupka's request), Matilda (and Mikhail, at Matilda's request), and Timothy Augustine (who Leon had resolved to invite).

Leon's phone call to Timothy had been interesting. He had not bothered to apologise for ignoring Timothy's calls of late, instead speaking as if they were continuing a recent conversation. Without mentioning Aneeka, Leon put it to Timothy that new evidence had come to light about the death of the citizen Proger in whom they shared an interest, and that there was a movement brewing to bring the Government to account.

"So, do you still want an opportunity to advance your ambitions?" he'd bluntly asked Timothy.

For a moment, Timothy had seemed somewhat nonplussed. Noting his hesitation, Leon commented on how impressively Timothy had dealt with his recent portfolio problems, citing comments made to him by some previously disgruntled citizens. Leon realised he was embellishing things somewhat, since in actuality only one citizen, Clovis, had given him feedback. He justified the liberty by assuming that Clovis's views would reflect those of his parents at least, whose property was in the affected area.

Timothy accepted Leon's positive feedback and rallied around to accept the invitation to attend the following evening's meeting, agreeing to keep its confidentiality.

Leon smiled as he ended the call. His pleasure came not from the prospect of aiding Timothy's rise to power but more from creating an opportunity that could give Gretel sufficient warning that she needed to resign. Better for her that it would seem to be by her own choice rather than through the public humiliation of being forced from office in disgrace.

Unlike the others attending the planned meeting, Leon played more than one hand in this game of attrition.

*

As Leon ended their call, Timothy smiled thoughtfully. He no longer felt completely aligned to Leon, his confidence and self-belief having grown over what he called his 'time in the wilderness' (when he'd seemingly been deserted by Leon). Under the recent guidance of his friend, companion and newly appointed political advisor, Frederick Kline, he knew he had matured and that he was rapidly gaining serious respect from those in government echelons, including, most recently, that of the President herself.

Still a schemer, but one not only wanting to best serve his own purposes, Timothy was coming to recognise in himself a surprisingly genuine desire to make the Government act in the best interests of its citizens. His 'meet and greet' experiences during the letterboxing project had given him a new respect for the ordinary folk who formed the citizenry. He had learnt to listen to the citizens, to respect them and to enjoy the discussions he'd had, even when some citizens (though not the majority) were critical of the Government. During Gretel's presidency, ministers of the Inner Cabinet had largely been isolated from the citizens they were supposed to serve. Timothy recognised that he, along with his fellow ministers, were living in a bubble. That had to change; ministers needed to consult and to be visible.

He and Freddy, just like he and Leon before, had engaged in many discussions about how the Government should be organised to achieve this goal. He was starting to be more and more convinced by Freddy's argument that RevDem had been a good experiment for its time – but its time was over. Leon had never supported Revised Democracy, that he already knew. Timothy was now coming to recognise that Freddy and Leon had views of not dissimilar shades, and that these were shaping his own views.

The people needed to be included in the Country's governance: a return to some form of political parties and democratic elections was needed. No single assembly of ministers aligned to one president should be rulers; instead, from the voting preferences of the citizens, he believed that coalitions should be elected to share governance, allowing a rotational system of shared presidency to be drawn from these groups. Politicians would need to become accustomed to working together through negotiation, compromise and a sense of common purpose and duty.

To be able to instigate his vision, Timothy needed to become Gretel's replacement. Leon had once shared with him that she was contemplating retirement, although Timothy himself could not see signs of that in her. He also suspected that – despite a thaw in tensions between them – Gretel still didn't see him as having presidential potential. The space mission seemed to have cemented Bethany into position as Gretel's preferred candidate. He had vowed to apply himself to the best of his ability, act in a more serious and dignified way, and not miss an opportunity to raise his profile to Gretel, but that may not have been enough. Freddy had been counselling him that he might have to wait till after Bethany's presidency for his own chance, advice that Timothy neither liked nor had resigned himself to accept. That Gretel was adding part of the Department of Finance and Treasury to his portfolio of responsibilities was, as he told Freddy, a good step forward. He was rising in her respect.

Coming back to the meeting he'd agreed to attend, Timothy recognised that it might give him bargaining options. If the evidence was bad, Gretel might have to go – leaving the presidency open. He could do nothing and let this happen, or he could do as he had done once before – warn Gretel of the movement against her, maybe thereby moving further up in her esteem and gratitude, and perhaps bypassing Bethany as her preferred protégé.

Warning her didn't exactly advance my cause the last time I tried that tactic, he ruminated.

Another possibility might be to strike a bargain with Gretel, where she anointed him as her successor in exchange for the information she needed to squash the movement before it did her real harm.

With some sternness, he pulled himself up over his thoughts. *These are not the plans of a true statesman,* he surmised, reminding himself of his promise to act with greater wisdom and dignity.

Let's not get ahead of ourselves for now, old boy, he counselled himself. He'd attend the meeting, see what was going on and leave any decision-making till afterwards.

CHAPTER 39

Following her evening with Gretel and Javier, Eva's spirits had lifted. Gretel's suggested position in mathematics would nicely fill the interim period during the time it would take Seb to navigate his craft to Earth, deliver Gretel's message and make his return journey home. This would likely take at least two years, with the possibility of very little direct involvement required from Eva. She was inclined to accept Gretel's offer straight away but, on reflection, she decided to wait until after the space launch.

She was packing her necessary belongings in readiness to travel the comparatively short distance to the launch site. A small aircraft would transport her to this relatively isolated part of the Country. The launch was set for two weeks' time, and Eva would remain on site for several weeks after that – or at least until she was confident the mission was successfully underway and she could pass over control to the bots.

The actual launch was one of the most hazardous parts of the mission, but it was also the most spectacular. It would be streamed live so that all citizens could witness the start of the historic mission. There was some talk that the President herself might attend the launch, but Eva thought that seemed unlikely; Gretel would come to recognise that she'd be an unnecessary distraction. *No doubt, however, her presence will feature prominently in the news coverage of the event,* Eva predicted.

Seb and Tanzi had spent long periods of time at the Space Centre base training for an event like this. No citizens lived permanently in the area surrounding the site, with all workers flying in and out as required, temporary accommodation provided for their stay. Eva knew that some way to the north lay the border that represented as far north as it was safe to travel. The border was monitored; should any Souls manage to cross to the south of it, they would quickly be detected and forcibly returned. It had seemed harsh to Eva as a young school girl but she had been taught that this harshness was justified by the concern that the Souls could carry a contagion into the rest of the Country. No-one was aware of any contagion affecting the North, but 'one had to be careful' argued government ministers and OCMs alike. Thereafter, Eva, like most of her fellows, rarely gave it any further thought.

Eva's car arrived, and she set off for the Departments. She would fly out to the launch site later that day.

*

Bruce had contacted his friend from the yacht club to ask if it was in order for Jockey to pass on the name of the minister.

"Quite understand, old chap, if that's out of order, but it could help me with a client of mine if I could sound out the minister's stance on a particular matter. Bit hush-hush, so can't go into details. But what do you think, can you help me out with this?"

Jockey seemed to have a memory lapse at first, but it soon came back to him when Bruce reminded him that he was referring to the minister who had warned him to stay away from a chap called Leon Hartland. "By the way, thanks for that, we dropped Hartland as a client straight away following your tip-off," Bruce had added.

"Glad to be of help, we need to watch each other's backs, Bruce. Now, let me think," Jockey had replied. He went on to recall that the minister was called Jacques. "Don't think I was told his full name or what his portfolio was, or maybe I've just forgotten," Jockey had said, recalling that the minister had apparently said to his friend's friend that he was acting out of concern for the good name of Oostends.

After the call, Bruce had done a search for ministers named Jacques. When his search didn't come up with any, he'd concluded that Jacques must be a member of the Outer Cabinet rather than a minister in the Inner Cabinet. He passed the information on to Aleck the next morning.

*

Aleck was grateful for Bruce's prompt efforts on his behalf. He felt a little guilty not being upfront with Bruce, and he was very tempted to include Bruce in the gathering to take place that evening. But, since Bruce had been warned against Leon, maybe Bruce wouldn't be comfortable joining them.

He'd mentioned this dilemma when he spoke briefly to Leon, telling him the Cabinet minister (or, more likely, member) was someone called Jacques. Aleck had been quite surprised by the mirth this revelation seemed to produce in Leon. "Jacques is an instrument of the Government, but I don't think he can claim ministerial status," he'd laughed, adding in a more serious tone that he thought it ill-advised right now to include any more in the group, but maybe it could become a good idea to invite Bruce at some later time.

The day flew by for Aleck. He'd left the office early to attend his interview with a representative of the education faculty, and he felt that the interview had gone very well. The faculty person had been keen to hear Aleck speak of his experiences during his Service days, where he'd been teaching students whose education had been interrupted for one reason or another. There would shortly be a new intake of trainees for the course, and the officer had also confirmed that it would be possible for Aleck to undertake his training on a part-time basis.

He'd visited Cameron, returned home, eaten a light meal and was now awaiting Leon's arrival so they could travel together to the aged care home.

*

Clovis was driving Leon to Aleck's house. Leon explained that they were going to look at an apartment in an aged care home, one that had belonged to Aleck's now deceased uncle. In mock severity, Leon stressed his interest was as an investor at this stage.

"Don't you dare report back to your boss that I've reached that stage of life!" he had joked. "If you were my driver rather than my shadow, I could have asked you to go with me rather than bother Aleck, but alas, you keep turning down my offer," Leon added.

He then explained that he was spending the night at Aleck's. "Up to you, of course, if you want to wait around to see me emerge the next morning, but I've told you what I'm doing – so you can knock off and avoid an uncomfortable night, if you so choose."

Clovis laughed and said he hadn't had a client who was so cooperative. After a companionable silence, Clovis said he'd have to follow Leon to the aged care home so that it could be included in his report, but then he'd disappear after that because he did have other plans. "As you wish," was all that Leon said in reply, before they talked of other matters.

*

Aleck and Leon arrived at the aged care home. Their arrival was meant to be staggered compared to the other members of the group. Matilda had suggested the names of some residents that the others could claim to be visiting when checking in at reception.

Aleck said, truthfully, that they were meeting Matilda in Charles Raine's former apartment. Ronnie, the person on the duty desk, looked up at Aleck and smiled. "Hey Aleck, I remember you; so sorry about your uncle, he was a very lovely person."

Aleck also smiled; he remembered Ronnie from his earlier visit, when Charles was still alive. He thanked Ronnie for all that he'd done to make Charles happy during his stay, and then he introduced Leon, saying they had come to give Matilda a hand with completing the removal of Charles's effects.

Leon and Ronnie smiled at each other, and Aleck said they were pushed for time, so there was no further chat. "Good to see you again, Ronnie," said Aleck as he led Leon towards Charles's apartment.

In actuality, his haste was motivated by the dread of Ronnie asking after Aneeka – he wasn't quite ready to deal with that type of situation yet.

*

Clovis strolled over to the care home's reception desk, asking if he could leave a message for an older man called Leon. The receptionist laughed, saying, "You do realise this is a home for old people, right? We have a few Leon's living here – which one did you have in mind?"

Clovis laughed amicably, identifying 'his' Leon as a non-resident who would have accompanied a younger man, Aleck.

"Ah, then you've just missed them, they arrived about ten minutes ago. I can give Leon your message; I'll phone it through to Mr Raine's apartment if you like."

"Thanks for that; just tell Leon to get Aleck to bring him home, as his driver is signing off for the night and will see him tomorrow," replied Clovis. "By the way, I'm Clovis, Leon's driver," he added.

"Nice to meet you, Clovis, I'm Ronnie. Unlike you, I'm still on duty for a few more hours."

Clovis sympathised: "Hard luck, Ronnie." He then thanked him for his help and departed, holding the door for a middle-aged couple as he left, feeling very pleased with himself that he had cleverly checked all parts of Leon's story, and pleased for both of them that what Leon had told him had been correct. He'd send his daily report to Jacques, and then he was off to the pub to meet a woman he had recently met for a second date.

*

Professor Kupka and Geraldine Geary had travelled together to the care home on Matilda's instruction. They checked in, claiming to be visiting a resident she had suggested, and she was soon able to intercept them both and redirect them to Charles's apartment. Similarly, over the next fifteen minutes, Rueben and Eric arrived, separately, to visit different residents. Matilda's knowledge of the inmates had proved very helpful, and her simple plan worked well.

Matilda had also been instrumental in ensuring that Timothy arrived undetected. To avoid the possibility that he might be recognised at the duty desk, it had been agreed that Timothy, rather than Mikhail, would arrive with Matilda. Telling Ronnie that her husband was getting some stuff from the car, she had signed them both in, avoiding the need for Timothy to be seen. Although disappointed not to be attending the meeting, Mikhail had understood.

*

There was only one chair left in Charles's apartment; Rueben chaired the meeting, so he got to have the chair, too. The rest of them had no choice but to stand or sit on the floor, something that may have helped to streamline the meeting. Matilda had thought to bring bottles of water and some biscuits, so at least there was something to drink and eat.

After asking everyone to introduce themselves and their connection to either Aneeka Raine or Claus Proger, Rueben laid out what he knew to be factual and presented his various conjectures that linked the facts together, acknowledging that some of these remained speculations at this stage. He then allowed each person to offer any insight they might have into the two deaths, which was followed by further discussion.

Steering the meeting towards a decision about the course of action to be taken, Rueben then posed questions about what should happen next.

"How do we ensure Eva Baritz is held accountable and brought to justice? How do we ensure the Government is censured for turning a blind eye to what she was doing?" he asked.

Leon, who had been remarkably subdued, spoke first, emphasising Eva's mental condition.

"One part of her is a genius, but her mental and emotional sides have a fragility that differ from the norm. She does not view people in the same way that we do – although she will never have meant to deliberately harm anyone, it should be said. No court could convict her of her crimes due to her mental condition."

He paused, then continued. "I suggest we should focus on targeting the Government for not monitoring Professor Baritz carefully enough, rather than targeting Professor Baritz herself. It is the Government that must accept ultimate responsibility. Accordingly, censure is insufficient; the President and those close to her must resign and possibly face the Justices. As for Eva, she needs to be retired to a safe place, away from people."

Rueben acknowledged Leon's position, and then Timothy became the dominant presence in the room, surprising Rueben with his burgeoning leadership skills.

Speaking with conviction, Timothy stated that he categorically agreed with Leon, and that it was the Government, through its presidential office, which must accept ultimate responsibility for the unintended deaths of Claus Proger and Aneeka Raine. He offered to act as an intermediary to liaise between the Government and the members of their group.

Timothy went on to point out that the space mission was about to launch. Eva was due to be on site for the launch. He raised the question as to whether those present accepted that this event should take place before they took action against the Government. He indicated that he favoured that view himself.

Timothy recommended that Rueben prepare a summary of what they had discussed, but that he withhold publication until after the launch. He also suggested that each of them should prepare to start collecting petition signatures from their colleagues, friends, family, neighbours and acquaintances in readiness for taking action against the Government, cautioning that this should be done quietly at this stage.

Timothy concluded his remarks by suggesting that, if everyone agreed, a subcommittee – consisting of Timothy, Leon and Rueben – should be formed to decide how to use the knowledge shared that evening and the petitions and publications that they would be collecting and creating most effectively. His words were met with nods of agreement and respect.

As the meeting came to a natural end, Rueben thanked them all for coming and exhorted them to keep in touch and share any developments or further thoughts. With some difficulty, those on the floor stood and stretched their limbs, then, as planned, they departed at different intervals.

*

During the drive back to Aleck's home, little had been said by either man. Leon sensed Aleck was troubled and knew he owed it to Aleck to offer some explanation for the stance he'd taken at the meeting.

Suggesting they share a night cap before turning in, Leon was relieved when Aleck agreed. After a search, Aleck located a bottle of port and poured them each a small glass. As they sat together on the quite comfy sofa that would become Leon's bed for the night, sipping their drinks, Leon quietly told Aleck what he'd shared earlier with Rueben. While Aleck made no immediate response, Leon was encouraged a little later by Aleck grasping his hand firmly and wishing him goodnight. He was hopeful that his words had given Aleck some explanation for his defence of Eva earlier that evening.

CHAPTER 40

The launch went exactly as planned. The rocket, after separating from the spacecraft, returned to ground level at the location planned by the trajectory analysts, seemingly in good reusable condition, although that would have to be thoroughly checked by the engineers.

Eva enjoyed the rocket launch. She admired the elegant, streamlined motion of the rocket, and the anticipation of what was to come added to her pleasure; she did not doubt that the mathematics would prove to be correct.

Tanzi and Seb were in fine shape and in clear communication with the ground team. The next challenge would occur when Seb's capsule separated from Tanzi's spacecraft. Eva had every expectation that this would go to plan too. The most crucial stage would be when the capsule entered the black hole to tunnel through to another universe and enter the galaxy in which Earth orbited, all communication lost.

Gretel had appeared on their screens to send her congratulations to all involved in the successful launch, and she had rung Eva personally to repeat that sentiment. Eva had felt quite chuffed by Gretel's actions.

*

Aleck would always remember the day of the launch, since it was the day that he was finally allowed to bring his tiny precious son home. With Leon's help, he had employed both a day nurse and a night nurse to help him – a fortunate situation, Aleck knew, one that would be denied to the ordinary worker lacking a wealthy benefactor. Parents of children with disabilities were given assistance, as were single parents, but any child who had all day and all-night around-the-clock help from qualified nursing staff had chosen their grandfather wisely.

Despite the blur of the first day, Aleck did stop to watch the space launch, finding himself caught between marvelling at its awe and majesty and weeping with the sadness it had brought to him personally. He fed Cameron some milk, having been shown by the nurse how to prepare the bottle and formula, and as the baby lay asleep in his arms, he murmured to his sleeping son that this rocket had taken the mother he would never meet.

Dabbing away his tears, Aleck switched off the coverage and gently stood, trying not to disturb Cameron. The manoeuvre was unsuccessful, causing his son to wake, his cry quite loud for such a little person. Now it was time for the first nappy change at home.

*

The day after the launch, a meeting of the subcommittee was held, with Leon, Rueben and Timothy linked together through telecommunication – Leon at home so he didn't need to devise a plan to mislead Clovis, Rueben and Timothy at their respective offices. Initially, Leon listened quietly as Rueben and Timothy shared viewpoints about the reporting of the previous day's launch. Rueben noted that media platforms were abuzz with editorials lauding President Nuewen's far-sightedness, Timothy agreeing, adding that according to the early feedback from the OCMs, citizens were feeling pride in their small country's ability to have reached this point, and particularly proud of the humanitarian nature of the project.

Leon had laughed when Timothy wryly observed that many, OCMs and even some ministers, were trying to imagine what their counterparts on planet Earth would be like, whether they might one day meet them, and to what extent the type 1 human form would resemble their own type 2 form. *Despite what they'd been taught, there would always be some who couldn't help themselves from fantasising that their twin existed on their sister planet*, Leon had thought.

"What about any negative reaction?" Leon asked.

Rueben suggested that a small undercurrent was developing, albeit just a tiny trickle at this stage. Some citizens were beginning to hear rumours of morally reprehensible experimental work conducted for the space mission, although he had added that some poo-pooed the rumours as just tales by those implacably opposed to whatever the Government did. Still, in Rueben's estimation, a slowly growing number of less zealous, more open-minded citizens were beginning to feel uncomfortable about the rumours.

"The excitement of the launch day may have helped these few to block out their concern, at least temporarily," Leon commented. "It's important we continue our efforts.

"How is your own writing going, Rueben?" Leon continued.

Rueben's reply – that he was on track to release his article soon after the space launch had taken place – was comforting to Leon. He commended Rueben for his efforts. *How brave and admirable this ill man is*, he thought.

The line wasn't all that good, but it was sufficient for them to come to an agreement about the next action to be taken. Timothy would approach the President, revealing much of what they now believed to be the truth. What Timothy would then say would depend on the attitude of the President, she needing to be in no doubt that her situation was untenable. Both Leon and Rueben expressed their confidence in Timothy's judgement to handle the situation, and their conversation concluded.

Leon reiterated this confidence to Timothy when he met him in person later that day, at what could be thought of as a subdivision meeting of the subcommittee. For Leon, this meeting was a 'passing of the baton' ceremony. For possibly the first time in his life, he had formed the judgement that there was someone more suitable than himself to deal with Gretel; for perhaps not the first time, Leon acknowledged to himself that he was getting older; and for definitely the first time in quite a long while, Leon recognised and acknowledged that Timothy had the qualities to lead the Country. Timothy would have his backing and blessing should he use the current situation to make a play for the presidency.

Timothy seemed genuinely humbled by Leon's endorsement, and as they parted company Leon reflected that Timothy was about to face the biggest challenge of his career so far. Timothy's earlier confrontation with Gretel over the Proger death had served its purpose without too much emotional cost - but convincing Gretel she must resign was likely to be a far more harrowing experience for both minister and president, Leon predicted – and a sobering part of Timothy's preparation and training for higher office, he added as an afterthought.

*

Gretel had been ecstatic throughout the day of the launch, and so she decided to host an impromptu dinner for her ministers the following evening. During the dinner, she gave a speech in which she was generous in her praise of the role played by Bethany. She was careful to make no mention of Eva, but she did warmly congratulate all those responsible for the launch.

Late that evening as they were getting ready for bed, she shared with Javier that she had been tempted to go off script and announce her pending retirement.

"Leave on a high and bask in the reflected glory of the launch," she mused, once again.

Javier smiled, but he commented that impulsive decisions were generally not wise and, besides, only the first stage of the launch had been successful so far, there would still be more to celebrate when the capsule set off on its own journey. She had to agree with his logic, so off to sleep they went.

*

When Javier woke the next morning, he picked up a message he'd missed the night before in all the excitement and celebration. It was from Jacques. He reported that Minister Timothy Augustine had met with Leon Hartland prior to attending the dinner at Government House. Javier was surprised to learn this, as he thought that Leon and Timothy had fallen out; only recently, Leon had spoken somewhat scathingly to him about Timothy.

Still, Timothy was a changed person in Javier's eyes, someone who was becoming increasingly mature and impressive. If Javier hadn't known that Gretel was planning to step down as president, this meeting may have alarmed him. Now, however, he felt no need to tarnish Timothy's rising star.

*

Gretel greeted her staff cheerfully as she arrived at her office on the third day of the space mission. The suite of rooms was still filled with the fragrance of the many congratulatory bouquets Gretel had received as a result of the successful launch. The only news that had come in from the Space Centre showed that all was continuing to plan, and the astronauts were still in communication with the ground staff.

Gretel's private secretary advised her that the Minister for Roads, Transport and Finance had asked if she could see him that morning. Assuming Timothy wanted to discuss more details about his new portfolio, Gretel agreed to a meeting, and an hour later he was ushered into her sunny office.

The meeting sucked out the warmth of the day, the beauty of the flowers, the joy of the events of the previous days.

Showing no arrogance nor pleasure in what he was doing, Timothy laid out for Gretel the evidence that had been collected, alleging that the space mission arose from the ashes of two innocent victims, Proger and Raine. He matter-of-factly told her that a movement of some powerful and influential citizens had already begun, and the Government would be targeted for its complicity and duplicity in ignoring the actions of its employee, Eva Baritz.

He was brutally frank with Gretel. Her presidency was compromised, the movement was growing; it was too late to try to quietly suppress it. He suggested she had two choices, as he saw it – turn the Country into a police state by taking brutal actions against her own citizens, or resign.

Timothy paused and, with sadness, apologised for not being able to warn her earlier, when her resignation could have been the end of the matter. It now appeared inevitable that some censure was likely to be meted out to her as the Head of Government, the severity of which he could not predict.

Gretel sat in silence for a time, and when she spoke, she confided a number of things to him. She told Timothy that plans were already underway for her to resign, that she had been planning this for some time. Not without irony, she commented she had nearly made the announcement at the dinner the previous evening.

"So, there you are Timothy, my choice was made before you arrived; there won't be, how did you put it, 'brutal action taken against my people'," Gretel said, with some force.

Collecting herself, she advised Timothy that she would like to continue their discussion with Javier present.

She stepped out of the room to tell her private secretary to cancel her next appointment and to tell Javier he must come to her office immediately.

On his arrival, Gretel quickly gave Javier her version of what Timothy had laid before her.

Javier immediately said to Timothy: "Is this what you and Leon Hartland plotted yesterday before you departed to enjoy your president's hospitality?"

Unprovoked, Timothy replied that yes, he had met with Leon to discuss how best to lay the situation before Gretel.

"However, don't think of this as something that Leon plotted. He is a member of the movement, that is true, but I suggest to you that he is the member most sympathetic to you. You may not want or value my advice, but I shall give it all the same – keep Leon close to you; he can, if not soothe, at least temper the anger of others in the movement. To be blunt, if there is a chance of some deal being made, you want Leon arguing your case."

Gretel addressed Timothy. "Once I resign, and it will be of my own volition, please understand that I will fight to maintain my legacy. Nothing I have done has been criminal; I know next to nothing about either citizen you raise. It is true that I have spent much of my presidency trying to look after Eva, and I acknowledge there have been times when the Government has had to patch over problems she has created. I personally have not known, nor ever wanted to know, the details of Eva's research – but due to our shared past, I have always accepted that I have a duty of care towards Eva.

"Quite recently, I spoke to Eva about ending her involvement in the space program. I offered her a teaching chair in mathematics at the university. I intended then, and it is still my intention, to negotiate with my successor that the current arrangements set in place to help and to protect Eva should be continued."

Gretel turned to Javier and asked him to share the plans they had for her resignation. This he did, at the end of which Timothy asked if Bethany had been confirmed as the most suitable replacement.

Gretel couldn't help herself; she laughed, briefly, despite the gravity of the meeting. Javier explained that three ministers had been identified as contenders by the Department of Security and Intelligence: "Bethany, Shinzo and you, Timothy."

Noting that Timothy had actually blushed at the revelation, Gretel commented that she had already accepted and concurred with the three names recommended, although she was yet to finalise the order. However, in due course she had intended to anoint and announce her preferred candidate, both to the Cabinet and the citizens.

"That was the plan," she told Timothy. She paused momentarily, before adding significantly, "and, perhaps it still can be.

"I'm willing and happy to go, Timothy. However, I need to negotiate as good an exit as is possible. The space mission must not be placed under a cloud, which is my paramount concern. Do not, I entreat you, impeach me or whatever it is the movement has in mind, until after that capsule has gone down its tunnel."

Proceeding, she sternly added, "I emphasise to you and your fellow plotters that I am the President, not Javier. He may advise me, but he does not make the decisions. It is against me, not Javier, that you may or may not have a vicarious liability case for ignorance and lack of due care. And please note that I say again that I will strenuously dispute such assertions."

She then enquired, less stridently, "Should there be charges against Eva, and in turn possibly me, when do you expect these to be laid?"

"Of that I cannot say, I do not know," said Timothy. "However, I do know that nothing can stop the release of the damning information about Eva Baritz. It will come out before the space launch is out of the news, and it is inevitable that questions about the role of the Government will start to follow.

"My personal advice would be for you to resign in a matter of days, if not today. And I say that regardless of whom you choose to appoint as your preferred successor," said Timothy.

He continued. "My other obvious piece of advice is to get yourself the best lawyer you can and to start talking to Leon. If I thought there was some way that I could help, then I would offer it. I am distressed to have been the one who has had to lay the situation before you."

Timothy prepared to leave, saying it was best for him to go now so that Gretel and Javier could continue the discussion between them.

"You have achieved so much for our country, Gretel. It is my fervent hope that a way can be found that allows you to retire in peace, reputation intact," he said, choking up. He embraced both Gretel and Javier and left, his tears now freely flowing.

Gretel continued the conversation with Javier, discussing briefly how best to handle the looming and very unwelcome situation. They both agreed that they would fiercely contest any allegations of impropriety, should they arise. Javier counselled that she should leave things to him; he would speak to their lawyer, he would have Security identify the people in the movement so they could judge how influential the group might be, and he suggested he could speak to Leon as well.

As Javier took his leave, Gretel vowed not to show any outward sign of being unnerved by Timothy's visit. Turning to re-admire the bouquets of flowers, she inhaled their scents and tidied up the few petals that had fallen, shedding much of her own tension in the process.

*

It didn't take long before the rumour that Timothy had been sacked swept through the corridors of power. 'So-and-so' had heard it on good authority that Timothy had been called to the President's office and that he had emerged in tears a good time later. Most who heard the news were astounded, having thought Timothy's career was on the ascendency; some few were pleased to learn Timothy had received his comeuppance, having previously suffered under his cruel barbs and taunts. The wiser heads kept their views to themselves, refusing to speculate on an unconfirmed rumour.

Bethany was one of those wiser heads – or maybe she just didn't have the time to gossip, though she'd certainly heard a few of her colleagues indulging anyone who would listen with their opinion. She was caught up in waiting for further news from the Space Centre. She would have loved to have been present at the launch, but she understood why she and Gretel had been dissuaded from attending. They would have been in the way, everyone else working with purpose and full attention, focused only on getting the launch carried out successfully.

Bethany had found her involvement so far in the space project exhilarating; she was a good communicator and had been an efficient chair of the many meetings held in the planning stages, and her arguments for greater government funding had been accepted without quibble. She had done all that was expected of her in that role. (Indeed, as one of her old school reports had so pithily but aptly written, 'Bethany does her best.')

Bethany had trained as an accountant, and she was quite well-known and respected in her local community. She had become attracted to local politics through her involvement with a number of community issues and eventually, after two failed attempts, she had been elected as a member of the Outer Cabinet. Once there, she did her best for her community and was content.

Some years later, she was astounded to receive an invitation to become a minister of the Inner Cabinet. This had never been an aspiration for her, and she had doubted that she had the qualities necessary to take up such a responsible and highly prestigious position. It was only Gretel's personal intervention that had convinced her otherwise, and so she'd finally accepted the offer. She had served as a minister in the only way she knew how: she gave of her best. And, as her confidence grew, she had become one of Gretel's better ministers – and a dependable ally in Cabinet meetings.

Bethany had never really understood how Gretel had singled her out from the relative obscurity of her OCM status, but she'd always suspected it was connected to that sorry business over the snatched baby.

Years earlier, Bethany had happened to be strolling down a laneway when she had noticed a well-dressed tall woman carrying a young baby pass by her, hurrying in the opposite direction. Two things had gone through her mind at that instant, the second of which being that she thought it odd how the baby was being carried rather than wheeled along in a pram. Her first thought, however, had been to admire the expensive clothes and the beautiful high-heeled shoes that the mother was wearing.

She had thought no more of it until a news bulletin reported that a baby had been snatched from its pram that same day. Naturally, she'd wondered whether the perpetrator was the person she had seen, although, as she was later ashamed to admit, she had doubted that such an elegant person could commit such a crime. Placing her own feelings (of how awful she would feel accusing an innocent person) above those of the frantic mother, she had decided to wait till the next day, strongly hoping that the baby would by then have been found. When the child wasn't, she knew she had to report what she had seen, and she duly did.

Later that same day, she had been relieved to learn that the baby had been found and returned to its family. But that was far from the end of things for her. A security agent had come to her home to interview her about the woman she had seen. The officer was charming, attentive, respectful and, to her mind, very handsome. A relationship between the pair of them had developed from that visit, and even now, many years later, Bethany considered Jacques (as the agent had called himself) the love of her life.

Jacques had shown her a photo of a person she would later come to know as Eva Baritz. He had asked her if this was the person she had seen, and she had agreed she thought it was. About three weeks later, when their relationship had deepened into intimacy, he told her that the woman she had identified had been charged. When she had asked him what would happen to the (as-yet-unnamed) woman, Jacques had looked very troubled. He told her in confidence that the person had a form of mental illness and had been placed under surveillance to avoid such an incident occurring again.

Bethany still remembered the scene well. Gently stroking her face, Jacques had said how worried he was for Bethany's own sake. He had explained that if proceedings against the woman went ahead, she, Bethany, would be the chief witness and therefore subjected to a gruelling experience from the defence lawyers. He had seen what could happen before: the lawyers would deride Bethany's identification as merely a jealous eye for a good pair of shoes, make jokes at her expense and trash her reputation. She could even risk losing her incumbency.

He had put it to Bethany that, as the woman she had identified had returned the baby unharmed, was receiving treatment and was under the watchful eye of the Department of Security and Intelligence, why would Bethany want to go through with a trial when only she would be the loser?

From time to time over the ensuing days, Jacques had gently suggested that she withdraw her identification by making a statement that she was no longer certain she could recognise the woman she had seen so briefly. He'd never pressured her, and she'd believed then, and had always continued to believe, that Jacques was only concerned for what might happen to her.

She had taken his advice. The case against the woman had collapsed and been withdrawn.

She and Jacques had continued to spend as much time together as possible. He usually stayed over at her place – that she had never been to his home did not strike her as strange till much later. They were very happy times, and she remembered them with pleasure; she had loved Jacques and had felt loved in return.

Some two to three weeks after the case against Eva had been dropped, Jacques had told her he had to go away for a while on business. Sad to be apart from him but anticipating the continuance of their relationship upon his return, they had said a fond farewell. Bethany had neither seen nor heard from Jacques since that day of parting. She had tried to locate him, fearing he had become ill or had an accident, but she'd simply got nowhere; Jacques had vanished. Six months later, Gretel invited her into the Inner Cabinet.

Bethany had always maintained her discretion on the matter, even when she'd realised she would be working with Eva. This hadn't been difficult, as Eva clearly had absolutely no recollection that she had walked by Bethany that fateful day.

CHAPTER 41

Two days after Timothy's forewarning, Gretel was still feeling aggrieved and angry that after devoting much of her life to the good of her citizens, and just when she was on the very cusp of resignation, her presidency could be in danger of being besmirched. Sighing, she returned to other matters, one eye on the newsfeed that Bethany had messaged her to watch.

The latest news from the Space Centre was good; the capsule had successfully separated from the spacecraft. Before too long, Sebastian (in the capsule) would lose contact with the ground control staff, and eventually also with Tanzi. The tickertape elaborated that ground control would continue to maintain a skeleton presence for at least the next two years, awaiting contact from one or other (but preferably both) of the astronauts.

*

Professor Kupka noticed the newsfeed as he and Miss Geary emerged from their meeting with the Hospital Board. They were both preoccupied, but they couldn't help but be interested in the latest space news. They had presented to the Board members their now strong opinions concerning Aneeka Raine's cause of death.

They both agreed that her death was likely due to the genotoxic effect of paracetamol on the strand of her DNA disturbed during her participation in an experimental gene editing procedure, the research being related, in ways yet unknown, to the space mission. He had asserted that the ingestion of the paracetamol had occurred before the mutated DNA could have had the time to repair itself.

It was probable, he had added, that another citizen, a Claus Proger, had died in not dissimilar, although not identical, circumstances, having undergone an earlier prototype of the procedure. The research in both cases was conducted by Professor Eva Baritz, he had stated.

The outcome of their representation to the Board was as they had intended. The Board announced it was in receipt of new information of a sufficiently serious nature to justify a new inquiry into the death of Aneeka Raine – and possibly a related case, also. The Judiciary would investigate whether or not negligence charges could be laid against Professor Baritz, and consequently against her employer, the Government.

*

A weary Aleck, supported by Erik, met with Bruce Daniels and laid all before him. Aleck again asked if Bruce would be his and Cameron's lawyer in the case, to be lodged by Aleck, against the Government for its lack of due care in the death of Aneeka and the consequent damages suffered by Cameron. Bruce agreed, saying he would also be notifying the trustees of Oostends to seek their support in the related case against the Government. Feeling his mission had been accomplished, Aleck set off to return home to Cameron, leaving Bruce and Erik to watch the latest space news filter through.

*

Some days after the launch, Rueben posted his articles. It was the first time in ages that he had published controversial material without checking it for approval from Jacques. He knew how unhappy Jacques would be, but he felt elated by the sense of freedom and power to do his job to the best of his ability. He was an investigative journalist and loving it.

Cancer has its upside, who would have thunk it! he half joked to himself. He also gave silent thanks to the space program, since any attempt by the Government to close the news networks down would also prevent news about its signature event being transmitted.

*

By the time Leon placed a return call through to Javier, he was confident that even if the Government orchestrated a later network crash, sufficient people would have picked up Rueben's articles and be relaying their contents through other less technological means. In Leon's mind, the movement to reclaim democracy was underway.

He apologised to Javier for having been too preoccupied to return his earlier call. An earnest conversation between the two men then ensued, at the end of which they both agreed they had reached a workable compromise.

*

Gretel's Cabinet ministers had barely slept in days. They had all been glued to their devices to keep up with the latest space news, while some had also been on their phones lobbying for support to switch portfolios or add Timothy's responsibilities to their portfolios. Bethany was surprised how many of the Cabinet believed the rumours that Timothy had been sacked.

Bethany hadn't slept well either, not that this was due to worries over Timothy's future. She had left her devices on so she could awake from sleep every couple of hours and check on the news from the Space Centre. In so doing, she happened to read one of Rueben's articles. Disregarding the time, she had immediately messaged Gretel to alert her to read his words. She had been unable to get back to sleep afterwards.

It was a tired, straggly group of ministers who assembled for their regular Cabinet meeting that morning. To the visible surprise of several, Timothy was present.

Gretel arrived punctually, greeting them all cheerfully. Afterwards, Bethany would always say that this meeting was Gretel's most consummate performance.

*

Gretel dealt with the routine matters first, quickly and efficiently, then referred to the latest update on the space program. On completion of these agenda items, Gretel gazed out at her ministers, a perceptible smile on her lips. Coolly, she said she hoped by now they had all read the other news of the day, but in case they hadn't, she would summarise the published articles.

The room was hushed, with all ministers fully attentive as she spoke. When Gretel concluded that the articles were, by and large, reasonably factual, there was a collective intake of breath.

Without elaboration, she acknowledged that there did appear to be some circumstantial evidence that the Government, through its ignorance, had failed to protect at least one of its citizens who had recently died. She paused for an instant before calmly qualifying that the allegation of there being two deaths, over which, as the articles claimed, the Government had a duty of care, could also be true, but this was yet to be firmly substantiated and seemed less likely. Nevertheless, as the Head of Government, she expressed regret and deepest sympathy to any of the bereaved families, her words being met with a subdued "Hear, hear" from her ministers.

Gretel then asked her ministers if they felt that the Government should reach out to the families of the deceased and provide some assistance if needed. There being a show of hands in favour, she nominated Magda (the Treasurer) and Grigor (the Minister for Health) to look into this.

Sensing a restlessness in the room, she acknowledged that many of her ministers would have questions they wished to ask, but she requested that they save these until after she'd completed her comments.

She proceeded to address her Cabinet.

"On the day following the space launch, we had the pleasure of dining together, thereby rounding off two perfect days for me," she began. "So perfect," she explained, "that I should have included something else in the speech I made that evening. Instead, I shall now be revealing that omission to this morning's gathering of my respected ministers."

Gretel breathed in, trying to quell the unexpected surge of emotion she suddenly felt. Once she regained her self-control, she smiled and announced with a clear, steady voice: "It is my intention to activate the process that will, in due course, lead to me stepping down as your president."

Almost all her ministers seemed genuinely surprised. One by one they stood to congratulate Gretel on her achievements during her presidency, their words culminating in a resounding round of applause echoing around the room.

After thanking her ministers for their generous words of praise, Gretel opened up the meeting for questions and discussion.

Many questions were raised about the approach that should be taken in response to the allegations that had been published, but there were many more questions about the procedure to identify Gretel's successor. Having dismissed the few questions that had asked whether her resignation was being forced as a result of the news articles, Gretel focused on the procedure for installing the next president.

There were now very few ministers with first-hand experience of this procedure, most not having witnessed the transition from Homer to Nuewen. Explaining that she intended to adopt much the same process, Gretel outlined a précised version for the benefit of the majority of her Cabinet.

"Already, a shortlist of three candidates has been recommended by the Department of Security and Intelligence. These names will be announced in the press release to be issued later today," she informed her ministers, noting that citizens could then, if they so wished, make constructive comment through the OCMs.

"Naturally, that applies to ministers too. You are welcome to express appropriate comments, although all of you should accept that one of the three persons already shortlisted will become the next president," she said, reminding her ministers that secret deals and backroom plotting belonged to an older system of government, one that had no place in Revised Democracy.

"In due course I will anoint my successor, and there will then be a period where I shall work with that person to help introduce this incoming president into matters of government, just as President Homer did for me. Then, when both parties feel it right, I shall formally resign."

In response to a question, Gretel intimated that the entire process could take about four to five weeks, perhaps less.

She was then asked who the three candidates were. Choosing not to list them in order of preference, Gretel gave their names in alphabetical order: "Ministers Augustine, Cresswell and Nagita." She asked the three shortlisted ministers to meet with her over lunch.

Noting with some amusement that her ministers seemed keen to discuss the pros and cons of each candidate with their colleagues, she closed the meeting.

Shortly afterwards, she released a carefully worded notice of her intention to stand down as President. An overwhelming wave of emotional fatigue engulfed her, one coupled with relief. It was done.

The immediate impact of Gretel's announcement was better than Gretel could have hoped. It delivered a severe blow to the gossip that her resignation would be forced – an immediate fall from grace, essentially a sacking, one linked to the implication that the Government was complicit in the deaths of two citizens.

Clearly, it was argued, the President had been intending to stay only until the space launch; she had released the shortlist of candidates (which would have taken some lengthy time to construct), and she must have been planning her resignation long before the recent news about the lack of the Government's duty of care.

On balance, Gretel thought she was winning the debate sparked by the notice of her resignation. She was pleased with the calmness and detachment she felt, now that she was on the pathway to retirement. She knew she had truly tried to do her best to improve her country and the lives of its citizens.

However, there was still the matter of the deaths. The concern over Professor Baritz's actions was accelerating, in spite of a conflicted admiration for the professor's contribution to the space mission. Gretel discussed this with Javier, and they decided it was best for Eva that she remain at the Space Centre for the time being.

*

Gretel held several discussions with her potential replacements, very keen to listen as they outlined their visions for the future. She knew Bethany would make a compassionate leader, genuine in her willingness to devote herself to the Country, and she would continue to administer Gretel's viewpoint – but Gretel thought that an incoming leader, while respecting the past, should also have new ideas for the future. Shinzo was keen to address the potential of the digital economy and the importance of maintaining data security, but Gretel didn't detect much empathy for the everyday lives of the citizens in his presentation. (In fact, as she would confide to Javier later, he sounded like an economics professor cum technocrat impatiently addressing a struggling student.) Still, without strong infrastructure, progress would falter – and Bethany's weakness was that she had shown no innovation, opting instead to maintain the status quo.

That left Timothy. His plans had taken Gretel by surprise. He was not in a rush to do so, but over time he planned to re-involve citizens in the selection of those in the Government. Ultimately, he wanted to refresh Revised Democracy with an updated version, one in which political parties would be reintroduced and citizens given back some voting rights.

At Gretel's look of horror, Timothy hurriedly said he was still thinking through how best this would come about and promised he would be treading carefully and taking lots of advice. He then outlined to her his current thinking, welcoming any thoughts she might have.

"Citizens would cast two votes, one to elect the OCM to represent their particular community's subdivision, the second to nominate the preferred party from which the Inner Cabinet ministers should be drawn.

"Each party's manifesto would provide the information on which the second vote would be made. As no single party would likely get all the votes, each party would be allocated the number of ministers in proportion to the number of votes that party received, forcing the Government to be one of coalition."

Since ministers would not all be drawn from a single party, Timothy argued, compromise, negotiation and working together – the hallmarks of Revised Democracy as it had become under Gretel's leadership – would continue.

Gretel smiled thinly, and Timothy continued to explain his vision.

"Once the ministers of the Inner Cabinet have been confirmed, they would elect one among them to become president. The party with the greatest number of votes would have the most ministers, and therefore the President might normally be the leader of that party – but not automatically, depending on the distribution of votes, the will of the ministers, and the advice from the Department of Security and Intelligence. However, once chosen, the President would have the power, responsibility and choice to allocate the ministerial portfolios across party divides," he explained.

"Flexibility to allocate portfolios to experts non-aligned to any party could also be permitted if there was good reason so to do, thereby increasing the size of the Inner Cabinet – not unlike the precedent you have set, Gretel."

When Gretel showed no reaction, Timothy added that some upper limit would need to be set to ensure this power was not abused. "The brains in AI can figure that out," he said.

She asked what type of voting system Timothy envisaged.

"My current thinking is that the first vote for the OCMs should be preferential but the second vote for the party should be first-past-the-post. Voting to occur maybe every seven years, but with the two votes to be staggered, although I've not really given much thought to that just yet.

"What do you think about these ideas, Gretel?"

Gretel rolled her eyes, saying that she really didn't know what to think just yet, she'd been taken by surprise. However, she added a cautionary reflection. "Hasn't history shown us over and over that allowing untrained citizens to make a judgement about the selection of their leaders doesn't work out well?"

Timothy grinned in response. "Maybe I have greater faith in our citizens than you appear to have," he said, adding more seriously, "I do think it's important for ministers to know and be known by their citizens.

"Oh, and by the way, Gretel, if appointed, I intend to instigate some reform to your otherwise excellent education system. Mathematics and the sciences will always be highly valued, but so too should Literature and the Humanities. Maybe we'll even ensure Politics is an essential learning field so as to allay your concern that citizens are not learned enough to make political choices," he teased.

Gretel quipped: "That could be the most sensible thing you've said so far." Timothy looked surprised.

Gretel continued. "Since we're being candid with each other, let me ask you a personal question. Why have you never revealed your connection to President Homer? I confess I have always been intrigued by this."

Timothy explained that if he were to become president, he wanted this to be in recognition of his own ability, not that of his relative. "Actually, Gretel, to be completely frank with you, I am also scared of letting the family name down if I reveal my lineage yet fail to become president. So, unless or until you anoint me as your successor, I'll not be mentioning my family background."

Gretel nodded, satisfied with his answer, her respect further strengthened.

"In turn, Gretel, since it's confession time, maybe you could tell me why you never took me under your wing."

"You want the honest answer, Timothy?"

"Yes, please."

"Because you were such a buffoon: conceited, arrogant and insufferable."

Sighing, Timothy quietly asked: "And is that what you still think?"

Gretel paused for a moment before she replied.

"There are things about you that I personally still find irritating, but you've actually been a very good minister and carried out your portfolio, one could say, with distinction. You and I are very different, but to answer your question, I no longer consider you a buffoon or insufferable, and I respect you for not advertising your heritage."

She smiled and stood. Timothy would have to be content with that appraisal, as their meeting time was over.

While Gretel was not particularly comfortable with Timothy's ideas, he was the only candidate with a vision for the future.

"Presumably, that's why Cabut and his AI services shortlisted him as the first choice," she remarked to Javier. He pointed out that Timothy was not being rash in his proposals; he had said he would not act immediately to change the form of the Government, which was both wise and gave hope that he could change his mind once he better understood how the Government functioned. Gretel found Javier's calmness soothing.

*

Contact with Tanzi on the spacecraft was becoming very faint. All contact with Sebastian had finally been lost, the fate of the capsule unknown, and it would remain unknown until the astronaut was able to re-establish contact – when, or if, that eventuated.

News emanating from the Space Centre would now virtually cease, which posed a danger for the Government – the fickle citizens might put the great achievement of the mission out of their minds. It could be a long time before events would rekindle their interest and pride again.

Bethany had been tasked by Gretel to avoid this by ensuring that updates were released from time to time – updates designed to remind the citizens of the excitement and the potential achievements of the mission.

Bethany decided to enlist Rueben to assist her with the task. She had taken an instant liking to the journalist when he had interviewed her about the space mission, although she realised now that he'd had an ulterior agenda. She would have to be more on her guard about what she said, perhaps, but – as she had reasoned with Gretel – there was an old saying about keeping your enemies close. Added to which, he was a fine journalist.

*

Rueben was surprised but quite pleased to receive an invitation to meet with Bethany and discuss the proposal she'd outlined. He understood all too well that his prognosis was poor – less than a year, nine months at best, his doctor had advised. He had yet to share the news with his wife, thinking dryly that he didn't want her to get overexcited. Not that he had much to leave her financially. He'd never gone down the cheque-book journalism pathway, despite some offers. He'd earnt enough to get by on and had no regrets. A small retainer from the Government, however, would be a nice way of seeing him out. He was definitely interested in the minister's proposal.

Their meeting was amicable enough, the only sticking point in Rueben's mind being that Bethany wanted to employ him for a two-year period, the timeline of the space mission. Not wishing to share with her the real reason why that was too long a timeframe, Rueben had suggested that since there would be a change of president before long, perhaps a six-month contract would be more suitable.

"After all," he had quipped, "this could always be extended either by you as the minister or, should you have taken a higher position by then, your replacement." Bethany laughed and agreed to his suggestion, inviting him to take tea with her.

As she poured the tea, she said matter-of-factly: "Not sure I'll be going anywhere, but six months would allow me to terminate our contract should you again write with an agenda you have not shared with me." He felt a slight blush across his cheeks.

CHAPTER 42

Stewart Weisman had been unsuccessful in his attempts to contact Eva. As her lawyer, he felt obligated to inform her of the news articles penned by Rueben.

With Eva likely to be out of town at the Space Centre for some time yet, he had decided that the responsible thing to do was to seek an appointment with Professor Kupka – Rueben had given him the doctor's name.

On returning to his chambers after meeting the professor, Stewart found himself feeling very sombre. Neither his exchange with Kupka nor the breaking news about the President's resignation was likely to be good news for his client.

He was now quite concerned for Eva's wellbeing. He'd made enquires to the minister concerned: Minister Cresswell had told him that the Government felt it prudent for Eva to remain for the time being where she was, but she'd refused to be drawn any further.

Stewart had decided to lodge a request to travel to the Space Centre to meet with his client. Unsurprisingly, this had been turned down. He understood, from his visit to Professor Kupka, the seriousness of the new information, but it appeared that his client was being denied legal advice. Consequently, he had lodged a protest on her behalf to the courts.

The Justices had noted his concern and referred the matter back to the Government, requesting an explanation as to why Professor Baritz was remaining at the Space Centre. The response from the Government was that she was critical to the space mission and could not be spared as yet. However, in an attempt to appease the Justices, the Government provided a statement (purporting to be from Eva) in which she requested a delay in any procedures until her role in the space mission became less critical.

Stewart did not feel reassured. He was glad when finally, at last, Eva contacted him. She repeated the Government's response and authorised him to act on her behalf.

"I really can't be bothered with such distractions," she said, while promising that she would in future return his calls.

Stewart couldn't convince her that serious proceedings might be filed against her. He explained that Aneeka Raine's obstetrician, Miss Geary, had testified that Eva had not explained the risk or the experimental nature of what she was doing, either to Aneeka as the participant, or to herself. Furthermore, Professor Kupka had given his opinion about why the experiment may have had a deadly effect on Aneeka, also hypothesising that a previous volunteer, Claus Proger, may have suffered the same fate. Both doctors had condemned in the strongest terms Eva's unethical use of citizens as unwitting guinea pigs, and their viewpoints had now been endorsed by the Hospital Board.

"This is getting serious, Eva."

"Oh, I'm sure you're up to the challenge, Stewart! Just explain that there wouldn't have been a space mission without my research," Eva responded gaily.

"Eva, if you are found criminally negligent you could face a period of detention," stressed Stewart.

There was a short pause. "Darling, you're being naïve. I've been under detention for years." And with that she ended the call, leaving Stewart feeling even more unsettled.

*

The Justices were being kept busy.

Bruce Daniels had just filed notice of a damages case on behalf of Cameron Raine, with Eva and the Government as co-defendants. As had been expected, the proceedings against Eva were dragging the Government along with her.

Javier knew it was time to take Timothy's advice and talk to Leon about the activity in the Judiciary Department.

On his arrival at Javier's office, Leon first congratulated Javier on his coming retirement now that Gretel had announced her decision.

"I guess I have no choice," he shrugged. "More time for cooking, though," he half smiled.

"Now, Leon, what are we – and I emphasise 'we' here – what are we going to do about Eva and her mental state?" he asked, immediately getting to the point.

Leon's reply was cautiously optimistic. "It seems to me," he began, "having thought a lot about this lately, that there's a chance that she can avoid conviction on the Proger case without revealing her mental state. That has the advantage of not raising any doubts about the safety of the space mission, too, something that would be troubling me if I were in your shoes." Leon glanced up at Javier, and he merely nodded to acknowledge the point.

Leon continued. "Her lawyer should be able to argue the case that Eva had no awareness Proger was a Soul from the North and that it is therefore not beyond the realms of possibility that his death was a result of his genes, not Eva's testing."

Javier frowned. "Doesn't that run the risk of shifting blame on to Cabut, the government official who recommended Proger as a candidate?"

"Just for a moment, consider what it would mean if this Cabut character was unwittingly blamed," replied Leon. "Gretel's retiring; neither of you need Cabut anymore. The next president would almost certainly prefer to appoint his or her own Security team, so Cabut is expendable."

Before Javier could protest, Leon continued. "Cabut made a mistake or didn't check the background of Proger carefully enough – something like that could be argued quite easily. Result: Cabut gets transferred to another department, where in due course he can be resurrected once there's no further interest in Proger."

"Doesn't this still leave the Government culpable as Cabut's employer?" argued Javier.

"To some extent I suppose so, Javier. There'd have to be some recompense, given the law about corporations being responsible for the actions, deliberate or otherwise, of their employees. That's just routine civil stuff that Stewart Weisman, Eva's lawyer, is good at handling."

"Okay, let's for a moment say that the Proger case can be handled. What about the Raine case?" asked Javier awkwardly. "There are things that puzzle me about Aneeka Raine: I mean, your daughter. What about Aneeka's parents? Why have they not come forward? Are they deceased?"

Leon explained that Kay and Ann had long been institutionalised with dementia. They were incapable of absorbing the news about their estranged daughter.

Javier was puzzled; dementia had been treatable for some time. Before he could question further, Leon elaborated. "Kay and Ann became recluses, so by the time their dementia was picked up, neither was in a position to sanction treatment for the other. It was up to their next of kin to give permission. I have recently learnt that their next of kin vetoed any treatment."

"You mean Aneeka refused to help her parents?" he said, incredulous.

"Yep, I think it was Aneeka's payback for their treatment of her as a child. I don't believe she ever discussed the matter with Aleck, despite how close they were. Kupka told me. By the way, Javier, Professor Kupka is a force to be reckoned with. He may be all sweetness and care towards the young, but he's not someone to be crossed lightly. It's his doggedness that has convinced the Hospital Board to reopen Aneeka's case."

"Thanks for the warning," chuckled Javier wryly. "Now Leon, my turn to put an idea about Eva to you. We have left her up at the Space Centre for the time being, but she can't stay there forever. We can bring her back to address the charges against her. Let's say we did and she more or less wins the Proger case. She almost certainly is not going to get off lightly in the Raine case, given what happened to Proger. We could plead mental illness – that's a viable option. However, what say you about not bringing her back, getting her assessed up at the Space Centre, and negotiating a settlement whereby she has to go into care?"

It was Leon's turn to look puzzled. "There's no suitable care possible up at the Space Centre, of course she'll have to come back."

Javier sighed. "There is a possibility of care further north of the Space Centre if you think about it, Leon. As I understand it, if he gains the presidency, Timothy has plans to open up the North, to start to acknowledge its people and to provide infrastructure and aid to them. It's a good idea regardless of who becomes president – although Timothy will prevail, that's certain – but I digress."

Collecting his train of thought, Javier continued.

"Eva could be placed in this area. Maybe, eventually, she could teach some of the people there. It would be good PR for her to be quoted as saying she was going to the North out of respect for Claus Proger and her regret that she may have unwittingly contributed to his death. While up there, the Aneeka Raine case can proceed, with some compensation to be paid as a gesture of goodwill, but with the settlement negotiated in camera between the lawyers, who accept between them that Eva is not well. No guilty verdict would be recorded, but Eva and the Government would both contribute to a compensation package for the young Raine."

"How can Eva afford to pay compensation?" Leon asked.

Javier smiled broadly. Wrapping his arm around Leon's shoulder, he said, "That is where you come in, my good friend. My guess is you've already offered to support your grandson, and my hunch is your offer has largely been turned down. Be that as it may, here is your chance to ensure the child is provided for without his father feeling indebted to you. You pay Eva's share and, while you're at it, benevolent donor that you are, you can chip in with a donation towards a northern infrastructure package. The Government will finance much of it by raising funds, but your bit will make sure that Eva is taken care of in the North."

Leon slowly shook his head. "I must be getting old, Javier – you had this all figured out before I got here. You only wanted to discuss me supporting Eva to cover when you and Gretel will no longer be able to divert government funding for that purpose. Of course my answer is 'yes', but can't you get Timothy to continue the Government's contribution?"

"We're hoping Gretel may be able to convince him to contribute something, but Gretel is of the opinion that he will reduce the amount set aside for Eva and, really, who could blame him for that? Eva is our problem, not the new president's."

*

In the car, Leon processed the feeling that, for once, he'd been outplayed. He really was becoming an old man, he realised. Soon he'd be forgetting names and where he'd put his keys and so on, the thoughts not lifting his spirits.

Leon said very little to Clovis, even though he was sat next to him in the front seat of the car. Eventually, Clovis broke the silence to ask if Leon was feeling alright. Pulling himself together, he cheekily replied that he'd be feeling much better if Clovis would reconsider his offer of employment.

"You do know that a new president may not continue to employ your boss, young Clovis, don't you? It would be strategic of you to have a back-up plan," Leon said, to which Clovis had replied with a touch of seriousness that he'd been wondering about that.

"Do you have any inside information on the chances my boss will go?" Clovis asked.

"No, I don't, but let me assure you that my job offer remains open until things become clearer in that regard," replied Leon. "Now, play some music to soothe my tired person."

CHAPTER 43

Stewart listened in silence as Javier outlined the way President Nuewen wanted the case of Proger versus Baritz to proceed. He could see the suggestions being made by Javier were good, but, as Eva's lawyer, he felt the case against her was fairly hypothetical.

In his opinion, there wasn't a lot of evidence supporting the claims made about the circumstances of Proger's death. Despite the high respect in which Professor Kupka was held, his was a retrospective theory, one based on a different person. Kupka had neither met, examined, nor had any involvement with the citizen Proger. His theory was more a conjecture advanced only after Eva's indisputable involvement with Aneeka Raine.

When Javier had finished speaking, Stewart also pointed out that no files pertaining to Proger had been found in Eva's records when her files had been seized by officials from the coroner's office. As well, she had denied at that time any knowledge of the name Claus Proger.

"I believe we have a strong case to have the charges dropped," Stewart said.

Javier patiently replied, "Perhaps, perhaps not, but it's not a risk the Government wishes to take," adding a moment later, "and don't forget there's that hospital orderly who bears witness to having seen a similar outcome in Proger as was noted for Raine."

The mention of the orderly reminded Stewart of another point in Eva's defence. "What about the surgeon who performed Proger's vasectomy? Why hasn't that person been brought into the mix?" he asked.

There was a pause before Javier replied. "Stewart, there was no vasectomy. In strictest confidence, I'll tell you that two Department of Health officials foolishly mentioned this in a response to the FOI request. The two officers involved were confused. They have been reprimanded and stood down. Apparently, they were trying to fob off those who were requesting information when there was none to give. Proger does not appear on any hospital records." Javier added he'd appreciate Stewart's cooperation in not going down that rabbit hole.

Stewart tried another tack. He felt that keeping Eva at the Space Centre weakened her defence of the case against her. He argued that she should be brought back to testify; she'd be an asset to the case, and then she could return to the Space Centre where she was needed to continue her brilliant work.

Javier decided not to accept Stewart's advice, stating that Eva was too important to the space mission for her to return for the Proger case. This left Stewart feeling disappointed: he would have liked to have talked to Eva in person.

"Let us now turn to the Raine versus Baritz case please, Stewart," Javier requested.

Stewart was in complete agreement that the Raine case needed to be separated in time from the Proger one. As it was the more serious case from Eva's perspective, he argued it should be heard only after the Proger case had been completed.

He was not shocked to hear Javier raise mental illness, but he again argued that it would have been best to assess her at the same time as she returned for the Proger case. However, as that was not to be, he had little room for manoeuvre; he could see Javier was firm on that point. Nevertheless, should mental illness be established, Stewart confirmed that he would be comfortable negotiating a settlement with Bruce Daniels, whom he knew well, and he was confident that a fair and reasonable outcome would result.

They decided to reconvene once Javier had arranged for Eva's mental health assessment.

*

Things went according to plan. The Judiciary were agreeable to separating the two cases, and Eva's presence at the Space Centre was accepted as an understandable necessity at this particular time in the historic mission. The Proger case was set to be heard by a single Justice, as Javier had intended.

Shortly before the hearing, the nominated Justice received a deposition from Gretel on behalf of the Government. The deposition noted that the citizen was an illegal immigrant, a Soul from the North for whom there were no records of entry. There were therefore no records of his next of kin, and no assessment appeared to have been conducted regarding his state of health upon entry or any potential health risks that he might have brought to the Country. That Claus Proger may have been a harbinger of hitherto unknown diseases could not be ruled out, and, on behalf of her government, the President had apologised for this failure of the Government to protect its own citizens.

In order not to raise alarm at this breach of protocol and possible public safety, the Government was prepared to make a compensatory settlement offer in return for the matter being quietly dropped from further investigation, if that so pleased the Justice. Further, there being no known next of kin, the Government proposed that the settlement should take the form of an increase in the funds allocated to the administration of the northern lands.

At the commencement of proceedings, the Justice asked Stewart to approach the bench. Javier looked on as Stewart indicated to the Justice that the offer would be acceptable to his client, on whose behalf he had been empowered to speak.

The case was over in under half an hour.

No finding was given regarding any contact Professor Baritz may or may not have had with the citizen. The Justice applauded the President and her government for acting to atone for the lapse in security by Border Control in allowing a Soul to enter the Country.

The Justice's concluding remarks also contained the recommendation that the Government should hold an internal enquiry into the workplace practices of the civil servant or servants who had either failed to identify, or who had ignored the background of, the now deceased Proger, with particular scrutiny of any who may have been in a position to entice the citizen to participate in any research or other such undertaking.

Javier left the hearing and headed back to the office to update Gretel.

*

The response to his reporting of the Proger case rather bemused Rueben. It was not a headline story, yet it did elicit a surprising number of comments. Some viewpoints, critical of the bureaucracy that had failed to identify the man from the North, were bordering on racist, Rueben observed: no concern for the citizen or what had happened to him, but more an outrage that one of those northern Souls had lived in their midst, thereby exposing the citizens to who knew what. Rueben sometimes despaired of the selfishness of his fellow citizens, and this was one of those times. Fortunately, there were other more nuanced comments, including from those advocating that the Government had a duty to do more to help the unfortunate souls segregated in the North.

Rueben's other recent articles, those covering the background of the space program, were being well received, and Bethany was fulsome in her praise of his writings. She'd particularly enjoyed reading his description of a now-outdated theory that both type1 and type 2 human doubles coexisted in the same time space but moved along paths invisible to each other – possibly, as one went from A to B, the other type travelled from B to A in another dimension. Rueben had likened it to moving along out-of-phase sinusoidal trajectories in different dimensions. At places where, in two-dimensional space, the curves would intersect, Rueben had postulated that those instances coincided with the instants of intuition that humans often felt but could never quite explain. He added a disclaimer that this had never been a credible scientific theory, and yet it had resonated with some of his readers, according to the feedback.

Rueben found himself looking forward to visiting the minister; gradually, an unlikely friendship of sorts was building between the two of them. It was nice to be in the company of someone who seemed to appreciate him and his work. If he were honest, he'd also have to add that it was nice to have some pleasant female company – to spend time with someone he felt at ease with and with whom he could discuss a variety of subjects.

Bethany also seemed to enjoy the breadth of the conversation that flowed easily between them. There was no need for Rueben to bring his articles in to her, but she did nothing to deter him, and this pretext gave them the opportunity to enjoy some time, and sometimes even some food, together.

*

Gretel had noticed that Rueben was appearing at Bethany's office quite frequently. She and Timothy had even shared a giggle about it during one of their own, by now very frequent, meetings.

She had announced Timothy as her preferred choice of successor. There had been some minor dissent from some of her ministers initially, but this had come to be outweighed by the more considered responses that had followed.

It was rare for citizens to respond with comments. On this occasion, however, surprisingly many did, taking the opportunity to express their support for the 'Minister for Roads', as some called him, having met Timothy in person and been impressed by his personality and his ability to solve problems to their satisfaction. Timothy seemed particularly chuffed by this, and she noted to herself that it added weight to his long-term plan to restore a democratically elected form of governance.

It was Timothy, rather than Gretel, who first raised 'the Eva problem' in one of their meetings. Gretel started to give him a condensed version of Eva's background, but he interrupted her partway through.

"Gretel, Leon has told me much of her story, so please don't attempt to patronise me or censor what you tell me. I know her past is entwined with yours, and Leon's, but it is not her past that I'm asking about; it's her present, and the potential impact that may have on the Government."

Gretel responded with some asperity. "My problem in discussing this fully is that you, Timothy, have your feet in two different camps. You've been part of the influential body that has cast doubt on Eva's integrity, yet, as president-elect, it is you who will be dealing with any aftermath if her case is not very carefully handled."

Continuing, she added, "Reality check, Timothy, the space mission is my legacy – and that gives me a particular incentive to ensure that Eva's situation is handled sensitively. Prior to your group's interference, I had a good plan for what to do with Eva, but that's almost certainly gone by the bye thanks to you and your non-government friends."

Since the start of their formal meetings, this was as close to an argument as they had come, despite sharing different political views on some issues.

Timothy seemed unruffled by her tone, and he responded evenly to Gretel's outburst. "You should deal with me as the incoming President, nothing more, nothing less. Let's come back to Eva's court case when you're calmer. But tell me, did some poor civil servant really get shafted over the Proger case? And if so, who was the unlucky victim?"

Gretel regretted losing her temper and resolved that it wouldn't happen again. She had chosen Timothy to succeed her, so she needed to discuss such topics with him; besides which, doing so offered her and Javier a form of insurance against any later criticism of their actions. Timothy could hardly turn on her if they could show that he knew about and was complicit in what had been going on.

So, she told Timothy in strictest confidence that Eva's private secretary, Cabut, had likely selected Proger for the testing, though whether the testing actually took place had not been established. Admitting that Cabut was on loan from Security, Gretel pointed out that his name could never be revealed, let alone published, and that at a later stage she might elaborate further about Cabut and his role.

Returning to Eva, Gretel went on to explain how the Raine case was going to be handled and settled out of court. "Thereafter, Eva will be retired and transferred into care in a purpose-built facility in the North, returning when the space mission achieves its objective," she said. "And, if you so wish, you could claim this as the first step in your plans for the North, Timothy."

Their conversation proceeded from there, with Gretel advising and responding as best she could to Timothy's questions. As they were about to break for lunch, Gretel suggested they resume in an hour, when it would be timely to start discussing security issues.

*

Bruce Daniels greeted Stewart Weisman cordially. Although they rarely socialised, they enjoyed a good professional relationship, one based on mutual respect and collegiality. Bruce was the more senior of the two, and so the meeting took place at his chambers. The two took coffee and chatted about other cases, mutual colleagues and even the personalities of some of the Justices, before they finally turned to the purpose of their meeting.

Stewart began by laying out the argument for the Raine case to be settled out of court. Bruce counteracted some points, but he nodded in agreement to others. Bruce felt confident that when he took Stewart's proposition to Aleck, he would come to agree, on behalf of his son Cameron, with the settlement sum the Government was prepared to offer. However, Bruce reasoned to Stewart, even accepting that Eva had a mental illness, Aleck would still want some blame to be laid upon her.

"He's lost his young wife, his son's lost his mother and has a disability as a result; you can't blame the fellow for wanting someone to be held responsible, can you, Stewie," Bruce observed.

They talked through various ways to reach a conclusion that would be acceptable to both parties, but they kept coming back to the same stumbling block. Aware that they weren't going to achieve a complete agreement that day, Bruce said he'd speak with Aleck, and then they could meet again to resume their deliberations once the psychology tests on Eva had been completed. The two lawyers shook hands, each reasonably pleased with their progress.

When Bruce later spoke to a still-weary Aleck, the response was much as he had expected. Aleck was happy with the proposal to settle with the Government and pleased that the suggested payout was quite generous. However, it wasn't money that he wanted from Eva – perhaps not even a conviction, if she was mentally ill. No, what mattered to Aleck was that Eva was truly sorry for what she'd done.

He held firm on this, though as Bruce pointed out, a mental illness would probably prevent her from feeling sorry, so she was unlikely to offer a genuine apology.

"Then maybe the Government could apologise on her behalf," retorted Aleck.

"Mm, maybe that's a possibility I can explore," said Bruce thoughtfully.

*

Aleck was loving looking after Cameron, despite the exhaustion he felt. He was grateful to Matilda, who had continued to drop off ready-made meals for him, and he was pleased with the professional help that Cameron was receiving. The baby was gaining weight, which was a good sign.

Leon dropped in from time to time, and Aleck laughed to see how besotted he was with his grandson. Their conversation hardly touched on court cases, government changes or the news of the day; it was always about how Cameron was getting on.

*

Leon was impressed at Timothy's discretion – whenever they talked, he was careful not to reveal the nature of his conversations with Gretel. The man was adopting the gravitas required of a president at last, he observed.

"Forgive me for asking, Timothy, but I'm curious. Can you explain when you left behind your youthful impatience and impertinence and morphed into the statesman I now observe before me?"

Timothy laughed. "You know, there was a time when I felt you had stopped believing in me, Leon. You weren't answering my calls – or if you did, you were very offhand, treating me as if I was just an over-pampered poodle. At the same time, Gretel was busy promoting people – notably Bethany, but there were others too – always overlooking me, or so it seemed. But then I came to realise that I needed to work out what really mattered to me. That soul searching, that lonely process, was what I needed to undergo."

Looking up at Leon, Timothy smiled.

"I decided to grow up, and Freddy helped me to do so. I no longer had expectations of grand rewards for little effort. The reward of effort is in having done your best for your citizens and for yourself. I was slow to realise this; my vision was too obscured by ambition."

Nodding his head, Leon returned the smile. "You and Freddy are going to be a great combination, both in government and in life," he said. And he embraced his former protégé.

CHAPTER 44

Eva was far from stupid. She knew what the tests she was required to undergo were about. So, she played a game, sometimes responding as the psychologists would expect, sometimes throwing in responses they would not expect, and even on occasion giving responses that reflected exactly her own thoughts. *Would these so-called experts be able to distinguish between my answers to their questions? Probably not,* she decided – her impression being they seemed very pedestrian.

Stewart had told her about the mental assessment of her emotional state. It seemed to Eva that he was hinting that it might be in her best interests to be diagnosed with some form of illness to help her with the court case that Aneeka's husband was bringing against her.

What a pity that Aneeka took the headache tablet, she thought crossly. *Everyone is quick to swallow a pill at the first hint of a twinge these days; a bit more stoicism would help.*

Mellowing, she remembered how pleasant Aneeka had been, and her interest in, was it genetics? She wasn't sure, but she felt a debt of gratitude to Aneeka for her role in validating her research. *I wonder how her child is, the son she was carrying,* she thought. *Maybe when he's older I can share with him that his mother helped pave the way to planet Earth.* The thought of the child caused a feeling of sadness to pass through her: the child would never know its mother. For just a nanosecond, she felt something else flow through her, something that resembled regret.

Her thoughts switched back to her own predicament. She had asked Stewart what would happen next if she was either declared to have a mental illness or declared to be of sound mind. Neither of his answers was particularly good, from her perspective. Disappointingly, too, it seemed that Gretel had withdrawn her offer of a university position. She could stay at the Space Centre, but two years with little to do was not at all appealing.

Stewart called a little later to ask her if she had any interest in the peoples of the North.

"It might be interesting to see what, if anything, those Souls have done with their territory – but other than that, why would I be interested in them?" she replied.

"Fair enough, I was just wondering whether a visit there could fill in some of your time. The North is not all that far away from the Space Centre," Stewart observed.

Later on, thinking back on Stewart's words, the thought of visiting the North did seem to have some appeal – after all, she had two years to fill in somehow or other, Eva reasoned.

*

The psychologists sent to assess Eva were somewhat confused by her. They found that she functioned in non-predictable ways, some of which came close to suggesting she had Asperger's syndrome. However, they dismissed this since other aspects of her behaviour strongly failed to support that diagnosis. The tests did confirm that Eva was highly intelligent, yet they suggested her emotional intelligence was varied. While she was capable of displaying empathy, she could also be single-minded and completely oblivious to the feelings and experiences of others. The strongest conclusion that could be drawn from the testing was that she appeared to enjoy sending contradictory signals. The psychologists felt that this personality construct was unusual, but they were unable to agree on a consensus view regarding her mental state.

For Stewart, this was not the best news for his client – and Bruce had concurred. It seemed that the case would have to be heard by the Justices after all. *This doesn't auger well for Eva,* Stewart thought dejectedly; there was a strong chance that she would be found guilty of some level of misconduct.

*

Initially, Bruce was relieved, though surprised, when the Government's Department of Security and Intelligence started to take a proactive interest in the case. He and Stewart were called in for an audience with one of its security personnel, who introduced himself as Cabut.

Bruce was unsure how he should address Cabut. *Should he be addressed as Mr Cabut, or what?* he wondered. So, taking his cue from Stewart (who seemed more at ease), he simply said, "How do you do?"

Adding further to Bruce's discomfort was his attempt to shake Cabut's hand. Cabut had held out his hand palm down – somewhat like, thought Bruce, drawing on his knowledge of old movies, an emperor expecting those that stood before him to pay homage by kissing his ring. Not that Cabut was wearing one … so perhaps he was like a dowager countess deigning to allow a feint kiss of her fingertips. The awkward manoeuvre resulted in only their fingertips touching. Bruce noticed that Stewart smoothly changed tack, lowering his hands to his sides – he simply smiled at Cabut.

Cabut was curt; no preliminary niceties were offered. He conveyed the message that Professor Baritz was actually Major General Professor Baritz, a high-ranking member of a top-secret agency, her work classified under the Secrecy Act. If she had made an error, the agency would deal with it internally, not the Justices – she was beyond their jurisdiction. Accordingly, Cabut instructed the two lawyers to settle the case by negotiating compensation between the two of them.

Bruce couldn't help himself; he rather patronisingly told Cabut that this was not the way the Country's legal system operated. At first, Cabut stared in silence at him. Then, in what seemed a threatening manner, he said that Bruce would do well not to meddle in matters of government security, and that he might require some re-education.

Declaring the meeting over, Cabut left the room. The two lawyers were shocked by his abrupt manner; Bruce, in particular, was most indignant. As they departed, Bruce remembered Jockey's government connection, Jacques someone-or-other. He'd report the surly, rude behaviour of this Cabut to Jacques. He messaged Aleck to see if he had his details.

Aleck's reply came in promptly. It said: 'He's not a minister, speak to Leon H.'

Bruce was blowed if he'd do that.

Normally a very affable person, Bruce had been quite riled by Cabut. He was the well-respected head of the Country's premier law firm, and he'd been dressed down by some officious public servant. This simply would not do. He had clout and he would use it. Bruce messaged his secretary to make an appointment for him to meet with President Nuewen.

By the time Bruce returned to his chambers, he was informed that while the President was unable to see him, perhaps another person would be able to help him if he could explain the nature of his business. And so, Bruce soon found himself speaking to Javier, the President's Principal Advisor.

Javier soothingly expressed disappointment over the manner in which Bruce and Stewart had been spoken to, and promised he would ensure that the Head of Security and Intelligence's attention was drawn to this matter. The colloquy between the two turned out to be doubly fortuitous: it allowed Bruce to take up the matter of the Government issuing an apology to Aleck, the one condition Aleck required in exchange for agreeing to settle his case against Eva. Javier agreed to discuss with the President the possibility of some public expression of government regret over Aneeka's death.

All in all, Bruce was satisfied by the level of deference and respect Javier had shown him. He rang Stewart to bring him up to date and confirmed that they should now be able to tie up any loose ends and settle Aleck's case out of court.

*

Stewart contacted Eva to tell her the good news.

"So, the wackos think I'm mad, do they?" mocked Eva. Stewart explained that was not the case; rather, the psychologists had admitted to being confused by her behaviour.

"Presumably, that's what you intended," he added. Eva gave a throaty laugh.

"Can I come home now, Stewart?" she asked, affecting a little-girl voice.

"I think, my dear, that rather depends on whether your employer thinks you are still needed where you are," said Stewart. "Take my advice and press to be brought home."

Stewart told Eva that Cabut had gone in to bat for her. He was interested that Eva expressed surprise at this.

"Fancy Cabut, who hardly knows what to say to me, coming to my defence!" she had exclaimed.

"What is his relationship to you?" Stewart asked, intrigued. "I know you work together."

"Ostensibly, he's my private secretary, but on top of that he also looks after my security – not that he knows that I know that," she said.

"Why do you need guarding, Eva?"

Eva sighed. "Why indeed? I guess it's because the nature of my work is such that it could be unsettling for the ignorant to learn too much about it while it's in progress. Then, when my work has been successfully completed, there might be some in the community who would take advantage of my work and use it for ulterior, even nefarious, purposes. Whatever, the upshot is that I live under surveillance – for my own protection, or so I'm told," she added wryly.

"Will this level of security continue now that the space mission is underway?"

"I had thought not; the plan was that I would take up a professorship in mathematics. I guess that may now depend on the new president," Eva speculated.

In his heart of hearts, Stewart knew he couldn't condone Eva's actions as 'the end benefits justify the means', although as her lawyer he would never acknowledge that thought, being honour-bound to do the best for her as he possibly could. However, despite his personal misgivings, Stewart felt a deal of sympathy for this highly intelligent but different person. Reflecting on their conversation, he wondered whether there was anything he could do to help Eva ease back into a normal life now that the case against her was as good as settled.

The thought of lobbying the incoming President on her behalf began to germinate in his mind.

*

Some days later, the Government issued a statement stating its regret at the unfortunate death of Aneeka Raine and offering its condolences to her family. Her untimely death was the result of unforeseeable events that occurred following her voluntary participation in a government research project. The President wished to record how sorry she was to learn of Mrs Raine's passing.

The statement was followed up by a personal visit from two ministers, bearing flowers, who were visiting to pay their respects to Aleck on behalf of the Government.

Aleck didn't feel soothed by the announcement but, in light of it, he stuck with his agreement and allowed the lawyers to settle Cameron's compensation payout. It was a very generous payment; Cameron would be well cared for, his legal costs were being covered, and, although he could never forgive or forget the circumstances of Aneeka's death, Aleck was quite glad to put the proceedings behind him. He did feel grateful to Bruce for all that he had been able to achieve on their behalf.

*

Following the Government's statement of regret at Aneeka's death and the subsequent settlement of both cases against her, there was a further announcement confirming that Eva would be taking the opportunity to visit the North while things were quiet at the Space Centre. Her visit would allow her to be instrumental in making recommendations to the incoming government of President Augustine for its planned future development of that hitherto largely neglected part of the Country.

Officers soon arrived at the Space Centre in order to escort Eva to the Government building in the North. Here, applications from northerners seeking to travel south were processed. The office employed only two staff, a married couple who lived on site. Above the ground floor of the Government building lay two apartments: one for the two staff, the other for the use of visiting government officials. Eva moved into the vacant apartment.

She realised she was essentially being placed under a form of arrest, a 'confined to barracks' type of thing, but she assumed it would only be for a short time. Besides, she was surprised to find herself becoming quite curious about this area of the Country she'd never before visited. So, she went willingly enough. She was allowed to take her phone, but she could only use this within the Government building – there was no signal outside.

She stayed in touch with Stewart, telling him that the first thing that struck her about the North was the difference in weather. The temperature was of a steady warmth, punctuated by short bouts of heavy rainfall and occasional lightning. The night sky was clearer than in the south of the Country, although not quite as clear as at the Space Centre.

She was free to wander and this she did, partly for exercise and partly out of curiosity. It was Stewart who first suggested she document her observations and include any recommendations or ideas for practical ways in which the Government could make improvements to this previously neglected region.

Eva felt a strange kind of freedom. Nothing was expected of her, and she happily filled her days. She rarely spoke to any of the people she passed, for that was her way. However, she did observe the diversity of ethnicity and the relative poverty of the people, judging by their clothing. There was little in the way of decent shops, just markets really. As her meals were provided for her, she quickly lost interest in the produce on offer at the food stalls. A new outfit would be good, she figured, since she'd been rotating the clothes she'd had with her at the Space Centre; however, her tastes were vastly different from the clothes on offer.

Not all of her observations were so shallow, and gradually she found that compiling her list of recommendations for the Government was an increasingly worthwhile activity. The officer on duty agreed to send her list to his superior back at home.

CHAPTER 45

The newly invested President was smiling for photographs; the era of President Augustine had begun.

In his inaugural speech, Timothy had conveyed all the right sentiments. He lightly sketched out his vision for the Country; he paid generous tribute to his predecessor, President Nuewen, expressing gratitude for her support and his humility and honour at being appointed to follow in her footsteps; and he gave thanks for the legacy he had inherited from both President Nuewen and President Homer, assuring citizens that Revised Democracy would continue to evolve under his leadership.

However, it was when he went on to explain that there was something more he had inherited from President Homer that he fully captured his listeners. He shared with pride that he was a blood relative of President Homer, a descendant through Homer's sister's lineage.

The effect of his words was electric. Bartenders were quoted as saying that citizens having a quiet ale on the way home from work had chattered of little else, some going so far as to claim that it went a long way to explaining why he had been so outstanding in his former ministerial role. There was much praise for the new president for having been so discreet about his genealogy, rather than using it to bolster his claim on the presidency. He was heartened to hear of the many toasts proposed to him, to the cheers of 'Go Timbo'.

Timothy was enjoying basking in the well wishes expressed by so many of his former fellow ministers and the good wishes of the various department heads. Of course, he recognised that many were being strategic in trying to bolster the chances of maintaining their positions, but still, it was nice to receive their congratulations, a sentiment he was sharing with Frederick, (as Freddy was now to be called).

"You know, dear Frederick, of them all, it's Bethany's generosity of spirit that I find particularly touching. She could so easily have been the one standing in my shoes, yet she has only shown genuine excitement and not a trace of envy in pledging her loyalty and offering me her support."

"There are so many people to whom I am grateful", he said, continuing his reflections, "Leon prominent among these – and of course never forgetting your own good self." Frederick seized this opportunity to divert Timothy's musings into more practical action – the composition of the first Augustine ministry needed to be finalised.

A few days later, Timothy allowed the cameras to record his first Cabinet meeting as president. He ensured that the portraits of the Country's past presidents, Homer and Nuewen, flanked him, with both clearly visible on the wall behind him.

He felt both pride and humility to be following in their footsteps – and a responsibility to govern wisely. *Was he up to the task?* The gravity of what he was undertaking had earlier struck him when he took his oath of office. *I will do my best*, he had said to himself then, and he repeated that promise now.

That evening in their new home as they ate their meal, a stir fry of some sort made with mixed vegetables and noodles, Timothy and Frederick were discussing the order of Timothy's agenda.

Unlike Javier, who was famous in political circles for his love of cooking, Frederick had no culinary interests, so they decided that their meals in future would be prepared by a staff person. "Well, that's dealt with the important item," Frederick joked.

Timothy had decided that while he was new and had wide support, it was a good time to face the disturbing security issues that Gretel had passed on to him. Not that she herself had been particularly informative, referring him to the Head of Security and Intelligence instead. He had met with Jacques a few times during his period of training and recognised that he ran a department that on the surface seemed excellent. It was the darker side of the Security Agency that bothered Timothy. Gretel had advised him to stay out of the Agency, as she had done, but he was the President now and ultimately responsible for the management of every department.

He wanted to appoint a minister that Jacques would have to report to. Under Gretel, Javier had nominally had this role, but it seemed to Timothy that Javier just handballed problems to Jacques and did not ask for accountability in return. Further, Javier was not a minister, so there had been no accountability to the Cabinet. Timothy found this all less than satisfactory. He wasn't even sure that Gretel or Javier were aware of the extent of the growing use of robots, together with high-tech equipment for surveillance and other operations within the Security Agency.

He had already discussed his concerns with Jacques. Although the man had been charming, he'd essentially told Timothy not to tread on his domain.

"As the President, there are some details of which you should remain unaware," Jacques had advised.

Timothy had questioned Jacques about the need for such high levels of surveillance when their Country was all that remained habitable on their planet – there was no unfriendly nation likely to cause them harm. Jacques had just smiled enigmatically and made no comment. Frustrated, Timothy had backed off, but now he was president, Jacques had to be brought to account.

Responding to Timothy's dilemma, Frederick advised that Henry, the Minister for Fisheries in Gretel's government, could be up to the task.

"I think that's a good suggestion, I agree with you. Henry is firm, a good debater and strategic. I'll offer him the post tomorrow," said Timothy, decisively. "Now, who do you recommend to take on the Fisheries portfolio as Henry's replacement?"

Frederick replied that most of the ministerial responsibilities had already been distributed and thought fair. "Let's not disturb things too much from what you've already announced. What about promoting Drake from Assistant Minister to Minister with full responsibility for the portfolio? Later on, it could give you a chance to introduce someone new to assist him, perhaps an OCM, for example. Initially at least, my bet is Drake will be prepared to take on the extra work just to demonstrate to his new president that he's capable."

Timothy couldn't supress the 'old' Timothy completely; he quickly shot back with, "Drake in Fisheries might fit the bill, but could I be accused of playing ducks and drakes?" He was prevented from expanding on his word play by Frederick rolling his eyes.

"Spare me your pithy bon mots."

"In that case, mon ami, what have we for dessert?" responded Timothy.

"You just sit there, Mr President, while I get it for you – on this one occasion. Just remember, however, that I'm your advisor, but neither your maid nor your cook," laughed Frederick.

*

Jacques was already wary of this new president, who insisted on knowing more than was good for him. After he was asked to report to a minister (so he was being treated like any other department head), Jacques felt his wariness had been justified.

He faced two choices: shut down some of the burgeoning AI-intensive operations so that his department was open and accountable to the minister as the new president wished; or, heighten his efforts to keep the Security Agency's work in motion, and by default maintain his own power, by dividing his empire into two sections. Cabut didn't seem to be required any longer to monitor the Baritz woman, so Cabut could head the more opaque and experimental side of the Agency (unbeknownst to either the minister or the president, with Cabut reporting only to Jacques).

But even Jacques felt a chill of alarm at ceding too much power to Cabut. Jacques' megalomania was nothing compared to the possibility of the acts an unleashed Cabut might commit, given too much authority. He had already been alarmed by the initiative and emotion Cabut had shown in dealing with, albeit not particularly well, the two lawyers summoned in as part of the hosing-down of the anti-Baritz movement. Javier had asked Jacques to deal with it and, while he in turn had instructed Cabut to meet the two men and make them feel uncomfortable, Cabut's behaviour had been unexpected. Signs of antagonism and resentment were notably displayed by the hitherto impassive Cabut.

Was that a result of being unfairly accused of not scrutinising citizen Proger properly? Jacques wondered. *Did Cabut take pride in his meticulousness – surely not? – or was he displaying a sign of possible loyalty to Baritz?*

Until then, Cabut had not been considered capable of displaying much human emotion. It had unsettled Jacques enough to resolve that he would have to find a way of keeping Cabut more submissive, despite Cabut being his best creation (his name being an acronym for Complex Android Body Under Testing).

*

When Eva's report from the North reached Timothy, he knew at once that he had a job offer for the professor. He ordered that she be returned home quietly so they could discuss his plan to employ her as his Advisor for the North. He was very serious in his intentions to absorb the North back into the Country and to be more inclusive towards its people. So much so, he had added the portfolio of Minister for the North to those he had inherited from Gretel and appointed himself as the inaugural minister. This reflected the action Gretel had taken when she initially took on the education portfolio on becoming President; like Gretel, Timothy expected to relinquish his ministerial portfolio once he began to find his presidential duties too onerous. Right now, however, he was young, keen, ambitious and full of zeal.

Timothy enjoyed gazing at beautiful objects, usually those confined to art galleries or the occasional young aesthete, and he had felt the aura that surrounded Eva when they met. More importantly, he had been impressed by her mind, her ideas, her enthusiasm and her person.

He later tried to explain this to Frederick but was disappointed that he'd taken his comment as a personal slight. Still, it had been very nice making peace with Frederick afterwards.

*

Eva was happy to be back in her own apartment and very glad to access her wardrobe. She had felt quite excited to meet the new president, who had been so perceptive and complimentary about the recommendations she had compiled. She'd taken her time and pleasure in choosing an outfit for their meeting, confident that her career was about to take a new and unanticipated turn.

Eva felt both she and the President had appraised each other keenly during their meeting, Eva concluding that he had the intellectual strength, the will and the capacity to instigate tangible reforms. There was also a frisson of attraction, she noted, glad that she had dressed elegantly for the occasion. It was her one conceit: she enjoyed being admired.

As she had left the President's office, walking to where her car would collect her, Eva had crossed paths with Cabut. Glad to see him, she had said a warm hello and expressed her pleasure at bumping into him. While Cabut had been his usual reserved self and their conversation had been short, it was only on the drive back to her apartment that she reflected on how physically close he had allowed her to be – so close that she had been tempted to give him a hug. She had checked the impulse at the last moment, not wanting in any way to embarrass him, aware how he could quickly become ill at ease over any personal interaction.

Maybe it's true that absence makes the heart grow fonder, she laughed to herself. Although quietly pleased to note Cabut's emotional development, the observation disappeared from her mind as she turned her thoughts towards working with the President.

Upon being returned to her apartment, Eva changed into her running clothes and went for a satisfying ten-kilometre jog. There were few others out running, it being the middle of the working day. She whispered to the stream along whose banks she moved that she was glad to see it again; the murmured reply of the gentle ripples of water as she passed by assured her quietly that the feeling was mutual.

Refreshed physically and emotionally, Eva returned home to shower, following which, on the pretext of saying hello, she did something quite out of character: she gave Gretel a call.

After congratulating Gretel and Javier on their retirements from public life and wishing them well, Eva steered the conversation towards the new president, sharing what he had proposed to her.

"You must think well of him to have recommended he succeed you, Gretel?" Eva half questioned.

Gretel agreed that she now did, although it had taken her quite a while to reach that position.

"Nor do I necessarily agree with all that's on his agenda, you understand Eva – but as he grows into the role, some of his loftier plans will die a natural death, I'm sure."

"Like what?" Eva asked.

"Oh, like returning to an old-fashioned voting system where the citizens are allowed to democratically elect the composition of the Government. We moved on from that outdated system yonks ago. Going backwards is never a way forward."

"Oh, so he's a conservative, is he? One of those who yearns for the simple days of yore, that never really existed?" asked Eva, feeling a little deflated.

"Actually, he's not, he's quite progressive in many ways. For instance, he's very keen to integrate the Souls from the North into the Country. But he's too green and idealistic to realise what a difficult task that would be. It would impose a great strain on our already delicate economy, our education and health facilities, and our social service support systems, all to bring an impoverished, ill-educated and possibly disease-ridden set of people into our midst. Our citizens would be outraged. I know that very well because I had surveys done to gauge the collective viewpoint regarding the northern peoples some years ago."

"Does that mean you wouldn't advise me to accept the position he has offered me?"

"On the contrary, I think it's a rather clever offer. You have a two-year break from the space program, and this will keep you occupied in the meantime. For reasons we both understand, I'm afraid the university position I had in mind for you is no longer possible since you need to be away from here, totally out of the public eye and memory. The North is perfect for that, and the work you do may even be helpful to the Government," replied Gretel. "I'd strongly recommend that you accept the offer as the best you'll get."

"Then I'm pleased to hear that, because I have already accepted the offer," said Eva. "Maybe you and Javier might like to consider visiting the North sometime, now that you're retired?" she continued, her suggestion quite well-meant.

Gretel gave a small laugh and said she didn't rule it out, but right now she was just enjoying the freedom of having time to herself, adding she had agreed to start writing her autobiography.

The conversation between the pair came to an amicable end, each quite content for the other.

*

Javier was interested to listen to Gretel relay her conversation with Eva; however, as Gretel could not help but observe, Javier was distracted. When pressed, he told Gretel that he'd had a disturbing conversation with Jacques during lunch at a nearby pub.

Jacques, it seemed, was disturbed at two levels, one of which was Timothy's intention to monitor the Security Agency more closely than Gretel had done. This irritated Jacques, who had no time for documentation, accountability and so-called 'proper procedures'. He operated on the basis that if there was a problem, he would attend to it, no questions asked. He did his job extremely well and very discreetly, as Javier acknowledged.

"I did counsel Timothy that there were some areas where it might be in his best interests not to know too much," interrupted Gretel.

"I know you did, my petal," said Javier, kissing her on the cheek. "Jacques has split security in two and placed Cabut in charge of the 'darker side', with Cabut reporting to Jacques alone. Timothy – or, rather, Timothy's minister – will not be in the know about this side of the security business."

"Nor should we know," interrupted Gretel curtly.

"Correct, I only mention this because it helps to explain what's really bothering Jacques."

"Can't we just leave it to him to solve his problems in future? He seems to have managed so far," commented Gretel, seeming anxious not to get involved.

Javier braced himself; leading Gretel by the hand, he sat her down on the sofa. "There's something I have to tell you."

"What is it, Javier? You look quite serious," said a puzzled Gretel.

Javier quietly repeated to Gretel what Jacques had told him about Cabut, adding that it was just a matter of time before Cabut would be beyond Jacques' control.

"Now you're both being melodramatic. Let me remind you, Javier, that Cabut may have a human form but he is only a machine. I may know very little about Cabut, but surely all Jacques has to do is stop allowing the recharging to take place."

"That's exactly what I said to Jacques, but apparently it's no longer that simple. Cabut has become very sophisticated; he's been programming and re-programming himself to improve his power and his ability to act as a human. He has reached the stage where he understands human thinking probably better than we do and has almost reached the stage where an outsider would find it difficult to believe he wasn't a fairly well-adjusted, normal human being."

"But he's not well-adjusted, he has no emotional side," observed Gretel, her brow furrowed.

"Apparently that is changing too. He's about to become a more complete human than any of us could hope to become in our lifetimes."

"Is that necessarily bad? Can't Jacques use this to good advantage?" countered Gretel.

"It is Jacques' fear that it will be Cabut, as the superior being, who will be using Jacques, and the rest of us, as he wishes. Jacques is in a great state of concern, I might add," said Javier grimly.

"Then it's up to the likes of Jacques to harness this new humanoid to work for the greater good. Altruism is a human trait too; Cabut may acquire it," said Gretel, warming to the thought that this development could become another great achievement of their civilisation.

Gretel looked at him thoughtfully, but then she gasped, with hand over her mouth. "Oh, my goodness, Javier. Do you remember when Cabut nominated himself as first choice for the presidency, but we thought it was a joke? What if it wasn't? Oh, my goodness," she repeated. "Do you think that Jacques should share that with Timothy?"

"I think you're starting to understand the potential enormity of the situation," said Javier gently.

Gretel turned to face him, tenderly placing a hand on each of his cheeks. When she spoke, it was with a more familiar tone of authority. "Just remember, darling: Jacques created this problem, so it's Jacques' responsibility to sort this out; it is not yours, Javier. I don't like to see you looking so worried."

CHAPTER 46

Eva viewed the variation to her life instigated by the new president as a welcome, and likely stimulating, interlude. She had set out on her return to the North, spending a few days at the Space Centre before journeying on to what was intended to be her home for the next two years. She had left happily, this time with a full suitcase of appropriate clothing and belongings, and with a full agenda to carry out as the President's Advisor for the North.

*

The new president was starting to bring small ripples of change into the citizens' lives; inadvertently, he had also caused a small but valued difference to Leon's life. Leon had at last gained a new employee, Clovis having been advised by Jacques that it was time they parted company.

"It was an odd conversation, Leon," relayed Clovis. "The boss said that something terrible was about to happen to his business and, as I'd been a loyal worker, he was warning me to get out while I could. I asked him what he meant, but he said it was best if I didn't know."

"What was he planning to do to avoid getting caught up in whatever the impending terrible event was or is?" questioned Leon.

"I asked him that too, because I was worried for him – especially as he's treated me fairly. He just said he had a plan and I was not to worry about him," said Clovis. "I don't know what's going on, but I can't help but be worried."

Clovis added that he'd later tried to contact Jacques, but the phone had rung out.

Leon's first thought was that Timothy must have implemented some change that affected Jacques. Perhaps he'd decided to dispense with his services, having somehow seen through his charming façade. If true, then Timothy rose yet further in Leon's estimation.

Later that day, on a whim, Leon decided to check if Javier was aware of Jacques' fate. Javier, it turned out, was not.

Sensing that Javier was ill at ease, Leon pressed him further. "Have you spoken to Jacques recently?" he quizzed.

"Of all people, why are you showing concern about Jacques?" responded Javier with some asperity.

"Just curious, that's all," said Leon, offering up the news that he had just employed a new driver – someone Jacques had let go.

But Javier could not be drawn to divulge anything, so Leon had to let the matter drop. Asking to be remembered to Gretel, he ended the call.

*

When Timothy learnt that Jacques had resigned as the Head of Security and Intelligence, he was very surprised but also secretly pleased. He hadn't liked Jacques, nor had he liked the way he operated, based on his early impressions at least. His instincts, however, told him that the man was ruthless and likely to operate outside the law.

On the recommendation of Henry, now his Minister for Security and Intelligence, Timothy decided to appoint Cabut to replace Jacques – but only as a temporary measure. He'd only met Cabut once and had thought him rather odd, but wanting to encourage his new minister, he had not wished to completely overrule Henry's first ministerial decision.

Something else about Cabut struck Timothy as odd; he seemed to only be known by one name. Frederick had said it was becoming a modern trend. "For instance, you are 'Timbo' to your citizens; few probably know your full name," he had joked, adding that at least it wasn't Timmy. This hadn't reassured Timothy, but for some reason it did remind him that during his difficulty settling into his first year of school, his mother had quite often referred to him as Timmy: her 'timid Timmy', in fact. He didn't share this with Frederick.

Timothy asked Henry to see how Cabut performed, and if he reported well of Cabut after a few weeks or so, then maybe he'd consider making the appointment permanent.

*

There was a serious problem, one that neither Timothy nor his new minister seemed to be aware of. It was the problem that Javier was starting to believe had caused Jacques to resign: the problem of how to keep control of and manage Cabut, now that his autonomous reprogramming of himself was reaching exponential proportions.

Javier was aware, but for now he was keeping his own counsel – at Gretel's firm insistence. "Don't you dare 'do a Leon'," she had urged, emphasising that neither of them should interfere in the workings of Timothy's new government.

*

By the end of Cabut's first week as the acting Head of Security and Intelligence, Henry reported that Cabut's intelligence capacity appeared to exceed that of many of his fellow department heads, yet he remained shy and his emotional awareness and empathy were not particularly strong.

By the end of the third week, he was openly commented upon within government circles. The acting Head of Security and Intelligence had quickly matured in his new role, was extremely competent and confident, and was growing more at ease with his minister and those around him. No longer the awkward nerd, he was someone to be reckoned with and respected.

In view of the feedback from all sides, Timothy accepted Henry's advice that there was no need to prolong the trial period. Accordingly, he asked Cabut to make an appointment to see him the following week, intending to confirm in person Cabut's appointment as the Head of Security and Intelligence.

Initially, Timothy had felt reassured as Cabut stood before him, Cabut having duly arrived at his appointed time. Once the offer of permanency had been made and accepted, and congratulations had been offered and acknowledged, the two of them conversed for a few more minutes – and it wasn't long before Timothy's uneasiness began to resurface. Deliberately prolonging the conversation in an attempt to identify what was concerning him, he asked Cabut a question, one he felt to be puerile but it was also one that Gretel had once asked him.

"Do you see yourself in this role for the long term, or have you other ambitions you want to pursue?"

He was a bit taken aback by the bluntness of Cabut's reply.

"I intend to become president one day."

Timothy gave a short, unamused laugh, but responded graciously.

"Well, that position isn't likely to become vacant for quite some time. I was more interested in your plans for the foreseeable future."

When Cabut did not immediately respond, Timothy asked whether, for example, there were requests about staffing or resources that Cabut might have. "You know, the sort of things that would help you succeed in your new role," he clarified.

Again, Cabut's reply was a surprise.

"I would like Professor Baritz to be seconded to my department. She and I have worked well together over several years, and I want that working relationship to continue."

"Professor Baritz has only recently accepted a new appointment of her own, so she is not at this stage available. However, I'm puzzled by your request, since the professor is an astrophysicist," said Timothy.

"That is exactly why I need her," countered Cabut. "The threats to our future security will be from civilisations from other planets. This current space mission, for example, could lead to an attempted invasion by the peoples from planet Earth. It is essential that we have the likes of Professor Baritz in Security and Intelligence."

Timothy thought for some moments, acknowledging to himself that Cabut might have a point.

"Right now, there are reasons, which I choose not to explain, that require Professor Baritz to be out of the public eye; added to which, the role she's been assigned is of importance. However, I take your point and will give it further consideration. As the space mission is not expected to be completed for some time, I assume we are under no immediate threat from planet Earth. Let us agree to review your request in a few months."

Cabut seemed unsatisfied by what Timothy had thought was a reasonable compromise, retorting that nothing could be more important for the Country than its security.

"You don't wait till the invader arrives before thinking that now's the time to address the problem," he said scathingly. "Where is Professor Baritz stationed? Is she still at the Space Centre?"

"Yes, she spends some of her time at the Space Centre and some time as my Advisor for the North. It is one of my goals to improve life for those in the North and to explore the possibility of assimilating the northern peoples with our own," replied Timothy carefully.

"Then that involves my department too and so is of interest to me. You see, Mr President, we – that is, you, me and Professor Baritz – are already working together," quickly shot back Cabut.

Timothy decided he'd had quite enough. *What is it about those in Security that irritates me so much?* he wondered. He had disliked Jacques, and he was not so enamoured with Jacques' replacement, even though he had only just appointed him to the role!

Indicating to Cabut that their meeting had already gone over schedule, he said they would have to reconvene to continue their interesting conversation at another time.

As was becoming an evening habit, Timothy debriefed the day's events with Frederick as they dined on the meal their newly appointed chef had prepared for them.

Grilled steak, synthetic of course, with salad and fries was tasty enough but not exactly haute cuisine, they both agreed. "Perhaps a quiet word to the new chef would be in order," Timothy suggested.

Frederick agreed to follow this up, then, referring to Timothy's other complaint of the day, Frederick commented that since Timothy felt so uneasy, perhaps he should swallow his pride as well as his meal and speak to Jacques to discover how best to handle Cabut.

Timothy grimaced. "Maybe I have no other choice," he sighed.

They moved on to the dessert course. Pleasant though fresh figs and cheeses were, their chef was hardly justifying his employment. Following completion of the meal, they retreated into their respective studies, promising that neither would spend too much of the evening locked away from the other.

The next day, unable to trace the whereabouts of Jacques, Timothy rang Javier. They chatted amiably enough about retirement plans and presidential plans before Timothy raised the reason for his call. Javier was unable to shed any light on where Jacques might be, but Timothy noted the hesitation in his voice.

"So, what is it about Jacques that caused you to hesitate before answering my question?" he asked.

*

Javier's last conversation with Jacques had caused him much angst, but Gretel had counselled him not to raise his concerns with the new administration. He had been tempted to share his concerns with Leon, but Gretel's words were still freshly ringing in his ears and had prevented him from doing so. He was a very worried man; only the previous day, Gretel had, with some curtness, told him to 'lighten up'.

Javier came to a decision. He explained to Timothy that there was a related matter he needed to discuss with him in person. He agreed to meet Timothy at Government House.

A couple of hours later, Javier was ushered into Timothy's office. Although his mind was on other things, Javier did note the new modern furniture and the eclectic collection of abstract paintings hanging on the walls. He offered a congratulatory comment on how well Timothy had transformed Gretel's former office, a comment that seemed to please Timothy.

Nothing else that Javier had to say seemed to be at all pleasing to Timothy.

Cabut had been correct in suggesting that any threats to the Country's future security would come from other beings; however, it was not so likely to be an invasion by a civilisation from another planet.

No, those hypothetical threats were as nothing to the actual threat that already existed – the rise of the robot in humanoid form.

"Why did Gretel not explain to me what Cabut really is?" an angry Timothy demanded.

Javier explained that Gretel had never allowed herself to become involved, pointing out that she had advised Timothy to adopt the same approach. When Cabut was no longer required to monitor Eva Baritz and had been returned to Jacques, she'd left it up to Jacques as the Head of Security and Intelligence to give a more informed report on Cabut to Timothy as the incoming president.

"I guess it's obvious now that Jacques was not forthcoming," said Javier, apologetically.

Javier described how, at first, all had appeared to be going well with AI research and development while humankind had been in charge. He acknowledged that while Cabut had shown higher order reasoning powers than those of his human creators, he had remained a servant, submissive as intended, up until the time he had finally achieved the ability to be indistinguishable from his human creators. The unintended blurring of the distinction between human and robot had suddenly happened.

"The repercussions and implications for our country are difficult to assess," a gloomy Javier said.

"Catastrophic, unless a means of tethering the power of these new beings can be found," responded Timothy. "Jacques recognised this I assume; maybe that's why he resigned."

Javier nodded in agreement, then started to share his fears about Cabut's presidential ambitions. Timothy cut him short, saying Cabut had already told him he planned to become president.

Timothy continued. "We urgently need the knowledge and expertise of Jacques to help us. Can you think of where he could be?"

Javier replied that unfortunately he couldn't offer any suggestions. "Then is there someone else who might help?" asked Timothy, seeming increasingly desperate for ideas.

Javier thought for a moment before remembering that a former employee of Jacques now worked for Leon. He suggested he might know something about the likely whereabouts of Jacques.

Timothy agreed that it was worth a try, adding with irony that he could hardly handball the problem to Security. He seemed surprised when Javier countered, "Why not? Tell Cabut you want to speak to Jacques about certain anomalies. As the Head of Security and Intelligence, it's Cabut's job to find him. And let's face it, Cabut's the one who's most likely to be able to do so."

*

By the end of the first month of Cabut's official appointment as the Head of Security and Intelligence, the relationship between him and Timothy had become very tense. Cabut continued to insist that Eva join him. There being no news of Jacques, Timothy decided to order Eva's return. Perhaps she, as someone Cabut respected, would be able to advise on how to handle him.

CHAPTER 47

The North was becoming crowded with expats from the South, joked Eva to her charming new companion. He was on sabbatical leave, keen to see once again the land in which a long time ago he had spent a couple of years recharging himself before departing to resume his career. He owned a property that was not in good shape; it had been loaned for local use during the years he had returned south, so he was temporarily staying in rented dwellings close to where Eva was living. The two of them had just happened to meet by chance.

That was over six weeks ago, and they were now very comfortable in each other's company. Jacques knew the countryside well, and together he and Eva enjoyed travelling around. The red dust, the gnarled trees, the sparkling water views, the refreshing night rains ... such landscapes and acts of nature appealed to them both. They also shared a desire to help the local people, who were impoverished but seemingly happy, and Eva was pleased to discuss the ideas she planned to recommend in her report back to the Government; in fact, she was grateful for the input that Jacques had offered.

After returning to the North, Eva again became aware of the sense of freedom she felt there, the feeling of peace that both refreshed and intrigued her. She had lived for so long under scrutiny, under pressure, but here she felt the joy of liberation, the kind of joy that she found it difficult to explain rationally. Jacques seemed to understand, he too confessing that the northern lands were his escape and salvation. It was this shared experience that had drawn them closer together.

But now Eva had been asked to return south, despite her two-year appointment having only just started, or so it felt to her. As they lay in bed that evening, Eva explained to Jacques that she was being ordered home at the President's request.

"Why?" was his first reaction, which was a question Eva couldn't answer: the message said she was needed on a matter of urgency, but the matter had not been specified.

Jacques enveloped Eva's body with his own, whispering that she should stall. "Reply that you would like to request further information, as your work here is going very well and you are most reluctant to interrupt it," he suggested.

She agreed, then Eva and Jacques gently made love.

*

After Eva had fallen asleep, Jacques took stock. He knew there would come to be a problem with Cabut – could that be what was troubling Timothy? But if so, why would that involve Eva? If there was any connection between the request for Eva to return and Cabut, then he was worried for Eva's sake. He definitely didn't want her to return home at this juncture.

As he lay there, feeling the warmth of her body next to him and the rise and fall of her breathing, Jacques recognised there was a strangely personal reason why he didn't want Eva to comply with the presidential order. He'd had many relationships before, some short, some carnal, some directly attributable to his work needs, pleasant though some of those became. An image of a young Bethany came to his mind. Under different circumstances that might have lasted, he had occasionally thought. Dismissing thoughts of Bethany, he realised that none of his previous relationships, whatever their origin or purpose, had caused him to feel as protective of, as admiring of and, yes, as in love with the woman who slept peacefully beside him. This unscripted, unplanned and unexpected relationship with Eva had just happened by serendipity. It had taken him by surprise, and it was overwhelming.

Jacques had first come to the North to avoid attention after his assignment with Bethany had come to its successful professional conclusion. He had come to love the countryside and made friends with many of the local indigenous folk and the descendants of other ethnic refugees. The lifestyle was cathartic, and he had toyed with staying.

He'd purchased his own home and had enjoyed welcoming his new friends to it.

But, of course, he hadn't stayed, and his normal life had resumed ruthlessly.

He'd always been good at blocking his emotions when carrying out his orders, but he was also able to turn on the charm when required. He had developed the Security and Intelligence department into an empire, the darker side of which the Nuewen Government chose not to acknowledge existed. Yes, there were some incidents that he wasn't proud of, but Jacques never allowed himself to dwell too long on ethics. Ultimately, the results had been all that mattered – the problems he was challenged to resolve were successfully 'taken care of', with the ways left up to him.

That thought caused him to laugh silently, his movement momentarily rousing Eva. Cradling her, Jacques rocked her back to sleep as if she was a child. It was ironic that he should know so much about Professor Eva Baritz yet he'd never met her in person until now, and he had fallen in love with her almost from the instant they had started to talk.

Would he ever tell her that they shared a history – that he had been receiving regular reports from Cabut as to both her movements and the progress of her research? He had admired that her approach seemed to match his own philosophy – the end benefit justified the means – and he had held a great deal of respect for her intelligence, but Eva had just been part of the job and she'd had no significance in his life. Until now.

His thoughts again centred on Cabut, the human-looking robot that he'd commissioned, never dreaming that this creature could program itself to acquire, or at least simulate, human emotions. Cabut was the start of a new type of being – a type 3 humanoid, Jacques belatedly realised, though at the time he had still been confident that Cabut remained under his control.

In fact, Jacques had been very excited at the future potential offered by such an AI-driven being. Would it have remained that way if Timothy had adopted the approach of his predecessor and not tried to understand the workings of the Security Agency? Possibly, possibly not. Maybe it would only have been a matter of time before Cabut realised he was the higher order creature, rather than the humans who, in their conceit and ignorance, sought to maintain power over him, allocating him a subservient position.

The day that Cabut had challenged him (politely, though with criticism) was the day that Jacques recognised an evolution was occurring. It became clear from that incident onwards that the power structure between the two had shifted. Jacques had swiftly alerted Javier of the development, resigned his position and travelled north, strongly doubting that he would ever again return.

How could he allow Eva to return to the Country, which was about to undergo a change far greater than that which The Disaster had inflicted on it? And how could he bear to be parted from her?

The next morning the Government provided no further clarification, just a repeated insistence that Eva return immediately, so she made her arrangements to depart that day. She seemed sad at leaving Jacques, but she was optimistic that she would return before too long, an optimism that Jacques did not share. As she disappeared from his sight, Jacques was aware that tears were rolling down his face.

*

Eva was met by a government car that took her directly from the small airport to Government House, where the President awaited her.

Preliminaries aside and coffees poured, he explained why he had summoned Eva back. He explained that relations between him and Cabut were strained at best, and he would welcome her insight into managing an effective working relationship with Cabut now that he had taken a senior role as Head of Security and Intelligence. He acknowledged her long-term experience of working with him, reasoning that she might therefore be best placed to ease him into the role; besides which, Cabut clearly respected her and had requested her for his team.

She was surprised to hear that Cabut had requested her involvement, although she did comment that she'd noticed that Cabut had seemed almost pleased to see her recently.

"Exactly why we need you, Eva. You are the one person he seems to hold a genuine regard for, so it is you who may be able to suggest a way to manage, or at least to temper, his behaviour. He wants you to be seconded to his department – you start tomorrow, and I will speak with you at the end of the day to discuss your first impressions of him in this role."

Back in her apartment, unable to discuss the surprising development with Jacques, Eva sat on the edge of her bed, staring out at the twinkling flashes in the sky. Eventually, she resolved she would treat Cabut just as she always had and hope for the best. Emotionally tired, she fell asleep fully clothed on top of the covers.

The next day started just like the old days; it was as if the visit to the North had never happened. A car arrived to pick her up and she was driven to the Departments, but instead of being taken to her own office, she was taken to Cabut's. Without saying hello, she matter-of-factly said she believed he had requested her secondment to the Security Agency.

"Why, and what have you in mind?" she asked, demanding an explanation.

Cabut invited her to sit down, and after a brief hesitation, she complied.

"Does this reversal of roles make you feel ill at ease, Eva?" he asked.

"You worked for me for years, so yes, this is awkward – especially given I did not apply to work for you. I had a very good short-term appointment that I was enjoying, and suddenly that was interrupted and I was summoned back here. The role you have for me had better be pretty darn good to justify this," Eva complained, noting with interest that Cabut had used her first name.

Without further ado, Cabut put forward his theory that should Eva's space mission achieve its goal, then the next likely security threat could come from planet Earth. He conceded that this would not necessarily happen, but he argued that there was a not-insignificant probability of it occurring. Either way, it was important to plan ahead and to be ready for any such eventuality.

Eva did not dismiss Cabut's theory outright; in fact, she was quite impressed by his desire not to be caught by surprise, to be ready for anything that might occur.

"Why didn't you raise this with me earlier, when the mission became active?" she asked, less aggressively.

Cabut dismissed her question, simply stating that it hadn't occurred to him then – he had not been in a position where he was required to consider such possibilities at the time. However, now that he did carry such responsibility, he was determined to do his job dutifully and with foresight.

"This means that I must now think about such dangers," he said.

Eva noted that although Cabut had become more articulate, he was still compartmentalising his thought processes. *Odd fellow,* she thought.

"Alright, that sounds reasonable," she said aloud, before continuing to argue her prime grievance at being brought back virtually against her will.

"We both know two years is about the earliest we could expect to hear from Sebastian, so why the urgency to bring me here right now? I am happy, flattered, pleased even to work with you along the lines you've sketched, but there is no emergency. Why don't we initially communicate from a distance, allowing me to complete the task the President has assigned me? Once that's done, I'll gladly return to work with you in Security."

There was a short silence, during which Cabut appeared to be processing Eva's argument.

Strange person, she thought again, though not unkindly, remembering many of the times when Cabut's odd behaviour had taken her by surprise.

Eva took her eye off Cabut as she reminisced about their shared past, managing to prevent herself from laughing at some of her memories of his unusual behaviour. Consequently, she jumped when she realised Cabut was standing behind her. He placed his hands on her shoulders; he had never invaded her personal space before, so this action quite shocked her.

"I want you here now Eva because I function better when I am with you," he said simply, his hands beginning to caress her neck and back. For a moment she froze, then quietly she removed his hands from her body, stood to face him, and said, almost inaudibly but very deliberately, "Don't you ever touch me without my permission again." Eva picked up her bag and walked out of the room.

Maintaining her composure, she walked with measured strides back to her car, ordering that she be taken immediately to see the President.

He was in a Cabinet meeting, but Eva said she would wait. When he appeared almost half an hour later, Eva was calm, cool and professional as she related matter-of-factly what had happened.

"I cannot help you with Cabut," she said, requesting to be immediately returned to the North to resume her work there.

The President prevaricated. He said his first duty was to ensure her safety, but he also had a duty to give Cabut the right to explain what had taken place from his perspective. He promised he would arrange for Eva to be placed in a safe house overnight while he dealt with Cabut. Only after that would he make the decision about what to do next.

"Is there a friend you can stay with?" he asked.

Eva almost suggested Gretel and Javier, but she thought better of it. Instead, she replied that there was no-one she wanted to risk inflicting trouble on.

The President looked thoughtful. He explained that as the Head of Security and Intelligence, Cabut would know the whereabouts of every 'official' safe house and could quite easily locate Eva, should he so wish. This meant they had to think carefully about where she would be safe and secure.

Eva frowned – she had no wish for Cabut to discover her location, and her apartment suddenly didn't seem very safe. Then the President leapt up, suggesting he had a possible solution. Excusing himself, he left the room to act on his idea, returning soon afterwards to announce that a car would collect her shortly and take her to a private destination.

"You'll be safe there for the time being," he assured her. He handed her a small phone, telling her that if she was worried then she should call him on the number already entered into the device.

Eva climbed into the back seat of a car, one with a real human driver who introduced himself as Clovis. He told her to place a veil over her face and lie down on the back seat so she wouldn't be recognised by any of the security cameras they would pass. "Have you done this before?" she asked curiously.

"Sure have, ma'am," came the reply.

They drove in silence for some forty minutes until the car entered an underground garage and came to a stop. Cheerfully, Clovis announced, "We're home, you can sit up now."

It suddenly occurred to Eva that she may have put herself at risk – she had no idea where she was or who her driver was. Her fingers searched her bag for the phone the President had given her, and she held it tightly. However, she was determined to maintain her sangfroid and not to appear discomfited by proceedings; it was only one night, and tomorrow she'd be returning to safety, back into the arms of Jacques.

Clovis led her through two sets of security doors before she was ushered into a living room and across to a bedroom with an adjoining en suite.

"This is yours for tonight, you are quite safe here," said Clovis, kindly. "If you would care to join the owner of the house for an early afternoon tea, you are welcome. Otherwise I shall bring you a snack, and perhaps later on you might feel like joining us."

"Give me ten minutes to freshen up, then I shall gladly join the owner to convey my thanks," replied Eva.

Clovis grinned. "Good, I'll lay another place at the table." He then departed.

Once refreshed, Eva wandered out of her room, curious to meet the person who was her host.

"Good afternoon, Eva. I trust you find your room comfortable?" greeted Leon.

Eva was so surprised that she was rendered speechless. Leon proffered his arm, saying, "Let us join Clovis for afternoon tea, my dear."

Recovering her composure, Eva took Leon's arm, saying with some understatement, "What a day full of surprises this one has turned out to be." She added, more gratefully, "Thank you, Leon, for helping me."

He smiled back at her and, in a chivalrous gesture, helped her to be seated. Clovis was already sat at the table and he smiled at her too.

Leon led the conversation, with Clovis happily joining in. Eva felt herself relaxing. Over freshly baked scones with plum jam and cream, Eva told the two men of being summoned by the President to work for Cabut, then being shocked by Cabut's behaviour towards her earlier that day.

"I've worked with Cabut for several years and, if anything, he's been super shy, awkward and withdrawn. That he's grown in confidence is a good thing, or at least I thought so until he started hitting on me. I've told the President I'll not go near him again, and I'll be returning to the North tomorrow to continue the work that he originally assigned me to do."

Leon seemed interested in Eva's new line of work and in hearing more about her impressions of the northern land and its people. He listened attentively as she spoke fulsomely about her short time in the North. It was Clovis who asked her why the President had recalled her so soon after she took up that position.

"I think he's worried about Cabut. He told me I was the person Cabut most respected, so I could help temper him, or something like that. I was extremely annoyed to be brought back so quickly, I can tell you. Anyway, it's blown up in his face now," she replied, accepting Leon's offer to top-up her cup of tea.

"I believe your former boss was rather worried about Cabut, too," observed Leon to Clovis. "Did he ever mention that to you?"

Clovis paused to think. "No, I can't think I heard him mention the name Cabut." With a laugh, he added, "Jacques wasn't the type of fellow to confide in the likes of me."

Eva stared wide-eyed at him, and Clovis stopped laughing almost as soon as he'd spoken. Eva's cup of tea spilled slightly as her hand shook.

She apologised for making a mess and rose to mop up the small spill. Leon assured her that everything was okay, to which she replied, "I don't usually make a habit of spilling my tea, nor do I have any neurological problem in case you were wondering. It's just that Clovis surprised me when he said he used to work for Jacques. I met a fellow called Jacques quite recently, I wonder if they are one and the same?"

On comparing notes, it became obvious that Clovis's Jacques was also her Jacques.

"How did you find working with Jacques?" Eva asked Clovis, now quite eager to engage him in conversation.

"He was always decent to me – helped me turn my life around, in fact," Clovis replied. "How do you come to know him?"

Eva was vague, simply saying that the two of them had struck up a conversation by chance and had kept in touch. She did add that she thought he seemed very nice.

Leon enquired: "How nice may I ask, Eva?" to which Eva simply smiled enigmatically.

Leon continued. "And may I also ask when you last saw him?"

Eva frowned; she wondered why Leon was asking such questions. She batted the question away, replying, "Oh, it feels like a long time ago."

Leon let the matter drop and they talked of other things until a phone call took Leon out of the room. On his return, Leon explained that the call was from the President, who had been disturbed by his interview with Cabut. As a result, he agreed that it would be better if Eva returned to the North. Putting the phone on speaker, Leon said the President had asked to speak to her as well.

Eva nodded, saying, "Hello Mr President, Eva Baritz speaking."

The President told her that she would first be returned to the Space Centre, where she should stay for a short while in case Cabut checked on her movements.

Eva felt disappointed she couldn't travel directly to the North, but she was agreeable and thanked him for his help. "How long do you think I'll be at the Space Centre?" she asked.

He said he was hopeful that after a few days a car would become available for her to complete her journey, adding ominously, "But that depends on your cooperation."

"My cooperation?" she snapped, somewhat exasperatedly. "What do you mean by that?"

"There are two people I thought I could rely on to help palliate Cabut: you were one, and the other I had no idea where to find. But I've learnt just now from Leon that you almost certainly know where Jacques is and that the two of you are in contact."

Eva glared at Leon, who stood firm, returning her stare but with saddened eyes. Clovis looked on uncertainly.

Eventually, Eva spoke. "This sounds close to blackmail, Mr President."

"Necessity, my dear, the situation is live and developing," he quickly replied.

Eva thought fast. "Okay, here's the deal," she said. "First, you get me to the Space Centre, then I'll consider my position and weigh up whether I'll stay there or trade my friend's whereabouts for my car north."

"Deal not accepted, Eva. You're scheduled to leave for the Space Centre early tomorrow but that will be cancelled unless I know how to contact Jacques," the President coolly replied.

"I don't know how to contact Jacques, he has never given me such information," she almost screamed at the little phone lying on the table, her nerves now starting to jangle.

At this point, Leon intervened, suggesting that he and Eva talk through her situation and that they reconvene in an hour.

The President reluctantly agreed to the terms, and they ended the call.

*

As Clovis tidied their dishes onto a tray, he observed to Eva that Jacques had never had any issue keeping his security personnel under his control. "The President is probably right to think that Jacques might be able to help," he said soothingly. He departed from the room, leaving Leon alone with Eva.

Eva was agitated, pacing the room. "Please sit down," entreated Leon. "We must talk this through." She grudgingly took a chair next to him.

"From the little you've said, it's pretty clear to me that you met Jacques in the North. That would explain why we haven't been able to find him, this time or when he's disappeared previously. Clever of him – none of us ever thought of the North being his escape."

Continuing, he added, "I'd also wager that you've fallen for his charms."

When Eva failed to respond, Leon spoke at length of his past association with and knowledge of Jacques, making no attempt to shield her from what he knew of Jacques' modus operandi. "At one time, I even foolishly believed that Jacques was a friend.

"The inescapable truth, Eva, is that Jacques uses people for his own ends. He manipulates, charms and, in the case of women, not only has them fall in love with him, but has them believing that their love is mutual. Once he gets whatever information it is the Government wants, he simply disappears – North, we may now assume." Eva stared silently at him, her emotions hidden.

"Now, let me tell you about Cabut."

Leon noticed a flicker of interest from Eva.

"Cabut is an invention of Jacques'. Up until recently he was a very well-designed robot with an appearance hard to distinguish from that of a human being. He was placed to monitor you by Jacques, acting on the orders of Gretel and Javier, not from spite but because they cared for you – let's say because of your background and troubles. Cabut not only worked for you but this robot reported on you to Jacques, who in turn would pass on anything significant to Javier."

Leon paused to assess how Eva was taking this. He could see he now had her full attention.

"To cut the story short, Cabut has been continually reprogramming himself, and Jacques only recognised this when it was too late for him to intervene. Jacques resigned immediately and cowardly ran away.

"There you have the facts, Eva. Have you anything you want to say?"

Eva observed coolly that she had often wondered why Cabut was always at the office no matter the time – she had assumed he must live close to the Departments. She gave a mirthless giggle. She reflected that she'd always thought his strangeness was due to some sort of personality dysfunction or disorder, but if Leon was telling the truth – and she had no reason to doubt him – then perhaps she'd been very unobservant and naïve.

"No, you were very single-minded, totally engrossed in solving the problems surrounding the space mission. Don't be too hard on yourself as far as not recognising Cabut for what he is: the few who did know had been warned in advance," he said reassuringly.

He moved on to Jacques, a more sensitive subject. "What do you think now of Jacques? Did he tell you he already knew so much about you?"

"No, he didn't," she said quietly. "I believed – probably still do – that he was in love with me. Whatever that means."

Refusing to meet his sympathetic smile, Eva confirmed that she had told Timothy the truth: she had no means of contacting Jacques, other than in person.

"The North has very limited technology, part of its problems and its charm, actually. Anyway, without going into all that, if I can return to my lodgings up there then I am confident that I would see Jacques. The best I can do for the President is to pass on his 'call home' request to Jacques, but I can only deliver that message in person," she explained.

"So, you haven't been in contact with him while you've been down here?" quizzed Leon.

"No, I wanted to be able to send him messages via the Government office, but he said not to because everything would have to be impersonal if it was going through a third party," she replied.

"Could the office deliver Timothy's message direct?" speculated Leon.

"Deliver it where?" scoffed Eva. "Neither of the two people who staff the Government's only office have met Jacques; they don't even know of his existence as far as I'm aware, let alone where he might be at any given time. Jacques was always very careful about such things. Even I don't know where his home is, for instance. I just accepted that remaining incognito was part of his 'cleansing and renewal' ritual, the reason why he had gone to the North."

"Do you mean you might not be able to contact him either, even if you're given permission to return to the North?" argued Leon, struggling to clarify the relationship between Eva and Jacques.

"Oh, I'm sure he'd know straight away that I was back. He has a good – very good, in fact – relationship with several of the locals who keep him in the know. The 'old system' of communication works well for the Souls," commented Eva.

Leon was incredulous – this was not like the Eva he knew. "Let me get this straight. You just wait around until he contacts you? That sounds an unlikely doormat role for you to be accepting!"

Eva laughed. "No need to worry about me being downtrodden, because I'm not. In fact, I have never felt freer or happier than I have during my short time in the North. You should go there and see for yourself, Leon."

"Perhaps one day, but right now we'd better get back to Timothy."

*

Timothy had been putting it mildly when he had said his interview with Cabut had not gone well. Cabut had been single-minded in his insistence that Eva be returned to him, eventually walking out of the meeting and threatening to overthrow Timothy if Eva wasn't in his office at the start of the next working day. Timothy was now so alarmed that he had started to assemble a crisis committee. He was desperate for Jacques to speak to the committee members.

Although it didn't allay his fears, Timothy reluctantly agreed to allow Eva to return to the North on the condition that once she had spoken to Jacques, she would report back to him on how Jacques had received the message, using the phone he had given her earlier. Eva agreed.

CHAPTER 48

Eva failed to appear at Cabut's office the next morning, so Cabut carried out his threat. He placed Timothy under arrest, together with the members of the crisis committee who had been with him in his office.

*

Clovis was preparing to drive Leon to babysit Cameron, which would allow Aleck to attend one of his afternoon classes. Their day did not proceed as planned, however. He and Leon were arrested by the Security Agency on the grounds of aiding and abetting the escape of a wanted civilian. The security agents were androids, so neither reasoning nor resistance was possible.

*

As her aircraft lifted off the runway, Eva felt relieved – she was on her way back North. She welcomed the time ahead her flight would give her, time during which she could mull over the events of the previous day.

What an eventful day yesterday was, she mused. Leon had aged, now older than his years, but still instantly recognisable. And strange that for the third time in as many months he, or his name, had popped up in her life after such long absence.

Surprising too, how quickly I came to feel at ease in his presence, Eva observed, wondering why that was since she had not welcomed all of Leon's observations. Not that she doubted his sincerity of motive - and she was certainly grateful for his protection the previous day.

Her thoughts moved to Jacques: Leon had warned her about him, but she trusted her own feelings. Whether or not to tackle him over his non reveal of his background role in her life… well, that was another matter.

Does it matter Jacques hasn't told me? she contemplated. *Would I have told him had our positions been reversed?*

By the time the fasten seatbelt sign had switched off, Eva had formed her answers: 'Yes', I probably would've told him, but 'no', it doesn't matter that he hasn't. *Could be amusing to learn what his impressions of me were, however.* She grinned at the thought.

Accepting the coffee offered by the steward, the thought of caffeine momentarily switched Eva's thoughts to Seb. She raised her paper cup in his honour, his progress unknowable, his bravery indisputable. Her thoughts segued to the message Seb would deliver to Earth and from there to Cabut's invasion warning – an interesting conjecture, but Cabut was one black hole from which Eva was very glad to have escaped.

Her thoughts moved on to the puzzlement she had felt the previous evening when Leon had raised the topic of Aneeka's death. The poor woman's demise was sad, tragic even, but they'd discussed it at the time of the inquest when she'd been so stunned to receive his call. *I'd no idea about his personal connection to Aneeka back then,* Eva reminded herself.

Poor Leon, she thought anew, still a little saddened for him. *To come so close to establishing a relationship with Aneeka after all those years – and then to lose her again.*

Eva felt her mood shift.

Should I be feeling aggrieved that he thinks it's my fault in some way?

Less out of conviction, more out of her debt of gratitude to Leon for the help he'd given her, she had offered an apology to him in case, in any way, she had unwittingly contributed to Aneeka's death. But, as she had stressed to Leon, late the previous evening, Aneeka was heavily pregnant; she should have known better than to take any medication without first checking with her doctor.

After the remains of her in-flight lunch had been cleared, Eva's thoughts returned to the other topic Leon had raised – whether she, in her new role as the President's Advisor for the North, could examine and possibly suggest ways to improve the exodus of any Souls south.

Leon had told her that he knew of at least one Soul who had circumvented the official procedure, sailing a very long distance along the coast without attracting the notice of the border guards. Although this person had managed to quietly absorb himself into the citizenry, eventually he'd been identified and had agreed to a deal: his chance to be formally assimilated dependent on his volunteering to participate in a research program.

Leon wanted to ensure no further illegal immigrant could be abused by those in power. Eva remembered looking at him sharply, but she had merely said that nothing was off her agenda.

She made a mental note to follow this up, now that she would be resuming her role in the North.

It had taken Eva most of the day to complete the return to her room in the North, the one above the Government's office. It was now quite late, and she had no expectation of seeing Jacques that evening. She took a shower and went straight to bed.

*

Two of Cabut's most trusted personnel – his clones, the Cabutarki – arrived in the North at around eight in the morning. Their arrival was noticed by certain locals, who reported back to Jacques. As a unit, the Cabutarki were well-known to Jacques; he had employed their services on some difficult cases that had to be kept out of the public eye. Puzzled, he had at first assumed they must be coming for him. *But why?* he thought. *How could his whereabouts be known?* It wasn't until he was told that Eva had returned to the North late the previous evening that he realised they must have come for her.

Eva was having breakfast when Jacques arrived. *She's so beautiful,* thought Jacques as they passionately embraced. "Get dressed, my darling, I need to take you away from here. You're in danger," he said urgently, breaking away from her arms and allowing her to dress. "Security agents arrived earlier this morning and will soon be heading this way."

Her response surprised him. "It's not me the President wants, it's you. I've been sent back to deliver that message to you," Eva explained.

With no time to argue the point with her, Jacques grabbed her hand and the two left via the fire escape. Reaching ground level, they ran a short distance to the rear courtyard of a nearby pub. They were awaited by some of the locals he trusted most, who helped them into the back of a cart. They were covered with cloths and straw, while someone quickly jumped up on the donkey to which the small cart was hitched. The cart moved off slowly.

*

It was hot and her skin itched, so Eva was glad the journey was relatively short. When they climbed out of the cart, she was surprised to realise they were already out of the town area, despite the shortness of the journey. They entered a small wooden shack that stood nearby.

"Welcome to my house, Eva," murmured Jacques. "Apologies for its state of disrepair."

Sat perched on a rough-hewn stool, Eva updated Jacques on all that had happened, explaining to him that the President needed his help with handling Cabut. She added that the President must have sent the security agents to force Jacques' return.

Jacques gave a bitter laugh. "These agents answer only to Cabut. My grave error was in not recognising that before it was too late and his power was complete."

Gently, he explained that there was nothing he could do to help the President. He fervently wished that there were but, had there been, then he would have already acted to subdue Cabut.

"All I can do now is to try and save you from Cabut's clutches," he said, anxiously. He asked her to stay put while he returned to the town to see what the Cabutarki agents were up to.

Eva clung to him, and when he finally unfolded from her embrace there were tears on the rims of both their eyelashes.

"Know this, Eva, I love you and I will keep you safe from Cabut," said Jacques huskily.

"And know that I love you too, Jacques," said Eva quietly, holding his gaze. There was no longer need for her to question his sincerity: she discarded the doubts Leon had planted.

Jacques set off towards the township, driving the donkey and cart.

Eva took stock of her surroundings and her position. The man who had brought them both to the shack was nowhere to be seen. She was alone, but not frightened. She had just declared her love for another man, the first time she had said those words since Nolé. She thought of Nolé and hoped he'd approve; she felt he would.

Jacques was not gone as long as Eva had expected.

*

The bush telegraph's call had reached Jacques quickly, the warning relayed hurriedly along the chain of communication. The Cabutarki were on their way. They would reach the shack in approximately half an hour.

What were they going to do? What might the Cabutarki do to Eva to force her cooperation, to force her to become the plaything of a higher order form of life? These chilling thoughts ran through Jacques' head as he turned the cart around and headed back towards Eva.

And what matter is my life without Eva? His cogitations triggered more thoughts until it finally dawned on him what they needed to do.

When he reached Eva, he held her close as he explained the only solution to their situation.

*

Eva slowly smiled, accepting one of the two tablets Jacques held out in his open palm. She felt no fear, no real regret that she wouldn't witness the success of her space mission; she knew it would be successful, she'd always known that. Instead, she felt only gratitude; gratitude for the three indulgences that life had granted her – the devotion of her parents, the joy of mathematics, the love of two men.

How do you spend your last thirty minutes of life? Together, bodies entwined, lain on a rough camp bed somewhere in the North, the frivolous challenge finally answered.

*

The Cabinet ministers arrived early for their scheduled meeting, disturbed by rumours that something was amiss. There was a nervousness, an unease, emanating from the assembled throng. Even the level-headed Bethany, still the Minister for Education but with Aged Care added to her ministerial responsibilities, felt on edge. She keenly awaited the arrival of the President and the calming effect his presence would bring.

The door opened, but it was not their president who entered.

Cabut strode into the room, flanked by his android automatons, and greeted the gathering by announcing he had taken over the presidency. If any of the ministers objected, they would be dealt with by one of his security agents. "Your choice," Cabut said.

*

There were two further actions required before his takeover would be unassailable, Cabut had reasoned. No-one who knew of his humble beginnings should ever have the opportunity to share that knowledge.

*

The pleasant afternoon at home Gretel and Javier were enjoying was shattered by the arrival of security personnel, forcing their way in to their apartment and placing them under arrest. They were told the charges related to their time in Government, then they were roughly bundled into the back of a van and driven away.

*

From the room in which he was being held, Timothy was struck by the irony of Gretel's message to the type 1 humans of planet Earth. She had warned against The Disaster, but her message had contained no warning about The Rise of the Androids, the beginning of the evolution of type 3 'humans'.

Then something more solid struck him, and his mind ceased thinking for all eternity.

"I am the Alpha and the Omega, the first and the last, the beginning and the end." ...Revelation 22:13

www.ingramcontent.com/pod-product-compliance
Lightning Source LLC
Chambersburg PA
CBHW060814030726
47503CB00002B/482